About the author:

Stevie Davies lives nea[r] [...] English Literature at Manchester University [...] leaving to become a full-time writer. She has published eight volumes of literary criticism, including two studies of the revolutionary Milton, two books on Emily Brontë, one on Virginia Woolf and a feminist reappraisal of Renaissance poetry.

Her first novel, *Boy Blue* (The Women's Press, 1987), won the Fawcett Society Book Prize in 1989; *Primavera* (The Women's Press, 1990) confirmed her literary reputation; and her shattering breakthrough book, *Arms and the Girl* (The Women's Press, 1992), received universal acclaim.

About her novels:

'Original and poignant . . . Stevie Davies' first novel, *Boy Blue*, won the Fawcett Society Prize. *Primavera* proves that it was not just a flash in the pan.' *The Scotsman*

'Her greatest strength – besides powerful writing, fine character drawing and splendid storytelling – is honesty.' *The Times*

'It is her sensitivity that impresses. Very gently she'll tease out a pattern, a meaning, a brutal truth.' *Scotland on Sunday*

'Davies' writing is uniquely beautiful.' *City Life*

Also by Stevie Davies from The Women's Press:

Boy Blue (1987)
Primavera (1990)
Arms and the Girl (1992)

Author's Covenant With The Reader

United Nations guidelines direct the developed nations to
devote 0.7% of GDP to aid to the Third World. The British
Government falls shamefully and unapologetically short of
this target. The author of *Closing the Book* covenants with the
reader that 0.7% of her royalty on this book shall be paid to
an aid agency in sign of protest against the refusal by our
political leaders to discharge even the most minimal part of
our massive obligation to the Southern hemisphere.

STEVIE DAVIES

closing the book

My book is for
Ann Mackay

First published by The Women's Press Ltd, 1994
A member of the Namara Group
34 Great Sutton Street, London EC1V 0DX

British Library Cataloguing-in-Publication Data
A catalogue record for this book is available from the British Library

ISBN 0 7043 4388 6

Typeset in 11/13pt Bembo by Contour Typesetters, Southall, London
Printed and bound in Great Britain by
BPCC Paperbacks Ltd
Member of BPCC Ltd

1

Ruth, without Bridie, sat alone in the shadowy study, with the curtains shut. Bridie's absence was a merciful silence. Ruth drank it in. She breathed in deep, cooling draughts of Bridie's absence: the peace of it, the rest.

All these weeks of turmoil and degeneration had come to their quietus. Bridie's anger, agony, loud imprecations had volleyed through the space between them, day and night, night and day, though where night turned into day had become unclear to both of them. Ruth's sand-blasted eyes registered endless sleep-deprivation; she rubbed them ceaselessly but they remained dry. Bridie's pain had begun to gall and madden her – like the endless, pointless crying of her babies sixteen and twelve years ago, when she wanted to hit them, kill them, for obtruding upon her needful sleep, and she watched an imaginary hand (her hand) raise itself slowly into the air and come down violently hard to brain the little bastard – whom she loved above everything – but she could not endure another moment. But she never hit the babies. Only wanted to: and then the guilt at being a bad mother; and then the anger at the guilt; an endless circuit of rage and remorse.

What right had Bridie to be ill, anyway? Bridie who was her lifeline, her life. Bridie was a strong person and that was one reason why Ruth had come to her, forfeiting Lizzie and Sarah (for the judge sitting on the fourth floor at Heron House had ruled that a mother indulging in unnatural practices was unfit to have care and custody, though she might enjoy fortnightly access). Ruth did not enjoy the access. Access was a penance, seeing Lizzie refashioned into an enragedly reproachful miniature of the judge sitting on the fourth floor at Heron House, and Sarah's eyes overflowing with tears at every parting. Bridie didn't particularly care for children. With her usual relentless probity, she never pretended to their mother that she would ever grow to love them, though she tried to be civil and friendly. Frozen Lizzie stared over her coffee cup at Bridie with baleful eyes, giving pert or ironic answers; Sarah tried to be nice, for Ruth's sake, searching to fit in but not quite knowing how. But Bridie would comfort Ruth when she cried at their leaving, holding her for as many hours as it took to love the immediate pain away. And Bridie, surprisingly, would stand up for Lizzie: 'She's got a lot in her, that Lizzie of yours. She has a right to her feelings.' Ruth always felt that Bridie saw things more justly than she could or would; her own perceptions seemed always coloured by the lenses of her wishes and fears, a filtered light that saturated all with feeling. Now she didn't see or feel at all, she looked into space. The sum of her knowledge was nothing; she herself was nobody, and Bridie was nothing to her.

Bridie had been carried out on a stretcher at 9 a.m. They had given her a calming injection but it hadn't had time to take. She was a large-boned, powerfully built woman, so that it took the ambulance-men quite an effort to hump her down the wide staircase, despite her emaciation, and every time the stretcher jolted, she shrieked out in pain or outrage, one could not tell which. Ruth had followed them down slowly, carrying Bridie's brown grip, with all her few necessities inside.

She made as if to follow Bridie up into the ambulance.

'You might be better stopping home and getting a bit of kip,' the hospice nurse suggested. He must have noticed Bridie's hostility to Ruth.

'No, I'll go with her. She's my –'

She's my – what exactly? Not my sister, not my wife, not my legal next-of-kin.

'You're black under the eyes, you're ill yourself. Give yourself a rest, poor girl. We'll settle her in, and then you can visit later in the day.'

Ruth stared up at the nurse. He called her 'poor girl' though he was only two-thirds her age. The kindly meant words, after all that bawling and raving of Bridie's, fell on her spirit like gentle rain.

'I feel I ought,' she resisted, less firmly.

'Take care of yourself,' the young man urged. 'From what I've heard, you've been through a tough time.'

Tough time was an understatement. Tough time was a joke. Hell was a playground to this. There was no language for what she had been through. It had been more than enough to bear when the consultant had told them Bridie was dying, and they wept together all night long, soaking each other's night-shirts with their tears. But suffused with tenderness, each trying to comfort the other, the shock of the obscene disease had been cushioned by love. Love seemed ample, love would tide them through. Ruth became strong for Bridie. She seemed to grow another, more abundant self where Bridie could find support in her dying. She did not look forward in time, to picture her own loss, but lived intensely within the moment. Only Bridie's well-being mattered; only Bridie's comfort. All her gentleness came through, gentleness born of her own vulnerability, as a resource upon which she could draw and draw. Gratitude to Bridie for the five years of stable happiness also rose in her, releasing energy: she had never expected to know this certainty and centredness, but the gift had been given. Even when, after the radiotherapy had been completed and the Christie said they could do no more to enhance the quality of Bridie's remaining life, and Bridie became withdrawn and tetchy, Ruth's courage did not falter.

But Bridie changed. She was not Bridie any more. Bed-bound, she became hating and hostile. Ruth cleared up her shit and she hurled more shit at Ruth for the humiliation. Cursing Ruth was the only thing she seemed to enjoy. Foul-mouthed and cruel, she found fault with all Ruth's ministrations. She used some of the last strength in her once powerful arms to hurl at the wall some vegetable soup Ruth had spent the morning making, to tempt her appetite. She laughed at Ruth's tears. She accused Ruth of killing her. She woke Ruth in the middle of the night to inform her that she had never loved her. She loved Elaine far more than Ruth, she told her; Ruth was a stopgap, a second-best. Elaine was her soul-mate, she went on, and she had thought of her every day, every single day, and dreamt of her every night.

Ruth winced. She scrubbed furiously at the soup stains on the wall. Yes. Yes. Second-best, second-best. She had always in her heart of hearts suspected it. Now her heart of hearts went cold, like a stone. She said nothing, leaving the room with the cloth and bowl, slopping the suds down her jeans as she dashed out of range of that raving voice that went on and on betraying her.

Only once Bridie woke up and, smiling like her old self, said, 'You are the good gift of the road to destruction', quoting Pasternak. She drew Ruth's face down to hers and kissed it tenderly. Though it was three in the morning, Ruth had not slept; she had forgotten how to sleep. If she dozed off, Bridie would wake her to impart some malicious phrase she'd dreamed up, to torture her. Now when the cherishing words and gesture were offered, Ruth responded, but doubted whether they were

4

meant for her. Perhaps Bridie in her confusion mistook her for Elaine.

At first she ached for Bridie, that she should be reduced to this; she mourned the loss to her friend of her dignity and reserve – those qualities that made her Bridie. But weeks of attrition ground away Ruth's loving kindness. The constant pounding and sleep–deprivation destroyed her balance. Exhaustion and a kind of hatred set in together – loathing of Bridie's suffering spread into abhorrence of the sufferer, so mindlessly committed to the transference of her pain to a victim.

I'll walk out and leave her.

I hate her, I hate her stench and her shit and her open-mouthed snoring when the morphine's in her.

Die, can't you – just die.

Ungrateful.

Bridie's cheeks caved in. Her skin was ashen. Her cropped grey hair, which had fallen out in clumps during radiotherapy, grew in bristly patches on her skull. Ruth turned and washed this body, fed and watered it, because she had to, and only for that reason. Bridie's intelligence flickered in the blue eyes that still knew everything there was to know about Ruth and her susceptibilities. It flamed up in recognition of the fact that Ruth had withdrawn her love.

'You rat. You've run away. Fucking coward.'

'I don't know what you're talking about. Drink your tea.' She stuck the straw into Bridie's mouth to shut her up. Her eyes were cold. Bridie spat the straw out.

'Can't face it, can you? Can't face reality. Never could. Always running for mother.'

'Bridie. *Bridie.* I'm just tired. Tired.'

'Poor little thing,' Bridie sneered. 'I suppose you want *me* to be sorry for *you.*'

'No . . . no. I just want us to be – sane.'

There was a short pause. Then, 'I never loved you. You never loved me,' Bridie observed, through parched lips.

'So you keep telling me. But it's not true.'

'It is true, it is true.'

'Have it your own way.' Ruth plonked the cup down on the bedside cabinet.

'Bitch. Cunt. Dyke,' Bridie began to scream.

'Whatever you say. Let me know when you want your tea.'

'Elaine . . .' murmured Bridie. 'Elaine . . .'

Downstairs in the kitchen, Ruth's hands shook convulsively as she poured boiling water onto a teabag for herself. Her teeth were chattering as if she were cold, and something was screeching inside her head, a unanimous voice that was neither her own nor Bridie's but a keening composite of both. She must get that woman *out*. She must be got *out*. The noise must stop. It must be made to stop. The scalding contents of the mug spilt over her fingers as she tried to raise it to her lips. Damn. Can't even drink a cup of tea in peace.

She rang the doctor.

'I can't go on . . .'

The doctor rang the hospice.

'Six weeks' stay. Give you a rest . . .'

She didn't dare tell Bridie. She packed the grip all around the bed where Bridie lay, her eyes swivelling about after her. Ruth could feel the eyes on her back, on her hands as she folded pyjamas, put comb in brush, fetched washbag and towel – but did not risk meeting the eyes of prosecution and judge.

'You're getting rid of me, aren't you?'

Ruth did not say a word.

'Good,' said Bridie. 'I'm glad. I shan't have to see your evil do-gooding po-face again, you sick little hypocrite, you parasite, you nobody.' She began to shout and holler, blaspheming against her Maker, her mother, her lover, in a high, rasping voice that was in no sense Bridie's voice, firm and contralto, except for the hint of southern Irish that inflected it.

'Stop – that – bloody – noise!' Ruth, hands over ears, ran out of the room. The noise pursued her down the stairs. It didn't seem to lessen. The further away she got, the more it blared in her ears, like a Walkman with the volume turned up. The noise was inside her. Bursting out of the back door, she staggered into the raw, wintry garden. Bridie was a keen gardener. She had left everything neat and right for winter, ready for the sap to spring again in the vegetation of the new year. The shaven heads of the three beech trees stood still like penitents in the greyly misty air, stock-still; the polled hedges and lopped shrubs stood their ground the length of the long narrow garden. A dead silence reigned out here, and in that funerary silence mingled the polluting fumes from the nearby main road.

The next-door neighbour, Mrs Mason, a widow, looked out of her bedroom window in astonishment. The red-haired young woman from number seven was clashing the lid of her dustbin against the metal rim of the bin like a cymbal. Beating and roaring like a mad thing, like something not human. The other woman, Miss McKearn, the eminent one from the Third World Trust whom you sometimes saw being interviewed on television about Ethiopia and global warming and suchlike, was gravely ill, she knew. Only this morning she had been browsing round the second-hand shelves in the Trust shop on the High Street and come away with a very nice camel coat in top condition, as good as new.

Because of her distinguished neighbour, Doris Mason felt a particular interest and almost a proxy partnership in the Trust shop, where she would go by preference even over the Help the Aged shop at the other end of the High Street. She had taken to the Trust all George's best suits, shirts, ties, woollies and shoes the week after his death – all the garments immaculate, precision ironed, as she always kept them for him. Even now, two and a half years on, she could not bring herself to open his empty drawers. She sighed as she turned away from the window into the hollow house, letting the net curtain fall. It did not die, the ache, but you learnt a partnership with a person's absence; you learnt to live on the light fare of memory and to keep busy, always busy. They were going through it next door, that was for sure. She knew, she knew. She had offered help – shopping, sitting with the sick woman to give the girl a breather – but the red-haired girl, screwing up her eyes against the light, had said, 'No, no, there was nothing, really, nothing.'

Ruth suddenly let fall the dustbin lid and tottered into the house. A migraine aura had started, God be praised. The merciful, blinding pain spread to her right temple and across half her forehead, spiking her eye. It deafened her to the noise and the silence both.

The hospice nurse led her back indoors by the elbow. She acquiesced readily. He had a gold ear-ring in his left lobe. Its gleam drew her eye, which then met his in supplication.

'It happens a lot, it's a common reaction – rage,' he explained. 'People take it out on those they love best. They trust them to bear it for them. You shouldn't really be hurt – in fact, the opposite.'

Ruth began to laugh. 'Sorry,' she said. 'I've got a migraine,' as if that explained it. The joke was *those they love*. That was a good one. She let herself be settled on the divan in Bridie's study, with her head on a cushion. It was good to be babied. This was a nice young man, if off his head: *those they love*. She agreed to rest or sleep, and to ring in during the afternoon. The ambulance drove off with its suffering cargo and left her to the quiet.

'Thank God,' she thought, and slept.

A premature twilight had fallen, though it was only mid-afternoon. Ruth's eyes travelled the surfaces of Bridie's study, resting on the familiar textures and shapes of the objects with which her friend had surrounded herself through decades spent working for and travelling with aid agencies and latterly running the Trust. This room was Bridie's inner space, private and solitary as the centre of Bridie herself, which Ruth had never reached; and she doubted if anyone had ever shared it, even Elaine. Simple and beautiful objects, a Shona pitcher of orange terracotta, pots and drinking vessels chiefly South American, sculpted wooden heads and figurines, lay on shelves and on the sill of the high sash-window through which what cindery light there was fell in and smudged each image. The house was an Edwardian semi-detached building on three storeys, built by a Manchester bourgeoisie which hadn't quite the lucre to match its genteel aspirations: the magnificence of the entrance hall, with its stained-glass door-panels and wood-panelled walls, was belied by the thin wooden doors in the interior. The whole house had a faded, battered air. Bridie loved it, not least because it was her inheritance from her mother. Lizzie indicted it as a 'right dump'. Sarah had never stated her opinion. Bridie's study seemed its core, its heart. One wall was all books, to the ceiling: well-read books, nothing for show, and each one seeming a fragment of a testament to Bridie's mind. Pot plants perched on every ledge, and hung from the ceiling in a wicker basket, but they had all died, since Ruth had no time for them. Bridie had a little long-spouted can with which she watered them every other day, whistling.

So strong was the sense of Bridie's presence in the room that Ruth, starting awake, had thought she detected her in the

9

shadow between the bookcases and the curtains. Unnerved, she jerked upright on the couch, staring, searching. But there was only the smoke-screen of Bridie's belongings, the things her hands and eyes had touched, conveying the fiction of perpetuated life. Her travel clock with its minute tick registered 3.35: Ruth had been sleeping for six hours.

'Oh Bridie.'

She spoke it queryingly into the quiet obscurity of the study. 'Oh, Bridie.'

How would Bridie counsel her now, if Bridie were still Bridie? What wisdom would she offer? But Bridie, whatever words she had found to say, would have offered the solace of her arms and the warmth of her breast, to supplement the counsel. That was always what Ruth craved and needed. 'Don't lecture me, Bridie,' she'd sometimes said (for Bridie could be a bit obtuse, a bit prone to imagine that all problems had rational solutions, if you just put your mind to it). 'Don't give me one of your harangues: *hold me.*' Which Bridie did without any further ado, saying 'Of course' and that she loved to do it. Speech that was touch was the deepest communication.

Bridie would have told her to hang on to what they had had; to remember her as she was and had always been, and to take strength from the proven fact that she, Ruth, had been loved on this earth, truly and fiercely loved, for herself. She knew quite well what Bridie *would* have said. But that person seemed a frail and ghostly illusion that had been whisked away, to reveal – the horror of that afflicted woman, out of her senses with pain and despair, who vomited abuse day and night and called out, 'Elaine, Elaine'.

She had failed Bridie utterly, utterly. Failed her in her extremity, in the Gethsemane of her need. Failed her friend. She recoiled from herself in revulsion, sprang from the bed and leaned over Bridie's desk.

Bridie would have understood and forgiven. She would have said, *My darling*.

Yes, Bridie, who was temperate and wise deep down under the sharpness and the intellect, would have forgiven, saying, *I laid on you more than you could bear*.

Ruth reached out with trembling hand to switch on the Anglepoise on Bridie's desk. At once the pool of brilliant light and its reflection in the dusty gloss of the wood created a circular focus to the room. It shone on the black electric typewriter, ponderously old-fashioned, which Bridie called her 'thinking machine' and on which she composed the first drafts of her reports, directives, appeals and the letters with which she flooded the press, working sometimes deep into the night and bedding down on the couch in here if she thought Ruth likely to have fallen asleep already. Ruth, unlike her friend, was not a sound sleeper; if awoken in the night, she'd get jittery, start thinking about Lizzie and Sarah, and be unable to drop off again. Beside the typewriter were stacks of files and neat in-trays and out-trays of correspondence, marked 'Today', 'Next week', 'Sometime' and 'Anywhen'. Bridie's method was eccentric but fastidious. She had made herself computer literate, but never become attached to the word-processor and the fax, which she kept in a more impersonal room.

Ruth sat down in Bridie's place and fiddled with the drawers of a miniature chest Sarah had designed and manufactured in class, and given to Bridie on her birthday to please her mother. She had neglected to supply the drawers with handles, so that you had to invert the whole thing to slide them open, whereupon everything fell out. Paper-clips scattered over the desk. Ruth left them where they had showered, catching the light, making the desk look used.

Through the transparent plastic cover of the typewriter, Ruth discerned the shimmer of white paper, the ghost of the last

11

letter Bridie had typed before she put her work away. She ripped off the cover. Perhaps some final message to herself.

and therefore the relationship between North and South, she read, *on the face of it so advantageous to the affluent North, is in fact a time bomb waiting to explode in our faces. The deforestation of South America and the desertification of large tracts of Africa, the arming of the Third World with hi-tech weaponry and the manipulation of political tensions by the First World are*

Are what? Bridie did not say. They just are. She had left them in being.

Bridie was her work. That was where you found her, if anywhere. But finding her there was to stumble upon something beyond you – something faintly terrible and threatening, like a spider at the centre of its web. For she was not ordinary or homely like Ruth. Ruth went to school and taught for six hours, came home and did her marking as rapidly as possible and that was the end of it. Not that she did not care, but she did not let it take her over. Whereas Bridie ate, drank, lived, dreamed the Third World, as if driven to atone for its crucifixion. And that pledging of herself was what was wonderful about Bridie and what one reverenced. But it was what also seemed to draw her to the edge of sanity: it was extreme and exacting, both to herself and to others. Heaving the unimaginable weight of the globe on to her shoulders. Sometimes it occurred to Ruth in heretical moments that it was Bridie, not herself, who was unbalanced. She made you feel a lesser person, and wasn't that pride? But because she bestowed herself on you, she also extended and expanded you. Ruth felt far more herself for having known and been loved by Bridie: so much so that she had the courage to question Bridie's unbending standards.

'You're obsessed. You ought to be able to just let it all go, and enjoy yourself. Enjoy the moment. Just being.'

'I know. I've learnt that through you. So many, many things.'

And then the huge, warm smile would come, making Bridie's face so much younger and more gentle. 'I'd made a profession of being earnest – being formidable. Trying to move mountains, I'd squash people all along the way. It's you have made me human, Ruth – made me lighter.'

Ruth quivered with the wonder of that confession. All those marvellous things Bridie came out with, she committed to memory, learning them by heart, to turn them over and over in the more barren passages when Bridie was preoccupied, or abroad, and bad dreams surfaced of the impossibility of this beauty lasting.

Now it was all shattered. She felt like a murderer. She had had Bridie in her last illness in her care, at her mercy – Bridie whose love had been boundless and whom she loved boundlessly – and she had failed her. Failed her, betrayed her, and finally got rid of her. The hatred and revulsion she had felt for Bridie only six or seven hours ago now seemed mad and so cruel – inexplicable. It turned back on herself. What if Bridie had barked at her? Hadn't she the right? She saw Bridie's stick-arms lying helplessly over the quilt, with the big hands out of proportion to the wasted muscles, like something stuck on to a puppet; she saw the sunken cheeks and the deep grey shadowings around eyes and temples; the poor vulnerable bottom she had had to clean, and the catheter tube hanging from the tender place between her legs.

A silent scream tore through her brain. She shrouded the typewriter in its cover, hiding away that last unfinished letter's testament to the fact that these horrors are, they *are*, and can never be undone. She left the intolerable study, to move restlessly from room to room, but there wasn't a corner of the house where she could bear to remain. She sighed deeply, moved on again, sighed again. Switching on the radio she caught the words, *Secretary of State Baker has warned Saddam*

Hussein . . . It meant nothing to her. The pain of her spirit drowned out all external messages, peremptory as hunger and somehow locating itself physically in the pit of her stomach. In the kitchen she rummaged for bread and pulled a hunk off the remains of a granary loaf. But it was stale, and her mouth so dry she couldn't chew it. As she wrestled it with her tongue, she felt the sobs welling up from deep in the constriction of her throat. But the tears wouldn't flow, couldn't. She stood at the window and stared at the bruised sky while the inedible food congealed to a dry paste between tongue and palate.

So this was all it came down to, the obscene confusion, remorse and pointlessness? The darkening sky said so; the blank wall said so; the smirking Venus in the Botticelli print concurred. There was no one out there. There was no love. It was as if she had been pleading for a parental voice to reassure her that, no, this was not all there was to say. The voice was never going to speak.

'Bridie!'

The wad of bread came away and fell into the sink.

'Bridie . . . I'm so sorry . . . I failed you . . . forgive me . . . I had the chance I did I had the chance . . .'

A keening arose; she stumbled about from room to room but still there were no tears until suddenly the dam gave and they poured out with violence, accompanied by racking sobs until she was empty and still, lying in the middle of the sitting-room floor and hugging a cushion. There was no noise, not even the revving of a car or the echo of a distant aeroplane. Nothing. Getting up carefully, she balanced herself at the centre of the nothingness. She picked up the phone. She must have help, support, love. She was too frail to carry this burden alone; she must get through to someone.

Ruth began to dial Gavin's number. Not the Gavin who had turned so nasty on her and removed her children with the collusion of the judge sitting on the fourth floor at Heron House; not the Gavin of Asher and Co, the family solicitors in Bramhall which was also branching out into estate agency; not the Gavin with the expensive suit and the shirt with the detachable collar which returned in a cardboard box with four of its brethren from the laundry every Friday. No, not him, but the earlier Gavin of their student days at Manchester University nearly twenty years ago, the gentle law student, tall, willowy and supple but endearingly gauche, and with the sweetest smile Ruth had ever (to this day) seen. Gavin the failure, who understood, without needing to interrogate or analyse, her volatile, ambivalent moodiness, because he was considered to be a bit of a dead loss himself: a Rugby schoolboy who hadn't been equipped to play the game, but who softly stole off to the edge of the playing-field, leaving his defensive position uncovered, there to lie and study the low sunlight in the grass while his fellows walloped up and down the pitch in their big boots. Destined for Cambridge, he had scraped into Manchester and was heading for a Third. That suited him fine, he cheerfully said, for he wanted to work in Legal Aid and you didn't need fancy credentials. He liked Ruth's passion for Causes; ferried her to demonstrations and picked her up from police stations; introduced her proudly as 'my best friend Ruth who used to be a Communist and is now a peace worker'. Entwined from the first week of their first term, they dawdled in coffee bars, discussing the universe and giggling over nothing, like brother and sister almost more than lover and lover. And though she found him incredibly beautiful (he wore a sort of sarong at night instead of pyjamas; he looked like a statue come to breathing life, delicate-skinned and golden in lamplight), their love-making was hopeless. But she expected men to be costive and trusted the tenderness of gazes and silences. This was the Gavin whose number she now dialled.

'Hello. Gavin Asher here.'

She instantly replaced the receiver at the sound of the rich, authoritative voice. That was not the Gavin she wanted, in whose young uncertainty one could be embraced.

Ruth dialled again, her mother's number in Cornwall, but replaced the phone before anyone answered. Her mother and stepfather had formally cut her off after what they called her 'disgraceful abandonment of husband and children'. That was no loss, at the time. An unhingeing childhood spent in a number of second-rate boarding schools had come to seem the measure of her mother's attachment to her. For the first time now, she consciously registered the loss. She must speak to someone. Must.

She dialled the hospice.

'I'm enquiring about a patient, Miss Bridget McKearn – she came in this morning . . . I don't know the ward.'

'One moment please . . . ward five. I'm putting you through to Sister.'

'I'm enquiring about Bridget McKearn. She came in today. I – live with her. I'm her . . . I'm her friend, closest friend. Like a sister. Ruth Asher.'

'Oh, yes, hello, Miss Asher. Bridget's settled in very nicely. She's quite comfortable and peaceful – sleeping now. Come in and visit whenever you like. There are no fixed visiting hours. You're welcome any time.'

Welcome any time. The words stayed with her as she poured herself a glass of water from the tap. *Welcome any time.* They had the power to assuage, like conditional forgiveness. The water slid smoothly and coolly down her throat; it tasted very good, and refreshed, simply. *Welcome any time* was the short-term blessing of unlooked-for reprieve. It implied that there was still time; that she would not be turned away. She drank again.

Elaine Demetrian browsed her way round the Trust shop in the suburb of her home town, Leeds, where she had settled to write her book on child poverty, her specialism. She had obtained secondment from UNICEF and a Dingwall Scholarship: the work was going well, though more slowly than she had anticipated. But she indulged her lack of attack, uncharacteristically: after all, she was a mere four years off sixty, most people's retirement age. She lived content and self-sufficient, petting her cat, Leah, taking stock to reflect. The Trust shop, she was gratified to note, was doing a roaring trade in the city, despite all the bad auspices, including the formal objections registered by all the neighbouring businesses without exception, on the grounds of unfair competition. The clothes shop next door had objected to the lease and only rescinded its complaint when the Trust promised to withdraw its stock of new T-shirts and sell only the second-hand article; Elaine laughed up her sleeve when, searching through the rail of clothes, she discerned new T-shirts cunningly dispersed amongst the old. The card shop on the other side had objected to the Trust's window display of recycled stationery, and the shop had been forced to agree to place on display only second-hand books, which in turn displeased the nearby bookshop, whose outrage was appeased by the withdrawal of the books and the substitution of dhurries made in India by a women's co-op. This had caused offence to the shoe shop on the opposite side of the precinct, for no other reason than that its vivid brightness solicited the eye of the potential footwear customer from its proper preserve. This objection having been turned down on the grounds of its patent absurdity, the lighting shop insisted that its sales of china shepherdesses and half-lifesize spaniels with lampshades on their heads would be prejudiced by competition from cheap bric-à-brac sold by volunteer labour with no overheads and made by a dirt-cheap foreign workforce.

This objection was just being investigated when a Trust worker got in touch with the local television channel and the newspapers, whose adverse comment not only gave the shop some free publicity but caused a boycott of the complainants, who smartly withdrew their objections. Thus the First and Third Worlds had settled into a state of peaceful co-existence.

Elaine fingered a small wooden box made of teak, with pretty carvings in an abstract design. Coveting the object, which had no earthly use, she at once hunted round in her mind for someone to bestow it upon. That nice girl Lindsay she'd met at the concert: it would do just right for her. Still she lingered, dawdling. Being here was bitter-sweet, always; brought back such echoes of Bridie, and their early, amazing partnership which, by the outspoken force of their joint wills had brought the charity into being, turning their small capital into a several million-pound annual turnover. *Fiat lux*, they had said together, with such absolute conviction, that there *was* light, it came into being. She could not now, under the inertia of growing age, conceive how they did it. And then the shock when Bridie rejected her. It seemed impossible. She just turned her back and went off with that pretty girl. Had Bridie minded, she asked herself for the hundredth time, about Elaine's several lovers? She had assured her that, no, she did not mind a scrap, why should she? For she herself seemed to have been born with a shortage of libido, and why shouldn't Elaine enjoy hers to the full? So she went ahead (to be truthful, she'd have gone ahead anyway) and after steady years of comradeship, the unquestioned centre of both their lives, Bridie just flipped. Raved of Ruth. Wept for Ruth. Needed, wanted, must have Ruth. *A late adolescence*, observed Elaine coolly, and took herself off, carrying nothing away with her but an electric globe they'd been fond of. Well, you got over it; fell in love again; but she could never write Bridie off, diminish her greatness to a low stature on which one could look down and say, 'Well, she wasn't so very wonderful, after all.' For Bridie was wonderful, incomparably so. She'd heard she was ill. It bothered her. She might phone. Yes, she would definitely phone this evening: she made a mental note.

Elaine queued with her purchase. The lady in charge of the counter was having some trouble with the computerised till, and apologised to the queue. Elaine took her mind off the arthritic inflammation in her knees, which always got worse if she stood for any length of time, by listening in to the conversation of the women who helped run the shop, and were now sorting donations of second-hand clothing behind the open door of the ante-room.

'I never trust them when they come in saying "It's all good stuff" – you know at once it's full of holes or filthy throw-outs.'

'Or when they come in with a great heap of rags saying "You might find something amongst all this, and if you don't, you've always got a good waste arrangement, haven't you". Saves them a trip to the blinking tip.'

'Oh yes, we got a load of stuff last week. She said, "Some of it might be some use", and she was off out the door – you couldn't see her for dust – and when we got it open it was filthy old sheets, someone'd wet the bed, tried to bleach it out and left a big blue patch – would you credit it?'

'I would, I would indeed.'

'But wouldn't you think – wouldn't you honestly, Joan? – they'd have more *pride*?'

Elaine, catching no answer, imagined the eloquent look that must be passing between eye and eye at the general public's unthinking equation of the Third World Trust with a handy rubbish tip. She could perfectly sympathise with their feelings. And yet it went deeper and wider than that. We were all of us implicated. We condescended to donate, if not our leavings, at

19

least only a minute proportion of our surplus to the needy in the name of benevolence, and felt better people for doing so. Elaine shifted uneasily from foot to foot. She handed over the teak box and had the price rung up.

'Pretty thing,' said the assistant.

'Isn't it? Are you sure it's only £4.50?'

'That's what it says.'

A bargain indeed, she thought, sardonically. From the first they had agreed, she and Bridie, that charities shouldn't be necessary, they should be obsolete. Bridie had insisted on the political dimension of the Trust, working to change structures, not to palliate queasy consciences. Even so she'd sometimes awoken in the small hours, defences down, and perceived with desolation how puny, even meaningless, all their effort was; how vain, in every sense. She and Bridie had presided like Victorian ladies at a grandiose bazaar while all the time the ships ferried chemical waste to dump on famine-stricken nations which handed back the revenue in debt repayments. She'd seen Bridie rage about that; rage with all the frustration of the implicated.

'Look here, it's better than nothing,' they'd comforted each other.

After putting her purchase in her pocket, she paused to write in her diary 'Phone Ruth re Bridie tonight'.

2

Bridie floated, very restfully, somewhat above the bed where the white coats (without faces) had laid her body. She had just been taken down from the Cross and bestowed within a quiet recess from which the shining attendants had respectfully withdrawn, leaving her to float on a cushion of air, inches above a surface.

'Rest now, Bridget, sleep. I'll be nearby if you need someone.'

All was well with her shattered body now. The worst that could be done to it had been done. Wiped clean of Judas kisses, her remains were being cared for by blessedly anonymous pairs of hands, skilful and effective. Nothing was demanded. Everything was guaranteed. She was so glad. It was an inexpressible relief, to have the long drawn-out torture over at last. Her legs and arms were lead-solid and immovable, and yet it was true that she floated freely, as if these limbs had all turned to liquid and her identity flowed out over the pillowing air.

And then from time to time she disappeared from herself; flowed back into herself, rather, and was lost in emotionless depths that still floated high (pure of aspiration) above the demand that she – for others' sakes – be anything at all.

Once, her eyes awoke and viewed an expanse of grey light, framed in transverse bars and bordered by a green velvetish curtain. The monotony of this nearly blank perspective pleased her incurious eyes, until a floral curtain was trawled across it and voices announced their intention to turn her.

'No hassle, Bridget. It won't take a moment. My, what a nasty sore. Poor Bridget, has it been hurting you, dear? Sue, just pass those pads, darling, will you – that's the way. There we go, pet. Tuck you in again nice and comfy. You have another good sleep, there you go.'

Lullaby lullaby. But when they grasped her armpits and shoulders (though as gently as might be) to drag her up the bed as well as over to her left side, she seemed to burst the surface as if she came hurtling up like a hoisted fish from the sea, to be gutted in a dazzle of light. So perhaps she was not dead after all, if such violence could still be registered. Peace was what she ached for, peace beyond all: not to be touched, ever again.

She groaned.

'It's all right, my dear. It's all over.'

She floated up again, just fractionally above the bed, but enough to give her the desired advantage over her conditions. Some such advantage she had enjoyed throughout her life, hovering slightly above it all, them all, giving all and giving nothing, free until latterly of the incontinent mess of a full commitment.

Later again, Bridie's eyes and mind opened both together and consulted briefly over the low bars which broke up her field of vision. Although her mouth was unpleasantly dry, she was aware of no pain in any portion of her body, and the absence of this pain had a positive and profound quality, like the aftermath of a deafening noise which has been suddenly switched off. Here indeed was matter for praise.

A glass of water arrived, held in a small, neat hand wearing a wedding ring, and with finely manicured nails. They seemed to know before Bridie asked what her needs were, and these needs and functions were efficiently catered for. Bridie asked no questions and volunteered no speech.

Now her body was propped against a mound of pillows in a partially seated posture. She could see that she had been placed in a bed next to a great curtained window, in a ward containing six beds, two of which were unoccupied. In the others slept or sat two elderly and one ancient women, minding their own business. To her left stood a TV set on a high cupboard but it was not switched on, and Bridie was glad of that for she wanted no invasion of chatter.

Her mind was at once clear and wildly meandering. The clear part saw beyond a shadow of a doubt that she had reached the end of the road; the meandering part viewed the road itself. From her present position, Bridie could focus her 'journey' as she had liked to call it, leading back in a long white ribbon like one of those chalky bridle-paths she had used to trot along over the moors at Stanley, between the high banks of heather and bilberry. Sometimes the heather had been burnt and the moors spread like a wasteland of charcoal miles across, and smelt of ash mingled with sour peaty water from the burns. In early autumn the heather flared out like a field of spring violets; and at times it lay dark and sulphurous, mined with reedbeds and cotton-grass, under a blasting wind and turbid sky. Always the bridle-way intersected the moor in a straight line running up the breast of a gentle inclination and disappearing in a dot at the horizon. As a little girl, Bridie trotted along between her father's dark-trousered long strides and their spaniel, Dragon, and marvelled at the purposive straightness of the chalky path which dipped into troughs and shouldered ridges but always headed straight onwards toward the centre. The centre was the middle of nowhere, which also (when you got there) was the middle of everywhere. Their destination was a cairn of limestone blocks about twice as high as Bridie, placed there on the draughty continent of moorlands for no recorded purpose, but meaningful to the child's eye, all the more so for being attached solely to herself and her father. For it was their cairn, Bridie's and Tom's. She scaled the pinnacle and let the wind bash her eyes and inflate her waterproof hood; Dragon tore up and down the sheep-paths that catacombed the forests of heather and had to be called off from worrying the sheep. Her father, crouching at the base of the cairn, tried to smoke his pipe, cupping his hand around the guttering match in the lee of the rocks. When he had got it to light, he sat with his legs apart, fostering the tenuous fire in the bowl, and looking in the same direction as Bridie, frowningly, and there they sat like people on a sea-shore who surmise the suspicion of a boat on the horizon. Bridie could see him now, with the collar of his tweed coat turned up and his cap down, so private and inward a man, so affined to herself. They were looking out of the same eyes at the same eternity, in the silver lightscape of the heavens, above the dark mass of the earth – but where he saw God, even at that early stage she saw power without glory, force without love. The glory and the love resided in him, and in her love for him. When he was gone, that light went out, leaving the godless and orphaned creation in its dark wake.

Up in the gallery of the Stanley Baptist Chapel, they had stood Sunday by Sunday, Mr, Mrs, and Miss McKearn, singing with passionately stirred souls, 'Nearer, my God to thee' and 'O Love that wilt not let me go'. The fellowship of the congregation was cherishing, emotional and claustrophobic. Sometimes members sobbed out loud during the service; the Spirit might inspire one or another to exhale a resounding 'Hallelujah!' or an ecstatic 'Yea, Lord!'; a woman might stand up and confess, with rapturous remorse, to being a backsliding daughter. Each worshipper was served with a beaker of unfermented wine and a crust of tasty bread. You consumed these morsels in the comfort and dignity of your own pew; Bridie relished the bread and wine and often wished for a second helping. Baptised by total immersion at twelve, she reverted from Paul to Saul at fourteen: that too was a paradoxical consequence of her upbringing. From her earliest days as the only child of puritan parents, Bridie had been permitted no intervening screen against the awareness of the suffering and struggle which constituted a norm for most fellow creatures. Now her father himself grew ill with the tuberculosis which was to kill him in her fifteenth year. No good God would have allowed that. Upon scrutiny of the offensive logic of the Creator's punitive and indeed homicidal or pathological creation of a world of pain and injustice, she refused the inheritance of her father's religion. But his exacting social conscience was a different thing. She was the willing heir of her father's concern to ameliorate that suffering. Proudly, she took it upon herself.

'My special girl,' he had called her. 'My one and only.'

Throughout her life Bridie had hung on to that specialness, an exclusive difference from other people. Like the Calvinist's sense of election, it was not always easy to affirm in the face of deep-rooted insecurities, but all the more it seemed essential for survival, a defence against disintegration. A tall, large-limbed, speculative child, Bridie had never fitted in with the girls of Stanley, nor those of Halifax where she and her mother moved after her father's death. Her mother, a unique blend of tolerance and piety, had rarely criticised Bridie's tomboy-ishness, observing that she needed and ought to be 'as God made her'. Bridie sheared her own hair short with sewing scissors and her remarkable mother did not bat an eyelid, merely remarking that she might consider wearing a balaclava helmet when she went out in the cold. Then she went on peeling the sprouts. Bridie however was unimpressed by her mother's broadmindedness. Mum just peeled sprouts and stirred gravy (which Bridie was not, however, above eating); Dad dreamed dreams and saw visions. Among the red-ribboned, petticoated village girls, Bridie with her close-cropped head and belling trousers looked a freak; and the southern Irish accent she deliberately cultivated, in emulation of her father's lilt, also marked her out from the downright speech of her peers. But nobody bullied Bridie; nobody dared. When the village boys ambushed her, Bridie with bleeding head picked up a jagged stone and simply walked back towards the gang (quite unclear as to what she intended to do when she got there) which, reacting to the combination of bale and moral courage in her eye, thought better of the whole thing and did a bunk. In later decades, Bridie smashed opposition on a regular basis by drawing on the same combination.

So Bridie's 'journey' forked and twisted away from the straight white ribbon of the bridle-path. But it had mattered to be classed as a good person, a proudly good person who went her own way and whose commitment and concern were exercised over a broad – ultimately, global – area. She undertook this mission on the basis of a precise stratagem: first a degree in Economics at Hull, followed by a degree in Middle Eastern Studies. She taught herself four languages, one for every continent. She did VSO in Botswana. If you were to take on the world, it was necessary to do so in its own terms, having qualified yourself in its methods and techniques. Later in her life, Bridie taught herself computer skills. Elaine and she co-founded the Third World Trust, and turned it into a worldwide organisation within ten years precisely because they had both brought to it worldly wisdom, political astuteness (Elaine more so than she) and a ruthless intellectual self-discipline. Elaine first focused them on women's issues as the basis for Third World change: empowerment through co-operative work, control of fertility, dissemination of medical knowledge, resistance to oppression on many fronts, particularly to the sexual mutilation widespread in Africa and the East. Elaine . . . It would have been much better to have stayed with Elaine. They made a team. Ruth made her throw all that out of the window – all that work and comradeship, the years and years of mutual endeavour. Just like that. Ruth opened her up and melted her into tenderness and vulnerable need; the soft tissue at the quick of Bridie was touched as never before since Dad and early days. For years she could hardly believe this was herself, this yielding, happy woman who sang in the bath and went on holiday, who squandered God-given hours talking blissful nonsense or idly lying with her head in Ruth's lap – even watching rot like *Brookside* or Ruth Rendell mysteries on television because her friend mindlessly enjoyed relaxing by the box.

The road now was hazy but shining.

'So this is life. *Life!*' she kept radiantly exclaiming. She hadn't thought of it as something possible to herself, nor the sensual tenderness that took her body (accustomed to a state of uncomplaining austerity, like wartime rationing) by storm. 'And you've given it to me!'

'We've given it to one another,' Ruth would always reply. 'But we've brought one another different things, I think, Bridie. I've brought you – pleasure.'

'Delight – not *pleasure*.' She burnt her hands by plunging them into the red-gold fire of Ruth's hair. 'Amazing beauty.'

'Delight, then,' said Ruth, delighted. 'But you've brought me stability and security. The floor doesn't rock any more. You've earthed me.' She'd set her hands on Bridie's waist and stand against her strength and tallness, quietly, as if listening.

'Perhaps. Something like that.' Bridie, usually so careful

27

with words, vaguely demurred. 'Anyway, who cares? We've got one another, that's all that counts.'

But it was not true that Ruth had brought her only carefreeness and joy: Bridie's pride forbade her to admit even to herself that Ruth had a monopoly on new security. She evaded the acknowledgement that Ruth had compromised her independence. Where before she had felt complete in herself, sufficient for the road, now she needed someone else to feel whole. She must walk accompanied. But she endorsed the fiction that she was the strong one; Ruth the weaker. The mutual illusion made it seem truer. Her need bothered her: those ridiculous states of jealousy when Ruth got into animated conversation with colleagues. Especially younger and attractive men and women; the desire always to be in the same room with Ruth, which she sternly resisted by staying away for longer than was strictly necessary, even sleeping downstairs when she might have shared her bed. Ruth was not to know that she had gained advantage over Bridie. She should not be so entirely safe as to know her power. For Bridie half-consciously resented the threat to her own autonomy that had been made by Ruth's invasion of the sanctuary of her self: she had no weapons against that dominance.

Ruth's children cast long shadows on to the road. They bothered her for reasons she avoided delving into, for it would have been too gallingly humiliating to imagine that she could entertain jealousy of a mere child. The elder girl, Lizzie, oddly troubled her less than the winning and occasionally fawning younger. One could respect Lizzie's unfeigned hostility, and her heart went out in a complex of ways to the tall, arrogant sixteen-year-old, standing so straight, brown eyes very sharp and sometimes narrowing as she gave Bridie the deliberately evil eye. Lizzie's amazing bush of curly hair was a bright chestnut colour, lit by a gleam of her mother's auburn. It had been worn in one long rippling silky curtain all down her back, nearly to her waist until she had it cut into its present bush. Lizzie, being insecure, did not yet know that she was beautiful; she would find out at some stage, and then the world might appear different. Now it was a fearsome place of sliding surfaces and floors that gave, which did not seem to like her very much; she was a great quarreller and loser of friends. Bridie let Lizzie insult her, for it was not the children themselves that hurt her, but Ruth's bond; that, and the fact that they were offspring of union with *him*, that man she didn't want to name aloud. That man Ruth had once tenderly loved. She could not bear to think of Ruth making love – no, not making love at all, but coupling, being penetrated and possessed – by any man at all. Some demon of perversity kept drawing her imagination to that act, like a tongue exploring the aching hole of a pulled tooth. This kind of emotional mess exasperated her: it was alien to her habits of mind and the hitherto well-regulated conduct of her inner life. She made sure not to let on to Ruth. The more clamorous her need, the more glacial her aspect, so that Ruth often went off feeling small, and as if Bridie were not made of common stuff like herself but operated somewhere above her, in a rarefied empyrean where values and principles surmounted personal wants.

And yet they were happy – buoyantly happy for months and years together, happier than anyone (said Bridie) has a right to be. The lesser gods, confided Bridie in their bed, had ordained this from the beginning, the beginning being 18th May 1952, Ruth's birthday – behind the backs of the Major Gods, the ones in control of the world. The Major Gods, jealous of all human happiness, would find out in the end and squash them flat, but in the meantime . . . there was this . . .

It was in the spring of Bridie's fifty-second year and the sixth year of their partnership, that it became apparent that they had been detected by the Major Gods. At first they received the news of Bridie's terminal cancer with something like an ecstasy of heroism: Ruth especially. Ruth seemed to grow in stature during those weeks; her challenged love rose nobly to meet the threat in a way that astonished, and later (as she declined) dismayed and finally estranged Bridie. They wept together, deep in the night, cheek crushed against cheek, so that their tears flowed indistinguishably down their joined faces, soaking the pillow. Then they turned the pillow over and soaked the other side. Bridie wept for Ruth's coming widowhood as well as for her own ending. She checked out the terms of the life assurance policy and went over her will with her lawyer, to make sure Ruth's future life should be comfortable and free. At that time it had seemed to her as catastrophic to be the survivor as to be the dying partner.

'You'll be all right, Ruth, even if you decide to or have to give up work at any stage – I've gone through all the papers.' She tried to get Ruth to attend to practical details, down to the disposal of her remains and the probating of the will. 'The balance in the building society is around £16,000 and I want us to transfer it into your name now, so that there are no possible complications later on.'

Ruth seemed to attend, but only because it was demanded.

'I'm not thinking of all that, sweetheart, I'm thinking . . .'

'Oh but you *must*,' cut in Bridie. 'It's absolutely crucial for my peace of mind, to be sure that you'll never know want or be at a loss for funds – always have a roof over your head.'

'I know, darling love – I know, and that will be okay. Let's not . . .' She squeezed both Bridie's hands in both of hers and put them repeatedly to her lips.

'Are you paying attention or are you not, Ruth?' Bridie withdrew her hands and jabbed her forefinger at the documents.

'Yes, sir.'

'Right then, do. Because it's important. Now look here, Ruth, I've written it all down for you, because you'll be in no fit state when I've kicked the bucket. By the way, if it ever happens that you get into financial troubles in your old age – yes, I know it seems far away *now*, when you're only thirty-eight, but it will come, and perhaps ill health, and the children might not want to support you – take out an annuity on the house. It's all set out here.'

'But I'll have my teaching pension.'

'But, you see, you might lose your job or the pension might not be enough to cover your needs – say you have to go into a Home.'

'Oh, *Bridie*.'

'I'm thinking forward over every eventuality, Ruthie – though I can see you're not going to give yourself the trouble.'

'I'm thinking about you and only you. You are my world.'

'You have to live after I'm gone.'

'It won't be living. *This* is living. I want us to make use of every precious moment, my dear beautiful love – make an intense eternity of now.'

Bridie severely rumpled Ruth's hair. 'You're hopeless – bloody hopeless.'

'No, I'm full of hope.'

Bridie wondered if Ruth simply did not register the death sentence as reality, but, no, it did not seem to be that. It was more as if Ruth realised with rhapsodic clarity the beauty of what had been granted and was able to live in the centre of the moment of possession.

All Ruth's thoughts were concentrated on Bridie's present comfort. As the weeks went by and Bridie felt strength stealthily ebbing, Ruth's solicitude became rather stifling.

'Let me be, Ruth – you're suffocating me. Just be normal, for

Christ's sake,' she muttered edgily. 'I want to get on with my work. I can't while you're farting about.' She drummed with her fingers on the typewriter cover. 'Can I?'

'No. Sorry,' said Ruth, and withdrew from the study at once. Even Ruth's patience was beginning to get on Bridie's nerves. Why did she have to be so goody-goody? (That was her own prerogative.)

But Bridie couldn't cope with the work. Her tired fingers slid from the keys; the nauseous pain in her back seemed to eat at her mind as well as body. She knew that the eavesdropping Ruth knew that no significant sound was coming from the typewriter, whose motor purred softly on as Bridie lay down on the divan and turned her face away from the laden desk. Somehow she intermittently blamed Ruth for knowing the helplessness of her surrender; and for knowing that she blamed her, which was patently and absurdly unfair; and blamed her even for summoning up the loving forbearance to absorb all Bridie's tetchiness. That was superhuman, a quality Bridie had always congratulated herself on manifesting. And such a sustained show of strength demonstrated that Ruth was well and hale. Ruth had the health which she had lost.

Pounds of weight slid off her. She surveyed in the mirror the bony body whose ribs stood out under sagging breasts; flaps of skin had replaced the once powerful biceps. She looked at Ruth running to and fro for her all day long and her eyes wandered over the fit, young-looking body in tight jeans and Greenpeace T-shirt. She suddenly didn't want to touch Ruth any longer. As Ruth bent to kiss her, she averted her lips, keeping them tight; and inwardly mocked the momentary hurt hesitation Ruth betrayed, before she covered up the hurt behind a rueful smile. Then Bridie hated her inwardly for her composure – she who cried too easily, at the least excuse, so super-sensitive that she could spend a whole day brooding and grieving over some flea-bite of a sharp remark you couldn't even remember making – she was bearing this horror like some insufferable self-elected saint or martyr.

What it meant was that, ultimately, she didn't care. In Bridie's time of need, she had severed herself from her, enrolled in the tribe of the living beyond the thick glass pane that separates the dying from the well and hearty. Bridie felt as alone as after her father's funeral, blasted by the torrential wind that swept over the moors when she made the pilgrimage back to the cairn without him; and there was nothing and no one there, just the rough raw earth and dark clouds hurrying away out of sight – meaningless.

She even said it one apocalyptic day, after the administration of the Trust had been finally transferred from the Manchester to the London office. She said, sneeringly, 'You don't love me, Ruth. You don't really care.'

Ruth looked aghast. 'How can you say that, Bridie? How can you even begin to imagine it? I love you everything.'

Their old, childish phrase, once so dear, now grated on Bridie.

'You're well. I'm ill,' said Bridie, petulantly turning her face to the wall, eyes tight shut.

'Well, I can't help that,' returned Ruth. 'Can I?'

It was the first even slightly harsh thing she had said since the diagnosis, and although Bridie knew perfectly well she herself had forced it on Ruth, who had meant nothing by it, it caught in her mind by a tiny hook, and continued to irk, for it was just the sort of gruff, outspoken riposte she herself might have emitted in similar circumstances. Ruth had taken her place; taken her self away. On this occasion, however, Bridie had the grace, after a pause, to see her mistake and to redress it.

'I'm sorry – it's my fear speaking, Ruthie – not me.' And Ruth crowded in through the open door with her love and re-assurance.

But as time went on her response to Ruth took on the aspect of a settled malignity. Whatever pain and humiliation were doled out to her, she passed – or sought to pass – automatically across to her carer, who had once been the object of her care. She forgot that there had ever been a time when she worried fanatically if Ruth so much as caught a cold or even knocked her funny-bone on the door; wound her long tartan scarf several times round her neck against cold weather, even if it wasn't really all that chilly, and generally fussed and fidgeted over her friend's welfare 'like an old hen – give over, Bridie', as Ruth said. She had loved to protect and succour Ruth, but she had no talent for receiving with dignity and grace what she had so plentifully given. Dependency diminished her, she felt. And though Ruth (getting thinner and quieter, black bruise-like marks developing under her eyes) was joint victim of this torture, and lived in the same prison, it was not Ruth's liver, spine and lungs the cancer attacked. Ruth would wash her hands and dry her eyes at the end of it all when Bridie was underground (underground – to be buried – *underground*), and walk off scot-free, to get fat again and as happy as Larry. She'd be well-off, given all that Bridie had left to her, which was all Bridie had in the world including her mother's house; she could live as she liked, and, being youngish, vital and pretty-looking in a simple sort of way, she'd take new lovers, even marry again and make a new life of it, leaving Bridie alone and neglected, in the unvisited past. Although she couldn't summon the sexual energy to imagine Ruth with new partners and stab at herself with jealous fantasies, she nourished a vague general sense of inevitable betrayal, which was enough to make her keep hitting out at Ruth.

Somewhere within this degenerate wreck of her self, with its endless tirades and its pathetic and counter-productive campaign of retribution, remained the Bridie who Bridie had always been – looking out in silent distaste at her present disintegration. Her heart went out to Ruth as she scampered out of the sick-room to avoid breaking down in the face of the rancorously dying woman's unkindnesses. And, latterly, when she had reduced Ruth to a rage nearly as crazy as her own but more under control, she looked on her own behaviour as if witnessing a rather bad film, and shook her head at the folly of it. The film went on and on, nasty, stupid and in contradiction of all she had ever stood for.

At other times, when night and day had confusedly elided, and she could not distinguish the burning of the lamp at her bedside from the burning of the sun in the sky; and the outside world seemed to have penetrated the interior in an unseemly way, and her mind to have burst the sealing of its skull and to have poured out, discharging its seething contents out into a void, an overwhelming fear took over. She knew her need in its totality. She could sometimes catch and fix Ruth's face then, stabilising herself by keeping its pale oval at the focus of her gaze and meditating the contours of its chin and the tendrils of bright hair that curled at forehead and temples. That face was inexpressibly dear. But by some irony built into their situation, this calming perspective would generally be broken by Ruth's failure to register its wordless significance. As Ruth gazed back into the gazer's eyes, she would detect there no reassurance to herself, but only a steady coldness which made her flinch and flush up, and either turn away her eyes or remove her person, so that Bridie fell back into the maelstrom with curses on her lips. And the curses confirmed the darkness of Ruth's surmise.

Once only, she awoke and woke Ruth up, and the right words came, floating up perhaps from some dream: 'You are the good gift,' she said slowly, 'of the road to destruction', quoting one of

Yury's poems in *Dr Zhivago*. The benediction came out of the blue, or out of the black, with the arbitrariness of grace. But the breakthrough made no difference. The next morning she found herself hard at it again – slandering, vilifying. No language was too coarse: indeed, she heard herself uttering filth she hadn't previously known she knew. The unconscious mind was certainly a treasure trove of wonders when you came down to it – a bag of ordure, just like the human body. She laughed out loud at the discovery that had taken rather over half a century for her subtle and civilised mind to divine.

'Shit-bag, shit-bag, shit-bag!' she cackled, meaning Ruth, meaning herself, indiscriminately. With our soiled hands, mouths, brains, behinds and private (that was another joke) parts, we were all in it excrementally together, in up to our necks, in over our heads.

She saw Ruth sigh and raise her hand to her forehead which was wrinkled up with concentration, and rub it with the tips of her fingers, as if speculatively enquiring of herself, 'Who is this disgusting woman? Is this Bridie?' and then, 'Why have I got to look after *this*?' And again Bridie laughed, neighingly.

Therefore it was an unadulterated relief to be released from confinement with that stranger who had presumed too close an acquaintance and pinned Bridie like a flayed specimen on a tray, anatomising her with magnifying eye. Dying without mortification was the easy option; dying without love, and, if that meant dying without Ruth, then okay, dying without Ruth.

A white-coated anonymity fed Bridie teaspoons of some rather decent-tasting savoury liquid and broke a crusty roll into pieces for her to eat, soaking each fragment in the soup. Bridie was surprised to find that she rather enjoyed the meal, especially in view of the fact that she was expected neither to speak nor to acknowledge the reality of any world beyond these pictureless and mirrorless walls.

An unobjectionable young man in a short-sleeved jerkin with epaulettes, punkish dark hair and a pair of gold-rimmed glasses which he recurrently pushed up the bridge of his nose, appeared and perched on the edge of her bed.

'What we'd like to do,' he said, 'is to get a balance of drugs that is right for *you* – so that you can be pain-free and at the same time lucid in your mind, for as long as possible.'

'Can you do that?'

'Almost definitely. But it's slightly different for each individual, and there's a certain amount of trial and error involved in getting the proportions exactly right for you.'

Bridie's eyes strayed to the next bed but one, where a white-haired woman in, perhaps, her seventies, was sitting up in bed and peeling an apple with methodical neatness, so that the peel dangled from the parer in one complete loop. When she had finished, she began to munch the apple with apparent relish. On the thin stalk of her wizened neck, her head appeared grotesquely large. Yet in the absorbed preparation and consumption of the apple, she was living a life. On the other side of the ward a crumpled old person in navy-blue sat collapsed in a chair, dozing. The apple woman addressed a few words to the person in the bed beside her, whom at first Bridie could not see but who levered herself up into view and gave a chuckle. The navy-blue woman in her permanent state of capsize slept on. *It's like being in a bloody geriatric ward*, thought Bridie. She felt mildly offended. Always having mixed with younger people, she had never felt her age; was indeed still awaiting her menopause, and rather proud of it.

'Only fifty-one,' she confided to the young man.

'I know,' he said, and paused, holding her gaze and as if waiting to see if she wanted to open up further. 'I know.' He hazarded no further comment.

'You're . . . a professional. Seen so much . . . dying. Your job: dying.'

'My job is to do with life. But acceptance of death.'

'The last of life.'

'The last of life. But life all the same.'

She couldn't stand people pussy-footing, prevaricating. Never had been able to. Gave them short shrift. Irritation brought energy.

'Well, try out your drugs by all means,' said Bridie authoritatively – as if on the phone to some agent of the Trust to whom she was inclined to give her head. 'But no drivelling vicars . . . or do-gooders . . . are to come anywhere near my bed.'

He laughed out loud. 'Don't worry. They only come on demand. I'd feel just the same in your place.'

'You are . . . all right.'

'Thanks. I take that as a high compliment.'

The needle dug its shaft into the protruding vein of Bridie's arm and faintness lapped over her.

'And I don't want . . .' she pronounced, but what she didn't want (which was a vist from Ruth) was never divulged, as all her muscles and joints relaxed, and an enervating warmth and forgetfulness seemed to drift along all her arteries and finally misted her brain, so that it didn't much matter what she didn't want.

Ruth travelled to the hospice on a roundabout series of bus trips through Stockport. She had never driven a car, partly through personal cowardice and partly through Green principles (which

Bridie once rudely said came down in her case to much the same thing); she had relied on Bridie to ferry her about, beyond the range of her mountain bike, but now the car had not budged from the garage for four months. It was ages since she'd been out of the house at all, except to visit the local shops, and the busy communal life that had gone on in her absence had taken on an uncanny feel in the midst of its familiar ordinariness – as if she had returned as a revenant, the ghost of her self. The spooked feeling intensified as the bus, passing the precinct with the Trust shop, arrived at the high school. It was five o'clock and the lights were blazing: a parents' evening, perhaps, or a concert. They had been generous in extending her compassionate leave to unpaid leave on an open-ended basis, with the promise of a job to return to. At least she had gratefully thought it generous at the time, but on consideration she could see that the financial cuts made any savings on immediate expenditure worthwhile. They had neither enough textbooks to go round nor basic equipment for the students, mainly impoverished children of the notorious Ardenshaw Heath Estate. So they fiddled the budgets to keep going. Through the grime of the bus window, Ruth registered with a pang the lights of the run-down school and the vague motion of people inside. She sustained such a vividly uncomfortable impression of her own absence, and the unimportance of that absence, that she breathed a sigh of relief as the bus pulled out from the bus-stop and carried on up the hill, through the sleety darkness. She turned her head away to stare out of the window, in case any of the large brown-uniformed girls who had boarded and were now raucously mounting to the upper deck, should recognise her. She dreaded to hear, *Oh look, there's Old Ashy – Hello Mrs Asher, have you left for good or what*? though in the past she'd been easy with the students – easy-going and effortlessly natural with them, yet not without the ability to keep order. Now she winced back from confrontations with people's eyes, and looked on at her own queasy forlornness with a critical eye. Upstairs, numerous pairs of Doc Martens were being drummed on the metal floor and voices were raised in bawling song.

'It didn't ought to be allowed,' objected the old woman sitting next to Ruth.

'And it never were in our day,' another agreed, shaking her head. 'It's the parents I blame. They don't keep enough of a strong hand on them.'

'Oh I don't know,' objected a mild-looking woman. 'They're not doing no one much harm, are they? Just a bit of high spirits.'

'*Well*,' said Ruth's neighbour and left it at that. She drew in her chin and glared indignantly at a place directly above the mild woman's head, where a poster advertised a cut-price coach tour of the Glorious Peak District. The symphonic voices aloft crashed on regardless, but as the bus paused at the traffic lights just above the town hall, the singing turned to hooting and catcalls.

'It's them again – them frigging anti-war buggers!' Piercing whistles were directed out of the windows.

'Silly sods!'

'I'd join up, I would. Like a shot. Tomorrow,' bawled a boy.

Ruth's glazed eye picked up an image of a cluster of dark figures on the steps of the war memorial (which was also, by odious contingency, the civic art gallery), demonstrating with home-made banners, candles and torches against the imminent war against Saddam Hussein. The sight jolted Ruth into sudden recognition that the world had been going on without her. Of course she listened to the news; her eyes automatically travelled over the headlines of the *Guardian*. But it was as if these events had been happening on another planet. Bridie's suffering had swollen to occupy the entire visible horizon; Ruth had neither attempted nor been able to see round the huge head that blocked the view and commandeered all attention. It was not unlike her mental state when Lizzie was born, and the baby's beautiful, imperious face had engrossed every waking moment, to the exclusion of other subjects of thought or conversation (she had resented that, too, the well-nigh uncontested victory of biology over brain-cells). But then there had been the wonder of genesis. The present travail yielded a hole in the world.

Now that the bus was making its right turn past the war memorial, and they were briefly alongside the demonstrators, Ruth could see that they were pitifully few – a handful of chiefly middle-aged or elderly people in duffle-coats and woollen hats, hardly more than twenty-five or thirty, standing in two lines on the steps and apparently singing something inaudible into the roaring traffic. It must be perishing cold in that driving sleet. An aged man with a banner was balancing on the kerb-edge, wagging his message at their window.

'WHO SOLD THE ARMS TO SADDAM?' his banner demanded of the passengers. Ruth gained a close view of his face beneath his cloth-cap: he must have been at least seventy-five, with a strong light of irony in his eyes. He flipped the banner. 'WE DID.'

The bus swept past, but now the mood had changed. The passengers on the lower deck seemed less inclined to take issue with the juvenile patriots on the top, and their continuing shrieks of 'Pacifist dickheads!' went unreproved.

Bridie didn't know there was a war coming. If she knew, she wouldn't care. That was unthinkable. In normal times, before their world had convulsed and begun to end, she would have rushed home to tell Bridie what she had seen: 'Bridie, what are we going to do about the war?'

And Bridie would have said . . . what would Bridie have said? . . . Well, nothing, come to think of it, for they'd have been out there with the protestors already. They'd have kept up with history and world events over the past five months and not abdicated into the world of their own concerns. Again Bridie's afflicted, horizon-filling face spread out across Ruth's vision, with that look of hopeless pain in its eyes – and Ruth's spasm of anger that such things should be was so intense that she banged with her gloved fist on the juddering rail of the empty seat in front. Anger with Bridie for taking her away from life; for ruthlessly dragging her down to the grave with her; for forsaking her and leaving her alone on this earth without anyone to turn to; for refusing to kiss goodbye.

Let people bomb each other. What was it to her? What did it matter? Nothing mattered. To hell with them all.

She had never visited the hospice before; any hospice. She didn't know how to behave or what to expect. There was a pause at reception while they looked up Bridie's whereabouts, and Ruth stared around her at the carpeted hall where brisk nurses passed soundlessly, and a vase of tall irises balanced beside a sofa, at the entrance to a chapel. Ruth squinted in: an octagonal room, the altar surmounted by a great pine cross. It was empty of worshippers or intercessors, though rows of hassocks awaited knees at pine pews, and a stained-glass Jesus carrying a lamb invited the bereaved to come for succour. *And to hell with you, you bastard*, said Ruth inwardly to Jesus, and the heartfelt curse energised her, so that the chapel had evidently done her good. (Though Bridie had some respect for Jesus: after all, *he* could not be held responsible for his Father's wickedness, she pointed out.)

Courage faltered again as Ruth reached the ward and had Bridie's bed specified. In every particular the place resembled a small hospital, save for the colourful counterpanes draped on every bed in an effort to make the room seem less institutional.

'Bridget's asleep just at the moment,' said the nurse. 'Such a journey will have taken it out of her.'

'So can I just sit with her?' asked Ruth timidly.

'Well of course. As long as you like – as often as you like. Are you family or a friend?'

'. . . Family. Sort of.'

'Yes, well, make yourself quite comfortable. Talk to her, do – yes, even if she's asleep. We'll bring you a cup of tea. Anything you want, or want to know – don't fail to ask.'

Ruth tiptoed across to Bridie's bed, but her boots squeaked on the lino. She was afraid to see Bridie in these new circumstances. Her heart hammered colossally, as if a revelation at once monstrous and alien were about to be made of something irretrievably lost. Bridie who had once belonged to her had now been given away, into other hands and a strange regime. Bridie was theirs now, not hers. They had acquired and appropriated her. She saw Bridie's bed as a far raft floating out to sea, and the raft contained all that she loved, and that had nourished and sustained her in life – and Bridie, though nominally still alive, was dead to her. She stood at the end of Bridie's bed, clutching the rail, and shook from head to foot. The stranger with the mask of Bridie lay asleep on her left side, one hand lying over the rainbow quilt and the other tucked under her cheek. Her short grey and stubbly hair had been sleeked back from her face, giving her a curiously bare and open look. The frantic quality had been erased from the face, by a profound and anodyne unconsciousness which no echo from the ward remotely reached. The shadowy skin was stretched taut over prominent cheek-bones. Both her eyes and mouth were slightly open. It was Bridie's body but Bridie was not there.

Ruth settled herself beside the bed and tentatively took the hand that lay over the quilt, caressing it with both of hers.

'My dear darling,' she said.

3

Ruth yawned and stretched. She had been sitting for a couple of hours in a too low chair at Bridie's bedside, hunching forward toward Bridie's unconsciousness, sometimes silently, at others pouring out a rain of murmurings, asking Bridie's pardon for her failures, assuring her of the depth of her love. And, although Bridie was deaf to these solicitations and avowals, Ruth derived some comfort from her own whispered testament.

The time crawled by. Visitors arrived and departed from other bedsides, bearing Lucozade bottles, peaches in brown paper bags, magazines and jolly cards, and, in the next space but one, a pink hairnet was handed over with some ceremony and received with complacency. In the intervals of her own silence, Ruth peered surreptitiously across Bridie's safety-rails, trying not to stare, fascinated and repelled, trying to get her mind round the thought that this was the place we came to die. Her nerves squirmed, her mind went blank. Time crept on.

Her back hurt from this awful chair. She sighed. There was a pause. Bridie blinked; went still. Ruth got up and travelled round the bed, rearranging the few objects on the high cabinet. More time passed.

Now they shooed her affably away. Bridie was to be curtained off and turned. Ruth heard her hoarse groan as she was humped from her left to her right side. Her mind seemed to curdle at the all-too-familiar sound; it flayed her scalp. She sighed again and, turning away – as if turning from herself – encountered the figure of a minister of the Church of England, large, well-fed and benevolent, hovering in the doorway as if looking for a place to bestow his tenderness. *Oh my God a dog-collar*, thought Ruth, and ducked back behind Bridie's curtainings.

Ruth sat down again. Bridie's face was more in shadow; her body looked askew and uncomfortable, but *At least you don't know you're hurting*, Ruth thought. A long silence ensued.

Then she said, 'My dear love. I love you so much . . .' but her eye was caught by the round-faced wall-clock over the door, reiterating the uniform passage of time, its second hand flicking an irritating division of time into fussy, busy units. The second hand was unnecessary. It was senseless. But it kept going.

Ruth stared blankly around the ward and thought, *All these women are condemned to death*. And yet they went on normally, sipping a cup of tea or eating a grape, and one said to another (who, in the absence of a nurse, had got out of bed and made a shuffling pilgrimage to the lavatory, on spindling legs, leaning on a walking-frame), 'I thought you'd left us and gone out to a concert', and the other woman laughed quite cheerfully as she hauled herself into bed. *And they're all so old – except Bridie*, Ruth thought. She didn't want to meet their eyes or speak to them. Her own health seemed an uncivil intrusion; but, more disreputably, she avoided their extension of Bridie's predicament into a world-view.

After the seven-thousand-two-hundredth second had gone by, Ruth got up to go. She left a brief, loving note sellotaped to the safety-rail where Bridie could not fail to see it when she awoke, and kissed her forehead as she left, at which Bridie's eyes opened quite wide but seemed to perceive nothing.

'How long?' she asked the staff nurse.

45

He couldn't say with any degree of certainty.

'Surely you've some idea?'

Months rather than years, was his guess.

'Yes, but how many months? Two or ten?'

More likely two than ten, but don't quote him on that; prediction was not an exact science.

'Weeks rather than months?'

It could well be. Indeed, once the cancer got to the brain, it was his experience that things tended to progress pretty quickly.

'Are you saying it has reached Bridie's brain?'

He couldn't say that for sure, but the X-rays certainly suggested it was well on its way.

These words stabbed Ruth; and yet she could not take them in or connect that obscene invasion with Bridie's mind – that fine brain, with its straight-line logic and yet the subtle and labyrinthine complexities it simultaneously harboured; and the delicate skein of emotions woven through warp and weft of her personality. When she thought of Bridie's mind, a picture came of Marvell's 'green thought in a green shade' – a copious, dappled garden-world, full at once of peace and commotion. But this was like rape, the thrusting of the tumour into the privacy of Bridie's mind.

'Look, it's for the best. She'll most likely go into a coma. She won't know anything about it.'

'Yes, it's for the best.'

Good: better: best: words began wildly fluctuating in this situation. They conferred no intelligence of reality, but either concealed it or flew up into a world of their own where they denied the meaning of what they had denoted before this curse fell on them. For what could be good in an evil world? What could be 'best' for 'Bridie', now that the worst had happened? One's tongue lolled and sank in the cavity of the mouth, like the useless flap of moist spongy tissue it was. There was nothing to say to the young man. Hands in the pockets of her corduroy coat, amidst the leavings of loose gritty dust and small change, she shrugged, turned, and left.

There, on the steps of the war memorial, she saw from the bus window, still stood the huddle of anti-war protestors, swollen now to a larger mass; and she found herself getting off at the next stop and walking back up the hill to join them.

The sleet had paused but, a sharp wind having arisen, the demonstrators gathered in close for warmth, shifting from foot to foot to keep the circulation going, while their candles guttered in jamjars hanging by strings from mittened hands. They were deep in spirited conversation, and all seemed to know one another. She approached them obliquely, walking beneath the wall bearing the inscription '1939' and a metal funeral urn. The dark figures of a man and a woman were standing up there arm in arm, with posters exhorting the few passers-by to trust sanctions rather than bombs. In the dusky yellow light of the street-lamps, their messages were all but illegible.

It was only then (just as she was beginning to falter and sheer away) that Ruth recognised the girl standing in the front line with a candle in one hand, next to a tall youth whose arm was round her shoulders. Lizzie's curly hair was scraped from her forehead into a bunch on the top of her head, leaving her face with an expression of fanatical radiance; and her anorak was undone – no doubt for fashionable reasons – despite the severity of the cold. With a kind of shyness, Ruth mounted the steps towards her daughter.

'Lizzie. Hello.'

'Oh – Mum. What are you doing here?' Lizzie first scowled,

sincerely, then pushed her features into the simulation of a smile. She made no further effort to disguise the fact that she was not greatly thrilled to see her mother.

'The same as you, I suppose. I didn't know you were CND.'

'I'm not. Martin's a Socialist Worker. He won't carry a candle because he says candles are bourgeois.'

'But you're carrying one.'

'I like candles,' said Lizzie simply. 'I don't give a monkey's if they're capitalist-imperialist-bourgeois-reactionary-how's-your-father, I still like them. I'm not here as a Socialist Worker, I'm here as a member of the League Against Cruel Sports.'

Humans, she had early decided, were a nasty lot. Squeamish about anything that connoted blood or gristle, she ran retching out of the biology lab when they brought out the pickled cows' hearts to dissect. The dead and rotting bird on the roadside left her sobbing. Vegetarian from the age of eight, Lizzie Asher saw with her own eyes and smelt out with her own nose quite clearly the principles it took Charles Darwin twenty reluctant years to formulate. Even the milk in her tea carried traces of previous suffering, however much they explained to her, 'The cow didn't hurt when it gave us milk, Liz. The cow *likes* to give us milk.' But Lizzie saw and smelt right through that. 'Who asked the cow's permission?' she wanted to know. 'Well, that's silly,' they scoffed. 'That's not facing facts.' But Lizzie was scornful in her turn. Hadn't she seen the sausages hanging on strings beside the slices of pigs' thighs and the cows' brains? Sausages don't tell lies.

'It's you that don't face facts,' she insisted. '*Can't* face them.' She tried to explain to them about the horrors of the poultry factories where the hens never go out; the pig cages where the sow can't turn round; the hormones injected into cattle; the abattoirs where the creatures are not properly stunned but travel in panic to their deaths hung upside-down from moving

48

rails. Once on a sunny day, she was standing on the local station and she heard a bellowing from the slaughterhouse behind Purdy's the Family Butcher's, and she knew the voice was that of a cow in its death panic. But tried to persuade herself otherwise. Surely they could not actually kill the creatures in there, it was too small, too suburban and disinfected. Then a woman said to her husband, 'Glad we're not having beef for dinner, aren't you?' in a nervously joky tone, and laughed. Lizzie could not get the horror out of her mind. The bellowing went on in there for days. No one would listen to Lizzie when she tried to tell them; no one would share the burden of her knowledge. Beside the Madonna posters on her bedroom wall, she hung posters depicting the hanging of live creatures from meat-hooks. Their eyes spoke to Lizzie. They told intolerable truths with integrity. The eyes of humans roved and winked and pierced and swivelled. They lived off other creatures' suffering and refused to see their culpability. Her father put Elizabeth's excesses down to a mixture of adolescence and her mother's disturbing influence: all those Green pressure groups and peace groups, ridiculously standing for the local council as Green Party candidate and polling a piffling eighty-eight votes. But Lizzie hotly denied such influence. She was almost as contemptuous of her mother's misty Greenness as of her father's worldly pragmatism; almost but not quite, for though her mother had hurt Lizzie by going off with that woman, she knew that in other circumstances she might have shared something deep with her. This only intensified the hurt of her mother's having preferred *that woman* to herself.

'Unnatural practices,' she overheard her father saying to someone on the phone. Unnatural practices, if that meant sex, did not bother Lizzie (though she did wonder what they might involve), in the light of how she judged humans' normative brutality to animals. No, it was not a particular problem, to know that her mum was a lesbian. Jealousy and loss were the problems – the loss especially of the possibility of sitting by her mother on her bed as she remembered doing, and confiding, 'I think this . . . I think *this* . . .', and knowing that what she had to say, whatever its deviance from the norm, would be fairly heard. Things which seemed mad and peculiar to other ears did not automatically seem so to her mother's. She had idolised her – and she had been left – dumped.

Hence she now stepped down to a lower level with her candle, not willing to stand shoulder to shoulder with her mother. And Ruth interpreted the gesture with dumb, remorseful understanding that dared not object to any course of action her child might elect to take. The numbing cold inserted itself into cuffs and collars; one's very eyes seemed to film over with ice. As the traffic lights released the straining cars, patriotic Englishmen flicked V's and pressed their car-horns.

'Lizzie doesn't seem much bothered about killing Iraqi people,' said Martin. 'Believe it or not, it's the sea turtles and the dolphins she's bothered about, and the camels.'

Lizzie, offended, said nothing, but her tensely upright posture said it for her. She shoved Martin's hand from her shoulder. Now she was standing with no one.

'Well, she has a point. All life is precious,' said a bearded man with a European accent. 'Unnecessary suffering – that is always something to protest about.'

'You have it there,' Ruth said. 'In a nutshell.'

Something in the depth and rawness of a voice habitually light and soft – too blandly soft for Lizzie's taste – touched a nerve in Lizzie, so that she turned abruptly to confront the haggard mourning face behind her; and, as she turned, Ruth momentarily caught in the roundness of her silhouetted cheek a trace of the baby of sixteen-odd years ago, and was shot through with a sense of her vulnerability. Lizzie stared appraisingly into Ruth's eyes, and Ruth, who mistook the straight look for belligerence, winced.

'Does Daddy know where you are, love?'

'He thinks I'm at the Methodist disco.'

'Will that be okay? How will you get home?'

'Oh, Mart will take me. Don't worry, I can look after myself.'

'Wouldn't you be better if you did your coat up?'

'Don't *fuss*,' she hissed. 'I sort myself out. Have to, don't I? Anyway, how's Roger the Lodger?' Lizzie didn't trust herself to call Bridie by her actual name: it made her more real, more threatening. Even to her face, she called her 'Rog', or 'Dick', or even, on one stomach-churning occasion, 'Dad', on the stated grounds that, as her mother's partner, she must count as some sort of stepfather. Bridie, who could be terrifyingly eloquent when angered, simply looked at her with a slight frown, and, turning, silently left the room; later Lizzie saw her hoeing the border outside, and for some reason felt chilled and frightened. Momentarily she perceived Bridie as a person – as someone who could be wounded. It was far simpler not to see that; instantaneously she switched off the recognition. She too felt with a pang the power of Bridie's charisma. Occasionally she saw her being interviewed on TV and, though she normally turned over the channel, the impressiveness of the celluloid persona glamorised Bridie's image and doubled her awareness of the power the woman exerted over her mother. All sorts of people rushed to Bridie like iron filings to the magnet. She herself pointedly refused such supine susceptibility to attraction; and she could see that Bridie respected her for that, which increased her sense of conflict and the necessity to caricature the extraordinary woman as monstrous.

For months now, she and Sarah had not visited their mother's house for more than a couple of hours at a time. Although she had never enjoyed the 'access' weekends, which she had sought to foul up for everybody, Lizzie resented the reduction of her time there. It had been as if, in making life as horrible as possible for the two women, throughout the forty-eight hour duration, Lizzie had been able to leave daubings of crude graffiti all over their nice clean walls. She knew her mother cried after she left; and perhaps, if she persisted effectively, she could break the pair of them up. But Bridie's illness had put a stop to this exercise of her arts and the project died a limp death. Their mother wore a glazed, distracted expression when they were there; cuddled Sarah a lot and seemed confused in what she was saying. Behind the sitting-room door, up the dimly lit stairs and beyond the landing lay a silence which was that woman. Lizzie had made scrupulously sure *not* to enquire into that woman's health. She gave no quarter, extended no clemency. The predatory woman could die for all she cared; in fact it would be a hell of an improvement if she did – not that she would, for that would be just too convenient.

'Bridie's . . . very bad, Lizzie. She's not at home. She's in St Marcia's Hospice – went in today –'

'But that means she's –'

Lizzie knew what a hospice was. It was where you went to die. She'd seen a feature about St Marcia's on the north-west news when Princess Diana visited to open the new wing. It was not possible to react to the news that what she had most wanted to happen was happening. Roger the Lodger was going to be got out of the way. Neither was it possible to respond to the ashen deadness of her mother's face which, in the smear of lamplight, seemed like the ravaged mask of someone far older. Lizzie turned her back on her mother and took another step down. She muttered something which Ruth could not catch. Then she took another step down, and another, more decisively.

'I'm off home, Mart,' she called, without turning. 'Coming or stopping?'

The young man charged after Lizzie, as she plunged across the road and down the hill past the Admiral Nelson. She had left her candle in its jar at the base of the stairs, where it continued to glow for a further hour.

By nine o'clock only half a dozen remained, huddled in a shivering knot; the white dove on the banner glimmered, a vague cloudy shape behind them. Few passed by, and those that did were drunkenly hostile: it was entirely unclear why they still hung on. They were standing there because they were standing there.

'You want castrating, you do,' yelled a young man from the Nelson to the five women and one man on the memorial steps.

'Nothing to castrate, mate,' replied his friend. 'Got no bollocks. Nothing there to spay. You're not *men*, you.'

'True,' observed the woman next to Ruth. A ripple of amusement went round the group, but there was nervousness too. Three other youths had joined their fellows.

'We're going to get you. We'll do you. Pacifist wankers. We're going to *kick butt*.' The first youth came part of the way up the steps and, when he paused, it could be seen that he was no more than sixteen or seventeen.

'It's only a bunch of women,' he informed his friends, derisively. 'Who do you think's going to take any notice of you? We're going to bomb them Eye-Rakis flat, just like what we did Hitler.'

'Told you: no balls.'

'Three years ago,' said the woman next to Ruth, 'Saddam massacred the Kurds. We were out here protesting. Reagan and Thatcher didn't want to know. We armed Saddam and now . . .'

'Get stuffed.'

'Fucking idealists. Prick-lickers.'

'No bleeding balls.' Losing interest in the political discussion, the group drifted off in the direction of the Wellington Inn.

'Well,' said Ruth's neighbour. 'Well well.'

Ruth stared with numb eyes at the spotlit clock on the town hall. The sky above was thickly black. Once in a while an aeroplane was heard passing overhead but you could not see its lights. It was the same sky as enveloped Baghdad and Basra. Iraqi women were looking up into that potent darkness. Ruth's mind, clouded and confused from the months of sickbed vigil, wandered from Lizzie to the animals to the war to Bridie and back again. The sleet-white streets were numb. There was nothing you could do; no court of appeal. You could just stand. The creation seemed to labour in one clenched ball of pain that spasmed through its whole nervous system; and that was reality, the reality you came down to. No wonder people stayed at home and watched television, and fabricated celluloid emotions, of soap-operatic ardours or machismo or sporting glory. Who in her right mind could want to know, really *know*? or to comprehend her own responsibility for passing the pain along the line? It made you want to go out for good and close the door firmly behind you. Death was preferable on any terms.

She yawned suddenly. She just wanted to be asleep. The yawn stood on the freezing air in a smoky cloud and then dispersed.

'I'm going home,' she said.

'See you tomorrow?'

'I'll try.'

'And bring your warm coat. And your lovely daughter.'

Tottering down the steps, her legs buckled under her. The cold had exhausted her utterly. How she made it to the station, she never knew.

The lassitude by the gasfire eliminated all thought and feeling, save the purring pleasure as the heat of the tea and the fire stole through to her bones. Curling up on the settee, she half slept. Bridie was all right; Bridie was being cared for by people who knew how to care for her. Now it was time for Ruth to care for herself. That was permissible; that was right. As her consciousness eased out, and the last tension in the muscles of her neck relaxed, Ruth slid down towards sleep.

The phone rang like an alarm bell. Ruth shot off the settee, heart pounding.

'Hello. Who is it?'

'It's me.' A very quiet voice, almost a murmur, but certainly Bridie.

'Oh, sweetheart. How are you, my love? I came to see you but you were fast asleep. Did you get the note I left?'

'No note. Elaine . . .'

'No, it's not . . . it's not Elaine, Bridie darling. It's me, love, it's Ruth. It's just your boring old Ruth.' She choked, gasped for air. She had let Bridie down, terribly but forgivably – but she must not do it again. Whatever or whoever Bridie wanted, Bridie must have – even if it killed Ruth.

'Who's there?' Bridie's voice conveyed querulous puzzlement, as if the phone was a suspicious gadget she had never tried before, which put her in touch with a faceless void. 'Who's . . . that? . . . Who *are* you?'

'Can you hear me, darling?'

'Yes. Hear you. But who –?'

'It's Ruth. Do you remember me?'

There was a pause. 'Who?'

'Ruth. Ruth Asher. Your lover, Bridie. Your friend. We've been together for five years. As family.'

Complete silence prevailed on the other end. Ruth examined a spider's web wafting in the draught from the door. Her eye travelled up and down the fine thread from which the spider hung, up and down, up and down. She was calm.

'Do you want me to come over?' she asked softly.

'Ask Elaine . . .'

'You want – Elaine. You want her to come and see you?'

'Who?'

The spider spun on its thread. The spider had as much right as herself to inhabit this space. More.

'Try to tell me clearly what or who you want, my darling Bridie,' said Ruth in a firm, resolved voice. 'And I will do everything in my power to get it for you. Everything.' In this emergency, she saw with sudden lucidity, she must try to act as Bridie herself would have done. For if it was the case (as it certainly was) that her own self had been emptied and turned violently inside out like a ransacked pocket, there still remained the fund of the years Bridie had given her. The abundance of that gift was still brimful, undepleted – though she herself, as unaccommodated Ruth, had been used up. Bridie's strength should now be her strength, transferred by legitimate right of the love they had shared through these years. *Nobody* could take that away, not even Bridie's present denial. 'Now tell me – do you want me to get in touch with Elaine and ask her to come and see you?'

'Elaine?' wondered the voice huskily, and though it was inflected rather as a tentative query than a demand, Ruth was sure of its meaning.

'I will get hold of her for you, sweetheart, I promise. I'll ring her as soon as I put the phone down. Don't worry now, I'm sure she'll come and see you as soon as she can. I love you . . . love you more . . . love you more than I can say . . . and I . . . am . . . so, so . . . sorry for letting you down, I never will again.'

No more was said at the other end, and after a few minutes the line went dead.

As soon as she had replaced the receiver, she began to rip apart like a sheet of paper tearing and tearing. Her strength was nothing, it was illusion, but before she could disintegrate completely she snatched back the receiver and began dialling Elaine's number. She could hear herself splitting and rending. Yes, Elaine would come over; could be at the hospice by early afternoon; wanted to know with every sign of solicitude how Ruth herself was, but with steady, level voice, Ruth cut short the conversation, saying she was somewhat tired.

The sheet of paper tore from end to end.

Lizzie's dad was lounging on the settee in the living room trying to give the nonchalant impression that he had not been fondling the person of his secretary and girlfriend, Valerie, but had been riveted to a programme explaining how best to grow leeks under cloches. Scrupulously ignoring Val's existence, Lizzie contrived to stumble with her heavy boots over Val's elegant high-heeled shoes. Without apologising, she made for the gasfire and planted herself directly in front of it, blocking the view of the TV screen and standing with her legs apart and arms folded, in a manner that intended to offer provocation.

'Oh, hi,' said her father, evidently swallowing the urge to shout 'And take those bloody boots off before you come crashing in over my expensive carpet.' How could a girl be so ungainly and clod-hopping? How could a mere five foot six inches seem to swell till it filled half the room with attention-seeking self? But he had learnt to deal circumspectly with his elder daughter, manipulating her with soft felt gloves, especially since his introduction of Val as a future family member. 'How was the disco?' he asked genially.

'Crap,' replied Lizzie. 'Utter crap.'

'DJ not up to much?' asked Val.

Lizzie affected not to hear. She pulled one boot off, and a sprinkling of grimy slush fell on the hearthrug.

'Oh Lizzie – do for goodness sake take your outdoor shoes off in the hall. It's such a mess.'

'*She's* got hers on,' pointed out Lizzie. 'You don't make a fuss about that.' She hopped heavily on one socked foot, dragging at the other boot. Val looked mildly affronted but wisely tolerant of Gavin's unsavoury offspring.

'*Hers* are clean,' said Lizzie's father. 'Yours have half of Stockport on them.'

'Okay, okay, nothing to get in a benny about. Anyhow I know when I'm not wanted, don't let me interrupt the cosy party.'

She flounced out, her father following her.

'Sorry you didn't have much of a time,' he conciliated. 'But no need to take it out on Val. She's been a good friend to you.'

'Like a kick up the arse,' Lizzie muttered.

'Pardon, Lizzie?'

'Nothing,' said Lizzie. 'I'm going to bed.'

She thumped up the stairs in a way she knew he particularly detested. Again, he followed.

'Lizzie, love, let's not have these tantrums.'

'What tantrums? Are you having a tantrum?'

'You know what I mean. Let's not fall out.'

'I'm not falling out. I just don't *like* her, that's all.'

'Try to.'

'I can't. She's a cow.'

'*Lizzie.*'

'Well, she is. I hate her.'

'But why?'

'I just do, that's all – and Sarah hates her as well even though she plays up to her.'

She glared down over the bannister at her father, standing irresolute on the stairs, holding on to his temper, still seeking (she saw that) to appease and mollify. He wanted something from her, something big she had it in her power to withhold, giving her unquestionably the upper hand. She looked down upon him with a sneer, fastening her eyes on the as yet minimal bald spot on the back of his head, a focus of embarrassment about which he was touchy. He mounted the last four steps. From here he could look down on her. But he did not raise his voice.

'You can't hate everybody,' he reasoned. 'Can you?'

'I don't hate everybody. I hate bimbos. I hate slimy pseuds. I hate women with lacquered hair and red nail varnish. Do you know how they make that muck she smears on her face? Do you know how they test for it?'

Her father groaned out loud. 'Here we go again.' Monkeys and bunny rabbits and bow-wows and the whole animal kingdom brought into every damned conversation on the slightest – or no – pretext.

'Well, I'll tell you,' went on Lizzie remorselessly, 'even though I know you don't want to know, and you wouldn't care even if you did know – they torture little monkeys with carcinogenic chemicals to make the red on her mouth – they make puppies and mice blind for her eye-shadow – they make mutations – on purpose – just to sell her that ugly mug.'

'Oh turn it off, Lizzie. We've heard it all before. Give us a break, can't you.'

'If you're interested, Elizabeth,' came a cool voice from downstairs, 'I buy *all* my cosmetics at the Body Shop – guaranteed cruelty-free products.'

'So now you know,' said her father with a sudden broad grin. 'That's put you in your place, Lizzie. Not a leg to stand on,' and he sailed down the stairs as lightly as she had stomped up heavily. She heard them sniggering in the hall, briefly.

'Nice one, Val. You got her there.'

'Oh, it's just her age. They're all the same at that age. She'll grow out of it, don't worry.'

'Her mother didn't.'

'She'll be okay,' went on the creamy voice. 'Just letting off steam. At least she's got some principles.'

'If I hear one more word about cruelty to budgerigars, I swear I'll brain the cat.'

Lizzie went into Sarah's room, slamming the door behind her. *You can't hate everyone*, he said. And sometimes added, *or they'll all hate you, and then where will you be? If you're lovable, Lizzie, people will love you*. But often she didn't love anyone; her heart was curdled and she saw people – all people – through a lens coloured bile-green with cynicism. Then she was afraid, because the mood had an immediate built-in backlash: through the two-way lens, she saw everyone – friends, family, people on the street – rejecting her for her bale and spite. Sarah was not like that. Sarah was the nice, presentable sister who knew how to behave – the one they brought out for public inspection, who passed all the tests because she was, simply and genuinely, a lovely child. Lizzie had made three attempts during their earlier lives to smash Sarah's skull in. Once, aged five, she picked up a paperweight and hurled it at Sarah's head: a big blue-black egg appeared on her forehead and took weeks to fade. Secondly, she thrust her down on a barbed-wire fence and Sarah had to have stitches; on a third occasion she went for her with a rake. All that stopped when she was seven. She remembered her mother's voice saying soothingly, 'Gentle down, Lizzie – you're all right,' and she cried not only because of the magnitude of her murderous trespass but also because she was not in her heart of hearts sorry for it, and because she was afraid her mother would see how far she lay beyond forgiveness. Her mother's leaving seemed to endorse that intuition. She had always wanted Sarah out of the way. She wanted it now, but less fiercely. Sarah was just an irritating extra that had to be lived with because it couldn't be evacuated.

Sarah was sitting up in bed, painting a water-colour picture of a mountainous landscape, her paint pots perilously balanced at intervals on the quilt. She was left-handed and all her pictures had a back-to-front strangeness and eccentric appeal which even Lizzie grudgingly acknowledged.

'That's quite good.'

'Thanks. It's supposed to be a copy of this but it didn't quite come out the same. What was up with Dad?' she asked sympathetically. Sarah's long blond hair was tied up and back in a complex system of plaits. Her beautiful dark blue eyes looked at her sister with a kind of calculated guilelessness, as if she were still pondering the twelve-year-old problem of how to win Lizzie over, and had still not given up hope.

'Oh it was just him and that tarty rat-face – getting at me as usual.' 'She's all right really, Lizzie, if you get on her right side,' Sarah blurted, and then regretted, expecting an explosion. 'Sometimes anyway,' she qualified hastily. 'Actually I think she's afraid of us.'

But Lizzie just shrugged. 'I don't give a toss.' She began to brush her hair.

'Feel free to use my brush,' said Sarah, with unusual asperity. She didn't like her neatly placed personal belongings tampered with.

'Thanks. I do. Do you want to know something, Sarah?'

'What?'

'I was at the vigil.'

'I thought you would be. I didn't say anything.'

'Yes but Mum came and stood there with me.'

Sarah looked up with a start, her face reddening; then covered her feelings by looking down again and dabbing at her picture with a blue wash.

'Did she? What did she say?'

'Not much. She said some stuff about the war. Nothing much. She just stood there. It was queer.'

'Did she say anything about me, Lizzie?' Sarah asked in a thin, muffled voice.

'Nah.'

A couple of huge tears gathered in Sarah's eyes and overflowed on to the wash of the picture. Generally she held on to her feelings, reasoning them away, using one part of her mind to persuade and compose the other; but she had been taken by surprise.

'If you want to know what she said, it was that that woman – that Bridie woman – is in a hospice.'

'What's a hospice?'

'It's where people go to die.'

'Oh.'

There was a reflective silence. Then Sarah asked, 'When that happens – will Mummy come back to us, do you think, Lizzie?'

'Use your loaf, Sarah. Of course she won't.'

'No, I suppose not.'

'Well, she's a lezzie, isn't she. She'd shack up with a woman.' Sarah winced. 'She wasn't once.'

'She is now. And anyway, her place has been taken. Titty Vally's in Dad's bed, isn't she? There's no room for Mum here if she did want to come back.' There was a hole in both their hearts where their mother had been, but there existed no corresponding gap in the world outside to mark her loss. Lizzie saw, scorchingly, how replaceable people are; how temporary. She sat down on the end of Sarah's bed, and looked at her sister blankly, without animus.

'I wish . . .' said Sarah, but suspended her wish in mid-air. It could be fantasised but not imagined, the return of Sarah's mum to Sarah's dad. She painted idyllic portraits of family groups, in which the four bodies of mother, father and two children were represented as one red or blue splodge of paint, with four idiosyncratically different faces emerging from the one lovely blob. But she knew that the picture was without foundation in the facts or even the theoretical possibilities of life.

'I don't want Bridie to die, Lizzie . . . do you?'

Lizzie considered, scrutinising her image in the mirror. If only she had long straight hair like Zoë Price rather than this wild disorder of curls; if only she could be redesigned with blue eyes rather than this brown stare, a straighter nose and a smaller mouth. What was dying anyway? Grandma died – her father's mother – and that was just like an optical trick or a vanishing act. Whenever she walked past the terraced house (which was every day, on the way to school), she peered compulsively in the net-curtained windows and had the distinct impression that Grandma was still in there, guarding her privacy, keeping an eye on them as they went past, the loud gang of girls. In the park with the scraggy roses and the scatter of beer cans and chip papers, where Lizzie strolled with her mates, skiving off to smoke a fag behind the indulgent backs of the great chestnut trees that encircled the rose-beds and benches, Lizzie often had a sense of Grandma's continuing presence. The skin on her neck prickled and she looked round anxiously. She hadn't liked to offend Gran by showing her truculent side; and Grandma had never missed much. So when Grandma died, she didn't die. She just became nominally absent. Hide-and-seek went on re-currently, through windows, round trees.

Did she want Bridie to die? She used to. If looks could have killed, if ill-wishing . . . there'd have been no Bridie.

'She took our mother,' she said remorselessly. 'Didn't she?'

Sarah made no reply.

Back in her room, she undressed for bed, playing a heavy metal record at high volume. She ignored the banging on her door and the shouted requests to turn it down. The decibels did her good, blasting out the complexities from her brain cells, replacing them with the stunning din of violence to which she now danced, in her black nightgown in the beam of a single spotlamp. She threw off the nightgown and danced naked, her eyes without their spectacles as nude as her body – sightless and self-loving. She knew that this was the necessary thing: to love herself. Once she could achieve that, everything else would fall into place.

When the music stopped, the silence was deafening. She climbed into bed, yawning, and burrowed under her pillow for the relic of a cotton pram-sheet which had been her comfort-object since babyhood, when it swaddled her body in a firm embrace. She only had to touch it to fall, magically, asleep.

Over her head, the dying horses hung from meat-hooks; the hounds savaged the quarry while the beefy huntsmen looked on enjoyingly.

Tomorrow she would go to the hospice and see that woman, for the satisfying of a curiosity and the settling of an account.

4

Bridie dozed. When she opened her eyes, Elaine was sitting there by the bed, with both hands and her chin on the safety-rail, staring into Bridie's face.

'Goodness . . . it's you,' said Bridie, puzzled. Her tongue was dry and ponderous in her mouth. 'You were different in the dream – not so . . . faded. Where did you spring from?'

'From home.'

'Where's home?'

'I came over by car from Leeds, Bridie dear – Ruth called me last night. I'm so sorry – so *very* sorry – to find you like this. I knew you were ill, of course, but I'd no idea how bad.'

'Bad? This . . . isn't bad. Been in hell, Elaine. Now just limbo.'

'Oh *Bridie*.'

Bridie studied the rather heavy face which had been handsome once, and still was arresting, with its strong jaw, rather beaky nose and intelligent eyes, with their interrogative look and their habitual smiling sadness underscored by wrinkles. It was a more tired and worn face than she recalled; familiar; but a shock. And looked shocked to see her thus, but covering it up with professional stoicism.

'All right,' said Bridie. 'It's all right,' meaning *you're all right*. 'Behind the barrier. Pane of glass – ten foot thick – pain divides us. You're outside. I'm inside. Far away from me . . . you . . . far gone . . . me. Long time ago too. No way to touch.'

Elaine reached over and took her hand, caressing it with her fingers, and Bridie remembered that, too – the practical, strong hand. Her eyes filled with tears.

'You *are* real – are you?' she enquired, with some timidity. The phantasmagoria with whom she recurrently cohabited were not only illusions but told lies.

'I think so.' The scorching eyes smiled. Elaine could always summon a smile. It was her form of conscientious objection to impositions she either could or would not oppose. Thus she had smiled, veiling and guarding her inmost feelings, when Bridie broke the news about Ruth, and how she was in love ('For the first time in my life, Elaine!'), barely able to conceal her ruthless ecstasy and excitement behind her guilt-riddled sorrow on Elaine's account.

'I dream things, you see. Seen you so often – but walking through walls and windows – and so I . . . reluctantly . . . decided you weren't there – after all. I've talked to you. But you haven't visited before, have you, Elaine?'

'No – this is the first time for – what? – five or six years. But I'm very solid and real, Bridie. Feel.' She squeezed Bridie's hand, and, raising it to her lips, kissed it briefly.

'Something damned funny about you though – what is it?' Bridie frowned. 'That's it – you've got dreadfully grey, Elaine – if you don't mind my saying so.'

'Speak for yourself.'

'Suits you though. It does.'

'Makes me look mature and dignified, is that what you mean? Well, I'm an old woman now, Bridie, and quite content with that. I even have a cat, Leah, I dote on her, and if I have to be away from her for a day I start fretting and pining. You'd be disgusted.'

'Have you brought the cat?'

'She's in the car.'

'Bring her in. Do. Let me see her.'

'But Bridie, you *hate* cats! Anyway, she wouldn't be allowed in, would she?'

'No, they wouldn't mind. Truly. Not like a hospital. Someone had her dog in earlier. Woofed all round the shop. Bring in your cat, Elaine, I want to see her.'

The old tabby curled up on the bed between them and, purring sonorously, yielded itself up to the fondlings of both women.

'My friends say this cat is my post-menopausal baby-substitute. But I take no notice. She evidently fills a need.'

'And how have you been, dear, over the years? How has your health been?' It was, to Elaine, a strange reversal, to be anxiously questioned about her well-being by the skin-and-bone wreck of her old friend; but she discerned the motives that made Bridie need to ascertain that she had not come to permanent grief at her hands. And besides, there remained in the supine skeletal body of this woman the peremptory spirit that felt dishonoured by weakness – a woman bred in Sparta to whom illness was indignity. Bridie got cross if you suggested she might be coming down with a cold or needed a rest. *No such thing*, she rapped, *don't fuss*.

'I've been basically okay,' said Elaine. 'The arthritis still bothers me, of course, but I can get around.'

'And – still – living on your own?' Bridie laboured on.

'Oh yes,' said Elaine lightly. 'But that suits me fine, you see. You mustn't think I've been unhappy or lonely, Bridie, if that's what's bothering you, since we were together. I've found my right habitat – my own place and plenty of friends – and work of course. Please relieve your mind of *any* unease on my account. Life has been thoroughly generous to me.'

'Relief to know that,' said Bridie, but then she looked at Elaine angrily. 'Tumours in me. Huge. Tumours. Eating me.'

Elaine choked. 'Do you have much pain, love?'

'Not now. Did have. Rotting away. And full of hate. Dry mouth, Elaine,' she complained irritably. 'How can I talk so parched? Can't be expected.'

'I've brought along some Newcastle Brown, but I don't suppose you're allowed it or fancy it?'

'Oh yes – anything I like – but I don't like anything. Let's try the beer.'

Bridie's hand quivered with the effort to raise the plastic mug to her lips.

'Should I hold it for you?'

'*No.*' She heaved the cup to her lips and took a swig. The froth stood on her lip as she lowered the cup carefully and successfully. 'Good beer,' she said kindly.

Elaine removed the cup from her hand. Bridie's eyes closed; her mouth sagged open. Now Elaine could suddenly see how close Bridie was to the end. The greyish skin in the ashen light made of Bridie's face a dead landscape of lunar hollows, with its sunken cheeks and temples, the sockets of the eyes shrunken, and all excess flesh wasted away. *Oh my poor Bridie*, she cried in her heart, *throw your weight around again, spin the globe*.

'Do you remember when we spun the globe, Bridie?'

'Yes,' replied Bridie, without opening her eyes. 'The beginning of everything.'

That was when, nearly two decades ago, they had conceived the plan for the Trust, sitting one night late over wine; and Elaine brought across the globe they kept as an ornament on the sideboard, and set it on the dinner-table, amongst the dirty dinner-plates and glasses in the candle-light. They'd both been shouting their mouths off at the misery of the world, and how intolerable it was that *we* had so much and *they* so little; and that what little *they* had *we* remorselessly exploited. Then Bridie reached out her hand and slowly spun the globe. Candle-light flickered on the great continental land masses, as the world spun round at Bridie's dictation. Then, 'I know – plug it in and light it up,' Elaine said, for it was one of those fancy globes with a light-bulb inside which you could light from the mains. And when the light came on, so did the many colours – white for the Polar caps, golden-brown for the mountains and deserts, and green for the fertile areas. There it magically glowed in the darkness, a world lighting their night, for Bridie blew out both candles and the globe shed the only brightness in the room. And still Bridie turned, hypnotically, so that you saw how immense was the turquoise Pacific, pouring over the eye's entire perspective from a certain angle; and then the enormous variegated land mass of Asia, Austral-Asia, Europe and Africa swam into sight, a patchwork of interconnected colours, with wrinklings of mountains where the continental drift had buckled and levered the Earth's crust; and then the Americas, sinuously stretching from Pole to Pole. It was not so very long since the American Apollo Mission had landed two men and implanted a flag on the moon. There the lunar cosmonauts had buzzed round in their moon-buggy and bounced here and there picking up bits of this and that in the cause of science. 'One small step for man,' the radio kept raving; *but not for woman*, Bridie and Elaine agreed, for different reasons. Elaine harboured mystical feelings about the feminine moon, the white goddess sacred to women in labour and the virgin warrior Artemis: she didn't like men stamping around on her, poking poles into her. But notwithstanding this, and Bridie's disgust at the insane waste of money and resources, they had both watched the TV pictures with some fascination. They had viewed our world from 'out there' for the first time and understood from the perspective of a foothold in space the frailty and pathos of its beauty. Now it was as if they too, light-headed with wine, were detached intelligences looking back at the whole luminous orb which was their home. The mother planet spun in the darkness of the dining room at Sorrel Avenue and lit the edges of wine glasses and cutlery with its bluish glow, and it was a beautiful, heart-stopping moment – but 'An illusion!' as Bridie said, snapping on the light so that all the enchantment dispersed into the commonplace proportions of a dining-table heaped with unwashed pots. 'Really the whole planet is crawling with poverty, disease and oppression, only we can't see it so therefore it doesn't exist.' And somehow from that denial came their project for the Trust, and the labour of twenty years. But what Elaine recalled was, ironically, less the recognition of reality than the dream of the bright lamp still turning and glowing in the inner space of both their minds. Soon Bridie's sharing of that memory would be blanked out, and she would carry it alone and uncorroborated until her own dying day, and then it would be extinguished.

Bridie said no more; seemed to doze. The cat slept curled on the bed with her hand still on its stomach. Elaine was glad Bridie seemed, relatively, at peace. The drugs, no doubt. Her work was done and she had become one with the suffering she had sought to ameliorate; had become that suffering, rather. Elaine desired to add to Bridie's peace of mind whatever she had it in her to bestow. But what did she want of her? It was not clear, for Elaine had never been like some people, who seemed to come equipped with sensitive antennae, abundant in intuitions.

Therefore when Bridie snapped alert and asked, crisply, 'Would you think of coming back to the Trust – take over from me?', it floored her.

'Oh . . . oh, I don't know, Bridie,' she said quickly. 'I've adapted, you see, to my present life – I've other commitments and responsibilities. I don't know if I can go back, dear. And surely,' she went on rapidly but softly, pleading with Bridie to understand and let her off, 'the Trust is in good hands – Robyn, Jess – you have faith in them?'

Bridie glanced sidelong with a trace of the old haughtiness and said, 'It was in *my* hands. Now – can't be sure what will happen. Work *with* the people, we said, no condescension, no bread-basket. Political action. *Justice*. Support them taking back what's justly theirs. Now I'll never be sure . . .' She ran down; it became unreal. She stared past Elaine's head to where the blind TV screen mirrored the comings and goings of a world deaf to all but its own processes and preoccupations. She had already forgotten what she was saying. 'Oh well . . . never mind. Worth a shot.'

'Talk to Robyn and Jess, Bridie. Confide in them – let them put your heart at rest as I'm sure they will.'

Bridie sighed. 'Yes – yes. It doesn't matter. Just that you were there . . . there in the beginning.'

'And what about Ruth –?'

'Oh, *Ruth*.' Bridie cut in with startling asperity, and jerked with her left hand as if brushing off a troublesome fly. 'Ruth's just – a schoolteacher.'

She looked at Elaine with a wry twist of her mouth as if that were an argument that somehow clinched things.

'I thought – and hoped – you'd been happy, Bridie?'

'Happy . . . happiness. What's happiness?'

'Well, I suppose . . .'

'I mean, what does it matter, happiness, in the long run? In the end, you're on your own.' Her voice was down to a thick whisper.

'No, my friend, no.' Elaine took her hand again and pressed it strongly. 'Not so neither.'

But wasn't it true? Elaine asked herself, getting up to leave after Bridie had been given a further injection, and finding that her arthritic hip and knees had stiffened painfully during the two hours of sitting on that uncomfortable chair. *Wasn't Bridie right about how in the end you're on your own?* She was leaving Bridie abandoned on that institutional bed while she could rise (with relief) to her feet and make her escape, and now, as she picked Leah up and felt the awakening cat's panicky claws snatch at her sweater, she was already wondering how the traffic would be on the motorway home; what she'd have for tea when she got there. She was thinking, *God, I'm tired*, and *I think I'll ring Lindsay tonight and see if she wants to go to the Endellion concert.* She was taking the road back to normality – a normality Bridie had been prised off like a limpet; a normality one must reassert in the teeth of all Bridie's exclusion meant. The woman on the bed had silently told her she too was made of the same decaying matter and must come to the same vile end. And one did not want to know those truths: they must remain at the level of cliché. She brushed down her immaculate black trousers, gathered her bags and walked rather stiffly to the door of the ward. Within the complexity of her mourning for Bridie was mingled the remorseful illusion of exemption.

Ruth, spying through the glass partition of the ward, made a dash for it when she saw that Elaine was getting to her feet and making preparations to leave. She had been standing there for twenty minutes watching the two of them, her heart bursting with anguish. Yet superficially she was remarkably steady, and when the staff nurse enquired did she want to go in she replied in a calm, neutral way that, no, she thought one visitor at a time was plenty; she'd just wait here if she was not in the way.

It was nauseating that, even at a time of such crisis, when one wanted to live up to the highest and most generous standards of conduct, littleness would keep creeping in. She noted, with a satisfaction that curdled and condemned itself in the moment of experience, how grey and stout Elaine had become over these five years; how middle-aged and somehow tweedy was the figure that bent to kiss the unconscious face of her friend ('distinguished' she might be, as Bridie insisted on pronouncing and it had rung in her mind ever since – but now look at the bags under her eyes and the suggestion of a double chin). And carrying a bloody cat. Bridie detested cats. She went running out and shooed them off her lawn for peeing on her primroses. At the same time, Ruth experienced a self-preening awareness of her own comparative youthfulness: the slim, supple body in its blue jeans and denim shirt; the shock of curly, red hair without a grey fleck to be seen. That cumbrous old woman couldn't stand up against her, not in a million years. She took off up the corridor, lightly, in her trainers, and hid in the chapel. But all the time she was looking at herself with contempt, wondering how – on this of all occasions – she could be so petty and mean as to view life as some sort of beauty contest – with Bridie lying there *dying*, for Christ's sake. *I am not a sufficient person*, she told herself, *I'm nothing but a child howling for reassurance.* And her own littleness seemed to prove her unworthiness to be loved and accounted equal by someone like Bridie.

No. No. Elaine had not taken Bridie away from her. No one could take a person away. They went of their own accord or you unconsciously pushed them. Or they went because some extreme crisis changed the balance of their minds and between the two of you. *It was not my fault*, thought Ruth, *not Elaine's, and not Bridie's either. We loved each other. We did. We both tried.* The disease was the enemy, the way it violated not only Bridie's poor body but the tender join between the two of them, levering them apart like an invasive tumour. She inspected the empty chapel with cold eyes. The cross bereaved of its tenant presided over a space where mourners had solicited comfort, and gone away either temporarily solaced or disappointed, with the taste of the sacred supper still on their tongues; and then another lot filed in and wept and prayed and left. The only colour in the room came from the stained-glass Jesus with his long curly hair and his lamb – and the crystal vases of formal flowers, so rigidly stood to attention as if to emulate artificial flowers. Ruth went up and sniffed and, yes, they were real, just about. They looked like left-overs from a funeral – as perhaps they were.

Outside on the chaise longue in the foyer, orderlies were piling bulging grey plastic bags, marked THIS BAG IS THE PROPERTY OF ST MARCIA'S HOSPICE: PATIENT'S POSSESSIONS.

'We'll give you a hand to get these out to the car,' said one orderly cheerfully to a middle-aged couple. 'Where are you parked?'

'Just over there. To the left of the forecourt.'

'Righty-ho.'

The orderly marched out with two bags in each hand, the couple with their strained faces trailing along behind, each holding a bag. They faltered over the thick green carpet and the automatic doors opened soundlessly to let them out. At first Ruth failed to comprehend the significance of the bags: then it dawned. The patient – *their* person – was now the deceased. The bags contained all the stuff the deceased had brought into the hospice – all that was left of him or her. Here, in this deep-piled place, this transaction was normality. Out would come Bridie's belongings in the same matter-of-fact containers, dumped on the sofa, shoved in the back of a taxi.

'Shocking weather,' observed the orderly brightly, as he came back in out of the rain, wiping his shoes vigorously.

The sinister and nightmarish became ordinary; and that was in itself sinister and nightmarish.

She sat by Bridie's bed. After all that conversation with Elaine, Bridie was apparently wearied out, and – though her eyes were open and scanned Ruth's face confusedly – she gave no sign of recognition.

'You just rest, my darling love, and I'll sit here with you,' said Ruth tentatively, as if in expectation of rebuke or marching orders. 'There's no need to speak. I'll just enjoy your presence. I'll be here, sweetheart, as you've always been there for me.'

A tear formed in the bud of Bridie's eye. It formed slowly, gathered and hung. Somehow it appeared huge from the near perspective of Ruth's own eyes, as if they magnified what they saw, while the eventless tranquillity of the ward slowed down any minor and inconsequent change which happened to happen. The tear, as Ruth bent closer to Bridie's face, reflected in its quivering pearly globe, at the final second before it fell, her own peering face in glassy miniature. Overflowing, it dissolved the mirror and, sliding smoothly down beside Bridie's nose, made its diminishing way across her cheek.

'Don't let me upset you, Bridie love. Don't. I love you so much. I love you with all of me.'

But what was the tear? Was it a mere secretion of the duct in response to light and chemistry, or was it a sign of feeling? And if so, what did it mean?

'If you don't want me, I'll go, my love. Whatever is best for you. Just let me know.'

Bridie gave no response. How could one divine what, if anything, was going on behind the mask-like face that had suffered enough? Just a single and indubitable sign of love, reconciliation, care, would mean so much.

Bridie stared at the face that presented itself to her. It was a distressed face, and a gentle one. Its forehead was wrinkled up with repressed misery. The pale skin was freckled slightly around the cheeks, and under the eyes were blue-black shadows like bruises – as if someone had been hitting and punching her, and Ruth had just stood her ground allowing herself to be hit and punched. Bridie knew, without asking, all that had gone on in the mind behind the face, for it opposed her own like a mirror.

'I need you,' said the face. 'I know it's weak, and I shouldn't ask for anything for myself, but I need you. And I feel – bereft.'

Bridie couldn't answer anyone's need. She had to be numb and blank. People mustn't ask her for anything any more: she hadn't got it to give. They must go about their business in the world where they belonged and had a place and function. It was none of her concern. She had tried, and failed, to heave her own workload on to Elaine's shoulders; but Elaine had also found her niche in the world, her nice flat, her work and friends, her pet. It only served to emphasise that *they* were the living; *she* was outside and beyond. A screen of plate glass intervened between her mortal disease and their healthy bodies. She lay supine; they got up, with a scrape of the chair, shrugged on their overcoats and walked out scot-free. No longer hostile to them for this immunity, she experienced a detachment from their doings and sayings. She could tick off their names one by one on her valedictory list. And this dear face of all faces must be guarded against. Bridie had sharp eyes and had detected it palely hovering outside the ward while Elaine was visiting. This face thinned the glass partition that saved her from the cruelty of interference from the survivors. These tender, wistful eyes made her long and long to live – and, if she let them, their light would altogether melt the plate-glass screen that divided them and defended her, and so let loose the pandemonium of pain that had shrieked along every nerve in her body, and which she could and would no longer bear. Nobody had the right, invasively, to ask or command that of her.

'Now go away,' she heard herself telling Ruth, with a hoarse, abrasive voice. 'You've done all you can but I don't want you here any more. Go away.'

'*Bridie* – please.'

'Go away,' went on Bridie. 'Live your life. Don't think about me. I won't think about you.'

'Oh Bridie – have some mercy.'

'I haven't any mercy to spare.'

'I understand that – I understand – I know. But don't cut me off Bridie sweetheart, don't – just let me come and be near you. I won't ask anything of you, I'll just sit near you – or, out of sight, or anything – but don't send me away and abandon me after all the love –.' The face was pouring down tears, and Bridie had never been able to resist Ruth's tears, although she'd grumbled, 'You're like a tap: you just turn them on to get what you want.' She hadn't wanted a hair of Ruth's head hurt, which was all the more reason to protect herself now.

'Don't visit me again. Just let me be. If you care for me at all, stay right away.' Her voice was husky and croaking, like a cough.

Ruth was silent, rocking herself to and fro in her own arms, the tears spurting out between her lids, her face slightly raised.

'Bridie, for the love of God, I've got no one but you.'

'Of course you have,' said Bridie in a no-nonsense voice. 'Don't be ridiculous. You've got your children. You've got friends. You'll have other lovers.' Her voice caught. She stopped abruptly.

'No – no. You can't understand. You're *killing* me, Bridie,' she broke out in a loud voice, and the old woman in the next but one bed looked up from her magazine and craned round a Ribena bottle to see what was up. A nurse turned in her tracks and stood watching, bedpan in hand.

'Killing *you*! That's rich!' Bridie laughed out loud.

'There's more than one way to die,' Ruth went on in a somewhat less frenzied voice. '*You*'ll be free and *I*'ll still be dying.'

Bridie reached down for the buzzer. Its alarm call brought the nurse over at the double.

'Mrs Asher . . . this woman . . . upsetting me, Nurse,' Bridie told her raspingly. 'Don't want her to visit me any more. No more visits. Would you please . . . make it absolutely clear to her? She's not to come.'

'You've tired yourself out, Bridget,' said the nurse. 'Come on now, dear. It's all right.' She led Ruth off weeping, a sympathetic arm round her shoulders. Bridie did not follow with her eyes, which were gritty and dry but she could not summon the energy to raise a hand to rub them. She felt nothing except seethings of exasperation – excoriation. This was what it had been like before she entered the hospice – no peace at all.

No peace for the wicked, sneered a small voice in her mind. She ignored it. Her body fidgeted and itched as if insects were crawling all over it. Her fingers picked at the quilt until, with the suddenness of an accidental tumble, she tripped down into sleep.

'Don't let it get to you,' soothed the nurse, still holding Ruth's hand. 'She'll probably have forgotten she said it by tomorrow.'

'I don't think so. I don't think she will. She's been like this with me for months,' Ruth sobbed.

'Do you fancy a cup of tea and a chat, pet? I think you could do with it.'

Ruth allowed herself to be sat down in the staff room, and swallowed some mouthfuls of scalding tea.

'You live with Bridget, don't you, Ruth?' If there was prurience in the woman's enquiry, she was hiding it efficiently. 'It has been very hard for you both. Sometimes people turn against those they care about most. It's not uncommon. But it's very hard to bear.'

Ruth nodded; but could say nothing. She had not envisaged personality change when the disease was diagnosed. She would rather die with or for Bridie than submit to this skinning and flaying of rejection. There would be nothing to remember than that Bridie turned her back on her. Their life in retrospect appeared a tissue of frivolous illusions – for which she had sacrificed children, family, identity, everything.

Lizzie stood at the bottom of Bridie's bed in a state of hypnotised terror. A hypochondriac since the age of three, she had courted medicines, eye-drops, ointments and bandages for the smallest, or non-existent, complaints – the more the better – but shunned the doctor's surgery like the plague. Injections for rubella or measles induced hysteria; one nurse had to grapple her down while the other inserted the needle, at which she fainted. When Lizzie's verruca had to be frozen off, she treated it as major surgery, withdrawing her foot in angry protest with every advance of the doctor's implement. Lizzie's hatred of hospitals dated from the time of Sarah's birth, when she was taken in by Daddy to view the new baby – a squashed-up monkey mottled red and yellow with jaundice, which puked as soon as it was picked up. It was horrible to think of what we were made of: bags of blood, heart, kidneys, liver, miles of gut, lobes of lung and brain – the entire contents of the butcher's window packaged up in one skin. Raw meat and offal. That was what we were. It did not bear thinking about. But she could not help thinking about it. While Sarah played with her dolls and fondled the kitten, Lizzie's X-ray eye anatomised the doll's essential hollowness and the kitten's killer-instinct. Such insight alienated her from the doll but not the kitten, for the creature resisted her sister's infantilisation of it by bolting out of the cat-flap and shooting up a tree. Lizzie liked the kitten but never petted it. She tendered respect and fellow feeling.

The sight of Roger the Lodger, tenant of a bed in this ward of old ladies at the end of the world, shocked Lizzie rigid. In fact you could hardly recognise Roger as the same person. She crept round to observe at close quarters. What she witnessed made her heart bang and her stomach heave. An emaciated greyish face with a consistency like a waxwork lay on what seemed an immense pillow: though perhaps the pillow seemed so big because the face was shrunken. Always this woman had bulked so large in her imagination – and here she was revealed so small and shrivelled. Windfall fruit decaying came into her mind, and something of that sickly-sweet aroma hung around her. The eyes were shut, the mouth open, and as she slept, she snored slightly.

Lizzie was at once revolted and fascinated. So *this* was dying? It was a piece of news to her virgin spirit that penetrated her with the force of violation. Of course she had seen plenty of mutilation, horror and death on the videos her friends rented, which familiarised them all with violence, domesticating it into a vague fun-thing which scarcely arrested the attention or aroused the pulses. In response to this cult of glamorised violence, Lizzie was more fastidious than her peers. She did not like it very much, and only watched to keep in with them. But nothing of what she had seen had prepared her for this bloodcurdling perception of death's slow processes as it ate a person, from within, second by second, minute by minute.

The spectral figure on the bed did not move so much as an eyelash. No pulse beat in its throat. Its left hand lay like an open claw on the counterpane, with Lizzie's mother's plain gold ring loose on the bony finger between knuckle and joint.

Perhaps it was dead already.

Lizzie put her hand over her mouth and fled. But, though a small and compact building, the hospice was designed in three wings and cunningly labyrinthine in construction. Missing the 'This Way To The Exit' sign, she blundered into side-wards where other bodies lay – everywhere bodies, with gaping toothless mouths, or strung up to strange contraptions, all staring at Lizzie. The more she barged about, the more she panicked.

She found herself in the hospice shop. A stout elderly man with a white moustache like a colonel looked up in surprise from his crossword puzzle.

'How do I get out? *Please*?'

He came out and pointed. Lizzie raced out of the automatic doors into the rain. When she got home, she said nothing to Dad. Her face was working as she filled the kettle to make herself a cup of hot chocolate.

'Hey, Lizzie girl, what's up?' he asked. It was not like her to display any emotion except anger so nakedly.

She shook her head vehemently. Unacknowledged tears chased one another down her flaring cheeks.

'Are you sure?'

'Yes.'

'Hey, give me that – let me do it for you. You'll have sugar everywhere. Look here, you can tell me. Come on – come on to your old dad, Liz.'

He held out his arms for her and she ran into them, grasping on to his body with battening arms as if to rescue herself from drowning. It was years since she had turned to him, and now it felt to Gavin, curiously, as if a stranger had come rushing in from the dark and launched herself into his embrace. He felt for the first time her slender, solid tallness, only a few inches short of his own height, and felt – not for the first time – how little he knew her, however hard and diligently he tried.

Still she hung on tight, sobbing into the shoulder of his sweater. It must be something really bad. He went through the mental list – hormones, pregnancy, boyfriend, exams, drugs, or had she perhaps found out that he and Val were to marry?

'You can tell me, love,' he said, and stroked her hair with a clumsy but loving hand. 'I won't be angry. I'll stand beside you. Trust me, Liz.'

'I'm frightened,' said her muffled voice, but resisted telling him more, till in the end he began to feel mildly irritated – coming home tired from work, to be leapt on by a tearful adolescent, before he'd even got his moccasins on.

'Well – you'll tell me in your own good time,' he said in a patient tone, knowing she probably wouldn't, and disengaged himself gently, to make her hot chocolate. 'You calm down now, Lizzie. Calm yourself. And get those wet clothes off.'

Lizzie paused at the door.

'Thanks, Dad,' she mumbled.

She shook her hot chocolate and three biscuits upstairs to her room, locking herself in, and resting the convector heater against the waste-paper basket so that it would blast hot air at her face. The warmth inside as she sipped the chocolate, and outside from the fire, soothed and calmed her. But, glancing up, she chanced to meet the eye of a horse in the RSPCA poster, hanging from the cautionary meat-hook; and the desperately sad eye held her own, pleading for all creaturely life that suffered unnecessarily, and pleading (now, for the first time she made the connection) for Bridie and those women in the hospice – for all of whom Lizzie, being young and ignorant and alone, could do next to nothing.

Forgive me, she mentally begged of the horse and the caged pigs in the next poster, and the fox being torn to shreds by the hunt in the next, as she took them all down and, carefully rolling them up, hid them under the bed, well out of sight.

5

Elaine sat down in the tiny restaurant which had recently been
opened in the back room of the Leeds Trust shop, and ordered a
mug of coffee. There was minimal room for people once the
four round tables and assorted donated chairs had been
crammed into the room, and one had to hold one's breath in
order to squeeze a way through the crush of furniture. No doubt
one was getting corpulent in one's old age, but even so . . . The
coffee was expensive but prodigiously good – really choice. It
was being sold to the Trust, so the notice said, by a co-operative
of Brazilian growers at a sum appropriate to the labour of
producing it rather than the plummeted price dictated by the
slump in Western demand. Elaine privately doubted the success
of the project. *If I were Director* . . . she caught herself thinking,
but the reflection petered out unconsummated. It was too huge
an *if*. How could she, at her time of life, and with her arthritic
disability, face such an upheaval, the shouldering of so onerous a
responsibility? It was not only unrealistic, it was downright
unfair. Bridie's hand, disempowered itself, was seeking to exert
a forlorn but powerful pressure through her. *Not fair, Bridie, I've
got my life to live*, she mentally riposted, in a phlegmatic tone, and
censored the image of the suffering face of Bridie that
extenuated the importunity of her claims. Fortunately, Elaine
had always been able to do that: measure things up, reason them

84

thus and thus, so as to take practical action based on her assessment and walk away from debilitating emotional hangups. Up till now.

Today she was irked by her inability to concentrate. Having got up with a zest for work, she'd opened the manuscript of her book and found Bridie retarding the pen. 'If the campaign of mass-vaccination could prove so successful in a country like Turkey,' she had written, 'it implies that . . .' but what did it imply? She could not hazard any conclusion save that she needed fresh air. She closed the book and wandered out. Coming in to the Trust shop happened as if by lazy accident but Elaine was perfectly well aware that no serendipity was involved. It was her homing instinct that brought her and set her down amongst the red and white check gingham tablecloths, wedged between the wall and the rim of the table: she had come here to meet Bridie, just as decidedly as she had yesterday driven down to visit her in the hospice.

'More coffee, Dr Demetrian?' asked the daughter of the manager who was helping out for the day.

'*Elaine*.'

'Sorry – Elaine.'

'Well, yes I will – thank you. It's really excellent, isn't it? Have you tried it?'

'I've *tried* it . . . but you can't afford more than a bean at a time. Worse than British Rail. We treat it like gold you know, we grind the beans individually . . . well, not actually, but you know what I mean. There you are, Dr . . . Elaine.'

She hadn't the human touch; not like Bridie. People 'doctored' her, spread out a red carpet for her; honoured her and kept their distance like those coffee beans that were a bit too pricey for everyone's taste. She and Bridie had both been high-powered but Bridie had that – what was it? – charisma or some quality that appeared astoundingly to lay its life out in conversation, seeming to gild with light the face of the other person, the recipient, so that they never forgot the exchange, however casual. Thus when Bridie made contacts with individuals or organisations, they became connections. And on TV, what a performer . . . even Terry Wogan had had his show taken over by her, and been riveted into dropping his facile mask by the splendour of her presence. For you could call it no less than that: splendour.

To have such command . . . was not . . . she had sometimes thought . . . entirely desirable. She had seen Bridie manipulating people – feeding them through a mincer – seducing them into believing themselves more important to her than they were. And yet there was still a quality of – she would once have said, of God – but now she knew no word for it. A striving self-giving on a base of sturdy egoism; a power of care. And now that she was a wasted body on a bed, no more than that, how could one deny her anything? For one was indebted: that was it, and it was why Bridie's request continued to harrow her. A debt was due. But why *should* there be a debt? Why? It was irrational. It was extortion; blackmail.

Elaine fiddled irritably with the pile of leaflets and booklets on the table. At the bottom of the pile was the Trust's quarterly bulletin, which she opened idly at page one:

Director: Bridget Rose McKearn, B.Sc. (Econ), M.Phil.

In a flash she had imagined her own name in its place. It looked wonderful; it looked eminent. It impressed her as a capable name, able to restructure, modernise, galvanise: a name that could stand alone, no longer the eternal collaborator: *Elaine Demetrian*. But along with this vainglorying, and a sense of home-coming to her proper inheritance, came a vexation that so much should be demanded, so improperly late in the day. It was ridiculous even to entertain the thought. As if she'd been invited, at her time of life, to undergo a pregnancy and assume the care of a child. *No!* she fiercely denied Bridie, springing to her feet, so that the table jerked and the melted gold of the coffee slopped over the table-cloth, *there are plenty of other people to do the job. Sorry, but no. I'm damned if I will.*

At which Bridie seemed to turn over in bed, clear as day in her mind's eye, and confront her with her caved-in, stricken face, saying 'But you were there, in the beginning,' at which Elaine, faltering, sat down again heavily, conceding, *Well, I'll think about it.*

A false lucidity and composure lay across Ruth's mind. There was nothing to hope for; nothing to fear. The worst that could have happened had now happened. The blow that had struck her must have concussed her. That would explain the insane normality with which she fitted the key in the lock to let herself in; the calm with which she switched on the lamp beneath which Bridie used to sit curled up reading. Without taking off her outdoor coat, Ruth seated herself next to the empty place and put up one exploratory hand to her temples. Her head was ringing. But silent. Once as a child, she had been whacked on the head with a spade by a schoolfellow who erroneously claimed that Ruth had stolen her best friend. The blinding shock as metal impacted on bone had persisted, it seemed, for weeks: the echo of the report rang in her head wellnigh to the exclusion of external stimuli, which seemed trivially incidental.

And yet, when she consciously listened, she could hear nothing . . . but no . . . it was not nothing . . . it was a roar of emptiness; the air trapped in the hollow of her ear roared like thunder . . . the self in the gutted skull was a deafening absence. And yet all was silent; was silence.

She should not stay in. She should go back out, for her health's sake. The slanting rain was kinder than that penetration by silence; it turned as she walked into the multiple cold pangs of hailstones, from the darkened skies that were also considerably kinder than the lights she had left burning inside the house.

The Trust shop was bustlingly full and doing a brisk trade considering the lateness of the hour and the incommodious weather. Ruth loitered in the alcove between the changing room and the second-hand goods. From the changing room came the sound of a tussle between mother and daughter over the desirability of a skirt which the latter grizzlingly opined was not the height of fashion.

'But it's such a good fit. Suits you so well.'

'It's *not*. It's *stupid*. I'll get laughed at.'

'Of course you won't, dear. Do stand still. Don't *flounce* like that. Stop it, stop dragging if off like that, you'll break the zip – *Sophie*.'

There was a short pause, filled with a sort of rustling scrummage. Then the mother's tensely patient whisper resumed: 'There you are – look at it from the back. Very suitable. You could even wear it to school if you . . .'

'You're joking aren't you? I'd rather *die*.'

'Oh well, if you . . .'

'Anyway, it's dirty. I'm not going to wear something *dirty*.'

'It's not dirty – where is it dirty? . . . Oh Sophie, that's not dirt, that's a shadow.'

'No it's not, it's a dirty cast-off, it stinks and I'm not wearing it.'

'Shush, keep your voice down. Take it off carefully – *carefully* I said. Someone else might want it,' said the mother, losing her temper, 'even if you're too damned snobbish for it, Lady Muck.'

'I'm *not* a snob,' hissed the child, and stamped her foot, sending the offensive skirt sailing out of the cubicle; the mother, diving out through the curtains and snatching it up, gave a quick, embarrassed look round the shop and dived back in again.

'Just get dressed, will you?' The mother's tone had changed to wearied resignation.

'Sorry, Mum. But it wasn't really . . . *me*. Was it?'

Out they marched, heads down. Ruth continued to dawdle at the second-hand bric-à-brac counter where you could stand and philosophise, marvelling at the inexhaustible inventiveness of the consumerist dream, that had originally conjured up and succeeded in selling this cross-eyed china goblin on a red toadstool; a miniature gadget for picking up crumbs from very small surfaces, advertising itself as a 'Crumb-Buster'; twin gilt boxes of indeterminate purpose, labelled 'His' and 'Hers'. Each of these throw-outs was going for thirty pence, as was a bottle of nail varnish remover, a xylophone with two notes missing, two unopened pairs of nylon stockings, several dozen coat-hangers and a marble ashtray. The works of Barbara Cartland shared space with a manual of car maintenance and an elderly copy of Dr Spock's *Baby and Childcare*. Ruth picked everything up methodically and scrutinised it; then she replaced it tidily. Each item entered into her archaeologising eye but died at the moment of seeing.

There was Beth Hatch behind the counter; she knew and trusted her quite well – well enough to catch the eye and transmit the message that she couldn't bear to be spoken to. Beth was in her sixties, still limping from her hip operation, diffident but with a lot of humour in her. Beth's people were Marxists for three generations, Yorkshire miners of whom she told many proud anecdotes; she ought not to have got on with Marjorie Speenham-Cooke, her fellow-worker whose original triple-barrelled surname she boasted of having cut down to the present modest double 'on the grounds of convenience, bit of a mouthful' – but they did get on. Marjorie was just now sorting donations in the ante-room and keeping up a high-pitched commentary on the items being brought to light by her researchers.

'Well, look at all this crockery – quite decent stuff, willow-pattern – I say, I wouldn't mind taking this myself, Beth, a *very* little chipping to a couple of pieces but, my word, this *is* in good condition, we could charge £5 the lot and cheap at the price . . . oh, it's *you*, Ruth – look, Beth, it's Ruth, hadn't you seen her?' Emerging from the back room, she charged across to Ruth (she had no tact, none, she cursed herself many a time for her deplorable lack of insight), then swerved as she registered Ruth's stony face and red, bruised-looking eyes, just in the middle of asking, 'How's Bri . . .?', and said 'Oh no,' and took a dash at the shelves which she made as if to dust with her handkerchief before retreating to the counter. 'Jolly good tea-service, Beth – shall we price it now? Get it out on the shelf straightaway?'

'Hello, Marjorie,' said Ruth softly. 'It's good to see you,' and she held out her hand, which Marjorie took and pressed with an abrupt, embarrassed motion as if on the wing, before returning to the sorting-room. Summer and winter, indoors and out, she wore a floral scarf covering her hair: one wondered, as Bridie had speculated, what lay behind or beneath the defences of that scarf which seemed as organic a part of Marjorie as the nose on her face.

'I bite my tongue sometimes, I do really,' came the muffled boom of her voice through the doorway. 'My great blabbing mouth wants taping up . . . Is she all right, she looks like death . . . Oh, I say, Beth, what's this, would you say?'

There was a pause.

'I don't know, Marjorie. Is it some sort of – torch?'

'No light though . . . Is there?'

'No. But it seems to be electric. Look, it comes apart –

batteries inside. Let's try twiddling the end. Yes, look, it's switched on – you can hear it purring. But whatever is it? Damned if I know.'

Ruth, looking in through the open door, recognised the thing at once. She went in and whispered.

'A what? A vibrator?' Marjorie's falsetto, though intended to be muted, seemed to shriek a broadcast message to all and sundry. 'I can feel it vibrating okay. But what *is* a vibrator? What's it for?'

'Oh Marjorie – do shush – it's a . . . you know . . . sexual thing,' whispered Beth. '*You know.*'

Light dawned. '*Well*,' said Marjorie, stumped for words, and with innocent curiosity she turned the object over and over in her hands. 'Well. You live and learn. Don't you? Never clapped eyes on such a thing till now.'

However long was it since Ruth laughed? – really laughed, as now she did, wheezing and snorting, doubling up, as Beth, who was in a similar state, hastily closed the door.

'I don't know what you're both guffawing about,' said Marjorie. 'It's most interesting. A sexual aid. But – tell me – what do they *do* with them, actually? Scientific curiosity and all that.'

'Well, I suppose,' suggested Beth, 'they . . . tickle themselves with it.'

'So . . . men . . . tickle themselves with these?' She tried it against her cheek.

'No, Marjorie – *women* do.'

'Do they really? Women?' Marjorie held the vibrator at arm's length, giving it a long, hard look. 'And where would you go to purchase such a thing?'

'To any reputable Trust shop, evidently!' said Ruth, and she and Beth again went off the deep end, sobbing with laughter in one another's arms until a timid tap on the door caused them to leap apart and Marjorie to shove the object of her studies into a heap of clothing.

'Oh yes, it's Mrs Dark with her pennies,' said Beth. 'Hello, Mrs Dark, I'm just coming.'

The octogenarian deposited her tin of penny and tuppenny pieces on the counter as she did every week. It was wellnigh her sole journey, navigating with her stick the irregular pavements, a trip which took courage. She sat now taking breath while Beth counted out her savings.

Ruth was still laughing . . . too much. The explosive laughter turned to tears; the tears dried suddenly and silence rang in her ears. Beth tried to catch hold of her saying 'There, dear' but Ruth slipped past: 'Must go.'

In the street she started to laugh again. For it all came back, the time when (married to Gavin, and sexual love being a sequence of ever lonelier disappointments) she'd rushed into one of those sleazy shops and purchased at random from the full range of colours and shapes, one vibrator; paid; rushed out. Locked in the bathroom she had unpacked a six-inch red rocket, surveying it with fascinated distaste. She kept it wrapped in a series of brown paper bags in a pencil-case at the back of a desk drawer.

Years later she had confided the existence of this instrument to Bridie, who had been curious.

'Can I have a look? I've never seen one.'

Embarrassed, Ruth had produced the pencil-case. Bridie observed the process of unpacking with grave eyes; she would never laugh at you if she felt your shyness was involved, even if a thing struck her as a hoot. That was so endearing about Bridie.

The red rocket emerged from the last paper bag and Ruth stood it in the centre of the kitchen table.

'A miracle of modern technology,' Ruth had said.

'It must be if it helped you. It's a funny shape though, isn't it?

It looks as if it was about to take off from a launching pad at NASA. And very – crimson.'

'Like a prick, I suppose. They must think – the manufacturers, I mean, that only a prick could give a woman pleasure.'

'That must be it.'

'So what shall we do with it?' Ruth had wondered. 'Keep it as a curiosity or get rid of it? Or bury it with an epitaph, RIP?'

'Perhaps we could think of some alternative use – recycle it – in the kitchen or the garden.' They both burst out laughing.

In the end, no inspiration being forthcoming, Ruth had thrown the thing away in the dustbin, still wrapped in the modesty of its paper bags. It had helped her once, to feel whole and autonomous, but it had also confirmed her isolation. Nobody had ever touched her. Nobody had reached her. Perhaps they never would.

But then with Bridie, she had found the real thing; had been persuaded that she was beautiful, utterly beautiful, and entire and whole and complete.

'How easily I could have missed you,' she'd say to Bridie, lying in her arms, dazed with joy that she might so easily have missed. 'It's awful. If you hadn't been sitting in the second row at the Lindsay Quartet concert . . .'

'If I'd stayed at home and read a book . . .'

'If I'd sat on the stage as normal . . .'

'Ah, but the Minor Gods arranged it,' Bridie would say buoyantly. 'It couldn't have been otherwise. We couldn't not have met.'

Ruth knew they could. The needful food would never have found its way to her mouth, to show her how famished she had always been. Bridie had been the thickset, middle-aged woman seated next to her in the music department concert hall at the university, with a score of the Schubert Quintet in her lap. She could see it now, standing at the bus-stop in the rain – the dark-brown trousered lap at which she kept glancing sidelong to view the open book with its inscrutable code, a five-lane motorway along which all those dots with tadpole tails travelled. She had been inquisitive partly because she half thought she recognised the woman and partly because it galled her when people ostentatiously followed the music on a score, flapping over the pages in a superior manner. It was an affectation. Ruth, who could not read music, naturally resented those who could. She had sized the woman up covertly. Harsh-faced and humourless-looking, with greying brown hair, short and spiked in the modern fashion; dark jacket and trousers. A professor, most probably: she had the look of a professor, sombre and ascetic. Where had Ruth seen her before? Having puzzled over it casually, she had soon forgotten about her.

The Lindsay, with an additional cellist, began the quintet. Ruth flowed away into the music. It was only now in the slow movement, when the pizzicato pluckings of the two cellos made a throbbing heartbeat over which the violins' and viola's tragic melody streamed, that she glanced involuntarily at her neighbour and realised that she had not turned a page of the score since page one. The woman met her eyes but as if in her sleep, without focusing on anyone. After the interval, Ruth said to her, 'You didn't follow your score?'

'No – I got carried away. It often happens. I mean to *think* more about the music, but the music prevents me. And the Lindsay especially. And you –?'

'Oh – I'm not literate. Can't tell a crotchet from a semi-breve,' said Ruth with a sort of pride in her ignorance. 'It's not really necessary for understanding – at least, I don't think so. Music is the place – of refuge – democratic, where anyone can go.'

'Yes . . . I know that feeling. Yes.' She slapped her score shut and thrust it in a briefcase, as if conscious that it had caused offence.

'Music . . . is . . . don't you think? . . . where one cannot feel lonely.'

The woman stared. Ruth squirmed. What was the matter with her that she went around soliciting intimacy – baring her heart to scrutiny, unable to accommodate to the polite norms? It was as if she were always half-consciously casting around for a match and mate.

'I have felt so too,' said the woman with simple dignity. 'By the way, I'm Bridie McKearn.'

Bridie had gone out of her way to exert her considerable charisma on Ruth, making sure she got Ruth's address and phone number. They went to every concert in Manchester, from the Free Trade Hall to the Northern College, the Cathedral, the Palace, the BBC. Baby-sitters had to be found three nights a week which Gavin quietly deplored on the stated grounds that she was behaving like a bad mother and the unstated grounds that there must be some man she'd fallen for. Bridie had hugged and kissed her goodnight, and Ruth found herself looking forward to the hug. She would spin it out, laughing and chatting as they embraced. Then one night Bridie had kissed her on the mouth, a faltering but passionately tender kiss, and touched her face with fugitive, exploring fingers; and Ruth knew – or rather, could no longer conceal from herself the fact of her knowledge.

'I've wanted to do that for so long,' Bridie had murmured. 'I've longed and longed to put my hands through your amazing hair – so beautiful,' and tentatively did. The wind whipped against their faces as they stood gazing into one another's eyes at the bottom of the dark, sordid staircase leading up to Oxford Road Station. A heroin addict lay slumped half-way up the steps, and two beggars with cardboard boxes sat foetally, patiently, just above them. Chip papers and an old beer can tumbled around in the wind, and shouting men spilt out of the pub, smashing a bottle on the cobbles. Bridie and Ruth, under the dusky orange lamp, must have appeared to the casual observer just like any other couple, kissing goodnight. But for Ruth there had been an electric strangeness and fearful shyness, mingled perplexedly with the peculiar sense of home-coming she felt in Bridie's presence, as if she'd lived abroad for a lifetime and, in returning, scarcely knew the language or mores.

'Oh Bridie – I ought to say – I've never loved a woman before.'

'But at least you've loved. I don't believe I ever have. You've given me birth, Ruth.'

Who am I? Ruth had wondered, ambling on to the platform to await the train, glittering with excitement, rocking with uncertainty. It had been like becoming an adolescent again. She sought her self in a hall of many mirrors: Gavin's wife? Sarah and Elizabeth's mother? The high school's history teacher? None of these. She had taken her scissors to the old bonds of love and her roots shrieked as she tore them up. The tender steady caring Bridie had offered did not entirely atone for the unspoken knowledge that Bridie would have found it wellnigh impossible (if the judge at Heron House had awarded Ruth custody) to accept two young children into her household. Ruth noticed that she had a fastidious distaste for infants, and averted her eyes from Lizzie, who was – to put it mildly – a sloppy eater, when the eleven-year-old came for her access visits and shovelled in her baked beans by the spoonful, talking all the while. But Bridie had tried with them; she did try. She bought Lizzie a kite shaped like an eagle, and ran up and down the road with her, flying it. She permitted Sarah to trampoline on her bed in the study, her sanctum, smiling a rather frozen smile. She left the room for considerable periods to allow Ruth to read with the children and cuddle them, and made light of the outrageous insults Lizzie offered her. At five o'clock on Sunday, when their father came (on the dot) to remove the girls back to savoury normality, Bridie left Ruth to lock herself into the bedroom; then, when she heard the bolt being drawn, she would tap on the door and ask, 'Shall I come to you?', patiently lying with Ruth howling in her arms, from remorse as much as grief, until she was quiet again.

Sometimes Bridie was edgy and brittle. She seemed to wonder about the age gap and made elegantly witty derogatory remarks about Ruth's few friends. In anyone else, you would have diagnosed pathological jealousy, but not with Bridie: Bridie'd never stoop to *that*.

Mostly there was a blessedness about their most commonplace activities. Ruth recorded their smallest doings in a diary and took down Bridie's most banal utterances. 'Went to Boots in Manchester for shampoo. Bread and cheese in Royal Exchange. Glorious day.' She drank Bridie in at every pore. It was clear to her that nobody was more beautiful or profound, and at the same time comfortable and dear. She reverenced Bridie and tried to live a life in keeping with her principles – though that was impossible. Bridie's greatness was out of all proportion. This beauty couldn't last; couldn't possibly. Inequality didn't.

And it hadn't.

The lights were all blazing in the windows of number seven, Sorrel Avenue, the curtains open. Anyone could see in, Ruth noted, as she walked heavily up to the front door, to the comfortable middle-class world of cultured people, a literate family with book-lined walls and objects of artistic interest scattered around. She peered in through the bay as if poking her nose into other people's business, and indeed the spacious, creamy room with its high ceiling and rust-red carpet seemed not only to belong to a stranger but to forbid intrusion. It was not her home but she needed shelter, for the time being. She scrabbled in her pocket for her key.

A dark face appeared in the bay of the adjoining house. It stared out from behind lined velvet curtains with an addled expression, as if awaiting a visitor who was now so late that he was almost definitely not going to turn up. The face stared straight past Ruth's and Ruth, frenziedly hunting the key, in turn looked right past the face until their eyes met for the fraction of a second; and as if caught in an electric circuit, winced and pulled away. Mrs Mason staggered back into her front room, letting the heavy curtain drop; Ruth turned the key in the lock and let herself in.

For Doris it had been one of those days; one of those awful days that came from time to time out of the blue, and made her feel there was no earthly point in carrying on; dragging out an existence (you could not call it a life) from day to day, wearing this smile and missing George so rawly, as if he'd passed over only yesterday, rather than two years, seven months and four days ago. It was the dreams that did it. How maddening, when you organised every waking moment so as to leave no space for self-pity, that you could not regulate your dreams. She'd never dreamed before George died. Never. Not been that kind of a person: steady, sensible, matter-of-fact. Now he came to her by night and sat on the end of the bed as large as life and always doing something ordinary like taking off his socks or lighting up a cigarette (only you knew he was dead; it was his corpse walking; a see-through quality to the flesh, a tell-tale lightness and greyness to the skin). The dreaming did vex her: she felt there must be a way to prevent it, by sleeping on your front, say, or not eating cheese after midday. She even thought of asking

Dr Ray if he could recommend any medical remedy but it seemed such a daft thing to say when she actually got there (and she had a suspicion that he nursed contempt beneath that affable manner, for elderly ladies' complainings): so instead, when he said, 'And what can I do for you, Mrs Mason?', she had told him about stomach cramps, and came away with some pills. Even so, she had felt, transiently, a little eased. She had been taken notice of, catered for, however minimally.

But oh, these dream-days, as she called them to herself. Her tactics and procedures for coping failed her almost completely on such days as this. This morning she had awoken at 4.20, with the duvet bunched at her back, and somehow the hot water bottle which had become entangled in the ruck of the quilt persuaded her that the warm mound was the supportive body of her husband, curled round her; and she felt sure that it was him; and *you've come back* she thought with huge relief; but the moment the conception formed, she knew she'd been betrayed. There was no body-warmth, only fabricated comfort. Wobbly with distress she teetered to the bathroom through the empty hallway. The Expelair whirred; the toilet-flush roared. Hours and hours to dawn. *You aren't here*, her mind cried out to George. *You've left me on my own*. But then, *Now now*, she admonished herself. *None of that*, and she went into action. Teasmaid on. Wireless on. A purring male voice was telling her about a war. She sipped the tea, accompanied by a Nice biscuit which she nibbled, and then another. All normal. Nothing to fear. But she wouldn't sleep again, she knew that. So she got up and did the ironing, and it was a relief when the milkman came and the postman brought the letters, but it was only junk mail promising Mrs Mason that her name had been specially chosen by the computer for a prize draw which could win her the holiday of a lifetime for two in sunny Florida. (Their daughter never wrote. She'd moved to Australia, with the grandchildren.

Occasionally she'd phone in a faraway voice that held her at arm's length, but you couldn't hold and keep a phone call like a letter. Still, she had her life to live, did Barbara.) The day had seemed so long after that, despite shopping trips and taking a neighbour's baby out for a walk. It seemed to go on for ever; and she was irritated with herself for her desperation; talked to herself rather sharply, reminding herself that George when alive had been rather a nuisance than otherwise – getting under her feet when she hoovered; finding fault. Still, he had been *there*. Like a rock, unbudgeably solid. And she kept hovering, waiting for him to come in, right through the evening, but he was detained.

The Bridie-less house was blazing with light. Wasting electricity, very non-Green, Ruth thought as a kind of reflex. She always went round after Bridie turning off lamps and appliances, scolding. Bridie's voice came back as she snapped the hall light off, but very thin and remote: *my grass-green girl, my evergreen.* Ruth toured the house switching off the lights, to darken all the spaces, so that it could not be seen that Bridie was not there, would never be there again.

She was calm, composed. The question was not whether but when and how to make an end of herself. It was the rational conclusion. Life was not in itself a good. The blessing of escape was within her power. Ransacked and disembowelled as she was, the thought of suicide was a powerful anaesthetic.

My grass-green girl, my evergreen.

Bridie and she would sleep together. Together again. It could not be too soon. In the earth, the earth, dreamless beneath the green.

But she would wait and see Bridie off, before she too packed her bags. While away the time till then. Feed the animal. She heated up a can of tomato soup and burnt some toast. Switching on the television, she settled down with her tray. Aeroplanes taking off and landing; soldiers running, under the denomination 'our boys'; an elated-looking pilot clambering out of a cockpit and declaring in an American voice that it had been a great day, as good as a football match. The picture switched to a bulbous, jocose general behind a lectern and microphones, tapping with a stick on a map and speaking of military objectives, 'Desert Storm', liberation of Kuwait. Ruth switched over. More planes; a view of the Saudi capital by night; news just in of Tom King's speech. There was something glittering and excited in the tone of all the speakers, from the newscaster to the general, something boyish and thrilled. So Bush had kicked Saddam's butt at last. It had begun.

Ruth put down her tray and crossed to the window. The sky was overcast and the moon invisible behind the cloud-layer. In Baghdad women were looking out of their windows at a sky that rained bombs; computer-directed missiles sailed along their streets, turned left or right at crossroads and entered the building of choice. *The same sky*, Ruth kept repeating to herself, *the same sky*.

'So the buggers have started dropping bombs,' said Lizzie to her father. The three of them were sitting round the morning-room table eating vegetable stew. At least it was allegedly vegetable stew, untainted by animal ingredients or chemical additives, but Gavin had cheated by using a home-made chicken stock as the basis of the casserole, heavily flavouring it with celery and herbs. He liked cooking for the girls, and took trouble over it. There were both pride and satisfaction in nurturing and sustaining the children, feeling that he had been able (despite his own conditioning in manly values) to play both father and mother to Lizzie and Sarah. Their sturdy young bodies grew like trees under his tendance and they were scarcely ever ill. As for Lizzie, he worried that her near-vegan eating habits would turn her anorexic (God knew, she had the temperament), so he occasionally used subtle trickery in inducing her to accept disguised animal products into her diet. But he was judicious: she would explode through the roof if she found out and never trust him again.

'Yes, it's begun,' he answered her, and sighed. 'I don't see how it could have been avoided but I wish to God it could have been. Let's hope it's over quickly. They are predicting a few days at most.'

'Overwhelmed by our superior technology and fire-power,' said Lizzie. 'Well, I think it *stinks*. They're a Third World country. All we want is their oil.'

'Some more stew, Lizzie? There's plenty.'

'No thanks. There's something funny about the gravy.'

'Thanks a bundle, Lizzie. It only took two days to make.'

Lizzie sniffed at a spoonful of gravy. She had relished the meal, but her fastidious palate had suspected the very tastiness that seduced it.

'You haven't put any meat in, have you?' she interrogated her father, anatomising him with disturbing eyes of darkest brown, stirring with her spoon.

'Certainly not. You have some more, Sarah?'

'Yes please,' said Sarah. 'As much as there is.'

Gavin ladled a steaming pile of vegetables on to her plate.

'Good girl. You enjoy it,' he said, and they smiled into one another's eyes, each knowing how to please the other, and mutually reassured in that knowledge. 'How was your day?'

'Okay. Harriet was crying because her brother's in the Army and she thinks he'll be sent to fight the Iraqis, and might be killed.'

'Making the most of it, knowing Harriet Wilbraham,' Lizzie sneered. 'Anyhow he's only seventeen. He won't be sent.'

'Yes, he is being sent, Lizzie. He got his orders.'

'Well, he shouldn't have joined up, should he – then he wouldn't be killed. It's as simple as that. Anyway he's a right trog, Malcolm.'

'It doesn't seem to *me* that things are simple at all,' remonstrated Gavin, mildly but firmly. You couldn't let a child get away with the sort of gross simplifications Lizzie was always coming out with. Sarah had more sense in her little finger than Liz in her whole head. You could *see* Sarah thinking, negotiating and balancing issues in her mind, coming up with nuanced responses midway between compromise and principle. Gavin had once expounded to her the fundamental philosophy of the Liberal Democrats (he was an enthusiastic supporter) and Sarah had seemed to grasp it immediately.

Or did she just play him along, uncannily fathoming what it was he wanted to hear and ladling it out to him like pre-cooked stew? Sometimes he wondered. Her repetitions of his choicest opinions could sound obscurely like travesty. Once or twice he'd overheard Sarah swearing to herself when she didn't think anyone was listening – some of the foulest language you could hope to hear. He retreated from her locked door and never mentioned it.

'Some wars,' he went on, piling up his and Lizzie's plates and passing round the trifle, 'are necessary evils. For instance, against tyrants.'

'Or butchers,' suggested Lizzie. Several butchers' shops in the area had been bombed last year by the animal liberationists. Lizzie nursed ambitions in this direction.

Gavin ignored this. Addressing himself to his rational younger daughter, he went on, 'You see, there is always a complexity to things. What will Saddam do if he isn't stopped? He's a megalomaniac like Hitler. He's already invaded Kuwait.

He might take over the entire Middle East. And he's near to making the nuclear bomb, you know.'

'Just like us,' sneered Lizzie.

'Yes, Lizzie, but we've got sane people in control of it – in a democratic state. It won't actually be used. It's purely a deterrent.'

'*I* see what you mean, Daddy,' said Sarah confidentially, adding her dinner plate to the pile and tucking in to her trifle. 'You mean that if Saddam got control of the Middle East we wouldn't have enough cheap oil for all the things we need. He's *got* to be bombed.'

Her calmly neutral manner gave such a cynical aspect to this proposition that Gavin felt faintly unnerved. He scrutinised her as she ate her way with serious application through the trifle. Her face was the picture of trust and innocence.

'Any more?' she wondered.

'No, that's your lot.'

Lizzie thrust back her chair. 'I'm off out, thanks for the meal,' she said, and disappeared out of the front door, slamming it behind her.

'Where do you think you're going?' he hollered up the street.

'Jane's. Back by ten.'

'Mind you are.'

Lizzie at the bus-stop wound her scarf twice round her neck and pulled on her gloves. Her mind, like a portable TV screen, seemed to be filled with planes taking off and people in gas masks, running.

6

She had been dreaming vividly of the moors in autumn: she and her father were wading out into the swells of heather and bilberry, purple and crimson that stung your eyes with a saltiness which brought on a queer notion that there must be a sea over the shoulder of the hill (though there was no such sea) but if you licked your lips there was salt from this no-sea. The crags were sulphurously orange-yellow from some chemical that was in the rock – so Dad explained – and the sky was turquoise; and it was lovely, and wild, and headily excessive, as the dreaming Bridie lolloped out in the spaniel's wake, high-stepping to get through the heather that grew exceptionally tall and fibrous in this area and whipped at her legs with its scratchy branches. Bridie had seen and hated those Japanese dwarf-trees in plant pots, *bonsai*, the size of an average geranium, a whole oak stunted to a tiny eyeful. This was the opposite: the heathers were outrageously aspiring to the stature of trees, their twisted stems covered in gnarled bark. Bridie so loved this place, with the sharp winds that flowed over the plateau winter and summer, and the peaty smell they drove into her nostrils. She loved the fact of Dad ploughing on behind, with his battered walking-shoes impregnated with dubbin, his cloth-cap and his knobbed stick; and the triangular gull-grey cairn she could, or thought she could, just make out at the centre.

In Bridie's dream, her father overtook her, and that seemed only natural in view of the shortness of her legs and the lankiness of his. As he drew abreast, he cast her a peculiar look, half mocking, half melancholy, and: 'You'll never catch me up,' he said.

'*Oh* yes I will!'

'Prove it then.'

'I will, so there.'

He was already yards ahead, seeming to float from hummock to tussock with enormous strides and bounding gait . . . a man in conditions of lunar weightlessness. *Of course*, Bridie realised, *he has that freedom because he's dead*. But the unfair competition did not deter her. On the contrary. Bridie wasn't going to be left behind, not on your life she wasn't. She barged forward against the thrust of the wind, breaking through the entanglements of the heather, and sometimes she would make headway so that she came so close she could view the individual black, brown and grey checks on his cap and coat, and observe the puckered back of his neck between hair and collar; and then he would bounce serenely off. But she didn't give up. Where he could go, she could follow. Catch Bridie McKearn giving up. Even when the landscape dissolved him to a distant blur, she kept labouring on through the obstructive dimensions of space and time. She'd get to him *in the end*: it stood to reason.

And there he was, suddenly visible, idly leaning on the cairn. A delicious smell wafted on the wind. Whatever was it?

Chips.

That was it, chips from the chip shop, eaten piping hot out of the newspaper, with plenty of salt and vinegar.

'Hey! Keep some for me!' hollered Bridie, but woke up with a jerk before she could claim her share.

There at the bottom of Bridie's bed stood the red-haired woman, wearing a green shirt and tight jeans, perched on the bed and eating chips. Her hair was a coppery mass of flame in the light that was falling from – nowhere, for it was a grey day (all days were uniformly grey in the ward) – from within, then, as – bold as brass she fed herself the chips, cockily looking round the room; crumpled up the papers and dropped them on the floor, wiping her hands on her jeans. The nerve of it coming in here, slumming round, dropping litter . . . Bridie would remonstrate with . . . that woman, who now walked across, so near one could see the scatter of childish freckles across her nose and cheeks, the greenish eyes, my God what a feline colour – but she walked right through the wall and was gone before Bridie could speak her name.

Then all was calm, for hours or days, until Bridie woke with a start (although she'd thought she *was* awake), and realised she was in London with Ruth; it was summer and they saw a couple on a park bench at Richmond, eating chips, and Ruth was smitten with such a hankering that they trailed around all over the place looking for a shop, in the baking heat, Bridie grumbling; and queued; and ate them greedily with their fingers in the street, the first of many times.

But now Bridie realised this was all in the past. Broide was there, which was Irish for 'Bridget' but no one could pronounce the name accurately, so they called her 'Breeze' which suited exactly. She sometimes sang but was not singing now; was taking Bridie's temperature, in fact, and smiling a very gentle smile.

'Awake now?'

Bridie did not venture an answer. Although in the past few days she had established a relationship with the hospice and its persons, she was not always certain of whether they had walked into her dream or she had strayed into theirs. But Nigel was there, and that made it more solid – the beautiful young man one would never have trusted in real life (because of his beauty) but who had a gift for treating you as a person rather than a sick woman. Even when she was not saying anything, he appeared to be listening gravely to that which was left unsaid. Nobody turned or bathed her with more tender and efficient fingers. He changed the catheter bag and wiped her bottom in the most humane way, and discussed her bedsores as a matter worthy of intelligent consideration.

She'd been in a war, hadn't she, and everything below the belt was shot away? No, that wasn't it. What was it then?

'Cancer in my spine,' she confided, at last. 'Can't feel a thing below my waist – don't worry. Doesn't bother me. Cross it off the list.'

The list had always been too long – the inventory of things to remember, commitments to be honoured, parts of herself to be held together. The list was getting wonderfully shorter, and the present paralysis rendered the account that much more tidy. Though sometimes the nerves in her legs went into spasm, and her feet jerked up and down involuntarily as if haunted by the ghosts of themselves. She looked down from her pillow and saw them, way down the bed, abortively dancing, and they did not seem to belong to her but to some twin tenant of the bed. The twin and she lay back to back in the night, and Bridie was frightened of the twin, because the twin was out of control; could not answer for her behaviour; could not deal with the terrors of the black vortex as Bridie herself could. But of late days, as the drugs had achieved the desired aim, both the fear and the twin faded together, and there could be a calm and a harmony, in which luminous people walked, and complementary colours rang like bells. And then again, there could come times of twilit ordinariness, the neutrality of everyday, in which, however, people might come out with rather unlikely propositions, such as this of Nigel's: 'What I'd really like,' he said meditatively, 'is for you to get up.'

'Pigs might fly,' returned Bridie.

'No – really.'

'Take up my bed and walk.'

'What I mean is, sit out in a wheelchair. Give yourself a change. But only if you feel like trying.'

'Think . . . I'll think about it.'

'Sure. Just let me know.'

'Need a crane. Archimedean system of pulleys.'

Getting up: she was doubtful. The toppling danger of being winched up to vertical made her cringe. As she was, she was basically just a head, with a pair of arms that waved around occasionally before her line of vision: a decapitated head. If they levered her upright, she would be required to put the head and decaying body together again as one, for the purpose of the exercise. The vertigo of looking down from the sheer precipice of uprightness appalled. *It would be quite a brave thing to do.*

'Have a go at that . . . getting up. But won't I be dizzy, too dizzy?'

'You might be, at first. In fact, you're bound to feel a little funny – but that would wear off. What do you think?'

'As I say, have a go. Nothing much to lose, have I?' she replied jauntily, but all of a sudden her mind felt crumbly; thoughts flaked off and fell away into the void which surrounded the island of the bed.

While she was fishing for them, Nigel suddenly blurted, 'You have led an extraordinary life.' But didn't know how to continue. He had seen Bridie McKearn from time to time on television arguing for the cancellation of Third World debt, the halting of the arms trade. He envied her that overwhelming drive and effectiveness; one who would not accept limitations but simply powered her way across boundaries by denying their legitimate and therefore their actual existence. All his life he'd tended to be too softly complicit in his dealings, agreeing with opinions which were the opposite of those he really held and then wondering, 'Why did I say that?' It was the spinelessness of wanting to please, and to share rather than dispute. He'd got round it by choosing a profession where he could live rather than debate his allegiances. But people like Bridie bowled him over. He'd seen her severely embarrass a minister of state by carving up the pitiful aid budget and comparing it with the debt repayment figures to show that the North was in surplus. To see her reduced to the shambles she'd been on admission was a sickening shock. 'I've always envied you,' he admitted.

'How so?'

'Because you had the guts and the know-how to fight the system – to take on the world. Something like that. It makes one feel rather small.'

'*You* . . . feel *small*?' She contemplated him with a mystified expression. 'Tell you candidly, Nigel – I could never do your job. Too near the bone . . . too real and personal. If you administer an organisation . . . don't have to deal with the muck . . . and bedsores . . . people vomiting all over you. Kept *well* clear of intimacies. Coward, you see.'

'Oh no. The great thing is to change things out there. Change perceptions.'

'In that case . . . I've signally failed –. But there you are.' She was lying propped on her right shoulder, pillows carefully wedged to take the weight of her head and to lessen the load on her spine. 'That's life. Comes down to kidney bowls and catheters. Nice of you anyway.' She shrugged her left shoulder.

'I get everything I can at our local Trust shop,' Nigel went on shyly. He wanted to tell her, to make it clear to her, that her life was still going on outside, on every high street in the country more or less, and it would go on with or without her bodily presence. 'I buy all my recycled stationery, presents for friends, clothes and so on there. I'm a walking advertisement for you.'

'And I . . . a non-walking advertisement for you.'

They smiled into one another's eyes. The warmth stayed with her as she lay in a half-doze when he'd gone. She looked forward to seeing him again and to holding his hand as she had been doing throughout the conversation.

'Any chance of chips for lunch?' she asked a passing orderly.

Nigel watched her being fed a few of the chips by one of the steady stream of visitors who came and went from Bridget's bed, and sometimes sat in silence while she slept, and sometimes conversed in subdued, cultured voices. They were intense, quiet, middle-aged and upper middle-class people. He recognised the Oxfam director, and the other woman, Elaine Demetrian, who co-founded the Trust. Then there was the ginger girl Bridget lived with and wouldn't see, who scuttled in and out with laundry and bottles of squash, her head down, red-eyed and hunted-looking. She phoned for news several times a day, and yesterday had brought in a Walkman, together with several music tapes at which, when Bridie received them, she cried out in a sudden abbreviated shriek of distress, and 'Put away', she said. That whole thing was bloody strange, and pitiful.

Bridie was hoisted gasping from her bed like a sprat on a line. It was a terrifying act of violence, though they were gentle and performed the operation with experienced smoothness. Her limbs seemed to jangle along behind her as she was manoeuvred into the chair and then propelled to the window. As her mind sank back into the skull from which it had seemed to explode, she began to register a framed section of the outside world. At first it was made up of busy dots of shadow and pin-points of light, which gradually subsided into an image at once drab and alien. Two moderate-sized fir-trees dominated an area planted with bushes; beyond this an expanse of wintry grass was sprinkled with fallen leaves, and surrounded by a wooden fence, on the thither side of which lay an estate of redbrick houses, with washing-lines flapping in the wind. A child's ball popped up in a regular rhythm above the fence but the thrower was too small to be seen. Bridie sat there, trussed up in the helpless parcel of what remained of herself, and stared at the view.

She sagged sideways in the chair. Someone came and propped her up again. This time she listed in the other direction. Her eyes drifted from the trees to the grass to the fence to the roofs and upper windows of the house. So that was it, the outside world.

Once a blackbird flew across the window.

Then nothing happened, and after that nothing again happened, and Bridie maintained her observation of the nothing that was happening.

Low grey clouds travelled from left to right at a monotonously regular pace.

Now a flight of black flecks thronged the grey sky, complicating its sobriety with a welter of implication. The flecks whirled about in the top central pane of the window and swept in an arc downwards over the rooftops in the direction of a remote blob of darkness which might have been trees.

The sails of men's shirts billowed on lines; the waste paper of the old year's leaves blew about on the lawns.

The windowpane was scored with infinitesimal scratches, dots of dried white paint and the reflections (and reflections of reflections) of objects both within and without, also the residue of soap from a window-cleaner's imperfect wipings.

Up and down bobbed the ball thrown by the unseen child, up and down. Then it all abruptly ceased, for Bridie closed her eyes, abolishing the world, and slumped sideways in her chair. She was relieved when they heaved her back into bed, though her ribs felt as if they might split at the violence of the contact with the mattress, tenderly though they eased her in. It was better here, less tensely painful for the mind, which found mercy, if not home, in neutral territory. So exhausted was she by the journey from bed to window that she fell into a deep sleep from which she did not awaken until the following day.

She surfaced to find a Godawful fuss going on around the next bed, which, previously unoccupied, had acted as a barricade against the rest of the patients in the ward, to which Bridie had been able to consider herself annexed rather than included. She had not been forced to participate in the discussions of operations and grandchildren which formed the mainstay of what conversation there was. Bridie's irritation at the invasion of her privacy was, however, mitigated by curiosity. For the person was young, very young – a fair-haired girl of hardly thirty.

'It's only for a short rest-period, you know, Pat,' said the husband in a loud whisper. 'Just to get your strength back – and then you'll come back home to me and your mam, and we'll get you fighting fit. Won't we, Mam? You'll be out there jogging again in your pink tracksuit – swimming at Cheadle Baths twice a week. You'll enjoy that, won't you, Pattie – you're looking forward to it already, I can see you are.'

No answer being forthcoming from his wife, the husband turned to the mother, a stout woman in a belted raincoat who was untying a headscarf. She pursed her lips, shook her head and replied tonelessly, 'Yes, dear.'

'There you are, even your mam thinks you're looking better every minute, and you know what *she*'s like – pessimism her second name. Tell you what, we'll take that holiday in Cyprus we always promised ourselves, won't we lovey, our second

113

honeymoon. Just you and me – Mam will take the children, won't you, Jean? – I said, you'll take the kids to let her and me get away a bit? That's what we need, a change.'

Bridie and the other patients all stared. They tried to look away, at their magazines or their Ribena bottles, out of politeness, but the husband in his distraction was far beyond all consideration of discretion. Indeed, he seemed deliberately to court the attention of an audience, as though witnesses would confirm the validity of his affirmations. He barged around the bed, smoothing the counterpane, rearranging the jars and boxes on the cabinet, pointing out that Pattie couldn't reach the tissues there, though as far as Bridie could tell, Pattie showed no sign of being able to move a muscle in any direction. Her slender, fair-skinned arms lay out over the counterpane, in a trough of stillness under her husband's perambulating fulminations.

Now he was at the bottom of the bed, whence he was removing her clipboard, which he studied suspiciously. Now he was wondering where to pin her 'Get Well' cards.

'There are fifteen of them. They don't seem to provide pin-boards. Maybe I'll ask a nurse to supply one.'

'They've got better things to do, Ken,' objected the mother. 'Do sit down and take your coat off. You're making such a stir. People can't rest with this bother.'

'How can she be expected to get well if she hasn't got a pin-board?' He wrestled off his blue anorak, frowning at the bare wall with an air of accusation. Every few seconds, he jabbed the bridge of his glasses with his index finger, to push them up his nose. 'Don't you *realise*,' he turned on his mother-in-law, 'we've got to do *everything* to get her on her feet again. We've got to use every means. It's a matter of attitude. If we all *believe* she'll get well, and *she* believes it, she *will* get well.'

'Okay, okay, dear. Lower your voice. Come and sit with her. She wants you to sit with her,' the mother implored.

At once the husband swept down into a chair and covered Pattie's hands with kisses.

'You want me, Pattie, you want me with you. Say you want me.'

Pattie said nothing, but the husband overrode his wife's unbearable silence by haranguing his mother-in-law over the bed.

'I never wanted her brought in here,' he hissed. 'It was you.' Then, seeing her distress, he went on, 'No, I know, you did it for the best – don't go blaming yourself, chicken – and we both of us could do with a few nights' sleep – and the kids were getting pretty frayed. But I view it more as a brief rest for Pattie, to recoup her strength, and make a real fight of it. You see, Pattie love, you've got to get up and *fight*. Don't let it take you over. Between us we can see it off, but not if you won't make an effort. Nurse, sorry to trouble you but would you have such a thing as a pin-board? We need to put Pat's cards up so that she can get the benefit of them.'

Bridie watched as the husband positioned the cards in a symmetrical pattern on the pin-board.

'Lovely, see? And mine in the middle, with the red roses – and I've left it open so you can keep reading the message, pet. "To my beautiful wife from your ever-loving husband, Ken. PS GET WELL SOON." No, I don't think that's quite right. *Now* we've got it.' He exuded, as he worked, an air of manic euphoria, as though each effort brought him a stage closer to ultimate victory. But, 'Not enough pins!' he exclaimed, and shot off to the staff room in search of them. Back he came, before the mother had had time to exhale the sigh that had been gathering in her.

The pin-board was on the wall. Now he looked round for other ministrations.

'Chocolate!' he interrupted. 'Did you bring the Black Magic, Jean?'

'Over there. But I don't think she wants chocolate. I think she wants a rest. Squeeze my hand if you want a little rest, my pet.'

'What will you have, Pattie? What can I tempt you with?' He showed samples of his wares, holding them out between finger and thumb. 'Montelimar? Hazelnut brittle? Strawberry cup? . . . Well, perhaps you're not hungry at present. Tell you what, pet, I'm going to leave the box here on the table, where you can reach what you want.'

'Ken, she's squeezing my hand.'

Ken took no notice. He finished arranging the Black Magic box to his satisfaction, sat back down and began to stroke Pat's hair lovingly.

'The point you've got to realise is,' he said in a voice that seemed to resonate round the aseptic silence of the ward, 'the whole point is that, just because you've come into a hospice, *it doesn't mean you're going to die.*'

The knowing eyes of the dying women looked away compassionately. It came to Bridie that it might be the case that there was no suffering like that of the survivor. Quiet death might be infinitely preferable to this living hell.

'Ken, I said she's squeezing my hand. I think she wants us to go now, so that she can get some peace and rest.'

'Well, all right – but we'll come back later, pet, and we'll bring the kids. Cheer you up a bit, won't they? My darling – my sweet darling.'

He choked as he kissed her forehead, and the tears ran down his face.

'It's all right, Ken – don't worry,' said the faint voice of the dying woman, speaking for the first time.

116

The mother shepherded the man away. By the time he reached the door, he had recovered himself and was blaring his way down the corridor, apparently inventorying the requisite actions they and she would need co-operatively to undertake together in order to restore his wife to perfect health.

The old silence settled on the ward in his wake – a silence made up of countless waiting pauses between events which never came to pass, so that the pauses connected other pauses, metered by the roaming second-hand and jerking minute-hand of the clock above the doorway. At a variety of rates the soundless tumours multiplied subliminally under the skins of the six stricken women dominated by that clock.

'Got an awful backache,' an elderly woman who never complained, complained to the nurse she'd summoned by buzzer.

'Backache *is* the devil,' sympathised Broide. 'Let me see what I can give you for it.'

She squeaked away over the linoleum, and squeaked back with a small plastic cup containing two pills.

'See how you go now, dear. If it doesn't go off, I'll come back and rub it for you. In fact, why don't I rub it for you now?'

Soon the patient fell fast asleep, the ache both of spine and of consciousness blotted out.

Bridie had been propped up and given a beaker of tea, which she was drinking through a straw. Her new neighbour, she saw, was awake, and looking at her with contemplative eyes.

'Hello, Pat,' said Bridie. 'I'm Bridie.'

'Hello, Bridie.' The voice was little and husky. She seemed to have difficulty in drawing breath.

This was the entire extent of the conversation, but it was more than Bridie had exchanged with any of the other patients and it continued, chiefly through their eyes. Bridie, being

117

fatigued from the exertions of yesterday, catnapped intermittently, and the newcomer also drowsed. When Pat was
asleep, Bridie considered her. It was a pretty, oval face but
horribly pale, almost blanched. She looked peaceful, asleep.
That was good, poor girl. When Bridie woke again, Pat was
looking at her across the void, from her pillow. She smiled, a
crooked vague smile. Her eyes glazed and she seemed to lapse
into a sort of waking dream.

'Where are you? Where have you gone?' she asked, in a voice
of sobbing anxiety.

'I'm here,' said Bridie, and that seemed to answer the need.
Then they were each turned, and lay back to back for a passage
of time. When they were reversed, it was early evening. Bridie
felt for the first time properly awake. The girl in the next bed
was curtained off, for dressings and bedding to be changed. This
made a sort of cubicle of Bridie's space, between the curtain and
the green velvet curtain of the window. Privacy: she found
suddenly how much she missed her privacy, lying there
exposed, her dereliction open to the eyes of all comers. It was
the first time she had wished to be anywhere other than the
hospice into whose impersonal no-man's-land she had settled
with such relief. It was the first time she had *wished* at all.

'Tell me truly,' she asked. 'How long have I got?'

'We can't honestly pretend to tell you exactly,' said Broide,
her namesake, sitting on the bed, holding her hand. 'We just
can't predict. It might not be all that long, Bridie,' she added
tentatively.

'Don't prevaricate with me, will you? Be straight, I need
you to be straight. I know I'm on my way. But need – to know –
how much *conscious* life I've got left – how long in my right
mind? Okay, you can't tell me – will anyone tell me? Dr
Howarth?'

'*I'd* tell you if I knew, Bridie. You're that kind of person.'

118

'But you don't know?'

'No – I'm sorry.'

'Would you then . . . guess for me, Broide? Please?'

'Weeks, not months, is my guess. You're very frail, Bridie, aren't you?'

'In a way, yes.' She paused. 'In another, no.' It was impossible to find words to communicate the process, even to herself, but to Bridie it was as if the time spent in here (however long or short that was, she had little idea) had been the retreat into a chrysalis. She was aware of stirrings, presentiments, minimal but undeniable, deep inside her. Something was still living in there, amongst the tumours, the wasted flesh and the garbled mind, signalled by the tips of nerves that tingled faintly, rumouring the possibility of life. Some queer dream of Dad was part of it; the girl in the next bed, that very lovely girl; Nigel and his ear-ring; the journey (abortive though it had seemed) to the window; and intimations of other persons so far unnamed. *Perhaps*: there was just possibly a *perhaps*. But if the journey to the window had required courage, how much greater the risk of committing oneself to the possibility of *perhaps*. No; it was better to stay here and rot quietly in a morphine haze than essay the terrible pilgrimage that led back home.

'Ah well,' said Bridie. 'Thanks anyway, Broide.'

The girl in the next bed was murmuring behind the curtains to her attendants.

'He won't let me die, he won't let go . . . he can't accept . . . poor Ken, poor poor Ken, how's he going to manage? And the children – at least they've got my mam. He's worn me out, he's worn Mam out . . . I can't do anything for him now, but how will he go on? . . . won't listen, won't accept . . . no, I don't think there's any point . . . but will you talk to him, I'm so tired, too tired . . . my mam knows, she's wonderful, she can cope . . . my only hope for the kids . . . but he's a good father, yes, but how will he go on? Perhaps he'll marry again, it might be best, but then they'll have a stepmother, will she be kind to them? . . . but there's my mam. What if she dies? Everyone might die . . . no, no, I know . . . if you could just get him to see, and I worry for him so much, he might go mad and no one could help him . . . but why won't he let me rest, why is he chivvying me . . . and harrying me . . . he was trying to make me get up yesterday and it was awful, he pulled me out of bed and he wouldn't believe it that I couldn't stand up let alone get down the stairs, he kept on saying "Come on, Pattie, you can make it – just try, try for me," and Paul standing there screaming at the bottom of the stairs . . . he's only six, he can't understand . . . it was awful . . . terrible . . . and that was when my mam phoned you . . . thank God, thank God . . . but it's only because he loves me and he can't bear it . . . but he's worn me out . . .'

Soothing voices gentled her down, at once coaxing out and calming the outpouring of confidences.

'Would you like to be asleep when he comes? And we'll have a chat with him and your mother, see what we can do to help?'

'Oh, yes please.'

When the curtains were pulled back, Pattie smiled drowsily at Bridie.

'Can't remember your name. I'm Pat.'

'Bridie. How are you now?'

'Oh yes – Bridie. Nice name. Sounds married.'

'No,' said Bridie. 'I'm single,' and then wondered at the shout of remorse her spirit gave. She saw Peter, Peter betraying Jesus in the heart-wrenching Bible story. 'Well,' she went on, to correct the lie. 'I've a close friend I live with. Ruth . . . her name's . . . Ruth.' She had said the beloved name. There was no going back. She had said it now.

'I've two children – Paul and Kirsten – six and four years old. Have you any children?'

'No – no children.'

'I've had a mastectomy. But it was no good. Wish I hadn't
had it now. Then at least I'd be a whole woman.' She looked
across the gap at Bridie hopelessly as if they lay at twin cliff
edges with an abyss between them.

'You . . . are . . . a whole woman,' said Bridie, and with a
towering effort she heaved herself up on to her right elbow, to
make her point, in a tone full of healing indignation. 'You *are*.
And so am I. And so are all these.' She collapsed back on to the
pillow with pain, but still the angry energy that had launched
her impelled her on, to say, as if to a child, 'And don't let anyone
tell you otherwise.'

'Kind, Bridie,' murmured Pat's voice, dreamily. 'I wonder if
they would push our beds nearer together. It's so hard . . . to talk
. . . across this . . .'

'Later. You sleep now. You're nodding off.'

'No . . . I'm not.'

In marched Ken at the head of his brood, wagging a bunch of
daffodils and carrying several plastic bags full of supplies. But it
was too late; the bird had flown.

'She's fast asleep, look – oh, that's good. Don't wake her
now, shush, we'll just sit with Mam awhile, shall we, while she
sleeps,' said the mother, lifting Pat's fair, curly-haired daughter
on to her knee, where she sat sucking her thumb and looking
morosely round the ward. The boy wandered off, without
looking at his mother, and disappeared into the corridor.

'Well, I don't know – they've put her to sleep,' objected the
father. 'She never sleeps at this time of day. Likes to sit up and
watch the news, see what's happening in the world.' He
hovered over her disconsolately; then put down his face to hers
and fairly trumpeted in her ear, 'Come on, wake up now, Pattie
love – it's me – I've brought Kirsty and Paul to see you – you've
been looking forward to it, haven't you, my pet.'

'For Heaven's sake, Ken. You'd wake the ruddy dead,' said the mother at this reveille, and then regretted it. Pat took no notice; she did not move an eyelash. Ken sat down and took both her hands in his. His face was ashen, the skin stretched over haggard thinness, his mouth and eyes tightly stressed. 'We'll just sit here with her, Ken-lad – keep her company – and be glad she's peaceful,' said the mother comfortingly.

'I don't like it here. I want to go home,' the little girl whimpered.

'But here's your mam, we've come to see your mam, haven't we?'

'But she can't see *me*.'

'Shush now, lamb, she knows we're here.'

The child arched her back, refusing to be held, and slithered down from her grandmother's lap.

'I want to go *home*.'

'Stop it, Kirsty.' Her father stared at her distraught. 'Don't you want your mam to get better?'

Kirsten, turning to her grandmother, buried her face in the lap of her skirt, screwing her eyes shut and sticking her thumb back in her mouth.

'Where in God's name is Paul?'

'Don't like it here,' Kirsten grizzled.

'Dad, there's a playroom. Can we go to the playroom? The nurse says we can.' The boy had come shooting in and had situated himself at the end of the bed, hopping from foot to foot, out of range of the disturbing sight of his mother.

'Don't you want to sit with your mam?'

Paul was already halfway to the door.

'Me go too,' lisped Kirsten in an infantile way and, wriggling out of her grandmother's hands, hared after her brother: together they sought refuge in the trustworthy world of make-believe.

Ken began operations, arranging the daffodils in a vase, and grumbling about the lack of space as he stowed a plenitude of unnecessary objects in the bedside cabinet. Every so often he looked over at his wife, frowning and biting his lip.

'It's not right. *Look* at her. How can she get better when she's under sedation? Look here,' he burst out, thrusting his chin pugnaciously at Nigel, who had paused near the group – but the eyes that arrested Nigel were scared and pleading. 'What do you think you're up to, doping *my wife* up into a bloody cabbage?'

'Will you come and have a chat? We can't really talk about it here.' Nigel succeeded in guiding Ken out of the doorway. Now only the mother was left in solitary vigil at Pat's bedside.

'My darling girl – my pretty girl,' she murmured to the sleeping woman, and kept up a low hum of endearments, in a crooning singsong, as if to lull herself and reach her daughter (if anything could reach her) at one and the same time.

There could be no grief, Bridie thought, like that of a parent pre-deceased by a child. She was glad she had never had children – not of course that she had ever seriously pondered it. It occurred to her, watching the grey head bending over the fair head, that her own mother would only have been seventy-five now, if she had lived.

Her mother. A pang of remorse quivered through her mind. She might as well have been born by parthenogenesis out of her father's rib, for all the notice she'd taken of her mother. Now she thought of Mum, off-guard, and a swell of emotion rose from the depths of her mind – depths long unvisited, and rarely or never trawled with the net of conscious thought. The emotion rose slow-motion over Bridie as once a freak wave had towered behind her as a child in the sea at Cornwall. Having panicked in its trough, she had had to let the ebbtide drag her into the heart of the wave, where she hung suspended until it broke, disgorging Bridie into a maelstrom of foam and pebbles.

And she had once said to Ruth – Ruth who now flamed up in her mental eye . . . she was not prepared for Ruth any more than the memory of her mother but here Ruth was and once she had said . . . what? . . . something like . . . she didn't know but there was some connection, eclipsed now in the shock of visual remembrance. Mum she had drowned but Ruth she had burnt. Ruth flared at the black centre of her imagination, violently, her hair a curling mass of coppery flame . . . not burning to death . . . for this immolation was Ruth's life, it was how she had to live . . . ardently, and Bridie had left her to it, for how dared one go near such a being, to get one's hands burnt? But she'd run to her, Bridie had, positively charged up to her without taking any real precautions, knowing that this was life itself that was being offered . . . and, yes, that was what she'd said to Ruth once which had come with the force of an epiphany, *You've given me birth, Ruth, you've given me life, I wasn't alive until I had you.*

And she'd rejected both of them, Mother and Ruth. Her mother had seemed a very ordinary woman, a no one in particular. Bridie had early contrasted her with Dad and found her wanting. Whereas Dad had passionate religious feelings and a highly developed social conscience, Mum knitted socks. Dad talked to Bridie about the constellations, he filled her in on political science and stirred in her ambitions of great scope and moral grandeur, but Mum merely offered a second helping of rice pudding. To Dad, the moors; to Mum, the back garden, where she grew cabbages, carrots and potatoes, runner beans climbing bamboo poles with their bright orange flowers, rows of raspberry canes Bridie crept out to filch before breakfast. It must have been from her mother that she derived her own green fingers, though she had never devoted them to lowly vege-tables. Bridie avoided the maternal skills and wisdoms that must, she intuited, domesticate and tame her. But there was something in her mother's watchful eyes (blue as her own) which arrested her even then. Mum understood. Mum let her be; let go, and made scanty effort to forge Bridie into a shape convenient to herself. She let Bridie be an imitation boy, without lamenting the destiny that had conferred on her a ruffian who was always up trees and down holes, merely allowing herself to comment wryly that it would be a right shame to climb so high as to fall down and break your neck, or so deep that you couldn't get back up. When Mum was dying, Bridie was at university. She dawdled, made no effort to hurry home, and when she arrived, Mum was gone. Smothering the sense of her own betrayal, Bridie reminded herself that there was work to do: a life's work. She deferred her mourning, indefinitely.

Once . . . when? she couldn't tell . . . in the bus, it was, rattling over the narrow, winding roads between Stanley and Keighley, the pint-sized Bridie sat with her face against her mother's green cotton blouse (she was an ample woman), in the lap of the valley between bosomy hills to either side. Closeness and safety were in the fold of her mother's arm, the scent of her presence all around her, and the drowsy blur of green upon her closing eye . . .

She must indeed have drowsed off, for the return of her neighbour's husband aroused her with a jolt.

'I'm taking her home, Jean, and that's that,' he informed the mother-in-law, no longer bothering with his previous stertorous whisper, but addressing the inmates as a whole, together with their relatives and friends. 'They're drugging her up to the eyeballs. When she gets out of here, she'll be a bloody heroin-addict – a junkie.'

'For God's sake, Ken, be reasonable,' the mother began.

'Reasonable – *reason* – don't you see they're *killing* her?' He

grasped her arm and then tossed it from him in contempt.
'You're in with them– you're all in it together.'

Several nurses had gathered by the bed.

'Mr Shaw – now, Mr Shaw – calm yourself, please,' said the
ward sister.

'You're – killing – my – wife.'

'Ken, she's dying,' said Jean softly. 'Do you still not realise,
she's dying. She's very near the end.'

'Oh yes, I realise it all right,' he shouted, and, swooping
down on Pat, lifted her torso in his arms where it lay with the
head dangling back, a mane of pale hair falling, oddly graceful
as the tragic climax of a ballet. 'And I know who's killing her.
You and your so-called drug regime – you and your tender care.
She's coming home tomorrow.'

'Not tomorrow, Mr Shaw. The consultant will have to sign a
release first. It will take several days at least.'

'I know my rights under law,' he said, but in a milder voice,
having gained his point. 'I know my rights as next of kin. She's
mine.'

'No one disputes it,' said Nigel.

'Then don't. Just don't.' He spoke it peevishly, as if the folly
of his behaviour had been to some degree borne in on him.

'Why can't they . . . let me alone?' Pat moaned out of her
unconsciousness.

'You see,' he perked up. 'She wants you to let her alone. She
wants to come home with me. You *shall* come home, my baby.
We'll have you strong in no time. No more quacks. We'll have
the homeopath in – all you need is a few herbs. These people
don't know a thing . . .'

'My sainted aunt,' the cracked voice of one of the elderly
women across the ward was heard to exclaim. 'Give the poor
lass a break.'

'We can't have this disturbing of the patients,' said the ward sister. 'Put your wife down please, Mr Shaw. You may come back tomorrow afternoon when you are more collected. Meanwhile, put your wife down. You may well break one of her ribs if you drag her around like that.'

A look of horror froze on the husband's face. He lowered Pat with all conceivable tenderness, laying her head in his palm so that it met the pillow with the least possible shock. She was still deeply asleep.

'I'm sorry,' he said. 'Sorry. So sorry.' He had turned his back on the group and was apologising to the wall. Turning clockwise so as to confront them by the slowest possible route, he met Bridie's eyes, into which he stared for a long moment. Familiarised as she was with pain, she flinched from those red-rimmed eyes, reddened in the very whites, like a sufferer from conjunctivitis. The hell within him seemed to scorch its way to the surface.

'Dad – what are you doing? Kirsten's wet herself – she's crying in the playroom – she's thrown the toys around. Can't we go home now? Gran, what's Dad doing? Can't we go home now? We've been here ages, I'm hungry –'

The child provided the means to remove Ken from the scene. The madness died in his eyes as he took Paul's hand, stroking his head and urging him to kiss his mother goodnight. Paul obeyed, staring for a moment transfixed at the mute, grey-white face of his mother, and then scurrying out of the ward. Ken strode after him, looking neither to right nor left; and finally Pat's mother, after an urgently whispered conversation with the ward sister, followed in their wake.

That night there were two deaths in the ward. One of the elderly women died at around 2 a.m. Bridie awoke transiently to hear a sort of gargling sound, and a flurry of activity in the lamplight which hemmed her curtained space; then a stretcher was hastily wheeled out. Later, when Bridie must have been deeply asleep, Pat mercifully made her exit. She heard and saw nothing of this, but found when she awoke that Pat's bed was not only empty but empty as if there had never existed a Pat Shaw to occupy it. Sprucely laundered sheets were tucked in with tight precision, and two plump pillows with the hospice monogram awaited a new head. Pat's name-card had been taken down and all her personal things removed. Bridie stared. At first she thought Ken had somehow succeeded in claiming her in the night.

'No, Bridget love,' said Lilith, a black nurse from Longsight. 'Pat died in her sleep – easy and painless.'

'I'm glad for her.'

But Bridie's eyes filled with tears. A splendour of quiet, enduring gentleness had passed away; a possible friend at the end of the road, whom she could not spare. But it was not that. Nor was it that she foresaw more clearly her own passing, for how could one desire to eke out this terminal suffering? It was less for the reconciled and now liberated Pat that she grieved than for the bereft survivor beginning the first penitential day of his appalling life-sentence. Again and again, she saw him lift the frail remnant of his wife in his arms as if he could haul it bodily, through main force, from its destined deathbed. The ancient stories the Greeks fabled about the return of the wife from the dead – Alcestis, Eurydice – haunted her mind confusedly, and there was something sublime and heroic in the very folly and futility of the man who had fought with his bare hands the fact of his wife's inevitable passing.

There was love. She had indeed seen love.

The ward was more moody than usual, more hollow and echoing; the nurses, orderlies and cleaners with their polishers seemed to turn the volume of their cheeriness up as if to compensate for this depletion. People bustled, emitting quips and snatches of song. Bridie missed the man's harsh voice, which had filled the void with the desperate anger of his loss. The bed beside her was so very empty. She too had the status of a survivor, and knew the survivor's pangs.

So oppressive did these feelings become that she asked Lilith to turn her to the window. She did not wish to view the place where that young girl had been.

Lilith padded away and all was quiet. Yes, Bridie had seen love in that deranged man. But she saw love here, in the quiet, too. There was love in Ruth's absence, more love than Bridie could ever merit – letting her be; giving up her claim; sending in the Walkman and the tape of the Lindsay playing the Schubert Quintet; not saying 'You are mine, I own you' but withdrawing and waiting at the margins because Bridie willed it.

7

Sarah, waiting at the bus-stop, jingled the coins she had extracted from her father's cash-box. Her fingers explored the gritty interior of the pocket – papers from several miniature Mars bars she had stolen that weekend from Kwiksave; other papers folded very small which contained coded secret messages to herself on topics now forgotten; an oval pebble; hair-grips and a bobble for making a pony-tail; the stub of a pencil bitten at one end; miscellaneous sticky items her fingers couldn't identify. Her hands ruminated pleasurably on this private mess. Sarah, outwardly so neat and clean, cultivated patches of waste ground in her life in which circumscribed but disgustingly filthy messes blossomed and fructified, and small caches of swag were stashed. She favoured this ulterior life as a kind of wisdom, to balance out the cost of the good-tempered accommodation she made to what all and sundry desired of her. Now she stood with her purple and green coat zipped up to the neck over her school uniform, her backpack over her shoulder and her thin legs straight together, one knobbly knee slightly to the fore of the other. A single labyrinthine plait stretched from the crown of her head to half way down her back, fed by two other tributary braids which caught the side hair up from her face. A fringe which she had snipped this morning hung at an angle over her strong eyebrows and startling violet eyes. Picking up her violin case, she boarded a number thirteen bus and asked for a child's fare.

When she arrived at her mother's house, the sky was already blue-black and the downstairs lights were on. She could hear music playing as she stood with her ear up to the stained-glass of the front door, and then, poking up the flap of the letter-box, got a view of the wooden panelling of the hallway. Sarah had never liked this big old Edwardian house; it gave her the creeps with its high ceilings and elegant picture rails, undermined by the capacious whitewashed cellars, with the original cooking range, eaten by rust, where once the cook skivvied for the *bourgeois* family above, and the sour-smelling coal-hole. She didn't much like the twin-roomed 'nursery' as her mother designated it, where she and Lizzie were put to sleep on the second floor – the old servants' quarters, with thin doors and a sheer drop outside the window that affected her like a scream whenever she looked out. She knew they were stowed up there so that their noise wouldn't disturb Bridie – but, as she was rarely guilty of making noise, she couldn't see why she should be out of the way. Lizzie, yes. Lizzie was stupid; stupid because of her barefaced integrity. Lizzie had no political skills. She was not a survivor. But she would go down fighting and Sarah could see the merit in that.

It was peculiar standing here on the outside of her mother's inside, with the wind spanking her legs between sock and skirt, and thrashing the ivy back and forth against the wall. For it came over Sarah with the force of a novel suggestion that her mother went on leading a life in there, on a day-to-day basis, regardless of where Sarah was or what she was doing or thinking. This thought had a spiteful, whiplash quality about it, as if someone had slapped her in the face for nothing. It rubbed in her unnecessariness in the scheme of things. At need, Sarah sometimes conjured up her mother to share a particular situation, such as when she fell out with one of her numerous problematic best friends or when, going along the hall to the loo in the middle of the night, she caught a sleepy glimpse of Dad's girlfriend sitting on his bed in a lemon-yellow, frilly nightie. Then the phantom 'Mummy' could be brought in, as it were out of the cupboard, and put away when she had served her purpose. But to witness with your own eyes that your mother had her own existence behind her daughter's back (was not just 'Mummy' but a person you didn't know, called Ruth) – that she was *real* – brought a nasty shivery feeling, like flu.

To banish the ache, she rang the doorbell firmly. A figure ran to the door, a blur of colours in the distorting waves of glass. Together with her mother, cello music and radiator-warmth opened to Sarah.

'Oh . . . oh, it's *you*.' Her mother looked caught off-balance, teetering. She seemed not to know what to do. Then she remembered. 'Oh Sarah, *Sarah* – my darling. Are you all right?'

'Yes,' said Sarah in a casual tone. 'I just thought I'd stop by and say hello.'

'Come on then. You've brought your violin – have you come to give me a recital?' She drew her in and hugged her.

'If you like. Well, actually I've come straight from school and I had my lesson from Mr Hammond today, he says I should pass Grade Four with no trouble but Dad says he's pushing me too hard.' As she chattered, she also registered the flood of music, warmth and her mother's embrace, all surrounding her; but also the dismaying height of the walls and ceilings, towering away from them, together with the cavernous stairwell, whose brown-panelled gloom no lighting could clarify. It had always seemed a place where something catastrophic might happen.

'Does he know you're here?' asked Ruth.

'Well – not exactly.'

'What do you mean, not exactly, love? He must either know or not know, mustn't he?'

Sarah unzipped her coat in the heat of the living-room gasfire. She laid it neatly over the back of a chair.

'Oh dear – all your plants have died. What's happened to them?'

'Oh – I'm not much good with plants,' said Ruth, looking round vaguely. 'I forgot to water them, I expect. Bridie's – away, you see.'

'I know. Lizzie told me.'

'Yes. I suppose she did. But what about Dad? Will he be wondering where you are?'

'Oh no. I told him I was staying on for orchestra. He always believes everything I tell him.'

'*Sarah.* That's not like you. What's the matter? Has something happened?' Ruth stared uncertainly at the orthodox little figure in her white shirt, dingy at the cuffs, her navy skirt, and black and gold tie. With the children she was never at ease and spontaneous; she wondered if she had ever said a natural word to them since the day she had staggered out of Heron House and all but fallen to the pavement five years ago, in the knowledge that care, control and custody had been awarded to Gavin. Since then, her tongue had been heavy in her mouth, as if weighted with the burden of remorse that was not and would never become contrition, since she would never revoke the vows that bonded her to Bridie. Now half of what had been forfeited was here in the room with her, and she hardly knew how to address her, but had to trust, as always, to the language of touch, gently massaging Sarah's narrow shoulders in both palms and bending her head to listen.

'Nothing's happened,' said Sarah, and gave a little petulant squirm. 'But Lizzie saw you at the war memorial and it isn't fair because I never see you.'

133

'I'm sorry, love. I've been through bad times. But it's not for want of thinking about you.'

'I know. I can see the bad times in your face,' said Sarah, with something of that adult-seeming insight, at once complex and compassionate, that had made her a force to be reckoned with since approximately the age of six. 'I'm sorry Bridie's ill, Mummy, and sorry for you. Bridie's a nice person. I like Bridie.'

The latter two statements, which both knew to be insincere, were repeated like a singsong creed.

'Well,' Sarah corrected her false note. 'I don't mean *nice*. She's not exactly nice. But she does good things. So I'm sorry.'

'Do you want some biscuits and a drink? There might be some squash. Shall I see?'

'Could I have a cup of tea instead? Two sugars. I don't drink much squash these days – I still go for coke and Tizer though Lizzie says they're full of chemicals and so is the tap-water for that matter – Lizzie says she can taste pesticides in it, and our nails and hair will go blue because of the aluminium sulphate.' Lizzie, with her blazing dissidence, seemed to her sister to inhabit a sort of science-fiction world, at once lurid and neurotic, but logically possible enough to make her peruse her nails on an occasional basis for signs of turquoise dye and to chew her helping of roast chicken with less relish at the thought that she was eating an animal's suffering. Her susceptibility to Lizzie's eye-view caused her to plant her two legs all the more sturdily on the norms, for security's sake.

'Do you think she's looking rather skinny?'

'Dad says she's getting anorexic,' said Sarah but, noting Ruth's look of alarm, went on, 'But she stuffs Mars bars when he isn't looking and she buys double portions of chips at the chippy after her lunch. *I* shouldn't worry if I were you. She'll grow out of it.'

Ruth laughed, passing Sarah her cup of tea and three biscuits, which Sarah dipped in her tea and sucked. 'I'm glad you came,' she said. 'But I'm a bit worried about Dad not knowing where you are. He might think I'd –'

The phone rang: a wrong number. People kept phoning – Bridie's friends and colleagues from the Trust and associated causes, international calls often from workers in Africa and Asia. Ruth gave out bulletins in an official-sounding voice, answering queries with apparent patience, but fuming inwardly, for she was always convinced that while these well-meaning people were hogging the phone, Bridie was trying to get through from the hospice. Elaine had twice phoned, enquiring not after Bridie's health but after her own, and implying that she would like to visit. Ruth cut her off, saying frigidly, 'I'm fine, thanks. Please don't concern yourself about me.' Afterwards she sat down and trembled from head to foot with a complex emotion of mingled rage and grief. This woman (how *dared* she?) had taken Bridie away from her (which she had the right to do, the bitch, since Ruth had first taken Bridie away from her) and now she had the gall to try to insinuate herself into her own life as well. *Keep your distance*, her tone told all enquirers, even Frances, her fellow historian from the high school, to whom she had been close for many years. She didn't want anybody to get near her; especially recoiled from sympathy. Even speaking to people in the shops or on the bus was threatening. She had established a routine for herself in a void, which consisted in a regular pattern of phoning the hospice, attending obsessively to Bridie's small bundles of laundry, standing for two hours each evening on the steps of the war memorial, and looking round for some message which she had got it into her head Bridie might have left for her in some secret place. The imaginary letter became so real to Ruth that she almost believed she had seen it. They had been used to leave

one another love-notes on an almost daily basis. Now she all but
took the house apart seeking the message of consolation, going
over the same ground again and again in case she had missed it
the first time at the back of a drawer or in the interior of a book.
But there was no message. No word at all, in the eery silence of
her home and brain. To cover the silence, she left the TV set on:
it yielded images of 'surgical strikes' like video games and
generals who had become overnight celebrities briefing the
press or striding across the sand between tanks. And beneath
these alarums and excursions too there was the same deep
silence, the silence of reason where unreason only was
broadcast and listened to.

She was waiting to go home to Bridie, under the earth, in the
earth, sealed over, asleep. How beautiful that seemed, how
fortunate a state. She never slept now. Sometimes she found
herself standing at the war memorial, but what she was standing
for she hardly knew. Some force was out of control in the
world: it was killing Bridie and causing us to kill each other. She
did not confide her thoughts to her companions, an odd jumble
of Quakers, CNDs, Greens, Marxists and one or two youths
who just came for a lark, and ran up and down on the parapets
gesturing lewdly at the traffic.

Sarah's appearance at the door had brought genuine human
contact for the first time for days. The simple actions of opening
up and brewing a cup of tea for her daughter reminded her of
the routine give and take of life, grown so unfamiliar.
Watching the child sip the hot tea, one leg crossed over the
other in composed emulation of adult manners, Ruth registered
the extent of her abdication from the land of the living, with all
its givens. There was something vaguely unfitting in enter-
taining this living child in a house that had become darkened
and staled with morbid preoccupation. And she felt a sudden
remorseful surge of anger with the whimsical and far-fetched

face of the child, lamplit and touchingly beautiful amongst the shadows. The child had a claim. She was an obstacle to Ruth's going home to Bridie.

'Dad's going to marry Val, by the way,' Sarah informed her mother.

'Shall you mind that?'

Sarah paused. 'She's quite a nice person when you get to know her,' she went on, cautiously. 'Though Lizzie doesn't think so.'

'Oh dear.'

'I suppose . . . there's no chance of your coming back instead, Mummy? . . . No, I didn't think you would. I just thought I'd mention it. Well, I'd better be getting home, I suppose. Thanks for the tea, I really enjoyed it.'

'Sarah, you know I did not in any way, at any time, leave *you*,' said Ruth, deep in the mire of equivocation, taking Sarah's slender hand in hers. Her heart tore. 'Don't you? I tried for custody in the court. But I didn't win. You know that.'

'Yes. But then we'd have been taken away from Daddy, wouldn't we?' Sarah did not remove the hand and looked at her mother without animus but with some rigour. The logic of it all had a mathematical inevitability, as she saw it. To multiply Dad and Mummy out into separate units was to cut herself into halves: there was no alternative. She had centred her weight on the half that remained with her father. Mummy was the wistful lost spiritual gentleness she always mourned and always would, but Dad was solidity, tea-time, pancakes, ironing your school shirt, up in the night with a bucket when you were sick, cleaning your shoes and grumbling. Dad was the body in the thick sweater with the slight paunch who cuddled you if Daniel Blakey whacked you; the keeper of the cat, the hamster and the tank of twelve tropical fish through which the light glowed, golden and green. Mummy was like a tender ghost which haunted Sarah's dreams, most precious but essentially bodiless or of a substance so permeable that the draught drove right through it.

Sarah pulled up her knee-length white socks and then carefully wrinkled them down according to current fashion. She zipped her coat and picked up the backpack and violin case. When she looked up again, all trace of undesirable emotion had been denied and erased from her face; it had been transferred through her nervous system into muscles rigid and quivering with tension.

'I'm all right, Mummy – you don't have to worry about *me*,' she said brightly, turning for the door. She looked like the picture of a little girl who had been perfectly primed to look both ways before crossing the road and always to clean her plate to the final forkful of cold mashed potato.

'Sarah – I'm always with you. *Always*.' The violin case dropped to the floor with a twang and a crash from within, as Sarah hurled herself into Ruth's arms. 'Why don't we call a taxi and go together? Let's do that. And see each other very soon.'

As she deposited the child at the end of the road, Ruth sat in the back of the black taxi and watched her disappear into the front door on her own latchkey. She had come and gone like a gentle messenger telling of an obligatory life above and beyond this underworld of foreboding and dark presentiment she inhabited. In Ruth's heart there was a prickling sensation, uncomfortable, like the shoots of grass that needle up through the tough crust of January earth.

Valerie settled herself on what she had tried to make 'her' corner of the settee by building a modest pile of books and magazines beside it. She fabricated an air of amiable ease, to convey the impression that she both felt at home and enjoyed an acknowledged right to be there. In this nest she found composure easier to fake, a psychological ploy which Lizzie had early sussed out. She made a point of dumping herself in Val's nest whenever she found it vacant. Not only did she brazenly occupy this roost but she sprawled there, lolling with her feet up on the coffee table, provoking Val to dispute her right of territory and behaviour in her own home. Seldom had Val come into contact with so crass a lump of girlhood. There was so much of her, an ungovernable mass of sulks whose tantrums once in progress seemed to echo into every corner of the house like a bombardment. She had once come across Lizzie punching a door with her bare fist.

'Won't you hurt your hand?' she enquired curiously. 'Wouldn't a cushion do better, in the long run?'

'Get stuffed, you old hag,' replied the pugilist, and let fly another loud blow.

'I don't like to worry you,' remarked Val to Gavin. 'But your daughter's punching her door.' She did not see fit to reveal the eloquence about the stuffed hag.

Later, when Lizzie appeared, somewhat embarrassed, with a bandaged hand, it transpired that she had had the foresight to confine the damage to her left hand. This got her out of PE but left her free to write. Val could not help but (privately) chuckle.

This evening, having laid claim to her place, she sighed and smoothed down her skirt, taking deep breaths as learnt in the yoga classes she had been attending, to smooth her ruffled mind. It was never easy being left in charge of the household when Gavin had to be away overnight at a conference. You never knew what palaver might erupt; and even on the occasions when Lizzie preserved an unbroken silence throughout the evening, not responding to any remark or question but looking straight through you to the wallpaper, the nerves were strung

139

unbearably. She turned on the six o'clock news and absorbed herself in the reports of the war. Kate Adie in camouflage uniform was reporting from a moving tank in the desert somewhere in Saudi Arabia. She looked rather good in that outfit, the wind blowing through her hair. Val tried to imagine how she might look in Kate Adie's place, the raffish green and black scarf at her neck blowing in the breeze, striking a bravado pose, wearing male gear in such a way as to emphasise your essential femininity. What Val couldn't work out was how Kate Adie managed to keep her hair so clean and nice, out there in the desert where the grit and fuel would get in everywhere. They could hardly have proper hairdressing facilities on the spot.

Now the picture changed to a male reporter covering the Scud bombing of Riyadh, the Saudi capital. The reporter, wearing an attractive cream wool sweater, and spotlit on a runway against a jet plane of some sort, was enumerating the precautions the brave citizens were having to take against Saddam's rockets. Those gasmasks must be most alarming to wear. She was sure she could never bear the claustrophobia of being inside one. Now Saddam Hussein himself (his black moustache reminding her of Hitler) was haranguing a rent-a-crowd. He must surely dye his hair, it couldn't be that colour naturally, like President Qaddafi, Ronald Reagan and the Queen, though her Majesty had wisely allowed streaks of grey to show at her temples of late years. She admired the Queen for holding on but wasn't it about time she stood down perhaps, in favour of Charles and Diana? *There* was a woman who knew how to dress though she was dreadfully skinny. Gavin always said he preferred women with a bit of flesh on them (and, please note, the wife was a *stick*); also that he had a preference for brunettes over blondes or redheads; and that, though he could in a qualified way admire a woman like Mrs Thatcher, it was femininity and softness that attracted him. Not that he was against equality, but that he was for difference. From the first day that she had come to work as his secretary, she had been drawn to him – his tact and civility, his caring ways that showed he thought about you as a person rather than an article of office furniture or a piece of crumpet, his lovely smile, his manly bearing and smartness. In fact he was the next best thing to Paddy Ashdown, as she later told him, and he grinned, flattered.

He was indeed a dream, and it was a pity that his elder offspring was a nightmare. It angered her for his sake, since she saw in him so affectionate and approachable a father, that Lizzie uncouthly resisted so many – not quite all – testimonies of love with what one could only call arrogant contempt. Sometimes she wondered and even calculated whether the dream was worth the nightmare it incurred, but the happiness of being with Gavin, the goodwill of the pleasant younger daughter and the prospect that Elizabeth would be got rid of to university or college within a couple of years, generally brought the balance down on the plus side. Meanwhile, both pragmatist and optimist, Valerie searched around for ways of recommending herself to the girls, claiming a nook in the family home. Often she felt secure, for wherever Gavin was seemed like home to her, and she still marvelled that so intelligent and distinguished a man should want and need a relative nobody like herself. Her first husband had been a very basic type; he drank and went to seed. Having lost his job as an estate agent, he took up with another woman and, when Val found out, he locked her in the wardrobe. *It's where you belong*, he had said. She'd quoted that on her divorce petition.

Gavin was a beautiful man, and not just physically. In him were depths beyond depths, one sensed that at once. He cared about people – the poor, for instance – and had a covenant with

Help the Aged; only he didn't advertise this – she found out by happening to glance accidentally at his bank statement. Val was not just moved but stirred. She began to reflect more about such things. She set up a covenant of her own with Save the Children for £10 a month, making sure to leave her bank statement open on a table where she knew he'd see it. She began to see that there were beggars on Oxford Road and in St Ann's Square and would cross the road to put her loose change into their hats. Previously they'd been either invisible or an embarrassing nuisance. A complex of motives underlay such charitable actions. Her newly awakened social concern was not the less sincere for its role in the campaign she fought against Gavin's first wife – for 'Oh,' murmured Gavin once, 'she was something special when she was young.' He said it with the appearance of tears in his eyes but that might have been just the effects of the cigarette smoke in the pub. Val disliked it when he said her name but would find herself chiming it over and over in her own mind: *Ruth, Ruth, Ruth.* What had he seen in that carrot-top? Whenever they passed a redhead in the street, Val would be sure to disparage something about her – not her hair but her handbag or shoes, and Gavin would good-naturedly agree, going on to compare Val to her advantage, for he was besotted with her, that was for sure. Unfortunately, she knew what Gavin had seen in Ruth: the soul beneath the transparency of a very thin skin. But she took courage from the fact that the woman was a lesbian, an invert – a mess, really. The lustre of her so-called spiritual quality was just the way her damage looked in the light of nostalgia and a glass of wine too many. And Gavin did belong to Val, being in her sexual power in a way that astonished herself, for she was neither sexually experienced nor particularly imaginative. But she seemed to know intuitively how to love him and how to teach him to love her. He was so grateful and emotional that once or twice he'd cried when he'd come inside her body, tears pouring down his face. You didn't really doubt a man who yielded like that. At other times he laughed, with wild and boyish extravagance, and she was certain Ginger had never known the secret of releasing such exultation. And once Gavin had described Ruth in her bedwear: a nightshirt striped like a convict's with a pair of stick-legs coming out of the stripes. *Oh don't be so unkind, Gavin*, she reproved, *she can't help how she looks*.

In came Lizzie, wreathed in uncivil smiles.

'Hi,' she said, towering above Val and rocking from the heels to the toes of her trainers. 'Watching the sport?'

'No, it's the news actually – the war in the Gulf.'

'That's what I mean. Sport. Blood sports.'

Val had no intention of getting involved in a political controversy with the cantankerous girl. She deflected the conversation.

'That reminds me, there's some post for you – I think it's from the League Against Cruel Sports.'

'Ta. So how are you enjoying the war so far?' Lizzie, having found her quarry, had no intention of letting go.

'Nobody's *enjoying* it. It's an unavoidable necessity. I hope it's over very soon. What would you like for your tea, Lizzie – veggieburgers or mushroom feasts?'

'Baked beans, please, but I'd like them *hot* not lukewarm.'

'I'll see what I can do,' replied Val brightly, determined not to be goaded but recalling with irritation the last occasion when she had cooked Lizzie's tea, only to have it shovelled into the swingbin on the grounds of being too cold to eat.

As Val rose from the settee to go and prepare Lizzie's meal, Lizzie with an adroit manoeuvre slipped into her adversary's place. She rested one black-trousered leg on the other knee and, twiddling her thumbs, grinned up at the supplanted Val.

'I think I'll have it in here on my knee watching the match,' said Lizzie and her grin broadened. 'It's cosier.'

'If you don't mind, come and eat at the table,' replied Val. 'Your father prefers it.'

'But he's not here, is he?' Lizzie pointed out, peering interrogatively round the room. Resisting the impulse to pity the hovering strandedness of the poor woman, she reminded herself of the fact that her father's girlfriend was a foreign body like a germ, who had no business here at all.

'No, Lizzie, but we'll go according to his rules. I'll let you know when it's on the table.'

Lizzie watched her high heels stalking out. Her feet must be size four at most. They positively invited your size eight boot to squash them.

'On the table, Lizzie.'

Lizzie pretended not to hear. They were talking about cluster-bombings on the television: a kind of hi-tech weaponry in which the Air Force scattered bombs on the enemy airfield, from which multitudinous 'bomblets' burst out on impact and blew craters in the runway so that the Iraqi planes couldn't get out of their hangars. *Dear little bomblets*, thought Lizzie. *Sweet darling bomblets*.

'Lizzie. It's getting cold.'

'Coming,' she grumbled, and heaved herself off the settee. The battle over territory seemed hardly worth the effort if it kept you pinned down.

She ate the cold beans with disdain.

'When's Sarah coming in from orchestra? Your father said she'd be home by now. Do you think I should ring the school?' Val asked with some anxiety. 'It's dreadfully dark out there.'

'No, she'll be all right. Sometimes they go on for hours.'

'What will you have for pudding?'

'A carrot. I think I'll have a carrot. What's the saying? – "If carrots grew in Kuwait . . ."?'

'You really want a carrot? Well, I suppose at least it's healthy – full of carotene, to make you see in the dark.'

'Yes, please, I'll have a great big long fat carrot, like a '– she paused – 'banana.' *I can already see in the dark*, thought Lizzie, *I don't need carotene to open my eyes to what you people can't see.* Her X-ray vision that pierced the walls of abattoirs, factory farms and laboratories also afforded a keyhole-squint into her father's bedroom at night when, waking in the early hours, she'd catch the squeak of a bedspring or a muffled giggle, which was enough to kindle detestable images of couplings between him and this woman, which she didn't want to entertain but couldn't turn off. Now that she had heard of *bomblets* they too were exploding in her brain cells; and across the dark conurbation, beyond office blocks and the station, the new neon-lit bowling alley, the M63 and the leafy suburbs, her anatomising eye could see through to a picture of the ruins of Bridie McKearn, open-mouthed, dead-eyed, on a glacially white-sheeted bed. It had made a difference, going there. She couldn't say exactly what. It had brought her transiently nearer to Dad, feeling the warmth of him, the crucial support that was there at need; but the very next day, a reaction had set in, for no sooner did she set foot bleary-eyed in the kitchen than she was confronted by his dressing-gowned figure with his arm round Val's shoulder as she buttered toast; and they were both laughing; and they turned their heads as Lizzie crashed in, with one simultaneous movement, so that they appeared for a moment as one two-headed person.

'The beast with two backs,' she said (having been studying *Othello* for GCSE).

'Pardon?' asked her father.

'Nothing,' she shrugged, and poured out a bowl of Frosties for herself.

'Cup of tea?'

'Don't bother.'

'No bother.'

'I'll get my own, thanks.' For she saw how unnecessary she was to her father's happiness and that three into two wouldn't go. And so she lost him all over again, and cursed herself for falling into the trap of trusting his tenderness. For he was a tender person. But out for what he could get.

Now she crunched her carrot with outrageous noise. Val said, in a small voice, 'Lizzie, couldn't we be friends?'

Lizzie stopped crunching.

'You see . . . I know it's hard for you to accept me but really I do, I do care about Sarah and . . . you . . . and I've been hoping you might get to like me, a bit. I can't take the place of your mother but –'

'No, you can't.'

'Well of course not, I wouldn't dream of trying, I wouldn't presume. But if we could – just settle down with one another . . .?'

Lizzie shifted round in her chair. She didn't like the appeal to her better nature. It threatened to rob her of the upper hand: the power (which was the only power she had left) to spoil what she could not share. Once she recognised this woman as a person, rather than an alien from outer space, she would have ceded in the face of human complexity the strategic advantage of her back-to-the-wall position.

'We're not very alike,' she objected mildly. 'We haven't anything in common. You like clothes and make-up and that, and *ballroom dancing*. My mother and I – we think for ourselves.'

Val was quiet, head down, fiddling with the handle of her cup.

'But if you talked to me,' she replied, equally mildly, 'I might be able to understand. Try to, anyway.'

This reasonable doctrine, together with the change of tone from pleading to thoughtfulness, caught Lizzie off guard. Nothing was the same as you had persuaded yourself it was. Nothing stayed fixed. The floor gave way under you. That was a shock but you got used to falling and decided it was the unalterable condition of things, and then suddenly you landed on a new platform; then it gave way, and you fell again. You decided to hate and get rid of Bridie McKearn but when she started to disintegrate horrifyingly in front of your eyes, you needed her to live. Having reduced Dad's girlfriend to a shampoo and set and a pair of ten denier tights, you caught a glimpse of timid human eyes peeping out of her face. The only thing to do to preserve the simpleness of integrity was to mutter execrable phrases like *ballroom dancing* – and think of something devastating in the way of bomblets to throw at the creep.

'Don't worry about my father,' she confided to Val. 'He isn't really a womaniser.'

She swept out of the room, thrusting the rest of the carrot into her mouth. For the second time she saw the point of reading *Othello* for GCSE.

Half amused, half jangled, Val cleared away the plates. Poor Lizzie. Poor gawky, transparent Lizzie. Upstairs, she looked in the mirror. She was thirty-five but looked twenty-five. Touching up her lipstick, she put a comb through her brown curly hair: perhaps a new perm was indicated. Her hair had always been rather on the thin side. It needed body and bounce. She would make an appointment at the hairdresser's tomorrow. Val dabbed perfume behind her ears. Certainly she was still an attractive woman, *good enough to eat* said Gavin, and *Who is that damned pulchritudinous girl?* asked his uncle that time, eyeing her bosom.

147

Lizzie smelt the perfume which wafted fleetingly into her bedroom as Val passed by.

'Odour of skunk,' she remarked out loud.

Later she heard Sarah come in, and she dawdled outside the dining room to hear their conversation. There was a false note in her sister's voice, she divined, indicative of untruths being told or truths being withheld.

'Lizzie was in a bit of a state. Poor girl, she gets so – violent,' she heard Val confide.

'I don't think she means anything,' Sarah replied blandly.

Violent! Lizzie thought, enraged, taking off up the street to Martin's house. Why was that woman calling her *violent*? It was them that were *violent* without knowing or admitting it. Just because she crashed around a bit and let fly with her tongue didn't make her *violent*. Their family cars were deadly weapons unloading asphyxiating filth into the atmosphere; their fridges and aerosols punctured the ozone layer; their nuclear plants killed babies with leukaemia; their hi-technology manufactured bomblets, and they sat at home insisting that they were nice peaceful people and she was *violent*.

'Do *you* think I'm violent?' she asked Martin.

'Nah. Who said you were?'

'Oh – no one.'

They kissed and cuddled on the corner of Greek Street in the doorway of a disused garage. Martin's hands swarmed all over her body, delving through bewildering layers of scarf and sweater in search of her breasts and grasping her bottom through her impenetrably tight jeans. The bitter gale acted as a passion-killer, and Lizzie was relieved that Martin did not guide her hand into his trousers as he had done on several previous occasions, breathing hard, to get her to fondle his – she didn't name it to herself – within his boxer shorts. She loved the kissing and cuddling; couldn't get enough of it. But his – thing –

reminded her of a sausage. It put her off to have to handle the sausage in his underpants, which somehow didn't seem like Martin, or to be part of Martin the person, but had a pop-up life of its own. She didn't know what exactly she was supposed to do with the sausage, so she just rubbed a bit and removed her hand. It was not for want of instruction in the facts of sex that Lizzie experienced this shock: indeed, her streetwise friend Cheryl had enlightened her in detail, with diagrams, when they were both ten, and Lizzie had gone home to explain the principles of fellatio, cunnilingus and buggery to a disbelieving six-year-old Sarah. Like the rest of her generation, she knew it all. But none of this had prepared her for the sausage.

And Freud, so she read in a copy of *Cosmopolitan* in the dentist's waiting-room, had stated that all girls experienced sausage-envy. *Pull the other one*, thought Lizzie. But the article went on to explain that you didn't know you felt this envy, because it was subconscious. And Freud knew all this because, being a scientist (and possessing the sausage), he could poke through to your subconscious, which he had penetrated though you could not. *Cobblers*, thought Lizzie, anxiously.

After a deep kiss, Martin pulled away in a business-like fashion, to consult his watch.

'What do you want to do?' he asked. 'Vigil at the war memorial or Socialist Workers' meeting at the college?'

'Socialist Wankers,' said Lizzie. 'Not likely.'

'What then?'

'I'm going to throw a brick through the window of Purdy's the Butcher,' she announced. She was sick of Martin deciding on priorities; and besides it was time she went for action rather than words. She had been called violent; and, in her heart, she had wincingly acknowledged the justice of this charge. Being no better than the rest of them, she would put her violence to a positive use.

149

'Go on,' said Martin, uncertainly. 'You wouldn't.' Then he paused and added, 'Would you?' He was fundamentally a gentle boy. At the vigil, he would have liked to hold a candle like the anti-nuclear lot, but a combination of Marxist and macho principle forbade.

'Just watch me,' said Lizzie. 'Come on. If you dare.'

The Animal Liberation Front had been at work in late months in the Stockport, Altrincham and Rochdale areas, bombing butchers and abattoirs, and smashing crates of factory-farm eggs. Lizzie had watched the local news bulletins with an elated sense of prescience. She didn't want to hurt people but she wanted people to stop hurting animals. She wanted them to know that when they went into the butcher's shop and asked for a leg of lamb, what they came out of the door with was an actual severed leg, which had been walking in a field the previous week. Brains, hearts, livers, kidneys, intestines, ribs lay on the bloody Belsen of the butcher's slab, and cried out to Lizzie for redress and atonement. And the stench of the place . . . couldn't the people smell it, didn't it turn their stomachs all queasy as they queued for their Sunday roast? Mr Purdy was just as bad as Saddam Hussein, or even George Bush, in Lizzie's opinion; but no one, not even her mother, or Martin, could see that.

Martin skulked behind the wall between Purdy's and the station, peering out occasionally and preparing to make a dash for it down the railway path if Lizzie got caught. The high street was deserted and dark save for smears of yellow light from the street lamps and the cold fluorescence of the shop window itself, which advertised in blue neon, 'Purdy's, The Family Butcher For Quality Meat'. The scrubbed surfaces of the refrigerated display shelves were bare, and the blue-and-white chequered floor was a model of disinfection. Lizzie, with bricks in either pocket, loitered shiftily, her eyes roaming around the street and the car-park opposite. Having waited for a break in the occasional traffic that swept downhill under the railway bridge, she lobbed her first brick. The brick bounced harmlessly off the pane like rubber, leaving merely a scratch.

'Damn,' said Lizzie, scarpering round the corner to join Martin. 'What shall I do now?'

'Give it up. It's unbreakable glass, most likely. Come on. Let's go. Leave it at that – you tried.'

'Not fucking likely,' Lizzie whispered. 'Not after all this.' To come with heroic purpose and leave as a laughing-stock was not an attractive option, though she was beginning to feel a bit foolish. 'Help me bring over that bit of rock.'

Together they manhandled the rock from the railway embankment; together they pitched it through the shop window, which shattered across half its surface.

Lizzie was at the police station; Gavin was in Birmingham; Sarah was crying upstairs; Lizzie's mother seemed to be out or at least not answering the telephone. Val, at her wits' end, left a message for Gavin on the ansafone and, depositing Sarah with a neighbour, drove to the police station.

'I can only say,' she assured the officer, 'that I'm – we're – so very sorry this has happened. She's a highly strung, neurotic girl at the best of times and I'm afraid she has some funny ideas.'

'We've been hearing about them from her,' observed the policeman laconically. 'I gather it was your daughter led the young lad on. *He's* in there crying. *She's* laying down the law.'

'Oh *dear*,' said Val. 'What's going to happen? Her father's away – I'm not her mother by the way. Is there any chance that, in view of her youth, the charges might be dropped? Just caution her? Of course we'll pay Mr Purdy for the broken window.'

The bright lights of the interviewing room created a

shadowless interior, in which Val blinked. A large youth was blubbering, head down on a table, with his aghast parents standing on either side. Lizzie was hysterically pouring forth a denunciation of the meat-eating public and the anti-vegetarian powers that be. Her head was held high and tilted back slightly in the truculent gesture Val knew so well, her arms waving about for emphasis: but behind the bravado it could be seen that her tears were rising, and her voice was beginning to falter.

Something at once absurd and profoundly vulnerable in the girl's defiant stance made Val's heart contract; she smiled to suppress the pang on Lizzie's behalf, an inappropriate response which she converted into a frown.

'Don't you laugh at me!' Lizzie bawled out, and burst into a flood of tears. 'I hate you!'

'I wasn't laughing at you, Lizzie, by the way,' said Val on the way home in the car. 'It was a nervous tic. But what possessed you?'

Lizzie made no reply. She would lose her pocket-money for two years, she calculated. *Two years.* It was a sobering thought, which made her somewhat rue, not the action itself (which was just) but the wholly inadequate precautions and lack of planning. And she didn't like to think of what Dad would say.

The wind soughed around the house in restless eddies, which from time to time seemed to lull and wane but never succeeded in dying; for they anguished up again in ireful blasts that shook the sash-windows in their frames and dashed the boughs of Bridie's copper beech this way and that, till they creaked and foamed, distraught. Then ebbed, then sank, blowing and sucking dreary monotones down the drainpipes. Ruth stared out of the window at Bridie's darkening garden, thrashed and tormented, and never still. That fence they'd patched was going again: it hung by a nail from the keeling post. The windy noise got into your mind; couldn't be turned off.

Beyond all this commotion, what lies beyond? She strained her eyes to focus the skies but they too were turbulent, dark bunches of cloud stampeding before the wind. Beyond this nether chaos there was the silence of space, the mercy of nonentity.

Her palm warmed the glass of a bottle of a hundred Diazepam, carried in her pocket wherever she went. It dulled her distress to count them out on a table, drawing them up in formations of ten: enough there, surely, to purchase peace.

The phone rang *again*. It wouldn't give her an hour's rest. The wind roared behind the gasfire and the ringing went on and on. She waited for it to stop, her scalp crawling, and downed a second glass of red cooking wine; it seethed on her empty stomach. The phone would not give over: finally, exasperated, she picked it up.

'Go away. Leave me alone.'

Immediately it rang again. Trembling with irritation, she waited for it to stop, then took the receiver off and laid it on the desk.

Please replace the handset and try again, advised a monitory voice, *please replace the*

When the wineglass smashed against the wall, the winestain bled down and soaked into the carpet.

and try again please replace the handset

'Damn you!' The phone was indestructible. It hit the wall in the wake of the wineglass but carried on with its advice.

again please

She circled the house nervously, up and down the stairs, from room to room; tipped the curdled leavings of the wine down her throat, grimacing, for it was old and nasty, having been opened last year for a casserole Bridie made for a birthday meal which seemed to be . . . she remembered . . . full of . . . bayleaves . . . and they both . . . and Bridie said . . . nothing . . . she couldn't remember.

Half slept, and woke with a jolt, to find herself at the bottom of the stairs and something horrible happening at the door, a newspaper thrusting through the brass flap of the letter-box . . . that was all, but it seemed frightening, a penetration . . . she couldn't bear it, things getting in. They must not get in. She threw open the heavy door with a clang, and a shout of air tore in through its wide-open mouth, and 'Don't *do* that!' she screamed at the amazed paper-boy with his fluorescent orange bag; then crashed the door, so savagely that the whole stairwell seemed to jangle with reverberations. She leaned panting against the door.

'Calm yourself – calm, my love – calm,' Bridie said.

Would have said. Was not here to say.

And Sarah would not let her die. Sarah forbade it. Sarah swelled to tyrannous proportions and, with all the authority of the law, condemned her to life. She upturned the empty bottle and tongued the neck, coaxing out a few drops, musty and powdery with cork.

'You'll be all right, you know. You will,' Bridie said.

She used to say. She had been so boundlessly reassuring. (Was that because she had once needed reassurance so much herself – her father dying – and had been too proud to ask for it?) If Ruth cried, Bridie's strong arms were round her at once, and even now in the shadow of her abdication it came back so tenderly, how she had laid her face against Bridie's throat through her tears and breathed in the dear gentle smell of her (Johnson's baby lotion mingled with Bridieness), hearing the assuaging words only Bridie knew how to give

but now she could not give

because she was not here

because she had turned her back and confided her self to others and to another world.

where I shall follow and find you.

A blast of wind seemed to shake the deep-rooted house. She started as if jerked awake. Doors slammed and a draught swept in under the front door to where she sat slumped on the staircase. When was the wind ever as bad? Yes, the storms last year, when the trees came down at Kew, ancient trees centuries old. For weeks on end the world seethed and pitched; walls fell; roofs blew off. They had been sitting one evening with a group of educated people at some Godawful dinner-party (Bridie enjoyed it) and the *coq au vin* was just being served when the gale got up, and Dieter Grünmann said 'Climate change' and Hannah Fisher said 'Judgement on us', and there they were gorging themselves while the world turned to an apocalyptic force field all round them, and 'It will come', said Johnnie Cartwright and 'I have long predicted it', looking smug. But 'What can we do?' asked Julia Grünmann, forehead wrinkled, and had to repeat the question which couldn't be heard above the wind. 'Eat up,' was the answer, and so the epicures went on to guzzle the *Apfelstrudel* while the trees twisted and slates flew. That night the garage roof made of corrugated plastic ripped off in strips and scattered around the whole area: Ruth came across a fragment next to a pillar-box a third of a mile away. All the fences were wrecked and Mrs Mason's chimney-pot fell. Ruth couldn't stand it; she went around in a state of edgy disquiet.

'What's up?' asked Bridie.

'I don't know,' said Ruth. 'It's the wind – makes me jumpy. I *wish* it would be quiet.'

'Don't think about it.'

'I can't help it – it gets into me.'

Ruth ventured out to work and her hair stood straight up like sheets of flame in the scalding cold. The wind banged her back toward the front door, taking away her breath, so she put her head down and butted her way forward, and, turning, saw Bridie at her typewriter looking out composedly through the window at her, a steadfast figure not susceptible to storm. An anchor, a roof over Ruth's head even if every other shelter blew off. 'Yea in the shadow of thy wings will I make my refuge': that psalm had rung in her mind then at the sense of sanctuary that had come over Ruth at the calming sight of her friend at the window. And how much more dangerous it was to depend on a mortal for your very being than to ride out the storm had not occurred to her then, nor the sacrilege that exalted Bridie into God.

Here in the kitchen she came upon the trove of a bottle of Moët, saved for some special celebration. She shook it violently: the cork shot the morning-room light to pieces. Ruth laughed. She scaled the precipice of stairs, bottle in hand. Their bedroom. Their bed. The cream-coloured duvet had two small frills running down either side, otherwise it was quite plain, against the equally plain dove-grey wall Ruth had lovingly painted. She lay down and rested her head on the coolness of the pillow. Rain lashed against the window from a grey-green sky. After they had made love they held hands, all four hands tenderly together, as one, and their cheeks against their hands, and sometimes Bridie's hands were on the outside, enclosing hers, and sometimes Ruth's embraced Bridie's in a stasis so beautiful that the tears might come, in Ruth's eyes, or Bridie's or both; but of their murmurings during these meditations, nothing could afterwards be remembered. Only you were changed in the aftermath, refreshed and blessed in spirit, as if you had both swum in the salt, cold sea.

O westron wind when wilt thou blow
The small rain down might rain
Christ that my love were in my arms
And I in my bed again

'Oh my Bridie – please – please – come here and love me.' The terrible tears began to surge up from the depths of that well where they were brewed and forever replenished, and the renewed consciousness of pain drove her from the bed. Reeling up, she came face to face with the mirror. A staring, mad face screamed *Bridie*! at her. Taking hold of the bronze Demeter her friend kept on the bedside table, she eliminated the face. Again and again she retrieved the missile and smashed the mirror out of its frame until only bare board remained, with a few shards of silvery glass lodged in the frame, and her hand and face were running blood, and a tinny echo sang on the air, diminuendo.

There was no face, there was nobody there, she had exploded and disintegrated.

Someone who used to be Ruth staggered downstairs and sat down confusedly beside the telephone which was saying *Please replace the handset and try again please replace the handset and try again.* Ruth complied.

What was this in her hand? Warm from her palm it was the statuette of the corn goddess they had bought at the souvenir shop at Eleusis. In her hand she held a sheaf of wheat, mingled with poppies; her archaic smile denoted neither joy nor grief but the harvest of both, fired in bronze. It was amazing she had survived intact.

The phone began to ring.

8

They were moving a new woman into the bed beside Bridie's: a small, grey-haired person in her sixties whose body in its pink nightgown seemed to hang in the air fragile as a bird's as they lifted her. She weighed next to nothing in the orderlies' hands and indeed seemed committed to causing the least possible trouble to anyone and to taking up a minimum of space. Bridie heard her apologising for the nuisance she was causing.

'I'm nothing but trouble to you.'

'Nonsense, Nell. Don't be so blooming daft.'

'I thought I'd have been on my way before now – I certainly didn't reckon to being back in here taking up valuable bedspace.'

'Is she always like this?'

'That's Nell all over. Can't abide fuss and giving trouble. You'll not change her now.' That must be the husband, a gaunt, bent man, wheezing and breathless, who looked as if he ought to be in bed himself, being nursed. When he said 'You'll not change her now', it was spoken with a placid pride as if she'd beaten them all. He coughed painfully.

'Now you get off home as soon as I'm sorted out, Jack, and have a good rest. You've overdone it terrible. Look at him.'

'Well, he loves you, Nell. He wanted to care for you.' That

was Broide, Bridie's favourite. There was a silence. Then they drew back the curtains and Nell looked about her.

'Gladys has gone then?' she asked Broide.

'Yes – last night.'

'Well, that's as well, poor girl. And she had a good long life of it. How old were she – eighty-one or eighty-two, were it?'

'Eighty-two.'

'She went quiet-like?'

'In her sleep, without knowing about it.'

'That's good then.' She lay propped against a mound of pillows, tranquil and accepting, as if she'd rid her mind of a great load in being no longer a burden to her husband. 'Now Jack, mind what I say – go round to our Deirdre's and she'll cook you dinner, then home and into bed. Have a good rest.'

The elderly man held her hand in his, tenderly caressing it with his bony rheumatic fingers.

'I'm off down the pub for a pint as soon as I get out of here,' he wheezed, and his eyes crinkled at her.

'You do that. Enjoy it – and I'll enjoy thinking of you there. And don't you bother a moment about me – I'm in good hands. You know that.'

When Jack had gone, shuffling out and leaning heavily on his stick, Nell shed a few tears.

'You all right, dear?' asked Broide. She took the hand that was brittle and veined like a leaf.

'Oh yes, I'm fine – don't you mind me. I should have gone, you know, Breeze; I should have been on my way two months ago – that's what Mr Mattingley predicted. He made no bones about it and I liked him for that. He said, "Six weeks at the most, Mrs Smithers", so I made all my arrangements and put things straight and neat-like – right and tight. I set everything in order and just sat back and waited. Blow me down, nothing happened. The date came and went and I said to Jack, "Hey I'm still here" I said, and he said, "The tumour's maybe dissolved, Nell" but I didn't reckon much to that. Embarrassing in a way. I felt I *ought* to have gone. I'd packed my bags and bought my ticket – no train. Hanging around twiddling my thumbs, I'm thinking "What possible use am I?" – and I see people fretting and grieving, and Jack getting more and more wore down. But he *would* have me home; there were no persuading him. Sometimes I've wondered if he'd pop off before me, he were getting so done in.'

'Well, he'll get a rest now. He's a lovely, caring person, Nell.'

'A good nut – a right good nut is Jack, all through. Always were – always will be. But I don't know what I'm doing hanging about, wasting your time and the precious bed. When I'm gone he'll be able to settle down and get his own health back – he's got our daughter to see after him and his mates round the pub and he won't be at a loss for company. Anyway, what am I rambling on for? I talk too much, he always tells me. I'm going to shut up now and let you get on with your duties.'

'Have you got everything you want?'

'Oh yes, I'm well content.'

It was strange for Bridie to see the unfamiliar face of the woman in Pat's bed; the new name-plaque; the alien sponge-bag, carton of apple juice, framed photograph of a family group. One by one they succeeded one another through this transit-lounge, souls awaiting their flight like the passengers dossing down at Manchester Airport last year during the European Air Traffic Control strikes. Some grumbled; some cursed; others sighed and took it philosophically or lightly, reading a newspaper to kill the time. In the end, they all got away. But the lounge was never empty.

Years ago, Bridie had visited a friend in St Mary's Maternity Hospital. All those babies: a living nightmare, so she had described it to Elaine when she had escaped, adding comic elaborations. Sucking nipples, squalling, comatose, swaddled in identical white sheets, they had come bursting through the door of life one after the other; and nobody had ever asked them, 'Do you want to live? Do you want to be mortal?' We called them in from the dark and condemned them to – *this*, thought Bridie, peering through the bars of the safety-panel toward the newcomer or returnee or whatever she was. Why did we condemn people so lightly to life? She could not understand it; never had understood it. Population control . . . that had always been number one priority. It had made her several powerful enemies. The organisation had been boycotted by Roman Catholics and denounced by a *Monsignor* in Brazil . . . what was his name? . . . she couldn't recall but saw him in her mind's eye with hallucinatory clarity. They were working side by side with the street-children who lived in sewers and were raped and murdered by the police; also with families who not only scavenged a living off gigantic heaps of refuse but actually inhabited corrugated iron shelters or boxes perched on the rubbish-heaps: ten, eleven, twelve, thirteen children born to the squalor, disease and degradation of life begun and ended in ordure and decay. Bridie staggered up the face of the tip to greet these people, her stomach heaving with rage as with nausea. 'How can life under these conditions be better than never to have lived?' she demanded of the *Monsignor*.

He, who worked in his shirt-sleeves amongst the refuse, and had a right to be heard if anyone did, replied, 'But they are all God's children, Miss McKearn. Every blessed one of them,' and looked her compassionately but steadily in the eye. His very goodness infuriated her. It shone from him. The children thronged round him, calling him 'Papa'. 'Papa' was the only name she remembered for him. But to her mind, this excellent man and the others like him were forces of reaction propping up the structure that oppressed the children they genuinely loved.

Labouring with these mighty issues, surly moods had often flooded her with distaste for the whole lot of them, the whole human race striving in its dearth, its do-gooding, its corruption and its blindness. A worm of indifference ate its way into the soft heart of her concern and she thought *Why bother? Let them rot.* At other times the scope and complexity of the problems appalled her into inertia; her jaded mind threw down its tools and said *I can't; how can I?* Next morning she might awaken to the freshness of the garden and she'd do an hour of digging before anyone was up; then she'd type some letters and reports before a breakfast of coffee and toast, and her mind was lit by purpose, and as if regenerated by the vision of that electrically powered globe she and Elaine had owned, the glowing beautiful planet which they spun that night they had the idea for the Trust. It symbolised their hope in their work; hope against all the odds. She noticed that when Elaine left, the globe was one of the very few jointly owned objects she took with her.

That *Monsignor* – she saw him now, quite vividly, down to the badger-grey beard and the fair hairs on his sunburnt brawny arms, under the harsh sunlight. He was quite an enchanting man. The laughter-lines around his eyes were deep but she had also seen him cry. Those children on the tips were *his* children, he told her, fostered for God.

'You must make a point of knowing each and all by name,' he said, and indicated the practicality of his doctrine by addressing scores by name or nickname. He sat down with a family amongst the tins, tyres, rotten fruit, excreta, jars, offal, slime and flies, and broke bread with them. The heat beat down and struck up from the flashing glass and metal into Bridie's face, and her nose was traumatised by the indescribable reek of the nameless deposits of deliquescence; even through the tiny holes in her wide-brimmed straw hat her face scorched and she nearly fainted.

'Won't you join us, Miss McKearn?' he invited her. So she sat and ate, and tried to smile into the thronging faces, and thought, *it would have been better for you if you had never been born*.

The truth was – or rather, one of many incompatible truths – she found it hard to love people; excruciatingly hard. Until Ruth she had never laid bare her soul. It was easier to fly cerebrally high above the revolving globe and, in taking the larger perspective (though it denoted a failure of personality, fuelled by pride and fear), to obtain a view not granted to those more humanly involved in the thick of it down below. That lapsed, melted look in the eyes of friends who took a year out to have a child baffled and dismayed Bridie.

'Don't you think – pardon me for saying – there are enough, not to say a superfluity, of children in the world already?' she heard herself asking Thérèse, on her visit to the maternity ward, not meaning to put the proud parent's back up (though she did have a certain knack that way) but genuinely curious.

'Oh but this is *our* son, Michael's and mine.' Thérèse took no offence, knowing Bridie's intense naïvety. 'You wouldn't understand, Bridie,' she added in a velvety voice.

Bridie had contemplated the squashed-up beetroot face of this new specimen of the genus *Homo sapiens*. She felt the proximity of the warm, shallow dream of parenthood that makes possible the reproduction of the species, and she knew you couldn't argue with it. No amount of tax incentive or birth control education with free condoms supplied would slow the population growth that would ultimately choke on its own excess, to invert the pattern and make us eat each other to survive.

'*You* wouldn't understand,' Thérèse said. But oddly enough, Bridie did come briefly to understand. Most bizarre of all the tricks love played on her when Ruth appeared was the phase in which she found herself longing to have a baby with Ruth. It was at the time when the ecstatic shock of Ruth was still so new that every hour brought its own revelation. She thought of a child made of herself and Ruth; she saw it running in and out of the house, with its red-brown hair and green eyes – it was perhaps two years old, wearing denim dungarees and blowing a toy trumpet. The image, conceived between asleep and awake, carried its own incontrovertible authenticity, as if she had been shown a photograph of the very girl.

'I imagined our child,' she admitted to Ruth, taking her warm, half-asleep body in her arms.

'We could always adopt one,' mumbled Ruth.

'Oh *no*,' Bridie came back immediately. 'That wouldn't be the same.'

So now she knew. It was nonsense, of course, on the low-grade level of fantasy; and it was not in keeping with Bridie's character to entertain such nonsense, quite apart from the risible little matter of biological constraints. But fleetingly she saw and comprehended how deep passion would desire to breed. And the little girl occasionally popped up in her mind with a toy or looking out of a window, and Bridie knew, *That was the child I could not have.*

Yes and once (to her starved senses that memory came glowing back with filmic brilliancy) they had been in Delamere Forest walking down through a glade, clambering over fallen timber and wading through ladyfern in a resinous haze of light. The forest became denser and more dappled, so that they walked through light to shade and back to light, thin-soled over the softness of the ground. Deeper they went, without speech. Inside it was strange and rather wonderful. They trod carefully, so as not to disturb anything, skirting spiders in their radiant webs, strung between tree and tree, dodging their heads under low boughs. They touched only with the tips of their fingers as Ruth led, Bridie followed, or Bridie led and Ruth followed, or they went different ways round the same tree and linked hands smiling. The quiet of the interior became more intense and they too remained quiet, not desiring to penetrate the forest, only to share its space. Now that the trees were so close together, they blocked out all but a residue of wavering light, and the darkness had a quality of sanctuary as if the trees were rooted pillars of some living temple, not man-made but whole and maternal. The labyrinthine complications of many pathways radiated around them, and 'We're lost', said Ruth rapturously, turning in her tracks to kiss her mouth. They stood and held each other, swaying slightly, their hands in one another's jeans back-pockets, listening to the stillness and to the rustlings that signified other lives than theirs, of which they were ignorant. The sense of their mutually tender, nurturing, listening love was so intense in that hour, she would always remember it, could never forget it, and how they stood face to face in that deep green darkness; and with gentle, almost reverencing fingers (as she afterwards thought) she undid the buttons of Ruth's shirt, and slid it from her shoulders, and there she stood in the privacy of the forest where the faint flutings of birdsong echoed the only sound, her breasts so tenderly beautiful in the dim light, with one nipple and the swell of part of the left breast caught in a glimmer of sunlight, that moved over her skin as the breeze lifted the treetops high above. Bridie bent slowly to Ruth's beautiful nakedness and softly brushed the delicate nipple with her lips, and took it into her mouth, caressing it with her tongue. Ruth's body was cool away from the scalding heat outside the forest; Bridie's cheek felt the silken cool of the skin as she laid her head between her friend's breasts, (Ruth's hands about her head as if in benediction) and she felt she had never known the meaning and the piercing sweetness of her love until today. For it was as if Ruth was clothed and she naked; and fast asleep and dreaming, the two of them dreaming the same dream.

And it was at that moment that the child burst through from the forest. In a patch of dappled light it stopped, wearing a pale yellow cotton dress, carrying a handful of bracken, its hair bronze golden where the light caught it, tense and panting. The child looked up at Bridie with a curious, cryptic look (she was not frightened, that was for sure, she was challenging rather, or so it seemed) and Bridie gave a small cry, reached out her hands to snatch the girl up – her daughter, their daughter – and, catching it by the waist, heard for a moment through the cotton dress against her face the wild heartbeat that drummed to be gone. And she was away. Lost. Lost her. Not a tame creature. But Ruth only had time to ask, 'What . . .?' and turn. And Bridie said, 'Did you see? Did you see her, Ruth? Our . . .' And Ruth, puzzled, said, 'What is it, love?' and Bridie said, 'Listen', and far in the distance you could hear the ring of a child's excitement as it pelted from tree to tree, so that Ruth said, 'I can only hear children – is that what you mean?' Bridie blinked the tears off her eyes and took her friend into strong embrace; sobbed on her bare shoulder with joy or grief or both, and later, with the sun going down, they walked languorously out of the forest where the silent light burnt in the tall stillnesses of yellow oat grass that were the colour, thus burnished, of the child's hair and Ruth's. Arms round one another's waists, they sauntered along the heather-lined path, and through the loggers' clearance, with its litter of sawdust and shavings and its pregnant aroma of resin, and out of the corner of her eye Bridie sought hints of her child through the grid of lengthening shadows in that penultimate summer of her life. But she never saw her again.

They had sat on the jog-trot stopping train between Chester and Manchester opposite a burly male reading *Viz*, Bridie remembered. And they, fresh from the recreation of their day, had dropped all semblance of decorum and lolled in one another's sunburnt arms, playing with one another's watch-strap, whispering and kissing one another's ear or shoulder; and whether their fellow-passenger eyed them with more amused speculation under cover of studious application to his reading matter, or they the big-boobed, walloping-bottomed cuties who straddled the cartoons and poked surprised-looking men in the eye with their appurtenances, was a moot point. His arms were hairy and much tattooed; his head shaven. Outside, the gold-green fields were grazed by cows with long shadows. The rich Cheshire farmlands undulated between gentle swells and dips, with occasional copses that had once been part of the original forest that had covered the whole area. The *Viz* reader disembarked at Knutsford, bestowing upon them a wink, a sideways leer and a clicking noise indicative of the wish to see them up and at it.

'Pity, he's taken his comic. I've never seen one,' said Ruth.

'Ah well, you'll get over it.'

'Been a lovely day.' Ruth stroked the fair hairs on Bridie's arm. 'You've caught the sun.'

'Feel gorgeous. Can't wait to get you into bed.' A beautiful lassitude seemed to flow over the surface of her skin. She would not say anything about the forest, the child.

'But isn't it sad,' said Ruth. 'Eighty per cent of the world was once forest – eighty per cent. In Shakespeare's day Michael Drayton was lamenting the deforestation. And now – it's very sad. Acid rain, logging. You can't go back, can you, Bridie? I mean, you think you can, but it's illusion. Where we were, the road was only a couple of hundred yards away. Illusion . . .'

Bridie paused, reflected. She, who could detect an illusion at a mile's distance before it hove into sight round a corner, was not ready to surrender to it today. The mother-world had been hacked back and ransacked but there were still (for their generation, at least) hidden sanctuaries and refuges.

'It wasn't illusion,' she said simply. 'It was real. Beyond the shadow of a suspicion of a hint of a doubt. You smell of fresh air . . .' She raised Ruth's hand to her face and brushed it with her lips. 'And resin and greenness.'

It all came back to Bridie not as a sequence of events but as if her mind were charged with the imperative of its colour.

'Would you ring home for me, Nigel? – ring Ruth, and ask her – please – to come.'

'Of course – but wouldn't you rather do it yourself? I could bring you the phone.'

'Oh no – no.' Bridie's voice faltered; she breathed hard and the unaccustomed mental excitement fatigued her. She was suddenly frightened; all but drew back. Her resources so depleted, how could she possibly cope with seeing Ruth again? The emotional effort would prostrate her utterly; she might be cruel again, rejecting; she might go out of control all over again. This awareness made her feel irritable.

'Could you tell her . . . it must be low key, I can't . . . cope with a scene but I do invite her to come – if she *will* come.'

Perhaps Ruth wouldn't come. Perhaps the hurt she'd done her was simply too violent. Perhaps it would be better to cancel her message now; press the buzzer *now*, before Nigel reached the door, keep quiet and safe in the semi-comatose privacy of the ward. Perhaps it would be better to ask for a knock-out injection; and whenever she awoke, ask for another. There was still time. Bridie's fingers dawdled on the buzzer, like a trigger; but she didn't fire. She sighed, turned her head away from the door as far as she could, and drifted off to sleep.

Bridie's dream was appalling. She knew that she was dreaming as soon as she slept, and looked for means to wake up, but when (by banging her head repeatedly against a brick wall) she did succeed in awakening, it was only into another dream. There was no option but to go through with it.

Her work . . . her work must be done . . . but she was behind with it, wretchedly, hopelessly behind. She would have to race to catch up with herself. But the work . . . was simply too great . . . not within her compass. She'd lost too much time hanging around here on the ward, letting it all pile up. She staggered on make-shift crutches and splints to the hospice door. Must have looked a fine sight stumping along, held together by bandages . . . but she got there anyway. Evidently though it wasn't the way out: 'No, Bridie,' they laughed at her clumsy wrestle with the doorknob. 'It doesn't open inwards. That way – see? – exit.'

But it was miles down a dark corridor, the exit; she toiled towards it.

'Got to get to work,' she told the nurse. 'No time to lose.'

'You've been dreaming, Bridget.'

'No . . . no. It was real.'

'Just a dream.'

'The seedcorn ran out,' she told the nurse. It seemed a message she was obligated to transmit. 'That was the whole problem.'

'Yes, dear. But all's well.'

She held the nurse's hand. What was real? What was the problem? It wasn't clear, it all fuzzed over and she slid down again. No question about it now: people were definitely dying (not her though, she was in the bloom of health). Pollution and radiation, these were responsible. Not a speck of green in sight. She couldn't suppress a sense of told-you-so complacency . . . but the silence was uncanny. A man in a white suit was standing at the hospice door when she went to enquire.

'You didn't tell us,' he accused her.

'I did. I did. You wouldn't listen.'

'You didn't shout loudly enough.'

It was true, she'd only whispered. Millions had been left to die because she'd only whispered. For her immunity, what atonement?

'I've had a rotten dream,' she complained to the nurse, expecting sympathy. But the nurse was actually part of the dream and could afford no palliative.

'What do you expect, in Chernobyl?' she asked. 'A holiday camp?'

The crops and the creatures . . . all perished. It was dreadful to see the extent of the havoc . . . and fellow humans of every tribe and continent filing through the hospice door, under the exit sign.

She went with them. It was the only way. Her garden was full of daffodils, cool and wet in the thick grass. She felt so free. They had dug her a resting place beneath the copper beech and Ruth was there waiting for her in a blue-green dress. 'At last!' she said, looking up from her watch and held out her arms for her . . . and Bridie wondered how it was that the contamination hadn't reached the garden but there was no time to ask for the sun was very low on the horizon.

She lay down willingly, without making a fuss. In a cross-section of the earth she could see the buried bulbs of daffodils and crocuses, as well as the network of roots from the trees in their garden. Considering these things, and having the sense of double presence – care above and mercy below – Bridie closed her eyes and slept.

And awoke.

'Where is she?' she cried out.

'I'm here,' said Ruth. 'It's all right, my lamb, I'm here.'

'Ruth,' she went on, panicking. 'Is there a shelter?'

'How do you mean, a shelter?'

'From the radiation. Is there somewhere we could go?'

'We're there – we're there already. In the shelter.'

'Are you sure?'

'Quite quite sure.'

'Oh . . . yes. Yes. I see.' But she did not see. Confusion was the only certainty, but her pulse calmed and she dozed, her hand in Ruth's.

When she awoke and recognised Ruth, she asked, 'How did *you* get here?' puzzled, and when Ruth answered, timidly, 'You asked for me, Bridie,' her face working to keep back her own tears, Bridie began to cry.

'Please don't let me upset you,' said Ruth, looking round in apprehension. 'They might turf me out for upsetting you.'

Bridie smiled through her tears. 'No bouncers here – don't worry.'

'I came out in such a fit when the nurse phoned, I locked myself out, Bridie.'

'Did you? . . . Stupid girl, aren't you?' said Bridie tenderly. What she could not understand, what mystified and appalled her utterly was how she could have done without Ruth for five minutes. 'But . . . how are we going to get back in?'

'Don't know. Hadn't thought. I just wanted to get here to you, be here with you.'

'Have to climb in the bathroom window – have we still got the step-ladder?'

'Yes, but it's bust.'

'Borrow one from next door. Then you can let me in by the front door.'

'Bridie, *please*. You'll start me off. You know what I'm like when I start bawling, I won't be able to stop. Bridie,' she was terrified of letting go of her emotions. 'Nigel told me I must keep calm.'

'Balls to that. I do mean it. I intend to come home. If you can . . . put up with me of course . . . Not been looking after yourself,' she admonished gently. 'Need me there to take care of you.'

'I might say the wrong thing,' said Ruth quietly. 'I'm very near the edge.'

'My darling.' A surge of pity rose in Bridie and broke like a wave. 'It's all right now.' She saw the edge Ruth was on. 'Come away from the edge. It's all right now.'

She drew her steadily away from the cliff-edge with her eyes. 'You'll be all right now. We'll be all right.'

She'd been there swaying and faltering on the precipice all her life till Bridie drew her in to safety – the sheer fall an inch from her feet; and she couldn't look down, daren't face that fall. Blindly feeling around with her foot on treacherous ground, she couldn't take stock. Bridie had seen that from the first; she saw it now from where she lay, with deeper compassion and remorse.

'My beautiful – not to fear any more. Here is your friend. Your friend for life. You know.'

Tears trembled on the rim of Ruth's eyes. Bridie saw that. Saw the burden of unspilt tears, concernedly; drew her face down with her own eyes and kissed the eyes, drinking salt.

'You can cry all you need . . . What did you do to your face, my love?'

'Had an accident. With a mirror.'

'You'll be all right, you know. You will. You won't fall because you'll feel me loving you . . . and you'll be safe and secure. You will.'

'Promise, Bridie?'

'Cross my heart and . . .'

'No.'

'Do you understand why . . . why I was so cruel, Ruthie?'

Ruth chafed and kissed the darling hand that seemed brittle like an old woman's and yet retained such a surprising power of grip; she adored the beautiful, keen eyes that were the same but utterly changed in the ravaged face, and would insist on telling the truth, dotting the i's and crossing the t's, even at this late hour on the edge of the world. She knew perfectly well why Bridie had denied her but she didn't want it spelt out, for then she'd have to remember she'd turned her back and, when Bridie most needed succour, evicted her. When she thought of these things – her jealousy of Elaine, her failure to go on loving in the face of Bridie's ill words – she believed herself unworthy to live, let alone to take this hand which now she enclosed between both her own, with its complex and unique tracery of lifelines and lovelines. But it was the cancer, the cancer that was to blame. They'd both been hit, and how could it be otherwise, being so close?

'Don't speak of it,' she begged. 'There's no need.'

'Need you. Couldn't bear to need you. Couldn't bear to lose you so . . . I cast you off. Terrible.'

'I know, it doesn't matter now, please don't . . .'

'Yes,' she cut in quickly, with hectic energy. 'It does matter. Forgive, I must hear you say you do. *Say.*'

'Nothing to forgive. Nothing in the world. We . . .'

'Say it, for pity's sake.'

'I do, I do forgive you, Bridie, if you say I must. And I'm . . . so sorry . . .'

An effort out of all proportion to her resources was now, she knew, required of Bridie, to atone for the hurt and equip Ruth for the road. She had seen people popping off in here, one by one. You never knew when it might be you: and though she felt stronger than for weeks and clear in her mind as an underwater swimmer can ever feel, to whom all objects flow and waver problematically in aqueous light, she knew she must pass across a message of love powerful enough to reach that face above the surface peering down into these depths.

'Ruth, you've been life to me. By which I mean you've been my life. If . . .'

'Bridie, can I come with you when you go?'

'No, Ruth, no. Listen . . .'

'I can't stay here without you.'

'You can. You can. You will recover. You will be calm, in time . . . and healing . . . will come.'

'No, Bridie, no .'

'I've learnt so much in here, Ruth . . . seen such incredible people. And it's not hard . . . to die. I met a man. He had to survive. *That* was hard. He loved her but he will get through – he had her children. You have mine. Somehow, I'm not being clear. Muddled. But you have my child. Inside. It will become clear. Wait for that.'

At this Ruth simply laid her head down on the counterpane and sobbed. Bridie reached down her left hand to stroke her hair and with a prodigious effort managed to heave the right hand over too, so that Ruth's head was covered in both of hers. She moved her hands in a gentle rhythm, using all her powers of co-ordination, to massage the tension out of Ruth's scalp; and it came over her to think (breathing hard with the effort, she couldn't keep it up long) that this was probably the first time she'd given anything to anyone, really given, rather than being on the receiving end, for months and months. And this was truly living – this profound caring which restored you to yourself as the person you needed to be. She was alive. Fully alive. Rooted and growing.

'You're wearing my old green shirt,' she said.

'Am I?' Ruth looked up, beguiled by the dextrous ordinariness of Bridie's words.

'Yes, and those baggy old jeans, aren't you?' She paused,

fiddling with Ruth's ring, pleasing her hands in touching the familiarity of Ruth's palm and slender fingers. 'So . . . it's you. This is you. I want to be . . . all you know as me. I'd like to come home, if there's time. I might be crabby, you'd have to accept. It won't be easy – I might not be much use to you any more, but I'd be . . . better than nothing.'

'Bridie, you've been life to me. You've been my life. Please do come home.' She kissed Bridie's eyes, slowly, tenderly, and placed her palm over the large forehead, full of kindness and intelligence. Bridie sighed, as if releasing a breath she'd been holding for weeks. 'You're tired, love. Will you sleep?'

'Ask Nigel – over there making that bed – to draw the curtain round us.'

Ruth lay down on the bed beside Bridie and held her as she slept. No one disturbed them.

'Well, Jack,' said Nell, the woman in the bed next to Bridie's. 'There's been such goings-on in here today, I can't rightly tell you, it's been better than *EastEnders*. In fact rightly speaking you don't need a TV in here which is just as well because they never switch it on. I just wish you could have been here to see it because you'd never believe it otherwise.'

It was evening and several groups of visitors were clustered round the beds. Nell's husband wheezed and coughed, and ate a grape. Then he stuck his pipe in his mouth, but without lighting it. 'Well, it seems to have perked you up,' he observed.

'You'd never believe it,' Nell went on, in a very audible whisper, 'but that woman in the bed behind you (no, don't turn round and stare – *don't*, Jack) is a lesbian like Martina Navratilova . . . Yes, one of them . . . Her girlfriend were in earlier and blow me if they didn't have a passionate love scene right here in front of our eyes, and the girlfriend actually got into bed with her – yes, really – a red-haired woman, sweet-faced girl actually, you'd never have known to look at her – and there they were laughing and crying and carrying on . . . Don't stare now, Jack – pretend to be looking out the window . . .'

'She don't look the type,' observed Jack, screwing himself round in his chair to study Bridie for several minutes, without hypocritical subtlety.

'No, I know, she looks proper respectable but my goodness, from what I heard – *well* –'

'Speak up a bit,' said Bridie. 'I don't think absolutely everyone can hear you.' She smiled pleasantly across the gap between territories.

'Now look what you've done,' whispered Nell to Jack. 'What did you have to stare like that for? Sorry, dear,' she said to Bridie.

'No offence,' replied Bridie. 'Glad to have given some entertainment. Precious little of it around here.' The delirious hope had arisen that she might after all get better. She felt so good in the aftermath of Ruth's visit that it crossed her mind to speculate that happiness might wash away the treachery of tumours. But that was fantasy. She could not allow herself the distraction of delusions. There was work to be done, hard work on Ruth's behalf, which would take every scrap of energy she possessed; plus a bit.

'So how have you been?' asked Jack.

'Can't complain at all – I've been spoilt rotten,' replied Nell. 'How about you, that's the important thing? Did you get your dinner from Deirdre?'

'Didn't want to bother her. I had what you might call a liquid luncheon down the King's Arms.'

'Now Jack. That won't do. When I'm gone there won't be no one to make sure you eat and take care of yourself so you're just going to have to fend for yourself. It's a terrible worry, Jack, it is really.'

'All right, lass, don't get all hot under the collar. I don't want much to eat anyhow. But when you come back home you can sort me out like.'

Nell scrutinised him cautiously. Why did he kid himself she was coming home? But perhaps he needed to pull the wool over his eyes: it was his way of coping. Or perhaps he thought she needed the comfort of it. She would not disturb the equilibrium of his inner negotiations. She knew very well she would never see the little terraced house in Oldham again where they'd lived throughout forty-two years of married life, with the well-rubbed brass door-knocker and scoured doorstep; the pillar-box red door, the 'Dunroamin' doormat she whacked with a carpet-beater twice a week; the teapot collection on the front window-sill, dusted daily, and the well-polished teak dresser in which was kept the best tea-service they hardly ever used; the ornately framed mirror above the mantelpiece in which she had daily greeted herself for four decades. She knew quite well that she would never again see the immaculate and familiar beauty of this tidy home; and, in relinquishing this (which was the world to her), she had as good as packed up and left the world itself already. Why she lingered on, a nuisance to everybody, she could not imagine.

God only knew.

9

Lizzie broke through taboo after taboo. She smashed her way through prohibitions one after another, and found beyond each fence yet another provoking fence, inviting her to bulldoze it flat by raw power of *will* and *won't*. The unnerving thing was, it was so easy. Each barrier splintered like plywood as she drove her weight against it; and with each victory she found herself more at sea than ever, less at home, both in her home and in the world. The fences, she discovered, were also protective devices, holding her in with the family and the social group, keeping her from flying apart. At times she felt as if the top of her head were exploding; in the face of which disintegration she wrapped herself in a long hooded black cardigan, pulling the sleeves down over her hands, and hugged herself in her own arms. She sat cowled and cross-legged on her bed, rocked to and fro, and listened in to the cracklings and clickings in her brain, like radio interferences. Puzzled, mortified but defiant, she watched her father's consternation pass into disfavour, his angry anxiety mount and harden. She observed Titty Vally wriggle her way further into the household. She discerned in her sister's quiet, methodical ways the timeserver's obsequious survival tactics. They all turned from her and she stalked off, head in the air, and her silence howled at them from behind the wall of her ire, but nobody heard.

After the butcher's shop incident, Martin had been forbidden to go out with her. He was grounded in the evenings and no longer frequented the haunts of the Stockport Reds. Lizzie was grounded too but she simply got out of her window and, clambering on to the flat roof of the kitchen extension, prowled off evening by evening to join a group of militant vegetarians she had contacted through a magazine. An incoherent mixture of fanatical ladies and bull-headed young men with pony-tails, they discussed the presence of rennet in supermarket cheese and dwelt at length on the right to life of the yolk in the unhatched egg. The three young men took little part in these discussions but sat them out politely before raising plans under 'Any Other Business' to picket factory farms and dump manure on the steps of the town hall. Lizzie's contribution to the manure-dumping expedition, in company with the three young men, was reported in the *Stockport Messenger*, the *Metro News* and the *Reporter*, together with a flashlit photograph of Lizzie with raised fist, trading words with a police officer. 'BRAMHALL SCHOOLGIRL IN MANURE OUTRAGE', read the headlines.

'Why are you doing it, Elizabeth? Why?' asked Gavin. 'Why are you doing this to me?'

'I'm not doing anything to *you*. It's nothing to do with *you*. Why do you always say I'm getting at *you*?'

'Of course you're doing it to me.'

'Well, I'm not.'

'Of course you are.'

'I'm not.'

'You damned well are. Don't talk back, you little madam. I'm a laughing stock in the neighbourhood – my business is suffering – I've a letter here from your headmaster, how the hell am I going to keep a shred of credibility on the board of governors, tell me that, when my elder daughter gets herself onto the front bloody page for shovelling horse shit on to the steps of the town fucking hall?'

'That's your problem.' A foolish and infuriating smile flickered on her lips. He stormed across the kitchen in his apron, a drying-up cloth in his left hand, and raised the other hand as if to hit her. It remained trembling in the air and he did not strike. He longed to clout her into kingdom-come. But the hand did not strike. 'That's right, hit a girl, hit a woman,' she challenged, chancing it brazenly, in the knowledge that he had never once raised a hand to her in all her life. 'There's a law against that. I could call Esther Rantzen on *ChildLine*.'

'How dare you?' he raged impotently. His eyes swept the room, bulging, as if searching for words. 'HOW DARE YOU?'

He brought his hand slamming down on to the worktop, causing herb bottles to cascade from their rack. The washing-machine raised its voice to a shrill whirring as it went into fast spin.

'Pick those up!' he shouted against the din, which was both outside and inside his own head, he was unsure which. 'Go on, pick them up.'

Lizzie bent lazily to retrieve a jar of mixed herbs. Lounging against the workbench, she poured some into the palm of her hand and sniffed them appreciatively.

'Put that back,' he yelled maddened. 'Pick those up and put that back!'

'Excuse me, I want a cup of tea,' said Lizzie, elbowing past her father and calmly fishing out a teabag. The kettle belched steam into the explosive, ringing room. Gavin brought his fist down again hard. More jars jangled, rolled and fell.

'You're having no cup of tea in this house,' he hollered absurdly, snatching the teabag from her fingers and stuffing it back in the box, 'until you start behaving yourself!'

'Okay, I'll have a cup of coffee.'

'Get your hands off that jar. Do you know how much Gold Blend costs?' he roared, habitual irritation with Lizzie's expensive tastes veering him wildly off the point.

'In Kwiksave or Tesco?'

'You little bitch,' he said quietly.

Lizzie's eyes narrowed. Their dark brown irises bored a hole in him; never in his life had he called her crude or offensive names. Though she had been out of control, he had maintained invincible control of himself, and hence ultimate contact with her.

'Pick up the jars,' said Gavin.

Lizzie picked them up.

'Put them on the rack.'

Lizzie put them on the rack.

'Anything else, master?'

'Yes – just bloody well get into line. I'll have no more of it. No more animal liberation. No more hanging around with those Class War hooligans. No more violence. No more vandalism. No more staying out after ten o'clock.' With each *no more* he jabbed her shoulder with his forefinger. 'And – no – more – answering back. Get it?'

'Yes, master.'

'And stop calling me master! I won't have it, do you understand?' His agitation competed with the vibrating washing-machine, now in its final throes. 'Why can't you be more like your sister? Why can't you be *normal*? It's your damned mother with her airy-fairy pie-in-the-sky opinions as windy as a fart and about as useful to the human race. Well, if you like her ways so much and don't like mine, you can go and live with her and that cross-eyed dyke in Y-fronts, and see how much you like that. You'd soon come running home then, oh yes, you'd soon see which side your bread's buttered.'

'Perhaps I will.'

There was a pause.

'She wouldn't have you,' he said cuttingly, between rage and fear.

Lizzie turned her head away, her cheek burning as if it had been struck. Another pause.

'She's dying anyway – she's dying.'

'What do you mean, she's dying? Who's *dying*?' he scoffed.

'My mother's wife, or husband, or whatever she is. Bridie – she's dying. In St Marcia's Hospice.'

'Don't talk nonsense.'

'I've seen her,' said Lizzie quietly.

'What?'

'None of your business. I wouldn't tell you what I've seen if you were the last person on earth.' She had sided with Bridie. It was so novel, such a green, fresh awareness that it brought all sorts of incongruent feelings into harmony just as it threw her out of true with her father at the deepest level. 'I'd rather go and live in a cardboard box on Piccadilly Station than come back to you.' Lizzie turned and left the room with dignity, then plunged up the stairs in a storm of tears, nearly knocking Val over as she attempted to come down.

'Oh dear,' said Val to Gavin. 'I don't think that was very wise. She needs kid-glove treatment, not the old boxing-gloves.'

Since the butcher's shop incident, Val had become noticeably more critical and detached from Gavin. He had seen her fluttering her eyelashes at the shock-headed junior clerk, Morgan. An apparent diminution in Val's worship had doubled his own sense of betrayal; his repressed anger, unleashed, extended in all directions, missing only Sarah, who ducked when she saw it coming, smiling tolerantly as if target-practice were only to be expected on a military range, and she was not inclined to take it personally.

The house was bedlam.

Gavin's awareness of having put himself in the wrong was now confirmed by Val's comment, which however hurt his *amour propre* so that he felt bound to deny it and to emphasise that what Lizzie needed was firm handling; he'd be obliged if Valerie would back him up rather than setting herself against him. Val's reply, to the effect that she was going out for a drink with the girls and didn't know when she might be back, rattled him. Off she minced. He watched her *mincing*. She didn't, couldn't, walk: she tottered, waddled, swayed, *minced*. Those high-heels. A stupid, artificial woman. Not like . . . But at the same time, he thought, 'Come back, Val: be good to me.'

The turbulence that seethed in the house had entirely put Gavin off his stroke, that was the trouble; otherwise he wouldn't think these hostile things. His failure of performance night by night at once fuelled Gavin's resentment against Lizzie and Val's growing conviction that living in this house of feuding generations was not likely to prove a conspicuous treat. Nor was Gavin's resemblance to the ex-commando Paddy Ashdown as impressive as it had once seemed; Gavin had a frazzled air and a habit of blinking nervously whatever was said to him. Paddy Ashdown would certainly have known how to handle the refractory Lizzie, catching her in a pincer between toughness and charm. Val vacated her perch on the sofa, tendering Lizzie right of occupancy. But Lizzie, deprived of provocation, lost interest, so that the seat remained vacant. Since the night of the butcher's shop, and increasingly since she had begun to detach herself from the fullness of her infatuation with Gavin, Val had grown to respect something in the girl. Anyone so vulnerable who would – at the top of her voice – take on a roomful of six-foot-two-inch police officers, was a young woman of principle, even if the principles were more or less deranged. Val could the more readily acknowledge this in that she was edging toward a position out of earshot and surrogate responsibility.

'Bye!'

Off she minced, on stilts. *Dressed up fit to kill*, thought Gavin, and hardly cared why. Having drunk half a bottle of Piesporter, he sprawled in a state of soothing dolour by the fire, watching our boys in the Saudi desert demonstrating the use of infra-red lighting equipment, in readiness for the land offensive. He was only mildly interested; watched the highlights of the war every evening as he had once lackadaisically kept up with Football League.

In vino veritas, he thought. That was about all he retained of his Rugby School Latin, that and the immortal *Post coitum homo tristis est*. But that was not strictly true: *femina triste*, Ruth had whispered to herself (though meaning him to hear), drooping on the edge of the turbulent bed in a white nightgown while Gavin fought the compulsion to sleep and made yet another hopeless effort to comfort her. And *I'm sorry I'm so inadequate*, he said wretchedly; but *no, it's me, Gavin – honestly it's me, or biology or something*, she would hasten to reassure him through her wanness or tears; then cling to him beseechingly. Passion might recurrently fail, but tenderness (which for him had always the seeds of passion in it) seldom did. He shared the birth of their daughters, the most profound experience of his life, and the wonder of it was that they were *her* children, his through her. He took pride in her lack of worldliness and in the gentle, generous temperament that strove to see round the cataract of egoism and the blur of her many hesitations and ambivalences for clarity of perception and emotional truth. His own ethical desires were modest: to be a decent fellow, an honourable business partner, a reliable friend, a loving husband and father. As he prospered, she came to seem a bit of a clown, in her dissident enthusiasms that had nothing to do with basics and the little matter of practicality. She made him feel his insufficiency: *femina tristis est*. But he had never retaliated with *You're frigid* in his shame and anger: she said it for him and he denied it. For she remained in his eyes lovely, rare and special. For years they communicated through quiet endearment, sharing the burdens of life, a sense of humour, saying very little about it.

All to no purpose. Along came the McKearn and explained the mystery of Ruth; explained her away. It was pathetic. Ruth had been a closet lesbian all along. At first it flabbergasted him. But he wasn't shocked or frightened. You couldn't take the McKearn woman seriously as a sexual rival – not in the way you would if there were a male lover involved. She was a joke. It was grotesque that his wife should have a preference for this male-impersonator over the real thing. Then Bridie opened her mouth in his presence, declaring her love for his wife most insolently. At once he felt the potency of her character: the ice-blue eyes and the dignified tilt of her cropped head gave the illusion of beauty. He wondered for a time whether to solve the situation by seducing Bridie (for he could tell she was rattled by his sensitivity and good looks) but soon decided there was nothing in that. When he looked from Bridie to his wife, he was staggered at what he recognised. He saw her melted in the dazzle of her love and desire; all his yearning, early love for her revived. He begged her abjectly not to go. She hardly heard his voice in the spell of the McKearn. Hardening his heart, Gavin fought her for the children. The thrill of Val drove her out of his consciousness and only the sentimentality of alcohol or a trick of the light on Lizzie's (or worse, Sarah's) face brought her back. He didn't miss her any more.

He was on the wrong tack with Lizzie; Val felt it, and he saw the truth of her observations. Loving a child was not as easy as it had seemed in the days of visits to the park, the pantomime and roller-skating rink. He recalled that closeness of touch and understanding with nostalgia. Even Sarah seemed to have grown a mask. And yet Lizzie was still the same being as the riotous little character he used to hoist on to his shoulders along the Goyt Valley, grasping one ankle in either hand, while she played on his head like a tom-tom. She was troubled. She might do anything. And if he was not her friend, who was?

'Liz – Lizzie – can I come in?' He listened timidly at the door. The low throb of her music could be heard but there was no reply. 'I'm sorry, Lizzie, can we make it up?'

'She's gone,' said Sarah.

'Where has she gone?'

'I don't know. I saw her burning it up the road on her bike.'

'Christ,' said Gavin. He wrenched out the cork of a new bottle. In the normal course of events he'd have been able to relieve his anxieties by expressions of wrath and ridicule aimed at his ex-wife's bedfellow, who had now rendered such revenges dishonourable by abdicating (allegedly) to a bed at St Marcia's Hospice – and where that left Ruth was strictly speaking none of his business but he could not persuade himself that he absolutely didn't care. So he took another swig.

Several hours later, after a drunken nap, he had sobered up and Lizzie was still not home. His heart misgave him. There were sharks around cruising for soft young prey like Lizzie. He began to ring round friends and acquaintances.

Ruth thought she saw Lizzie flash past on a white mountain-bike, hair streaming; but it probably wasn't. She was seeing things all over the place these days. For instance, looking into the Norweb showroom window, she spotted the shadowy face of Elaine looking over her shoulder; and Bridie in the prime of health came striding along the high street towards her, tall and dashing, hands in the pockets of a navy jacket she hadn't worn for years but which was so very 'Bridie' she sometimes foolishly cuddled it in her friend's absence. When the woman came up close, she was a man and didn't look anything like Bridie. Once Ruth even caught sight of Gavin's girlfriend, and, to her surprise, it *was* Gavin's girlfriend, staring into a jeweller's window – a pretty, prefabricated woman caked in make-up. But mostly Ruth was seeing illusions and failing to register palpable facts, such as the lamp-post which came up and whacked her astoundingly on the nose and the plate-glass door of the bookshop which presented itself (until too late) as thin air.

Bridie was coming home. Joyous serenity alternated with a mad efflorescence of fears, grief, diffidence, unworthiness, and a peculiar, shameful wish to turn over in bed and go to sleep on the whole vile thing. Let it be someone else's nightmare. In an advertisement in the travel agent's window, luscious sun-tanned women with copious flesh invited you to join them under palm trees on white sand in the Canary Islands. Their eyes were closed; their lips and legs were parted, and a little dusting of sand smeared the inside of their thighs and the skin between armpit and bikini. *An easy lay*, thought Ruth; she'd like to lie easy, to be laid, to take her ease, to be lying easy on those shores far from reality beside the turquoise sea. The Manchester rain poured down. She jerked as if awakening from a half-sleep in that cheap fantasy-land. She was shivering. *Am I catching a cold?* The fear had become obsessive. Vitamin C; she must buy Vitamin C. How could she look after Bridie if she had a virus? If she gave Bridie a virus? She looked with morbid suspicion at her neighbours on the bus for signs of sneezing or Kleenex.

Bridie. Is. Coming. Home. She had informed Elaine of this last night over the phone, in a quiet, friendly manner, and in the ecstatic aftermath of the reconciliation between Bridie and herself, her sense of guilty malice toward Elaine had sunk down so low you hardly knew it was there.

'So don't worry,' she had assured Elaine. 'She'll be well taken care of. And on the same drugs régime as in the hospice. So no pain, which is the main thing. I'll keep in touch, of course.'

'And you, Ruth,' had replied the enviably firm contralto voice. 'How is it with you? I am *most* concerned for you.'

'Oh – fine,' she had sung. 'Don't worry about me.' The anxiety hadn't dawned then. That was still to come, after the hectic night lacking sleep.

'Did Bridie say . . . mention to you . . . anything she had asked me to do?' The voice had become uncharacteristically hesitant.

'No. How do you mean?'

'She seemed concerned, when I saw her, about the continuity of the Trust. I wondered if she'd mentioned it?'

'No . . . no. Nothing.'

'If you need anything . . . ring. Any time.'

Yesterday had been brimful of wonder because *Bridie is coming home*. But for the very same reason, today was hazardous, overwhelming. She told herself the news and the pavement slid out of true. In the tide of the crowd she stood nervously, nudged by oncoming elbows and shoulders. She breathed hard and it annoyed her that her heart beat so high, using up precious energy. What had she come out to shop for? God only knew. Painstaking effort had gone into compilation of a list of all the things Bridie might need but where was the list? She delved in her pockets fruitlessly.

The black cloudscape pressed down on the city, promising snow, and dark-coated people in caps and headscarves passed like mourners, heads low against the sleety wind. She might fail Bridie again, or Bridie might turn against her again, she might catch a cold and give it to Bridie, and, God, if she was worn out already, how would she cope at all?

The list. What would Bridie need? Bread, butter, tea, orange juice. Incontinence pads, talcum powder, stuff for bedsores. You couldn't get it all on prescription any more. She came out of the chemist's with a bulky bag, having thought to buy in addition some jars of Milupa semolina and other babyfood in case Bridie just couldn't digest a normal diet. It felt a lot better to be weighed down by bags of solid items Bridie might need. The bags held her down to earth as the wind drove her along the high street. Again a girl sailed past on a white mountain-bike, threading the parked cars and buses with death-defiant flair. A bus hooted, drawing out, as the mountain-bike sped past it. The cyclist's red scarf unfurled like a streamer. She bobbed out into the centre of the road without signalling, and executed a right turn just as the traffic lights turned red. A Post Office van blocked Ruth's sight.

She stood still in her tracks. The ghostly cyclist streaked across her inner eye again and again, fading each time. Dark bodies muscled past. The shop windows reflected shadowy images of these fleeting bodies. 'Cheadle Hulme couple commit suicide,' she read on the newsagent's board. Bridie passed Ruth without stopping to pass the time of day, dissolving into the crowd.

In the Trust shop, there was a quiet, browsing air after the roar of the street. Only the gentle jangle of a mobile made of translucent honesty pods in a delicate silver setting qualified the stillness, like that of a library or shrine. A few customers were musing over rushmats and dhurries, painted wooden bowls and ornaments, and appeared to have been loitering there forever, with nothing to do but fondle the pretty things with their eyes. Ruth blew on the mobile. Its gauzy leaves fluttered, tinkled and were still.

'Bridie's coming home,' she told Beth Hatch, softly.

'Oh, my dear . . . And is that good for you both, dear?'

189

'That is very good for us both. *Very* good, Beth.' The simplicity with which this could be said to the gentle Beth somehow sorted out the good seeds from the bad. For Beth in the wisdom of much caring (for her octogenarian mother dying of Alzheimer's and then for her husband with his stroke) knew most of what you might have to confide without its having to be spoken out loud. And if Ruth, laboriously, had tried to spell out the details of her remorse, inadequacy, anger, Beth would have said, *Well, that's natural, dear.* And so the confusion fell away in the course of the momentary dialogue between their eyes, and there stood the little heap of good seeds miraculously sorted from the discarded bad. 'Yes, it's wonderful,' said Ruth, and took both her hands. 'Things are ever so much better.'

'I'm glad for Bridie. Glad for you.' She returned the pressure of Ruth's hands but would say no more. She knew the finesse with which the tightrope-walker must balance and the dimensions of the abyss beneath.

'By the way, Ruth,' trumpeted Marjorie. 'That what-jamacallit – that vibrator thing – it sold within the first half hour. Thought you'd like to know. One pound fifty and a bargain at the price, I told the young man who bought it – and we had another jolly weird thing in after that, a long piece of flex with suckers coming out of it – I said to Pamela Quilleashe who was on with me at the time, "Do you think it's another of those *sexual aids*, Pamela?" but she said no, she couldn't see any such logical use for it and we sold it as a chest expander. Cup of tea, Ruth?'

Ruth declined the tea but stayed to browse. She bought a plain black pottery bowl as a 'welcome home' present for Bridie, and on the way out caught sight at the florist's of several bunches of daffodils which she would arrange in it, so that it would light the bedside cabinet like a lamp.

In her wake, a blast of traffic noise penetrated the shop; and in its aftermath the wind-chimes took up their dulcet, failing, inconclusive theme.

'You don't mean it,' said Elaine in a fury.

'I assuredly do,' replied Robyn Wilkie, with a sigh of what seemed to Elaine to be resignation, and angered her still more. 'Mind you, we've seen it coming for a long time. As surely you must. Ever since the Charity Commission began to murmur about Oxfam's political activities, we've just been waiting for our turn to come.'

'Look here,' said Elaine, and Lindsay looked up from her book at the rasping tone that had come into her friend's voice, clenching the phone till her arthritic knuckles whitened. She had not seen this side of Elaine and it interested her. Their book had made no progress at all in the last weeks. Lainey had simply put her pen down. Lindsay understood why, or thought she did – poor Bridie McKearn, principally, but also there was the sense of Elaine gathering her resources, reformulating her direction. Whatever that might turn out to be, Lindsay hoped to have a part in it. 'Now look here,' Elaine went on. 'This must quite simply not be allowed to happen. Have you tried . . .' and she went on to enumerate a number of courses of action from which Lindsay deduced that the Charity Commissioners were threatening to withdraw the Third World Trust's charitable status.

'What we must do is . . .', said Elaine.

'Yes, but I don't think you see the level of difficulty,' replied Robyn. 'We are being accused by the Government of destabilising the political set-up in our Asian work. You'd need to see all the paperwork. Shall I fax it through?'

'Yes, do.'

'You see, Bridie always said . . .'

'Well, I know that, Robyn,' riposted Elaine with some asperity. 'That's understood. But the business about women doing two-thirds of the world's work and receiving one-tenth of the world's income is not particularly the Trust's analysis, is it? – it's the official UN position. I think it needs to be put to the Charity Commissioners as follows . . .'

Lindsay closed her book and went into the kitchen to turn the oven down. Through the open door she could hear Elaine talking on, calmer now, thinking on her feet.

'Yes . . . yes,' she was saying. And toward the end of the conversation, she said, 'You see, if I'd been in Bridie's shoes at that time, I would never have angled things in quite that way.'

At length Elaine put the phone down and, accepting a cup of tea, she plumped down in her armchair, the cat instantly springing into her lap where it curled, purring in reverberant tones.

'This will not be allowed to happen,' she told Lindsay. 'Over my dead body.'

Lizzie freewheeled downhill toward Stockport Station, in the fumes of rush-hour traffic. Where she was destined or to whom she might turn she did not know and had scarcely considered, her only aim having been to pedal away from *it*. But *it* had tracked her through Heald Green and Edgeley, fixed to the back of her bike like a mocking fellow-traveller on a tandem as she ploughed through sleet and wind, scorching up the yellow line through puddles or weaving in and out of traffic jams. She had the impression *it* had been there from the beginning, but partially obscured by protective presences – her teddy bear Archie in her cot, and when she woke screaming in the night her mother and father in their dressing-gowns grumbling, 'What is it now, Lizzie?' She could not answer for she did not know what it was. She only knew *it was*. In those days *it* could not survive the snapping-on of the light. Company scared *it* away. With Sarah's birth, *it* got more of a hold. With her mother's departure, *it* nosed closer. With all she had learnt of the sufferings of the animals and the cruelty of our species, *it* had loomed tall and towering. In the hospice, *it* took the piteous form of Bridie McKearn, and sent her running for the cover of Dad and Dad said 'I'll stand by you – trust me, love', which Lizzie almost did; but Dad had turned against her and Mum had turned to Bridie McKearn and was part of *it*; and Martin was spinelessly in collusion with *it*.

On the grass verge beside the war memorial, several torches could be seen bobbing about. Lizzie coasted to a halt in front of the steps. NO BLOOD FOR OIL, their banner read in the sickly light. She wondered if her mother was there; a pang of longing that she should be there squeezed Lizzie's heart. If only they could stand side by side, in common cause, even if at a loss for words, *it* would draw off, baffled. But, no, Ruth was absent, and indeed numbers seemed severely depleted.

'Hello, Busy Lizzie,' said the old man who patrolled the kerb with his idiosyncratic home-made placards, which he waved at the passengers of buses pausing at the lights. He was being charged for non-payment of poll tax, Lizzie knew; was what they called in the area a 'character', practising mild forms of civil disobedience in Stockport precinct every Saturday morning of the year by mounting one-man protests against poverty, homelessness and the dismantling of the NHS. Occasionally Lizzie had stood by him to keep him company of a Saturday. 'Coming to join us, are you?'

'I wasn't,' said Lizzie. 'But I will if you like.'

'Come on then. Want to hold my placard for a bit while I light up?'

'Okay then.' Balancing her bike against the wall, she took the placard and waved it vaguely at the traffic.

'Get stuffed, you pacifist wallies.' A lorry driver took aim, with pursed mouth, and spat. The patriotic gob of spit landed just short of Lizzie's foot. She stepped back a little.

'You ought to be called up, you,' his mate shouted. 'They ought to fucking well put you on the fucking parade ground, you wankers.'

Lizzie waggled the placard up at them. She had a sudden image of herself and Frank Neild being called up; a very young girl and a very old man marched out across the Arabian desert to facilitate the war effort. The lights turned green and the wildly hooting lorry set off down the hill.

'Good soldiers we'd make, you and me,' said Frank and winked. 'Good deserters, any road.'

Lizzie giggled. *It* had drawn off. 'Not many people here tonight,' she said.

'No – it's a shame. The Socialist Workers said they couldn't conscientiously come any more. An ideological objection. No, not to candles . . . Gina said to them, "No selling newspapers", and they said it was their democratic right to sell their paper where they liked and Gina said, "If you want to set up as a newsagent's kindly do it elsewhere" so they all voted unanimously to censure Gina as a bourgeois lackey and Gina said, "I don't give a monkey's if you want to call me a bourgeois lackey, that's fine by me, but this is a peace group protest against the Gulf war and not a propaganda stall, sorry" – so off they went. Pity really. Now you're the only young person left.'

He finished his pipe and took back his placard. Lizzie was offered a candle in a jar, which she accepted, and stood on the steps with the main group. The scent of mingled pipe-smoke and candlewax disguised the traffic fumes. Talk was of the Allied bombing of the air raid shelter in Baghdad, from which the cremated corpses of women had been lifted throughout the day.

'So much for their "smart weapons". So much for their so-called "surgical strikes".'

'Do you think they didn't know it was a shelter? They said they thought it was a military installation.'

'Of course they knew.'

'I don't think they knew. If they'd known they wouldn't have bombed it.'

'Oh, come off it.'

'No – really. They don't want the bad publicity. They'd never have courted a bad press.'

'Saw something about *you* in the papers, Lizzie, didn't we?'

'Mmm.' Lizzie shifted in embarrassment, staring at her candle. The manure exploit had brought a humiliation which heavily outweighed private glory.

'By all accounts she dumped a load of ripe horse-dung on the town hall doorstep.'

'Coals to Newcastle,' someone said, and they all laughed.

A car drew up with a screech of brakes. The driver slammed the door and stared up through the gloom. He bounded up the steps and grasped Lizzie by the wrist. 'How *dare* you?' he roared. 'Don't you know she's underage?'

'I *beg* your pardon?' said Gina.

'Damned irresponsible birdbrained do-bloody-gooders exploiting susceptible young people.' Gavin's voice was high and frantic. 'I've been looking for you for literally hours. *Hours*. How *dare* you?' he turned on Gina.

'She comes with her mother. We naturally assumed . . .'

'You assumed! You *assumed*! Well, there'll be no more assuming.' He yanked her viciously down the steps. 'Assuming,' he stated madly, 'is over.'

'Wait a minute – I've left my bike, Dad – my bike – over

there against the wall.' As he involuntarily released her wrist, she broke away, vaulted on to the bike and made off down the hill. Gavin ran but could not catch up. By the time he had got the car going and driven in her wake to the roundabout, the white bike and its shadowy rider had disappeared.

Lizzie raced head down, through a labyrinth of ill-lit back-alleys. She no longer knew where she was. The bike sailed her over cobbles and down kerbs into the black mouths of unknown alleys, past dustbins that gleamed in the moonlight, and round corners into areas of grosser dereliction, where terraced windows were boarded over, and the gardens and paths were strewn with refuse, old cardboard boxes, broken glass and tumbling papers and cans, through which the bike wheels forged their path. A vandalised housing estate stretched out before her, with eyeless sockets where the windows had been. Over all lay a reek of smoke from small fires started either by the council or by vandals to destroy the belongings the tenants had ditched. Lizzie stopped by a still smouldering fire, in which the charred remnants of someone's household could still be discerned: a wardrobe, a vacuum cleaner, a mattress reduced to its metalwork. Lizzie inspected the fire in the cold fluorescence of one of the few lamps not yet stoned out of its fitting.

She swept the dark horizons with her eyes. Running north to south on a raised embankment was the railway line, on which a train was rattling its way from Manchester, each window a cell of yellow light. Over Manchester the black clear night was brightened by a sulphurous glow, and a stippling of orange lights stretched south as far as the eye could see. The derelict estate lay in a basin of viscous shadow, a site for human and material waste. The burnt-out shell of a joy-rider's car stood at an angle to an uninhabited and uninhabitable house with a stoved-in roof; but to her surprise Lizzie saw that people were still living in the adjoining semi. Lights shone from net-curtained windows and canned laughter from a television show could be heard. Further down the street toward the railway line, the demolition squads had been in: half a dozen houses were reduced to rubble.

At least she knew where she was. She'd looked down upon it before from the train, for this was a common place for the signal box to maroon local trains while the Inter-City expresses burst past. She'd seen it as a community with washing on the lines and an elderly man who kept rabbits in a hutch; watched it collapse, as home after home was boarded up; she'd seen the iron demolition ball on the chain smite the flimsiness of the walls and all the children on the train shrieked 'Oh!' in delight and, pressing their noses against the grubby pane, cried out for more. The lads had been scavenging and committing arson, blatantly, in full light of day, and one lady said, 'Goodness me, they can't be more than ten or eleven years old', and a pin-striped man with plump hands and a heavy gold signet-ring mentioned Kenneth Baker and said it was a public scandal, their parents should be fined for not keeping them under proper control – gross irresponsibility – they should be locked up in his opinion. Nobody replying, he raised the *Telegraph* against the unwholesome sight, banging out the fold, and Lizzie studied the hairy space between his navy blue sock and his trouser bottom. She looked at the court news on the back of his paper and learned that Queen Elizabeth the Queen Mother had been wearing a lemon-yellow coat and hat while visiting an Army barracks.

The moon slid from behind a cloud; it cast a milky light on Lizzie's white bike and on the mist of her condensing breath. It was raw and cold, and what was she doing here in this godforsaken hole? The cold numbed her memory of earlier events: anger and grief were displaced by hunger and cold.

People slept in cardboard boxes, she knew that. Homeless people with nowhere to go and nothing to live on but beggary, theft and dole. She had thought, when it was solely an abstraction dreamed in the luxury of a centrally heated interior, that she could easily endure such privations. But it was not so. She could not imagine bedding down famished in one of those vandalised houses. The very thought made her want to retch. The strangeness of the place, and the world beyond the abandoned place, and of herself small as a microbe on the great blue eyeball of the globe, which itself was tinier than an atom in the expanse of space, annihilated her sense of self. *It* was here. *Its* home was here. She would have run for her life if her knees had not been melted by the combination of cold and fatigue. No other thought than self-preservation occupied her mind as she forced her jellied muscles to grapple the bike back up the hill and out of the estate.

There was a call-box but it was vandalised. Lizzie thumped the coin-box with her gloved fist. Outside a shadowy man loomed, with a lopsided grin on his face. A shaven, stubbly head; a leather jacket. She took a deep breath and plunged out. There seemed to be another man behind him, or was it only a tree? The man barred Lizzie's way, and when she moved in silent terror sideways, he moved as well, as if nimbly dancing. Alcohol was on his breath.

He spoke and she screamed. Abandoning her bike, she took to her heels, heart pounding, legs dead weights. She dared not look back to see if he was following. Echoing footsteps pursued her down a labyrinth of alleys.

There was another phone kiosk on the junction of a deserted side-street. If he trapped her in the call-box, she'd be finished. She ran past. Then tore back.

'Dad. It's me. I don't know where I am.'

'Lizzie. For God's sake – where are you? . . . it's Lizzie, Val

'. . . on the phone. Lizzie, will you please, please, come home? . . . she's crying . . . Liz, it will be okay, I promise. Where are you, love? Just tell Dad where you are?'

'I don't know. I don't know the place. I'm in a call-box. I can't see a road name. I think there's a man after me. I don't know though, there might not be. *Dad!*'

'I'm coming, lovely. Just tell me the general area. We'll find you. Be calm, love. Tell me the phone number.'

'*Dad!*'

'You're all right – you're all right. Can you tell us where you might be near?'

'Near the estate you see from the train. *Dad* – the money's running out.'

'Just stay there. I'll ring you back. If there's a man, knee him in the groin. Very, very hard.'

'I've lost my bike,' she wailed.

'Just stay put – someone will collect you. I'll ring you back. We'll soon have you home.'

Sarah, with a certain constitutional scepticism, observed the palaver as the prodigal daughter was received home at the hands of the police woman and the fatted calf in the form of toasted granary bread with peanut butter and hot chocolate was served up. She was naturally glad for Lizzie's sake that she had avoided getting murdered and consigned to the Ship Canal in a black plastic bag – though being an only child had significant attractions and she had often fantasised Lizzie's removal. She did not particularly resent the attention her sister had melo-dramatically wrestled from their father, for she knew herself to be hands-down his favourite without having to compete. But she had minded seeing his pain and knowing that she could do nothing to alleviate it. She had come over to where he sat and smoothed his forehead with her palms but, though he said 'That's a good girl', he seemed not to notice her. She went behind him and massaged the tense muscles of his neck and shoulders with her thumbs. His eyes were staring and his eyebrows raised in stress. He started at every knock and phone call, and chain-smoked cigarettes which smelt nasty and which he had given up years ago. He shouted on the phone at Sarah's mother and ranted at Val who had come in rather tipsy and was irritated at the hoo-hah.

'I shouldn't waste your energy worrying over her. She'll come home when she's hungry – she likes her creature comforts, does Elizabeth,' she advised. *Bald*, she thought, *he'll be totally bald in ten years' time.*

Then after all this rumpus, in came Lizzie, looking dazed and stupefied. Wrapped in a tartan blanket, she had been placed by the fire with a steaming drink and coddled and cuddled; and Dad cried, and Lizzie cried, and he half carried her up to bed like a baby with unbelievable fuss, and nobody asked her *Why? Why did you put us through all this?* In return for all the trouble she'd caused, Lizzie received a display of unearned and unqualified love. It was hardly fair.

10

So it was an ordinary, everyday thing, to die. Each day millions of candles were blown out and millions of new tapers were lit. We knew this; we had always known it perfectly well. Why then, when our turn arrived, or that of the person we loved, did it come as such a bombshell? 'It is impossible – it literally can't be true,' we thought, and right up to the ineluctable end, we refused to believe it. Ruth pored over the sleeping Bridie like a reader over some very absorbing book, a book which she must finish and commit to memory now if ever, for it was a vanishing text whose meanings must pass away. The face in the dim golden lamplight had lost its deathly colour and waxen texture; on the left side it was gilded, on the right in shadow. Bridie looked very quiet, very peaceful. That was good. That was comforting. Ruth fed in sips and crumbs at the parsimonious left-overs of life, and found she could live, even thrive, on these emergency rations. The repose of Bridie's face held something of the quality of a Dutch portrait, a Rembrandt: the quiet that included and transcended ultimate suffering. The shadow of her hair on her forehead confirmed the light.

Time had come to a spacious and merciful pause. Whereas elsewhere the marching armies of clock hands might be advancing to their metronomic beat on every front, here in Bridie's study the clock didn't tick. The travel clock had been allowed to run down ages ago, just after the plants had died. Then Ruth had been too preoccupied to care; now she didn't need the time of day. Living profoundly and calmly in the moment could dilate the secret eternity latent in it like a dormant seed in its husk. Looking attentively at her friend's face, learning it by heart (for time would resume all too soon), Ruth focused her contemplation on every nuance of Bridie. Those gentle eyes, the strong jaw, the individual arch of the eyebrow, the faint down on her upper lip, the high forehead very little lined, the grey cropped hair: all these were due to be erased. It was hard to credit. The day was coming when this beautiful person would no longer be here. Or anywhere. She would be nowhere. Would not be found, however indefatigably one searched. Would not be. And this was ordinary; banal; warp to life's weft. She shook her head and the movement changed the light on Bridie's face, revealing the corner of her mouth, which seemed to smile enigmatically in sleep.

What if anything did that mean? What did it actually mean to be Bridie? All their five loving years, Ruth had puzzled over that query. If only one could, for five minutes, move out of self and into the body space of one's friend, seeing through those eyes and feeling with those nerves: that would be truly to *know*. Not seeing through a glass darkly. She had aspired to that condition. In the passionate tenderness of their lovemaking there had been a sense of mutual journey, across infinite reaches toward the inner space of the other person. Sometimes through whole days they had lain there entangled in one another, just looking, witnessing, seeing deep into one another's eyes – seeing – what? – you did not know afterwards what exactly you had seen. It was not her own reflection in the pupil of Bridie's eye; it was not Bridie's mirroring vision of herself that she saw. But something beyond, within. There were no words: words were crass, demeaning, for they depended on a fiction of someone's having done something to someone else. But the vision faded, unmarked. *The middle wall of partition*, Bridie once said, *is down. A house not built with hands*, she said. *The living tables of the heart.* Ruth remembered these Biblical phrases. They were more apposite than any other words, and if there was God (which there was not) God was there in those words; or rather, those words were all there was of God.

'Hello . . . is it you . . . my darling – have I been asleep?' Bridie's heavy lids opened.

'Fast asleep, and so peaceful.'

'What's the time?'

'I don't know.'

'How is it with you? Why are you crying?'

'I didn't know I was.' Ruth rubbed the palms of her hands against her cheeks and found them wet.

'Don't have bad thoughts.'

'I don't know that I was. In fact I'm sure I wasn't. I was looking at you and thinking how beautiful you are – *how* beautiful – and oh Bridie I was feeling such a peace in my heart . . . that we've had one another . . . we have one another . . . in life.'

'Well, I'm home to take care of you, Ruthie, so you needn't have bad thoughts or if you do wake me and tell me, I rely on you to do that. My dear darling. I'm sorry I was grouchy earlier.' Her voice was hoarse and breathing a struggle, but her mind seemed to herself a marvel of clarity. Life had an aim and purpose, to which her whole effort was directed. To take care of Ruth. She could do this, though appearances were all against it. Ruth must not be left with nothing. *Must not.*

The journey home had been a fearful ordeal. As they fetched her up into the ambulance, the shock of the fresh air after the removal from the ward's dull haven had felt like a violent uprooting. Her roots came away with an inward shriek. As the engine started, her body throbbed, and each swerve and stop jolted her unbearably. They carried her in to her home that was not her home, for it was all precipices and jagged edges, and busy patternings that played on her eyeball in a phantasmagoria of lurid colours. Nigel went, and she did not want him to go. Nigel knew how to care and cater for her. But Nigel went. He left her stranded on a bed that was hopelessly wrong: too soft, too unsupportive. Skewed at an angle, she had to instruct the nerve-shattered Ruth in how to lay her comfortably. Finally, six pillows were wedged around her and 'It's not right,' she muttered peevishly, 'but if it's the best you can do . . .' Ruth in her agitation was near to tears.

'Let me try again. I'm sorry.'

'No, it's okay. You did your best.'

She looked round the room: desk, typewriter, lamp, phone, bookshelves, ornaments, Anaglypta wallpaper painted a garish rust colour. She didn't like it. It was all too demanding on her eyes. It wasn't like the nice nullity of the hospice. The daffodils on the bedside cabinet were especially unacceptable. They burned in the vase like naked electric light bulbs held up to a naked eye. She tried to blink them off but they left an afterglare.

'Can't you take those things away?' she asked Ruth irritably.

'What things?' Ruth looked round.

'Those flowers. And all the other things. There are too many *things*.'

Thus Ruth brought a cardboard box and loaded it with all the supernumerary items condemned by Bridie. When the room was stark enough, Bridie said, wearily, 'That's better. That's quieter,' though she didn't much like the dark wooden shelves left exposed by the removals; but accepted that you couldn't start dismantling fixtures and fittings, and perhaps she'd get used to them.

'Shall we have a cup of tea?' Ruth asked; and Bridie knew that Ruth had gone off to have a good cry, though not that she went and screamed into a towel in the cellar, to work off the anguish of her fear of inadequacy and hurt at the rejection of her loving offerings.

When Ruth returned with the tea, Bridie was much gentler and less disorientated. She sipped her tea through a straw with every appearance of enjoyment.

'This is what I've missed,' she said. 'Ruth Asher's best PG Tips. Do you remember . . . when we had that Cambridge chappie over and he wondered whether it was Darjeeling or Assam? . . . And you said, "Well actually it's Co-op Own Blend." His *face*.' Ruth laughed, and then Bridie, feeling for her hand, said, 'Just give me a little while to settle down, my dear – and never you worry – it'll be *all right*.' And the kind, ordinary way she said 'My dear' reassured Ruth more than volumes of protestation. She slept until the nurse came, and then she slept again. Ruth could hardly permit herself to go out of the room without wanting to rush back in, saying to herself over and over in her heart, *Bridie is home, my Bridie is back.*

Bridie awoke from curious dreams of being at home, to find herself at home. In her dream she had scrambled up, yawned, stretched and rubbed her eyes, and, wrapping her maroon towelling dressing-gown around her, crossed to the window, peering through the gap between the curtains to see dawn breaking on her garden. The dew was on the grass and swathes of mist lay under the apple trees like an exhalation; the earliness of the vaporous bluish-grey light drew attention to the absolute stasis of trees and bushes, flower-beds and fences. It was her last day . . . she should appreciate it. Bridie's eye roved, free as it seemed of her body. She had encouraged ivy and honeysuckle to wreathe each window: now they were hung with beads of moisture, suspended in the timeless second before falling, and all containing fortune-telling images of the refracted face of Bridie. The gardener in her stirred. She would very much have liked to wander out into the damp chill of the early morning garden, in her muck-encrusted old boots that stood by the fridge at the back door, making a dark green trail out over the dewy turf. But . . . it came to her with the shock of the obvious . . . although so early, it was already too late. She withdrew, to re-enter her sleeping body.

She awoke to a heaving sea of consciousness on which she tossed and drifted, flotsam without mental aim or purpose. All was garbled, a churning welter of words which had lost their designation and floated spuriously on the surface of her mind. It was all *Unsinn . . . néant . . . nox . . . nichts . . . njet . . . nowt . . .* a sea of unmeaning. From time to time she went under: the curdled waters closed over her and she dozed before emerging, to be once more at the mercy of the brew of thoughts that led nowhere.

She had not the energy to sigh. It was all folly, it was all vanity and filth, and all she wanted was to be out of it.

Later she woke again, her mind amazingly clear. On the pillow next to her Ruth was fast asleep, having worn herself out with hovering, tiptoeing, laughing and crying, and generally turning herself inside out in the bitter-sweet thrill of Bridie's homecoming. Ruth's face was in shadow, turned towards Bridie's, the lamp behind her so that the rings and curls of hair burned with a coppery glow. Bridie, with a deep pang of tenderness, read the testament of the thin-skinned face which seemed to her, from this perspective, so open to injury. It was better and easier for herself, a thousand times easier, that she would never know they had parted. *How will you fend, my lamb?* All she could do was to bless her from the depths of her heart and commit herself again to putting everything into making these last days and weeks a time of benediction.

She might go mad again, for all that. She might turn against Ruth and spew gall and hate over her. She might well. She could feel the sick part of her brain churn, even now, with the vomit of abuse. If she went out of control, she might . . . Perhaps it would have been better to stay in the hospice and let Ruth see her go gracefully, at a distance. But no, no, the drugs would stop it. If there were the slimmest chance of a good God, she would humble herself to pray to him for help, but there was not; Elaine had thought a goddess . . . the earth . . . from whom we came, to whom we returned . . . she might try applying to a goddess. But she doubted it. One must fall back on the practical, down-to-earth resources, such as morphine. Such as partnership that bore it out to the bitter end.

Ruth turned slightly, so that she was lying on her back, one hand open on the pillow beside her cheek, palm upward. Bridie saw the plain gold ring on her third finger, the marriage ring they liked to call it.

They had bought identical rings in Samuel's in the Arndale Precinct in Manchester. 'Your cheapest wedding-rings, please – one each,' they told the assistant, who gave them such a look. Bridie had stared him seriously in the eye, but Ruth had burst out laughing, and 'Yes, we're going to be spliced,' she informed the assistant, who went and muttered to his colleague, and came back with a navy-blue velvet tray and the colleague, who made an elaborate pretence of dusting some silver carriage clocks while listening in. Bridie had tried to get it all over and done with. She could not see the necessity of any prolonged performance. Ruth, however, tried on and took off, hummed and hahed, and compared the £22.50 plain band of gold with the

£19.90 plain band of gold, until an impatient queue of would-be brides and grooms had gathered.

'What do you think of this?' Ruth had asked the assistant, displaying Bridie's reluctant hand, with the £22.50 version.

'It depends on Madam's preference,' said the young man, fingering his cufflinks and disguising his snorting giggle as a cough.

'But don't you think,' Ruth went on, 'it's a little *broad*?'

'What does Madam feel?' the young man enquired of Bridie. 'Is it the sort of thing Madam had in mind?'

'They both look exactly the same to me,' Bridie muttered. 'Let's get on with it.'

'Oh no, Bridie, this one is thinner – see? – and it's got to suit both of us. After all, we're both getting married.'

The young man choked.

'Well, you choose, Ruth – or rather don't choose. We'll take the cheaper one. What did you say – £19.90. Yes, two of those.' She submitted to having her finger measured, glaring severely at Ruth who was in one of her manic phases and was looking over the shoulders of the fiancés next to her and observing, 'God, I wouldn't pay £150 for *that*.'

'I could cheerfully throttle you,' she said to Ruth when they'd got outside the shop. 'I hate *fuss*. Why did you have to make such a song and dance about it?'

'Don't you think it's worth a song and dance?' Ruth asked, and went high-flying along the precinct like a balloon on a string.

'I don't know why we need rings anyway,' Bridie had grumbled, stomping along behind. It was only ever the inner truth that mattered. And why would they want to conform to the certificating practices of the heterosexual world in any case? And yet she found that she not only got used to the ring but that her hand felt wrong without it. Now, looking at the ring on

Ruth's finger, and the identical ring on the wasted flesh of hers, which only didn't fall off because of her bony joint, a gentle feeling of peace descended upon her. She managed to reach out her hand and rest it on Ruth's, which squeezed it in her sleep.

But now she was falling again, her mind full of ill-digested matter turning over and over, tumbling down through endless space. It was a horror all too familiar. She tried . . . to keep . . . her eyes . . . open . . . so as to stabilise herself. The bilious room rocked, it rocked from side to side. *Peace, be still*. She lay in her cold sweat and tried to . . . and managed to . . . focus on the window, with its statue of Demeter and a vase full of dried yellow grasses, next to a bookcase piled with files and loose papers. She steadied the image by force of will but suddenly (just as she was beginning to find repose) the whole thing tilted bizarrely leftwards. She closed her eyes; hung in space; fell.

No, said Bridie to herself, *can't have more of this*. She arrested her flight and again opened her eyes. *Yes . . . my study* – but its atmosphere was no longer friendly. Something had collapsed within her that allowed her to feel at home here. There was no meaning or orientation. The room was all dots and blurs, messy smears of light and shadow. No centre . . . there was no centre. But it was not frightening – just pointless and infinitely dreary.

But I am Bridie, Bridie McKearn, she reminded herself.

It was all humbug . . . it was all illusion . . . Bridie McKearn included. She saw that. Her forehead seemed to bulge forward, balloon out, with this pregnant knowledge. Her mighty brain knew it all. Her head was so big it would surely burst.

She quickly shut her eyes to allow the head to shrink. She was falling through fathoms of water into depths of cold ignorance, with the silt and detritus of perceptions dropping all around her, perceptions that died in the second before they could become thoughts. Abortive queries eddied and sank down, and all was silent in Bridie's mind.

'Bridie,' she thought a voice said, and she thought she opened her eyes to attain a shallow form of vision. She viewed the surface skin on the world but not the interior modelling which might give it mass and meaning.

'Bridie, your injection,' said the voice.

Then a hush fell on Bridie's inner mind. Its depths composed themselves. There was no question of fear.

When Ruth awoke it was broad daylight, and for once not raining. Bridie hardly stirred, even when she gently turned her to relieve the pressure. She looked serene lying there. Ruth kissed her temple and smoothed the hair back.

Ruth brought a pot of tea back to bed. The first full day of homecoming. Five years ago she had awoken for the first time in bed with Bridie, to find her leaning up on one elbow looking down on her with cherishing eyes. The novelty of it came back inexpressibly. She had gazed back into Bridie's gaze with a profound knowledge of her security in this love, this bed. Neither spoke aloud but there seemed a kind of far-fetched, long-lost communication of the eyes. They dwelt upon one another's faces. From earliest childhood there had been difficulty in holding a gaze. You looked away, or towards, or at, but seldom unreservedly into a person's eyes. Only when transiently breast-feeding Lizzie had Ruth recalled with a tender shock the circuit of that exclusive gaze. All the beauty and acceptance in the world were to be found there; for she saw, with absolute authority of conviction, that the gift she had tentatively brought was considered worthy and most welcome.

'So it's you,' Ruth had said, breaking the spell.

'It's me – and you.' Bridie had leant down to kiss her sleepy mouth and spoken hushed words of endearment, and Ruth had felt the morning-warmth of Bridie's full breast through the cotton of their night-shirts. The sensuous kindness of her touch, as Bridie's hands rippled through her hair and stroked her neck and shoulders, had filled her with wonder. She kissed Bridie's eyes, cradling her head in both her hands, and they gazed again, and tenderly loved again, until finally Bridie sprang up, saying, 'I'm starving, aren't you? – we'd better eat,' and when she was gone the room seemed full of radiance. Sunlight pooled on the wall next to the bed, and leafy branches cast wavering tendrils of shadow on to its reflection. The light cut out a triangular segment of a print of Pissarro's *The Hermitage*, intensifying the brilliance of its green pasture. Ruth sat up in bed, arms clasped about her bare knees, and marvelled.

Later had come the shynesses and hesitations: the difficulty of dressing and undressing in front of this new person; Bridie getting flustered over the boiling of an egg, because she felt awkward about cooking, so she said, always had and always would.

'Well, let me do it,' Ruth had urged, amused. 'I don't mind cooking.'

But no, Bridie would not have that. *She* wanted to do it for Ruth; no argument. And so they both sat down to bullet-hard eggs, and Ruth wondered how you ate such a horrible egg politely, and Bridie, digging in her spoon, remarked, 'Reminds you of those marble eggs you can buy as souvenirs in Athens.'

'At least we know the salmonella's cooked out of it.'

'You don't have to eat it if it's too awful.'

But Ruth loyally did eat the marble egg. She ate the love in the egg, as she consumed the spirit of five years of Bridie's culinary abominations. Afterwards Bridie had gone off to her study to type up some recommendations for the funding of projects in Bihar for health, pure water, family planning and opposition to the dowry system. Ruth had realised for the first time the extent to which she would have to share Bridie with her work. It had not disconcerted her. There had been a goldenness as she heard the typewriter murmuring in the room above; then silences which were Bridie thinking, then further bouts of thrumming. In the pauses and in the audible passages Bridie was intuited and known. Even now, when Bridie would never again sit at her desk, one naturally thought of her as getting on with her work.

Today the sunlight remembered those earliest days. A sense of *déjà vu* lay over the garden as Ruth drew the curtains to see the weak sunlight of late February temper the rigour of the trees with implications of the green to come. She had not previously noticed that the crocuses, with their silver-streaked leaves and candle-like buds, had already made headway through the soil and were standing in clusters ready to unfold. 'You go around with your eyes shut, you who are supposed to be such a Green girl,' Bridie had joshed her. 'And if I didn't point things out to you, you'd never know they were there.' That was true too. She saw the shadow part of the dappled world, the negative rather than the positive. The hole in the ozone layer met her upturned eyes rather than the blue glow of the air; the species that became extinct every hour absorbed her mind at the expense of present beauty.

That must not be. It was an absurd error of judgment. Bridie still slept soundly. Downstairs, Ruth slid her feet into Bridie's heavy gardening-boots, which had stood half a year by the fridge, still encrusted with last year's soil. The boots, which were two sizes too large, lacked laces. She shuffled out of the back door. The sun had paled behind a skein of cloud but the forsythia hedge, with its hosts of yellow buds, gave the illusion of a sunny day. Further down the long narrow garden, Bridie's lily-pond gave signs of ulterior life, as bubbles popped at the surface from undivulged lives in the mud. Her own face met her with a ripple of a smile: a shadowy, staring woman in a striped night-shirt with folded arms, bending low. A black and white cat shot away, scrabbling over the fence into next door's garden. She plodded on again in Bridie's clodhopping boots. Birdsong from the beech and apple trees mingled with the quiet. Down here there were buds of crocuses literally everywhere. It would be a sea of colour in a week or two's time. So thickly did they grow that she had to navigate the boots carefully amongst them to avoid crushing them. How did such delicate creations manage to survive, wrapped only in thin-spun sheaths? They didn't last long.

Perhaps she could carry Bridie out to view the crocuses before they perished. Turning, she looked back to the house. The distance seemed disproportionately long. Bridie's window on the first floor was a blank, black pane: the drainpipe to the left curled like a question mark on the redbrick wall. Something about the expression of the house agitated her with a sense of Bridie's helplessness in there. What was she doing, prowling off? An aeroplane roared in the sky in a long, slow arc, trailing double streams of smoke. A breeze shivered the parchment leaves of the beech hedge; the rustle began at one end and eerily passed Ruth by as it blew in one gust the length of the hedge. Taking off the impeding boots, Ruth raced back barefoot through the wet grass.

Bridie was coughing up phlegm and blood. The saturated pillow was scarlet. With trembling, icy hands, Ruth took hold of Bridie, whose coughing had turned to spasms of retching. Later she told Bridie about the crocuses but Bridie just looked, with exhausted eyes that were directed toward Ruth but appeared to focus on a point just beyond her head.

The district nurse came, and shook her head.

Ruth turned her face away.

'It's for the best,' said the nurse kindly.

'Yes,' said Ruth, meaning *no*.

No. She had it firmly in her mind that Bridie must live to see the crocuses. If the crocuses were still there, it was not the end.

'It'll be a blessing, the sooner it comes. She'll be out of pain,' said the nurse, seeing Ruth's face struggling.

'Yes,' said Ruth, but she thought *no*. The longer she had Bridie here, the better. Every moment of Bridie's life was of fabulous, priceless worth.

'I'll look in again. The injection should give her several hours of sleep. And, look, I'll leave you this pain-killer. Be careful with it now, it's strong. No children in the house, are there?'

'Oh no.'

She took the bottle of red mixture and placed it in the bathroom cabinet. She could not seem to blink its bloody colour off her eye.

At four o'clock Bridie awoke and smiled at Ruth.

'Had a bit of a turn,' she whispered. 'Okay now. You okay?'

'Yes, my darling. Yes. Have you got any pain?'

'No.'

She lay and looked at Ruth as if deliberating.

'Crocuses?' she asked. Her head was pillowed on Ruth's palm; their ring-hands were joined. She gently fractionally stroked Ruth's hand with her thumb. Her breath was laboured but she was very much herself. She had heard about the crocuses; heard and understood.

'Yes – pools of them, Bridie love – down the far end under the trees. I don't think they've ever been so profuse.'

'You saw?'

'Yes, I went out in your old boots. I want to take you out to see them when you feel like it.'

'Good.'

They gazed into one another's eyes.

'You are still the strong one – the healing one,' said Ruth, and the tears ran down. 'I need you so much.'

'Both of us . . . sheep and shepherd both.'

The nurse came in again.

'Well, she's rallied. I'd never have believed it. Her pulse is steadier.'

Triumph shone from Ruth's face.

'Don't build your hopes too high. I mean that kindly. It can't be long.'

'I live – we live – in the moment,' said Ruth. She saw, with astounding lucidity, that the moment had always been the only place to live, but she had never until now stumbled on that truth.

Sarah and Lizzie watched the news in silence. We had won the war.

'It's nice that they're free,' said Sarah, as the Kuwaitis in wild scenes of jubilation welcomed the first of their liberators into Kuwait City. They flung their arms around their American brothers and kissed them. They leapt, sang, fired rifles into the air, pressed their car-horns and capered in the tank-strewn streets. 'Isn't it nice, Lizzie?'

Lizzie didn't say anything. You couldn't talk to Sarah about real things. Sarah was just a child. She couldn't see behind the thin film of celluloid which screened our vision, neither could she hear the high-pitched scream behind the creamy voices which broadcast the things we wanted to hear. She drummed her fingers on the table, staring moodily at the box.

'*I* think it's nice,' said Val. 'It must be a super feeling to know you're safe and the country's free. And hardly any lives lost – that's the great thing.'

Lizzie, who had more or less stopped speaking to Val since her attempt at escape, shot her a look of scornful pity. The resident lunatic – Dad's performing monkey – it was hardly worth contradicting such a creature's jabber. More like a parrot on its perch actually, in that red, blue and yellow outfit, with nails like claws.

'Pretty Polly,' remarked Lizzie.

'Ooh, look at that.' Sarah winced at the sight of the oil fires' billowing black smoke. 'They say you can't see the sun, they say it's midnight all day long, and the children will die of lung cancer.'

'Wicked. Such a wicked waste. Eight hundred fires,' said Val with awe.

All that money going up in smoke. And then the way the Iraqis had released millions of gallons of oil into the Gulf, fouling the water and killing the wildlife. 'And those poor cormorants,' she added, shooting a cunning look sidelong at Lizzie. 'And the turtles. They say many species will be wiped out altogether.'

Lizzie did not respond. She chewed at a hangnail with an air of indifference. The woman was a creep in a nation of creeps. She thought no lives had been lost because only about eight Brits had died; she could look at the thousands of cremated bodies of the fleeing Iraqi conscripts stretching mile after mile up the Basra road and not see human beings. The 'turkey-shoot', the pilots called it.

'Gobble gobble. What about the turkeys?' she suddenly enquired, piercing Val with a hawk-eye.

'Really, Lizzie, I wonder about you sometimes. You can be very childish.'

'You worry about the turtles. I worry about the turkeys. That's all.'

Val shook her head. 'I'm sorry, Lizzie, I don't know what you're on about. Probably some private joke I'm not in on.' She smoothed her skirt down over her knee with one multicoloured arm. She was not absolutely sure about this sweater: it might be a bit garish. Still, it was spring – almost.

'Pieces of eight, pieces of eight!'

'*Lizzie*,' Sarah hissed, jabbing her sister with her elbow. 'Stop it.' Behind the severity lurked a giggle, waiting to pop.

'Who's a clever girl then? Pretty Polly!' squeaked Lizzie.

Sarah burst out laughing, trying to smother it behind her hand.

'Cut it out,' said their father, and sat down next to Val with his pipe. Immediately Lizzie cut it out. Tricky and inconclusive negotiations were underway since the occasion of Lizzie's last enormity, between their love for and hostility to one another. Somewhere in the middle of this had been the uncertain quantity of Val, whose swervings about between the intention to quit and the attraction of staying had been partially resolved by the renewal of Gavin's ability to make the bedsprings quiver.

'He's made a big mistake, has Bush,' he confided to Val. 'A big mistake.'

'How so?'

He had on his rugged ex-commando air, which made Val think of her Paddy Ashdown fantasy; made her remember his maleness shafting (she savoured the word, *shafting*) into her, from behind, last night, and how she watched them in the dressing-table mirror as he knelt up, thrusting. She blushed. There were two Gavins, one in the apron holding a spatula, cooking for the girls; the other the muscular hero commanding entry.

'He shouldn't have stopped. He should have gone all the way

through to Baghdad. Having started, he shouldn't have given way until he'd finished Saddam off. No matter what the cost. That's the logic of war. It sounds tough, even brutal, but in the end it would make the world a safer, more peaceful place.' He sat back, biting on the stem of his pipe.

'As a matter of fact, I think you're right,' said Lizzie. Everyone stared. 'Once you've stepped into blood that far, you might as well go on. You can't go back.' Her class had moved on from *Othello* to *Macbeth* and his New World Order; they had been to see the play at the Royal Exchange Theatre and she thought it very realistic, which the teacher had said was not the point.

'Anyway,' put in Sarah smoothly. 'It *is* nice that the Kuwaitis are free.'

Outside Ruth's front window gangs of youths passed that evening, swigging from beer cans and singing the National Anthem. They were brandishing a huge Union Jack. The neighbour over the way who had put out bunting to celebrate the victory hastily took it in again, so as to dissociate himself from the football crowd atmosphere of the section of the nation's youth which was at large in the avenue.

'Rule Britannia, Britannia rules the waves . . .' bawled the chorus of patriots.

'Bri-tons never ne-ver NEVER . . .'

They vanished round the corner, diminuendo. But soon they were back, crooning of Jerusalem in England's green and pleasant land. Celebrating by bestowing chip papers and beercans on a selection of law-abiding lawns and hedges, they faded away again, never to return.

It was only by way of this outburst of spontaneous public feeling that Ruth surmised that the war had ended. She had stopped listening to the radio or watching television. There was no energy to spare for attention to matters beyond the immediate nucleus of need, which seemed to her to be the world's centre. Bridie had gone into a fitful coma; had drawn therefore one step toward her freedom. Ruth could not let go. It seemed to be by her willpower alone that Bridie retained her power to breathe and be. If she relaxed her vigilance for one hour, Bridie would have a chance to escape. Which there could be no excuse for. She lay beside the unconscious Bridie and watched her chest's faltering rise and fall as the corrupted lungs laboured from one breath to another. At times she counted the breaths and measured the intervals. She bent all her concentration to the task.

She lived on milk, drunk on the hop, and spoonfuls of sugar; or frozen peas and corn eaten straight from the freezer. She didn't seem to need any further sustenance. Didn't answer the phone or the doorbell except for the nurse. Felt light-headed and mad or dizzy when it came to any other occupation than watching Bridie. She suffered from constipation, which made her furious, for it stuck her in the loo when she should have been watching and caring. She crouched there with her fists clenched and eyelids screwed up, bearing down, and it wouldn't come, she could have screamed. Dashed in to find Bridie still alive. Found some ancient laxative at the back of the medicine cabinet. Did the job, with excruciating bowel-gripings. Back in. Bridie still alive. Nurse arrived.

'*Not* much longer, dear,' said nurse.

Oh yes, moment by moment longer, Ruth insisted, and half-pushed the woman out of the door so she could get back to the massive task of wrestling for Bridie's soul.

Bridie awoke. She moaned in agony.

'My dear – my darling love.' Ruth was bending over her, angling for Bridie with the cruel line of her detaining love, and

219

the fish thrashed on the hook desperate for release to the open sea. 'I love you so much.'

'Help me go – help me die,' she begged, and began to howl, on and on, like a helpless animal caught in a trap.

'No, Bridie, no,' Ruth besought her through the noise.

Bridie's howling increased; then died down into a hopeless sobbing moan which brought to mind the television pictures of a skeletal Ethiopian child, four years old or less with aged face, pattering across emptiness in search of the parents who were not there, the food that did not exist.

Bridie cried in despair, gargled in her throat: 'Help me, Ruth.'

She brought the strong medicine from the cabinet, the red stuff. What Bridie wanted, Bridie must have. Bridie would never see the crocuses. Bridie would never know about the war. Bridie wanted freedom. Ruth would free Bridie.

Bridie swallowed; choked; swallowed again.

She went still. Her forehead was clammy. Ruth kissed her temples and eyes, kissed her mouth and the tip of her collar-bone. She did not weep. In the earth, the earth, they would be together, under the green.

Bridie was quiet.

Ruth tipped the rest of the medicine into her own mouth and lay down with her cheek against Bridie's. She arranged Bridie's arm around her own shoulders and fell asleep in those arms which gripped rigidly in their common unconsciousness.

The doorbell rang and went on ringing. It would not take no for an answer. The ghost of Ruth fought off the crook of Bridie's dead arm and made its way to the front door which it threw open. A blast of daylight burst in. She staggered back.

'I couldn't get an answer on the phone,' said Elaine. 'So I thought I'd better come and see how you were.'

'She's just sleeping,' said Ruth tonelessly. 'And you've woken me up.'

'I'm sorry.'

Elaine stooped over Bridie's body and immediately knew. 'No, Ruth – dear – she's gone, she's been gone many hours, she's out of it now,' said Elaine with quivering voice, and sought to put gentle arms round Ruth but Ruth shoved her off in vexation.

'*No*,' said Ruth. 'She wouldn't go without me. She wouldn't, I tell you – she just wouldn't.'

She fought Elaine to get to the body. Elaine was bigger and strong, and Ruth enfeebled with inanition and the drug.

'Come out, dear – come and sit down.'

'You've taken her,' Ruth shrieked. 'You've taken her away from me – she was all I had – she's my life and you won't let me near her. But she's mine, Elaine, she's mine, not yours, and this is my home, not yours, get out of my home –' She ran against Elaine to drive her out but Elaine caught and held her, and rocked with her, swaying, weeping into the younger woman's hair.

All that was hers in Bridie Elaine had long since ceded to Ruth: her security, her home, the day-to-day comradeship of her greatest friend. All but one thing, and she saw it now, spinning silently in the midnight of inner space – the bright globe they spun together which conceived the Trust. That frail lamp should not be allowed to fail until consciousness itself died in her. *Bridie, it shall not*, she pledged in her heart to whatever vestige of Bridie's spirit still hovered under the roof preparing for its long flight. That was the inheritance, the testament, the book that should never be closed.

11

There was no lack of widows in the avenue. Widows were indeed in abundant supply wherever you went, but you did not notice them particularly, nor did they seek to make themselves conspicuous. They endured their longevity with all the stoicism society demanded of them, covering the bleeding hole of their partner's absence which constituted an intrinsic part of their identity with a stoicism composed of one part seemliness to one part courage. Occasionally a widow had engaged Ruth in conversation on a bus, and she had courteously listened to narratives of Arthur or Tony and said, perhaps, 'I'm so sorry – I do hope you feel better soon'; and privately wondered why such women had not greater resources in themselves to fall back on. Sometimes they were left literally helpless by the partner of their life, ignorant of how to sign a cheque or pay a bill. Their pariah's isolation was compounded by penury and communal intolerance of any grief lasting more than a statutory six months. They were required to pull themselves together; buck up, go out – which they did, rallying the selves that were excess to requirements to undertake voluntary work or free baby-minding. Several widows worked in the local Trust shop; indeed the network of shops would have folded without them.

Now that Ruth stood in their shoes, she no longer felt inclined to question the widow's lack of inner resource. She only wondered how one dared to continue living. Extremes of dread and horror possessed her: she had no words for the emotions which seemed off the map of experience. She looked round for herself and there was no one there. She was lack, she was nothing. The world stretched around her in a silent infinity of perspectives radiating meaninglessly from the hole where she was. The hole was herself. The hole had no name. 'Ruth' they called her, and 'Ruth Asher' signed the death register, the probate forms. But 'Ruth' could claim no kinship with 'Bridie', that other hole in the world. She could not assume the title of 'widow', which at least attributed an existence to a prior bonding and warranted the official reality of the past. She was a relict with no title, like a mistress or an illegitimate child. She envied Mrs Mason, the woman next door, with her comings and goings, her visits to the Post Office and the hairdresser; her regular hooverings of the house on set days of the week. There was nothing in her life but routine. But that meant there was not nothing in her life. Mrs Mason drew a pension by right of her attachment to the late Mr Mason. But Ruth was 'only a friend' of Bridie McKearn, unmentioned in the newspaper obituaries in which Elaine Demetrian figured largely.

Mrs Mason knocked the second day after Bridie's death.

'I brought you a bit of stew,' she said. 'Heat it up and it'll make you a nice little dinner. You've got to take care of yourself – for your friend's sake, love.'

Ruth could not speak. But she stretched out her hands to receive the Tupperware dish, sealed with a foil cover; as she did so, the tears spilt down her cheeks. Her eyes had become half-closed with the endless crying, the crying that brought no release but only a proliferation of itself. She held the bowl carefully to her breast. She did not really register what she had been given or what she must do with it, but she knew that she had been given something.

'I know – I know. I hear you through the wall, poor lamb. You let it out: that's the only way.'

Ruth tried to speak but nothing came out. She shut the door. She took the bowl through to the kitchen and placed it on the counter-top. This was food. She must cook it. She must eat it. She was like a fully adult newborn, aborted into a foreign unmediated world where she must learn all things for herself from scratch.

Waiting for a break in the tears, Ruth heated the meal in a saucepan and ate it from the pan with a teaspoon. She drank a glass of water. The phone rang but she did not answer it.

Bridie was lying in a coffin at Johnson's the Funeral Directors, her darling body embalmed with chemicals.

They told her Bridie was at rest. They said Bridie was out of pain now, free. They assured her that Bridie's work would live on. They were admirable, eminent people, the cream of the caring intelligentsia, who one by one came and took Bridie away from her, a slice at a time. 'I remember,' they said, 'back in 1983, Bridie and I . . .', or 'Even as a teenager, Bridie was, I recall, a character to be reckoned with . . .'. But one woman, Fran Saxeham, came from London; she only stayed twenty minutes, and at the end of a conversation of many pauses she said, 'I came to see the woman Bridie loved. Well, now I've seen – and I understand why.' Oddly enough, Ruth could not put a face to her afterwards; her memory had painted out the features and retained only the frame of black curly hair, a rust-coloured silk scarf at her neck – and a pair of tapering, ringless hands folded on an elegant lap. But no face.

Next day Mrs Mason was back with a tray of roast beef with two veg, a covered bowl containing stewed pears and a jug of custard.

'Meals on wheels,' she said.

'Thank you so much,' said Ruth.

'The lady over the way did it for me. It helps a wee bit to get something nourishing in you.'

'I –'

'You just eat it up, there's a good girl.' She patted Ruth's arm with one plump, arthritic hand and turned away. 'I'll collect your pots this afternoon, you just put them on the doorstep, I won't disturb you.'

Ruth could not sleep. She begged the doctor for sleeping-pills but the doctor was reluctant. He had a principle against addictive pills: let the patient get through naturally if she possibly could, especially in these suicidal early weeks. He counselled gently against. Ruth began to shout. He wrote out a prescription.

'By the way, you can't kill yourself with an overdose of these. It wouldn't work. You'd just make yourself sick.'

Ruth took two pills and went out like a light. She dreamed that Bridie was needing a cup of tea, but that she herself, having shamefully fallen asleep, could not respond to the request. Over and over Bridie appealed to Ruth to relent and bring the tea; she was dying of thirst, she said, and explained that she could not get up to make it for herself because of her indisposition, she had to *rely* on Ruth; and over and over Ruth denied her. For how could she do otherwise? She was asleep. Finally Bridie clambered out of bed and began to crawl across the floor. Ruth in horrified desperation bit her own hand and bent it back to awaken herself; and did wake up, to find that there was no one there who needed a cup of tea. But she got up and went over to the window, and, looking out into the garden, saw Bridie out there in the glimmering dawn, fit as a flea, wearing her patched gardening-jeans and raking leaves under the beeches. Ruth's heart leapt and she threw up the window, but just as she was about to call to her friend, the figure turned to meet her eyes, and, no, it was not Bridie at all but a dark strange man who had

225

raped Bridie. Raped her and buried her under the mound of autumn leaves. Ruth woke up sweating.

Gavin arrived on the doorstep with the two girls, each gripping a bunch of daffodils. He cleared his throat.

'I'm so sorry – believe me, I'm so very sorry,' he said, and his face had a rueful look about it, as if it bothered him now, that he'd called Bridie the insulting names men call lesbians, for he'd found that she was mortal, a fact not previously comprehended. But he gasped as Ruth's disfiguring grief looked him in the eye, and choked on a mumble of inadequate commiserations. This had been his best friend, closer to him than anyone but his mother, this broken human. 'If there's anything we can do . . . just say the word.'

'Mummy,' said Sarah, extending her bunch of flowers with one hand and with the other hanging on tight to her father's hand. She hoped that Ruth would understand her sympathy from this one word. She could think of no others. Her mind went blank. She had awoken the day after Bridie died in serious doubt lest she had contracted AIDS from Daniel Bowen-Jones in the copse near Circle-K, he having rather surprisingly thrust his tongue into her mouth and waggled it about while they were dividing a packet of love-hearts on the way home from school. Then he pushed his tongue in her ear. In her *ear*! Why should he want to do that? This, she pondered, must be a form of sex; she just hoped it was safe sex, but feared the worst. What if she'd got AIDS? What would Dad say? What would be your symptoms? The more she thought about it, the more she felt a sore throat coming on. And somehow the AIDS had got all tangled up in her mind with Bridie's dying and her mum who came out on to the doorstep with her face all puffy from weeping, and, twisting a sodden handkerchief between her hands, enquired, 'Flowers?' much as to say 'What are flowers?'

Through her ugly weepy eyes she stared at Sarah, as if trying to place her.

Lizzie had got her heart's desire: the eviction of Roger the Lodger. It was as though she herself had done the deed, so curdled was her heart with remorse. She could not look her mother in the eye. Standing a little distance apart from her father and sister, she scuffed her Doc Martens on the doorstep with an appearance of bored detachment, surveying her muscular thighs in their purple leggings. *I've only come along because they made me*, her attitude said.

'Give your mother your flowers, Lizzie,' her father instructed her in an even tone.

Without coming up the steps, Lizzie obeyed the letter of the instruction, leaning forward at full stretch in a madly balletic pose. She made it seem as if her mother's grief might be contaminating like radiation or meningitis. She saw quite well she was being horrible. But contrition only bred further resentment, and resentment more remorse. And anyway, what did it matter how she behaved, since her mother did not give a sod one way or the other? If she had cared, she'd never have gone off with Roger in the first place.

'Thanks, Lizzie. They are. . .lovely.'

'Now don't forget,' said Gavin in a valedictory tone, pulling on his driving gloves, jingling his car keys. 'Anything at all we can do. Don't be afraid to ask. Any time.' He was sensible of the urge to run from the stricken figure of his ex-wife; at the same time he was arrested by an impulse to throw his arms around her and crush her body against the comfort of his own. The impulse was experienced as a spasm of his own need rather than a passive reaction to hers. *Don't despair because I can't bear it.* The stirring of long-quiet depths alarmed him. He gave a nervous cough and turned away. For what could you do? She'd have to get over it. God knows, she'd caused them all enough trouble.

And anyhow she always cried very easily. Could keep it up for hours, despite all attempts to appease her, and then suddenly you'd hear her laughing from another room, where she'd be found larking around, jouncing a baby in her arms. He followed Lizzie towards the car; looked back and she was still there in the doorway, her arms full of cold daffodils, looking dazed and very young. She had been a delicately pretty girl, and she could be very kind – kind beyond the common run, and there was a gentleness...Should he go back, stay with her? But what could he say? Just be, be with her. She should not be alone. And yet he opened the door to let Lizzie in the back and waved.

Val had been somewhat brittle about their coming here.

'As you wish,' she said.

'I don't wish,' he said.

'As you don't wish.'

'I feel we ought. She's their mother.'

'Whatever.'

'But you don't mind?'

'Why should I?'

'No reason at all.'

'Well, then.'

'Val –'

'Look, I am not even faintly interested. You are a free agent, Gavin.'

Gavin didn't much like the sound of that: it implied that Val was reciprocally a free agent. He was now in a hurry to get home.

Ruth laid the daffodils on the sink-drainer, where in the course of time they shrivelled and died.

She wandered the house vacantly, looking for something mislaid. Where was it? Something had gone astray and she could not rest until it was located. Through empty rooms she roamed, fagged to death with the effort of travelling to and fro, to and fro. But the moment she sat down, she had to be up again pursuing the search. Then recognition clicked. What she was looking for was not something but everything. It was not a part of the whole that had gone missing but the whole itself.

The hole where the whole had been. If one could find the entrance to the hole, one could disappear down it and find the way through.

She pitched around on the rocking deck of the house in her exhaustion.

Infantile voices sang *Cold. Cold* as she blundered up the stairs to the landing. But then, *Getting warmer* they enticed, as she paused outside Bridie's study. She had not entered since Bridie . . . since Bridie . . . since . . . she . . . no. The door was closed which had stood always ajar. She eyed the bare wood door and circled the knob with uncertain hand. Turned it: *Warmer still*.

The sickly, stale smell surrounded her like the remnant of a gas leak and, as she threw herself on the tell-tale stained mattress in an explosion of weeping, the voices all chanted together, *Cold. Cold*.

It was a riddle. She sat up and puzzled it out head in hands. She could say Bridie's name – 'Bridie, Bridie' – for Bridie's name had been left behind, intact. But Bridie, having been severed from her name, would never come again; never come again; never come; never again. If ever she had needed Bridie to hold her, it was now, tight, tight, wrapped round her, and summoning the helpful words in their private language which Bridie had always been able to supply. So she needed Bridie to explain the absurdity of her disappearance. But that was ridiculous for there was no Bridie any more to comment, and when would she come to understand that there was no Bridie?

Her head ached and agitated. It was a hot, excruciated burden in her hands. Its problems were weighty to the point of absurdity. If there was Bridie last week, why not today? Even in her illness, she had seemed so eternal. Made of some durable tough stuff, Bridie's personality had seemed and been so remarkable that nothing could dissolve it. Even when she had beaten Ruth off and flayed her with words of rejection, and Ruth had run yelping for cover, that only made Bridie the more authentic. No one like Bridie had existed before nor ever would again: that eccentric rarity could not, surely, be annihilated, just like that. Yes it could. It would have been better if she had died and Bridie lived. Or if she had continued to endure the penance of rejection in return for Bridie's survival. So she fatuously bargained, and evening fell, on the day before Bridie's funeral. She sat on Bridie's bed, elbows on her knees, chin in her hands, and a queen bee batted its head against the study window, whirring angrily, as Ruth pursued her negotiations with God.

Who didn't exist.

Like Bridie.

How lucky Bridie was, how bloody unfairly lucky, Ruth raged, looking up, to be asleep while she could not sleep. She'd been nodding off in Bridie's arms when Elaine malevolently woke her and made her live. Damn that woman, without whom Ruth's mourning would have been mercifully terminal.

The bee gave up its futile bombardment of the pane and took off.

Bridie was in that box, that blond box on the platform, with brass handles and hinges. Dark shapes loomed like many shadows. No officious clergyman was present to authorise the transaction. Instead Robyn Wilkie, looking sombre and distinguished, read the manifesto of the Trust in a sonorous voice. Jess Geddes, with a heavy cold, read poems by Wilfred Owen and Emily Brontë. The Schubert Quintet was played by a group from the college. Elaine sat well back in the gathering so as not to obtrude on Ruth's vision. Ruth had not noticed her.

The automatic doors of the chute to the ovens opened and slowly the box slid through. The doors closed. There was a silence. Ruth felt nothing. She put her hands out slightly in front of her and perused the ring on her wedding finger.

With my body I thee worship.

Love blazed and boiled in the apocalypse of the furnace. It flamed through her own body, from the soles of her feet to the roots of her hair. Together they burnt to ash and the disease went up in smoke. Ruth alone got up and walked away from her own remains into the crowd.

'A beautiful ceremony – a tender celebration of who Bridie was.'

'Her work . . . her work lives on. We must . . . redouble our efforts.'

'We are with you.'

'Phone us.'

'Keep in touch.'

'We won't forget.'

'Work to be done.'

'The Kurds.'

'I saw the reports.'

'Horrific.'

'There's Ruth . . . must speak to her . . .'

Ruth dodged to avoid people who broke from the crowd to offer condolence; ducked their threatening wooings of 'Ruth . . .' She carried a quietness and balance out through the crematorium gates, past the pruned rose-bushes and inde-terminate shrubs. Nobody was in the lane. She looked back at the tall chimney of the crematorium, then turned right and began to walk past the fallow meadows where cows were feeding under the cold sky. She stopped to look at one of the creatures through the barbed wire; in the stillness, the soft rasp of its mouth and teeth as it cropped the grass was clearly audible. Over to the east was the Manchester conurbation, picturesque with distance. It was a clean picture, neutral, scoured of pain: unbeautiful as all life would be unbeautiful now that its core had been gutted. But there was a sense of purification and release, as if Bridie had got away at last. She was glad for her, glad for her. She walked along steadily, wishing to see no human face.

A shriek ripped through her as she woke up; sat bolt upright. Where was her mother? Where was home? Where was Bridie? She ran round and round the room in her nightgown, her feet pattering on the floor, cannoning into sharp edges of desk and bookshelf. A bloated face kept bumping into itself in the glass frame of the Rembrandt self-portrait, with a look of terror. Rembrandt, with his bulbous nose and fleshy face (the last portrait before he died, having outlived his lover and son) looked over her reflection's shoulder from the tenebrous depths of layer upon layer of paint and varnish, with unflinching insight. That mad face imposed upon his sanity was Ruth-without-Bridie. Ruth-without-Bridie would always be that faceless face, running away from its own deformities. She burrowed back for safety under the duvet, clutching a pillow into which she thrust her tear-sodden face, biting right through the cotton to the feathers.

By and by she steadied herself.

'You are safe now, my dear love,' she said aloud. 'You are a free woman now.'

Free as air. But Ruth-without-Bridie was neither safe nor free. She was craven. She crept about, full of dread. Sat inert.

Had to force herself to undertake the smallest functions. *Wash your face, clean your teeth*, she told herself. Just raising the flannel, inducing the toothpaste on to the brush seemed an extraordinary effort. She sighed repeatedly. Sat down after the effort, fatigued. Sat and sat, twirling a loop of hair round one finger; sat stiffly, without changing position; needed to go to the loo; sighed; didn't go. The pressure in her bladder built up painfully. *Go to the loo.* But she didn't go. She just sat.

Suddenly she bounded up and found herself in the bathroom. Relieved herself. That was better. Now she could have a drink; she realised she was parched and went to make herself a coffee. But only a few grains were remaining in the bottom of the jar. And only loose change in her purse. Damn, she'd have to go to the bank and buy in some provisions from the shops. It was so hard getting out of the door that she almost couldn't. There was a hair-raising strangeness in the ordinary. She took courage and plunged out into that turbulence. The street, which she knew to be flat, had risen against its conditions and now inclined uphill. And the grey sky was pressing lower. Between the pavement and the sky she laboured deeper into the narrowing wedge, breathing with difficulty. The next door dog, normally an amiable, dozy creature, came padding towards her and she quickened pace, fearing that it would snarl at her, turn on her. A woman in a headscarf crossed the road when she saw Ruth coming. Cars rushed past, their noise and motion unduly fierce.

But then, at the junction, everything . . . just . . . stopped . . . froze. Cars . . . a blackbird . . . a banking plane . . . stopped dead in their tracks . . . and her windswept hair standing out on the wind did not fall. In photographic stillness the world drained of colour and meaning . . . and that woman over there was caught in mid-stride . . . the tossed boughs of the ash failed to bounce back.

Thunder broke as the traffic leapt forward; the blackbird

flicked away from its suspension; the woman carried on walking up the normality of the pavement, and Ruth fell back against a telegraph pole, her forehead and palms cold with sweat. For she saw it now, as if for the first time – the meaninglessness. Nothing made sense. That was the secret. We pretended that it did, and we sincerely felt that it did, and that was how we carried on. Our footsteps repeated over and over their small journeys to the shops and back, to school and back, to work and back, leaving the illusion of a warmly personal Wenceslas-trail. We could follow in our own footsteps with assurance. Until we saw through it to the pointless truth: there was no love, or intelligence, or worth out there at all, nothing at all.

She staggered home through the terror of the street; her key scrambled in the lock. Indoors she was under some shelter. She drank a glass of water in lieu of coffee. Bridie's roof was over Ruth.

On her doorstep appeared a box of provisions. Ruth saw it through the glass panel of the front door and was quick enough to spy the delivery man in a navy overall getting in a van. In the box were enough basic foodstuffs to keep her going for a month: tea, coffee, sugar, cheese, margarine, loaves, Ryvita, baked beans, potatoes, cans of beer. She unpacked it all onto the counter-top in wonderment. So much. Who from? There was no note. Running out of the door again, she peered up and down the road but the van was long gone. The surprising and necessary gift opened a space for comfort beside the grief which crowded her mind; made the grief budge over and yield ground. And curiosity was aroused. Who would think or care to send the staples of life? They sent slivers of sympathetic paper in recycled envelopes; they had flowers delivered, white and yellow tokens of emotion, heartfelt but unsustaining. Bridie would have been glad the food had been sent to her; Bridie would have grieved to think she was terrified to go out of the house alone. Bridie had loved her and that did not go for nothing. And somehow, eating a wedge of bread and cheese, and swilling it down with coffee, it was as if Bridie were also comforted that she was fed.

'I shall be all right for food,' she reassured Mrs Mason, who was off on holiday to Majorca with her friend Elsie with whom she played golf on Mondays and Thursdays. 'I've got plenty in – thank you so much for all you've given me. I really do appreciate it. I think I'd have starved without you.'

'You're very welcome. It helps a bit, until you come round from the shock.'

'Will you come in and have a cup of tea?'

'Well, I won't stop long – I've still some packing to do.' She looked round curiously as she stepped in through the hallway. She had always been intrigued about Miss McKearn and her do-gooding, highfalutin friends. George had not approved of them (though he had a sneaking regard for his eminent neighbour and was tickled to be on 'time of the day' terms with her). Being a lifelong Powellite Conservative, he had always maintained that foreign countries should look after themselves in a spirit of free competition. When the Oxfam or Christian Aid collectors had come round, to the front door, he had sent them off with a flea in their ear. Doris had not disputed this attitude with him – although she had been moved by the newsreel pictures of the Ethiopian children and was shocked now to the quick by the sight of the millions of Kurdish refugees climbing the mountains. That Saddam Hussein had a lot to answer for. Her husband would have had a few choice words to say about that Arab Hitler. Still, you could not take the whole world upon your shoulders. There was a limit. She felt a duty to supply practical help to the pain on her doorstep, and how many other people could put their hands on their hearts and say the same?

'So how are you feeling now, dear?' She stirred her cup of tea, inspecting the little bronze Buddha at her elbow, who badly needed a good polish. The whole place was covered in several layers of dust. This poor girl had evidently gone under completely. Odd how differently people took things: even when her George had his last stroke and needed constant attention, she'd found herself assiduously dusting and tidying right up to the last day. Partly house-pride; partly habit, and the comfort of routine. Most probably these intellectuals didn't know a duster from a dishclout.

'Up and down – not very up but very far down.'

'I know – I know. But you've got to cling on to the good memories, my dear, and remember how your friend wouldn't have wanted you to keep on and on grieving. You'll get through it, never you fear. My George said to me, "Don't you fret and mope, Doris, and that's an order. Get out and enjoy yourself. God knows," he said, "I've been getting under your feet for long enough – now just you mind and cheer up – get out of yourself – marry again." Bear in mind, I was sixty-three at the time and no great beauty at twenty-three, that was a bit far-fetched, but I didn't contradict him. Mind you I rarely did, he was quite an overbearing man, was George, and liked you to know who wore the trousers, but we got on well for all that, and it was a dreadful blow. But you have to go on living, don't you, dear? I mean, you just do. So I put a brave face on it, and I get about – bowls, golf, WI, holidays abroad – keep on the move.'

'Yes . . .' said Ruth vaguely. 'Yes. But the time seems so . . .

236

incredibly long. Each day . . . so long. Endless. Days that will never seem to . . . end.'

'That's why you have to keep busy. Make jam, sweep the floor, get out and about. If you don't mind my asking,' she added uneasily, but feeling as if she'd paid for the right to be a bit nosy, 'were you related to Miss McKearn?'

'Oh. Not legally.'

'Ah. I wondered if you were sisters, you seemed so close?'

'No . . . no,' said Ruth, and seemed inclined to supplement this with no further information.

'Just friends then.'

'Well actually,' said Ruth, and a wraith of her old spirit seemed to fizz up in her, 'we were lovers.'

Doris stared; swallowed some tea; choked and uttered a small, decorous cough.

'I hope it doesn't offend you. You've been so kind.'

'Certainly not. Each person is free to live his own life . . .' said Doris in a tightly proper voice. Though not entirely surprised, she could not deny to herself that she was shocked. One did, of course, get to know a certain amount through the walls of these old Edwardian semis. Bursts of laughter; rompings and larkings-about; rows and crying; a raucous pillow-fight on the stairs; then again, the view of the two women lying in the summer sun on a tartan blanket in what they took to be the privacy of their back garden, wearing very little, rubbing one another's backs with sun-oil; and through the murmurous afternoons of bees and distant lawn-mowers and a somnolent haze of sunshine in which she sat out in her lonely deckchair, she had caught the drift of conversations made up solely of endearments. Fragrance of sweet peas had wafted over the fence from Miss McKearn's beautifully tended garden, and with it had swum the scent of a liaison at once deliciously tender and profoundly private. Well, so it was not in itself a surprise; rather the words for the deeds were a bit of a shock.

(She couldn't wait to tell Elsie. 'Do you know, Elsie, they were a pair of lesbians next door – yes, she admitted it quite freely – mind you, I had my suspicions . . .' Elsie's face would be a picture.)

'Well, my thanks for the tea,' she said. 'I'd better organise myself for tomorrow.' Stooping to replace the mug on the tray, she picked up her handbag. 'You take care of yourself,' she said. 'It will take time. You'll be all right, you know.' She squeezed Ruth's hand encouragingly. After all, she had evidently loved the woman. 'Don't do anything silly.'

'Safe journey. Have a lovely holiday.'

Ruth closed the door on her visitor: that word, *journey*, it rang in her mind. That was Bridie's word, from her Nonconformist childhood. Your life was your journey. You were on your way to some meaningful destination; every so often, you paused in a lay-by to examine your state of progress. You referred to or corrected the bearings of a map you had drawn up yourself out of your own head; for each person's journey was unique and carried its own authenticity.

But Ruth had cadged or been awarded a free seat on Bridie's journey. Where Bridie had gone, she had been content to follow, like her namesake in the Bible with Naomi: 'Whither thou goest I will go; and where thou lodgest I will lodge: thy people shall be my people, and thy God my God.' Thus for five years of her life she had walked accompanied. Now if she were to go on (which was in doubt) it must be alone and in a void, trusting in her own self which, not yet fully born, was still labouring in solitude to be delivered.

Standing amongst the opening crocuses at the far end of the

garden, she pegged out washing on the lines that ran between three apple trees. She thought, 'I want to live.' But with that thought, the sunlight darkened, and a sense of insecurity welled up in her, as if she were riskily consenting to quit a trusted and proven friend in order to wander after new acquaintance. With Bridie she was safe, if only with a spectral safety; Bridie's grave fitted them both snugly. like a motherly embrace. And to say even for a moment 'I want to live' was to leave Bridie alone and unaccompanied. It was an adulterous thought.

Ruth pegged up another sock. In this goodish drying wind, the sheets on the longer of the two lines gently billowed. She hadn't washed or cleaned for ages and suddenly this morning, after peculiar dreams of God-knows-what, she had realised that she must be beginning to smell. The second load of washing was at this moment going into its spin stage, and she had scrubbed the kitchen floor and thrown away a mass of accumulated junk which suddenly she couldn't stand the sight of any more. The endless flow of tears, she noted, seemed to have been staunched, though you could never be sure when it might start up again, a tedious, useless drizzle. From the boredom and inertia of grief, she was relieved to have moved into action. 'I want to live,' she had thought as she scoured the bath and washbasin with Ajax, bleached the loo, threw open the windows. The light revealed grime everywhere, triggering an attack of the obsessive hospitality that precedes the arrival of a visitor, the need to make things decent and presentable. The only time she could recall such a ferocious fit of nest-cleaning was during the last fortnight before Sarah's birth when, grotesquely bulky, she had lumbered down on her hands and knees with a view to wiping every speck off the mirror of the kitchen floor, and 'Don't we possess a mop?' Gavin had wanted to know, and 'Yes, but it doesn't do the job properly,' she had replied without looking up; and 'Good grief,' he had observed, 'we'll need some kind of a crane to hoist you up again.'

A stiff wind spanked the washing and flapped the multi-coloured socks like bunting. Ruth watched from the kitchen window as she peeled two potatoes for her tea. An hour later, having eaten, she took down the washing from the line and, burrowing her nose into the sheets, sniffed in their freshness. It was then that, raising her head and looking round at the garden, she saw her.

Bridie. Most clearly and yet abstractedly. Saw her in the darkening green of the grass and the blue-grey of the air. Saw her in the quilt of open crocuses, with the saffron tongues of their stamens just showing through the lip of petals, silky purple, white and yellow. Saw Bridie in the complex angles of intersection in the boughs and twigs of silhouetted apple trees and just-budding beeches. She remembered Bridie's last kind-nesses and how Bridie had, with laboured breath, passed across the promise, 'Healing will come . . . it will, Ruth . . . wait . . . you will be whole again,' and, vividly recalling the tone of voice in which Bridie had used to say her name, she was able for a moment to . . . not grasp, but glimpse, just glimpse . . . that the promise might, one day, be fulfilled. For all this was Bridie, this garden with its brimming presence.

Indoors, she hastily dumped the washing on the kitchen table and fetched the tape of the Schubert Quintet from the cassette box. The music flooded the room from wall to wall. Bridie was in the music as surely as Bridie had been in the garden. She was speaking and Ruth was listening.

It didn't last. Nothing lasted. Nothing was conclusive. The horror fell like midnight at daybreak. Again she prowled the hollow house through rooms which echoed the drumroll of rain. For hours and hours until she could bear it no longer. From the top floor she looked down a vertiginous drop to the concrete drive; dragged up the window and leaned out with a thrill of frightened desire. For she didn't want to live. She leaned out further. The frenzy of excitement gave way to a mind that was cold and numb. Sitting on the window-sill, she shuffled her weight out; looked down, poised, holding on with one hand.

The earth seemed to rush up at her toppling eye.

The postman looked up, his mouth open wide.

'Just cleaning the window,' Ruth explained. 'Don't worry.'

Huddled in a corner of the nursery room, by the airing cupboard, she trembled and sobbed with delayed terror, stuffing her handkerchief in her mouth to stifle the screaming. Every time she sought to rise, an attack of vertiginous jitters forced her back into her corner again; she wavered over the chasm of air and the drive rushing toward her, on which her body would have smashed, her skull spilt its contents. On all fours she crawled toward Sarah's bed; the floor rocked beneath her. She reached for the moth-eaten old teddy bear and cradled it in her arms.

'It's all right, it's all right,' she assured herself, aloud. 'You won't fall, you won't.'

Heavy rain turned to hailstones, which bombarded the skylight and sloping roof of the attic room. The swathe of murky light from the skylight dimmed to become all but indistinguishable from the prevailing gloom. The hailstones relented and were replaced by the pattering monotony of steady rain.

She made her way carefully downstairs, a tricky negotiation, for while some steps flew up to meet her foot, others shelved away. The stairwell yawned. Although the ground floor was stabler, her soles sensed the empty space of the damp, stale cellar beneath. She picked up the mail and added it to the weary pile of unpaid bills and unanswered condolences.

The doorbell rang; she shrank into a corner. People: no. Faces – eyes – mouthed words: no. The fuzzy image of Beth Hatch – so mild, undemanding and respectful of your distance, why not let her in? – lingered diffidently; an arm reached out from the blur and rang again. Ruth started toward the outstretched hand but then winced back in. No. She was afraid of Beth (why be afraid of *Beth*?) just as yesterday she had been afraid of familiar Frances. She was too raw for them, too raw: and ashamed, shy of showing her hideous disfigurement, her face with the skin off. Beth faded and withdrew, and Ruth was sorry then, and wanted her, but made no move to pursue her.

A face appeared at the sitting-room window. A child's face. A little girl. Then it bobbed down. Ruth stared but did not distinguish it from the other strange faces which, in combination with a range of faceless voices, had imposed themselves on her hospitality during the days since she had nearly fallen from the third-floor window. These voices sometimes crept up out of nowhere just behind her right ear, to impart messages at once preposterous and portentous: DARE TO HEARKEN TO THE WHEELS OF THE WHERE. The bookshelf complained that its books were all being carried for nothing, for no one was bothering to read them. She took down a book and found in it the stub of a ticket for a Lindsay Concert in 1988 and a return railway ticket. She studied the tickets before putting them away in her pocket. From the kettle issued an authoritative male voice. It spoke on and on, a rigmarole of suggestions for energy-saving and conservation: POPULATION CONTROL STARTS AT HOME, it counselled, and the kitchen knife glinted on the breadboard.

She watched a spider for what seemed many hours, working its way conscientiously up and down its thread. This spider seemed to her a happy enough being but by and by it grew a big brown face with multiple eyes which came up close and told of the bloody end of the world, exemplified by the fly now ceasing to struggle in its web.

Apart from animate objects and garrulous insects, human beings came and went, and – because she knew at one level they were unreal – she took them and the menace of their cryptic suggestions with a pinch of salt. Nevertheless, she could neither predict their arrival nor control their utterances. And indeed it had occurred to her that they ought to be tolerated because Bridie might come. But Bridie did not come. She seemed to be the only person resolute in staying away.

Sarah's head bobbed up again. Her outline wavered through the uneven flow of the old glass. It was certainly Sarah, to the life. Pressing her nose up against the pane, she breathed on the glass. Now she knocked, hesitantly, gesturing to her mother to go round to the back door and let her in.

Ruth just sat and stared. She was used to all this monkey business. These stale tricks of her mind left her cold and disillusioned.

'Go away,' she said listlessly. 'Do go away.'

'Mummy, it's me,' mouthed Sarah, pointing at her own head, pointing to the door. '*Me*. Can – I – come – in?' She was wearing a purple tracksuit with a hood, which Ruth had not seen before. Crossing to the window, she stared into Sarah's eyes. The child's palms were flat against the window, so that you could make out the web of lifelines and character-lines with their complex intersections. Ruth placed her own palms upon the cold glass between them: the barrier began to warm. But there was something wrong with this child. She did not blink. Her serious, haunting eyes played ice-blue stare-you-out with her mother's. Ruth broke away; threw open the back door and dashed into the garden. No child, no sign of a child. A black and white cat was stalking along the window-sill.

Under this window was Bridie's herb garden, in the shape of a wheel, its spokes marked out in brick, and between them rosemary, lemon thyme, mint, lovage; all sorts of Elizabethan-sounding names – comfrey, camomile, feverfew – she liked the sound of and felt must do you good. On summer days they'd crouch and pinch the leaves, sniffing the fragrance from one another's fingers. 'Try this – hey, what about this, this one is really gorgeous.' This spot took the last of the afternoon sunlight, auburn on the rusty brick. A faint drift of aromatic herbs was on the air even now as she stooped where the tiptoe child must have stood to squint in at the window.

Evidently, however, the child had not been real. She had imagined her, like all the strange voices and faces that had thrown their echoes and shadows upon the emptiness of her mind. She held her temples between her fingers. She must be going round the twist, seeing things, hearing things. Even now, Sarah's voice was ringing in her ears: 'It's me,' she was saying. 'I'm real.'

'No,' Ruth replied wearily. 'You're not real, Sarah. You're in my mind.'

'I – am – real,' Sarah insisted obstinately. 'It's ridiculous to say I'm not real. Santa Claus is not real – Peter Pan is not real – Jesus Christ takes some believing in – Bridie McKearn was real and isn't now – but I am just as real as you, or more so. I live in the real world, unlike some people. You could reach out and touch me. If you wanted to,' she added with hurt feelings.

Ruth fled to the phone and dialled.

'Gavin – was Sarah here just now?'

'Oh, Ruth. Hello – no, she's in bed with tonsillitis – on a

244

course of penicillin and making the most of it, I'm bound to say. Are you okay?'

'I thought I saw her – but evidently I didn't. I'm sorry she's ill. Give her my love. Sorry to have bothered you.'

'No, dear, don't go. *Are* you okay? We're all so worried about you. Did the food reach you? I've ordered another delivery for Friday.'

'Oh, was it you? . . . How . . . how very . . .'

'Well, I knew you wouldn't feed yourself properly. It seemed the right thing. I remember – all sorts of things – and I'm so sad for you. And after all,' he added, in a quiet voice, 'they're our children. That doesn't go away. But tell me how you are.'

'I'm without a . . .' she was going to say *face*, but, recalling that normal people might not make much sense of this, she began again. 'I'm alive.'

'Just about. Well, hang on. It will get better. It will take time . . .' His kind, reassuring voice at once offered tentative comfort and seemed to solicit absolution. She knew what for. For all the names he'd called Bridie: *randy dyke, male-impersonator*. It didn't matter now; to be candid, it hadn't mattered much then, except for the fear he'd say it to the children. All that was in the past.

'Yes, I know.'

'Who is it, Gavin? Who's that you're talking to?' She could hear the magnified whisper of the girlfriend's voice.

'Ssh. Just a friend.'

'Well, hurry up. Sarah says she's going to be sick.'

'Oh God. Sarah's threatening to be sick, I'd better go. Hope she aims at the bucket this time. Take care of yourself.'

She sat down by the pile of unopened mail and began a letter. 'Dearest Sarah, I'm so sorry to hear you've been ill, I hope you feel better soon . . .'

The voices receded, the faces retired. When she looked up from the letter and licked the envelope to seal it, the uninvited guests had been shown off the premises. The pavement to and from the post-box was well-nigh stable under her feet.

She slit open letter after letter. Each was filled with reflections of Bridie. From their pages, in italic script in blue-black ink, in semi-legible ballpoint scrawl or in word-processor type, one could glean fragments of many narratives of Bridie. One told of Bridie as a little girl scrumping apples from the neighbour's orchard and fighting local boys for possession of a football. They called her 'Vixen'. Another wrote of Bridie in Africa during the drought of 1984 touring the refugee camps, and how he'd taken encouragement from her anger. Some told of Bridie's gentleness, others of her implacable determination. A Methodist minister felt that at heart she had remained a dissenting Christian, *very* dissenting, it was true, but never cut off from her spiritual roots. However, a well-known member of the Humanists' Association claimed her as a fellow-humanist, a lover of reason and a believer in human possibility. An ecological Bridie was constructed, alongside a radical feminist Bridie. Many different Bridies debated in the pages of the letters, and the further Ruth read, the deeper grew both her concentration and her breathing. She began to be fascinated with the mystery of her friend's total life. The agony of cancered flesh and the indignity of catheter and syringe no longer seemed conclusive; they assumed the status of a few contingent minutes out of the full twenty-four hours of Bridie's life-day.

She had thought she knew Bridie. Knew her through and through. But now she wondered. There was so much more to learn. She spread the letters out, open, on the morning-room table, where they aligned like a wonderful jigsaw of parts, none of which quite fitted with the others. A4 typewritten sheets were queried by blue Basildon Bond and recycled Greenpeace paper; testaments written in black ink on narrow-lined filing-paper negotiated with newspaper clippings and photocopies of cuttings going back years. Photographs of her friend never before seen fell out of envelopes and she stared, with poignant excitement, lips parted, at the novelty thus disclosed. One Bridie, thirty years back, had long, shaggy hair, tied back in a pony-tail, and this stranger who was also Bridie was smiling from young, shy eyes into the camera, amidst a group of young people from International House in Manchester. A black and white print, blown up to eight by ten size, was a study of Bridie deep in a book. This portrait seemed a reading of the light and shadow in her character, for she sat in lamplight against a dark background, chin resting on hand, with half her face and half the book illuminated; the other half in profound shadow. Ruth stared and stared. She cherished both the photograph and the sender.

So there was more of Bridie to discover; far more.

She stood up and, with one finger tapping her lips, contemplated the labyrinthine paper riddle on the table below her – the one person with so many faces. An enormous feeling of pride and worth swept over her: for this much-loved Bridie had loved her, Ruth, indisputably, indissolubly. And although she individually possessed only a fragment of the truth of Bridie, she was in a position to harvest far more.

There on the pin-board was a picture of Bridie standing between her parents in a park nearly half a century ago, holding both their hands. She must have been about three. She was grinning broadly and one cheek was enlarged, not – so Bridie had attested – with mumps, but with a gobstopper. The mischievous grin was very much the woman she knew, but so was the portrait of the adolescent Bridie on the Yorkshire moors, so shivery-looking and lonely, gazing out towards a

pale-grey dolmen or cairn in the distance. How did you know a
person, in the end?

Ruth's back prickled with the mystery of it. She crossed to
the window and looked out at the garden.

Who were you really, Bridie?

Deep in the night, she was still feverishly writing: 'Bridie said
. . . Bridie wore . . . she used to . . . She often . . . she loved . . .
When I first met her she used to . . . but then she changed her
mind and . . . Bridie often seemed . . . said . . . I saw then that
Bridie . . .' She wrote on until her wrist ached, and the more she
wrote, the more she knew there was to say. She laughed and
cried inwardly, and the voices dictating in her mind flew ahead
of her chasing pen. As cramp set in, and dawn, she put the pen
down. The birds were beginning to stir under the eaves and a
small rain was falling into the pool of light in the bowl of the
garden. Nobody but Ruth was awake. She did not feel lonely.
She stretched and yawned. She was still young and healthy.
Time and purpose remained. So much to do, not only, she
realised (turning from the window to the spotlit dishevelment
of papers spilling over the table) to write down her loving
thoughts of Bridie but to carry on with some of her work. For
the work was the deepest Bridie of all.

She read through a few lines of what she had written. It was
inadequate, paltry. But it brought a shimmering reflection of a
living person into the room. The Bridie she recognised was
here-and-now, not a discarded handful of ash and bone. A surge
of what could only be called joy at the beauty of a life so
generously lived squeezed her heart and drew tears to her eyes.
Tomorrow she would write again. She closed the book and lay
down on her bed, too weary to undress, falling without struggle
into sleep.

12

The Kurds toiled barefoot, family upon family, up the mountainside. Behind each million followed another million, as far as the eye could see: the refugees were climbing through mud and rain, up the precipitous mountain passes into the freezing zones, toward the Turkish and Iranian borders. Most had only the clothes they stood up in, plus a few bundles and containers. Men carried their elderly parents; mothers carried suckling babies and packs on their backs. Children carried their dying siblings. They slept under polythene sheets if they were lucky; without any shelter if they were not. In the night, the weak froze or starved to death and their bodies were left to putrefy by the roadside. In the stink and filth of insanitary camps amongst pools of diarrhoea and the carcases of rotting animals, Médécin Sans Frontières fought disease. And still they kept arriving, thousand upon thousand, pouring into the television screen, so that one's whole view seemed filled from dawn to dusk with the obscenity of their suffering. If the hi-tech war had resembled a video game, offering the small and pointless gratifications of zapping the adversary and moving on to a higher level, the aftermath threatened to overflow the TV screen, from which the refugees processed out of the box's containment and trekked relentlessly across the sitting room night after night.

The family watched in silence. Sarah stopped chewing her peanut butter sandwich. Tears overflowed Lizzie's eyes. How could people bear to let it happen? How could they? How could we?

Val said, 'Mr Major is upset about it. He will take some action. He won't let this go on. He's calling for safe havens. It'll be all right, Sarah – you'll see.'

Nobody answered.

Gavin wrote a cheque for £150 and sent it to the International Red Cross. It didn't make him feel any better. The sight of the refugees appalled and sickened him. He had no doubt in his mind that the war had been just and necessary, but he had some doubt as to whether we had 'won' it. He went and put his arms round both the girls' shoulders.

'Perhaps you oughtn't to watch?' he queried. 'If it upsets you like this?'

'I think we ought to watch,' said Lizzie. 'How can we not bear to know if they have to bear to be there?'

Sarah choked on her sandwich and had to have her back thumped; by the time this manoeuvre had been performed, the adverts had come on. Three beefy men with vacuum cleaners were dancing daintily backwards across a carpet, scattering cleaning-powder before them. Then a sultry, half-naked woman on a tropical island introduced a phallic chocolate bar between her lips. After this, a sex-mad car was driven up a mountainside by a power-hungry maniac, and was said to be a bargain at £18,000.

'We're mad, us,' said Lizzie. 'We're sick.'

Nobody said anything.

'Well, aren't we?'

'It's only adverts,' said Sarah.

'Only *ad*verts,' mimicked Lizzie. 'What do you mean, only adverts?'

'Oh no,' sneered Lizzie. 'That's why you were going round Kwiksave the other day singing "Captain Birdseye" and got Dad to buy you those Fishieburgers – vomitburgers, I'd say. Do you know what they put in them? Do you?'

'Now now,' cautioned Gavin.

'Do you know how much filthy farting muck comes out of those car-exhausts . . . do you? . . . those dickheads are trying to sell you . . .'

'Lizzie,' said Gavin.

'I'd like to get a brick and smash this TV set.'

'That's rich, coming from you,' said Gavin. 'Now I think I've heard it all. Considering the hours and hours you sit glued to the thing. I thought it was your bosom pal.'

'It feeds us pap, mum said. They use it to control our minds.' She glared at the one-eyed monster, through whose window she had stared for what must have added up to at least a year of her life, sucking ice lollies, watching *Neighbours*, eating licorice, watching *EastEnders*, drinking coke, watching *Top of the Pops*, eating Mars bars, watching assorted entertainments such as the destruction of the rain-forests, the lifestyle of the mandrill monkey, Captain Cook and the Starship Enterprise and nudy ladies with wobbling tits on the beaches of the Côte d'Azur . . . and on and on and on, she had sucked and watched, sucked and watched, taking it all in, while its big mouth yattered and its eye stared. 'It feeds us pap, and it feeds us crap,' she pondered.

'Language,' objected Val.

'Turds then.'

'Really, Lizzie, how childish can you be?'

'Is that a challenge, Polly?'

'My name is *not* Polly.' Val bristled. It was quite intolerable. She got all the ridicule, all the sneers. The tension was becoming unbearable again and Gavin did nothing about it; seemed downright scared of offending the girl. Lizzie was working up to some new outrage, she could feel it, and Gavin went pussyfooting round the great. brat, in wool-lined moccasins on a thick-piled carpet. 'My name, Elizabeth, is Valerie, and please to call me by my name.'

Lizzie gave an uncouth sniff. Gavin coughed behind his hand. He looked uneasily from one to the other, wondering whether to intervene.

'Think I'll go and get that brick,' announced Lizzie, and slouched out of the door. They heard her stomp through the hall, singing 'Polly-wally-doodle', and out of the front door.

'Do you think she's really going to get a brick?' Sarah, wide-eyed, asked her father.

'She'd better damned well not. There's £400-worth of television set there.'

Every day he meant to tell them that he and Val had named the date; but every day, some new obstacle presented itself. He sought to catch Lizzie in a pliable mood, in order to break the news with the least possible carry-on, but every day she became more surly.

'You should come down on her hard,' Val chivvied. 'Before it goes too far.'

'What am I supposed to do, tell me that for God's sake?' he snapped. 'First you tell me I'm not strict enough, then you tell me I'm too strict, now you go back to square one – I can't get it right, can I?'

'Well, I'm not standing it any more.' Val in her turn flounced out. Gavin poured himself a gin and tonic. He sighed defeatedly.

'Women . . .'

'Dad,' admonished Sarah. 'That's sexism.'

'True.' They sat and watched harmoniously together, Sarah's head nestling into the warm cleft beneath his arm. This was how she would have liked it to be forever, just her and Dad together, the rest of them having been beaten out by their own stupidity; and Mum could visit, and together she and Dad would heal Mum's wounds by their combined love . . .

But the Kurds were back again. They toiled uphill in the fullness of their desolate actuality, beseechingly raising their skeletal children to the cameramen to beg bread. Their menfolk were viewed fighting one another on a plateau for possession of a parachute-drop of US Air Force ration-packs comprising Chicken-à-la-King and french fries, so the commentator said, plus apple pie for desserts. Sometimes the parachutes fell on refugees' heads and killed them. A mother sat in a medical tent, her daughter in her lap. The daughter was dead but the woman did not believe this. She waited with passive patience for assistance to revive the child. She wore a turquoise veil round a young, thin face of dazzling beauty; from her large brown enduring eyes, tears welled. Beyond the tent, surging queues had formed, which Turkish soldiers were beating back with truncheons. Sarah flinched as blows fell on women's heads and shoulders.

Lizzie came in with a brick. She saw the Kurds and sat down quietly. She put the brick down on the floor and forgot about it, so engrossed did she become in the view through the screen and the complex sadness of her inner thoughts for which no words existed. They made everything into a show, these television people, but this sight they could neither fake nor manipulate. Her mother's dead friend had understood such things but it was too late now to talk to her.

'Lizzie!' yelped her father. 'What are you doing with that brick?' He leapt to his feet.

'What brick?'

'What do you mean, what brick? That brick there.'

'Oh – yes. Nothing.'

'Take it out immediately. How dare you go bringing bricks

into my house and threatening to smash the TV like you smashed Purdy's window?'

'Keep your hair on, Baldy.' She reached for the brick, to take it out of doors. 'What there is of it.'

'Don't you touch that brick!' Gavin hollered. He grabbed the thing from her hand and a clod of mud flaked away, to crumble on the rug. 'Look at that! Just look . . . I said, look.'

'At?'

'At that filth you've brought in. *There.* Don't go and tread in it! Christ! . . . If you want to live in my – and Val's house, you're going to have to live by civilised rules.'

Her eyes narrowed. 'It isn't Val's house.'

'Not yet, but it will be by the end of the month. We're getting married and you had better damn well like it.' This propitious announcement was succeeded by a chasm of silence.

'If she stays,' said Lizzie, her voice quivering, 'I go.'

'Lizzie, don't be absurd –'

'I mean it. I'm not living with that tart.'

'Don't be so sure, Gavin,' intervened Val, bursting in and waving her newly-painted fingernails about. 'Don't be so sure that I'm staying *here* to put up with *this*.'

'Let's settle it once and for all,' said Lizzie. Crashing up the stairs, she threw open her father's bedroom window and wardrobe doors. Sweeping a row of dresses and coats off the rail, she flung them out of the window, whence they sailed down languidly, to lie in a picturesque heap topped by a royal blue silk blouse. After them she sent a stream of flimsier items, panties and tights, bras and negligées, which caught on the wind and fluttered out, like magnified primrose and pink shiny petals. Now she began to shovel the entire contents of the dressing-table, cosmetics, perfumes and sweet-smelling femininities; but her father prevented this by seizing her wrists and thrusting her back on the bed. He was bellowing at the top of his voice; Val was shrieking.

Into this uproar, Lizzie bawled, 'That's right, use physical violence now. Coward. Hit me, go on. Go on, hit me.'

Val came for her with her red nails, but Val was a head smaller and not built for combat; Lizzie booted her and butted her away from the bed. Gavin grabbed Lizzie by one leg but she lashed out with the other and booted him too in the groin. He spun round, roaring with pain. Lizzie made for the door. Sarah had already left.

'Ruth,' he groaned. 'They've both gone. There was the most awful row. She doesn't hit it off with Val. Val's packing her bags. Anyway – they may one or both come to you. Will you ring *at once* if they do? I think Lizzie will come to you, I think so definitely . . . I don't know how to cope with her, perhaps you could . . . at least hold on to her. I think she needs counselling. She's smashed things up here good and proper . . . I've tried, honest-to-God I've tried . . . Yes, yes, okay.'

On the Manchester train, Lizzie counted out her money: £7 and some small change. She was appalled at herself and yet not surprised. It was as if the whole thing had been inevitable and foreseen from a long way back. And yet it made no sense and was not what she wanted. In no way. She wanted something to be stitched back together that had come adrift at the seams way back in the past, she was unsure when. Before Val came; even before Bridie came and Mum left; before that even, back before Sarah was born and came between her and the rapt exclusive attention on which she'd founded her ego; before her own birth perhaps, when the gene patterns had been laid down; before her

255

self at all, when the cruelty of the planet was first invented. At some epoch, during or before all this multiplying complication there had been a oneness, a warm and breathing closeness to whose security she was always fighting back. But it was something you couldn't have by fighting for it; violence alienated it still further. You were more lost than ever, after you had attacked the shop-window, the screen or the intrusive face.

Val wasn't actually such a bad woman. She knew that perfectly well, had known all the time. She was all right. She meant quite well. A bit superficial, a bit frilly. But not a bad egg. Knowing this did not help at all. The complexity made things squirmingly worse.

From Oxford Road Station, she made for the nearest pub. The barman didn't raise an eyebrow at the possibility of her being underage: she looked about nineteen, and a raving beauty, as people kept saying. They'd begun to say it so often, and cast such admiring looks, that she'd almost begun to believe it. It was a nice feeling, after you'd been convinced all your life you had a face like a pig's back-end. She found a seat under the strobe light. Music pulsated in her ears, just the raw decibels and beat she liked. The lager soothed her into a dizzy blur. Two large young men sauntered over and sat one at either side. They spoke to her nicely and bought her several drinks. She struck up a pleasant comradeship with Micky and Lee; she got giggly and tipsy, and agreed to go on with them to a great pub they knew which had a neon pair of green and red kicking legs outside, and there she danced and Micky and Lee danced with her and someone gave her a pill which was Ecstasy. Ecstasy they kept saying, and she lost all inhibition, letting herself go as she did in her bedroom with the door closed and her clothes off; and Micky and Lee took it in turns to neck with her, and then they all three piled out into the street, and Micky and Lee took it in turns to screw her in a dark alcove in a backstreet, and she knew they didn't use a condom and she knew it hurt like hell and they were rough and stoned and they laughed and reeled away, and one of her contact lenses fell out and she scrabbled around on hands and knees looking for it in the dirt amongst the chip papers and calling for her parents, and she could not find it, and she was alone and weeping, with warm stuff oozing out between her legs. She crashed asleep in a shop-doorway, whose owner, opening up first thing the following morning, had a shock to see a sleeping youngster sprawled out on his doorstep. Unable to awaken the girl, he called the police.

Sarah came to consciousness in the nursery room at her mother's house, with a giddy sense of steepness. She sat up and looked round. The cliff-edge feeling was not a dream. It belonged to this high room in which, when you looked out of the window (which she tried not to do) your stomach turned over and over, and your mind whirled up to the roof of your skull. Horrid. And yet the room itself was comfortable and homely. It had a wallpaper frieze of speedwell and bluebells, to go with the curtains. Her mother had decorated it especially for her the first month she came to live here. She liked the room better than her more cramped bedroom at home: but not the drop. And the drop came with the room.

She had bolted, simply, from her father's to her mother's house, to escape the storm. And it was as if her mother had known she was on her way and was waiting calmly at the door with her arms open. Sarah shot up the garden path and into the arms.

Sitting in the living room with a cup of hot chocolate, she had heard her mother out in the hall conferring with her father over the phone.

'Yes, she's fine – fine. I think she just got a bit upset – from what you say, it was quite a dingdong. I'll keep her here overnight, shall I? . . . No news of Liz? – No, oh well, she's done it before, she'll come home, not to worry . . . Yes, I'll ring you.'

Sarah dressed and went downstairs. Ruth heard her coming and ran up the stairs to meet her. She was almost ashamed of the sense of relief she felt at having Sarah under her roof, the blossoming reality of the familiar child with her particular personhood, her eccentric expressions and gestures. Someone to touch, kiss and hold, rather than the smoky shapes of imaginings and memories. Your hand did not go right through her; she sustained her shape in resistance to your pressure.

'Lizzie's been found. It seems she ran off into town. Kipped down in a shop-door. Dad says she's okay, just about. I hope . . . I hope you didn't get too attached to Val, Sarah.'

'No – not really,' replied Sarah, with her usual circumspection.

'Good – because she's cleared off.'

Sarah dipped toast in the yolk of a soft-boiled egg and looked out of the window to the garden whose yellow forsythia hedges made it seem like one of her more original paintings in which she coloured all the greenery yellow and the sky, say, red. This was the radical palette of Bridie's garden.

It was strange without Bridie.

You kept expecting to see Bridie clumping in with mud-caked boots and jeans, with shirt-sleeves rolled up above the elbow, showing her brawny arms and hands that were sometimes stained bright green from clearing the grass-mowings from the blades of the machine. You felt she must be out there somewhere, potting stuff in the greenhouse or turning over the earth; and would come in shortly, gasping for tea, and dump herself down at the kitchen table to drink it. She had a redeeming habit of dunking her biscuit in her tea and sucking it.

Sarah didn't think Bridie liked her all that much; she called her 'Sweetie' rather sarcastically and had a way of looking *in* to her rather than at her. But (not just for her mother's sake) she very much wished Bridie had not gone away.

So Lizzie had got rid of Val. She'd be jumping for joy. She'd be on Cloud Nine.

Gavin crouched outside Lizzie's bedroom with his head against the locked door. It was the nearest he could get to his daughter, and even this proximity afforded some comfort. It was entirely silent in there; he wished to God she'd turn her music up full-blare and rock the house to its foundations, thump away at her dancing and sing to her Walkman; any of the old aggravating, couldn't-care-less, hit-back, I'm-myself habits. Anything but this moroseness and despair. There was no reaching her, no obtaining the comfort of comforting her for whatever bruise had blackened in her mind, from whatever source, during that night. He sat with his head against her door and called, 'Lizzie, Lizzie – I love you – please come out'; and wept at the silence she preserved. It was terrifying, the extent to which your child could wound and disempower you, if you loved her; and how you could fail and wound her, however much you loved her.

'Go away, Daddy,' came the muffled voice, with no tears in it, but a great shudder where the tears should be. 'I'm all right. Go away.'

'Please, Lizzie. Let me help you. Let me say sorry to you. Work things out and try again. It's not the end of the world. We can try again . . . I care about you, Lizzie. I want things good for you.'

There was a pause.

'Daddy – just go away,' came the flat voice. 'I'm all right.'

'All right. I'll leave you to it, if that's what you want. I'll bring you a cup of tea and some cake or something and leave it outside the door.'

An hour later, the mug of cold tea and the plate of toast were still there; she must have thought it was a trap. Or was just sitting obliviously staring at the wall, or at the hovering goldfish in the bowl, in a state of lassitude, as she'd been ever since she got home.

'Give her time, give her room,' he thought to himself as he hunted round for things to do to while away the time and fill in the space left by Val's departure. He mopped the kitchen floor and mixed the ingredients for a cake. Rang up Ruth and said, 'She still won't come out. Won't speak. Won't eat.'

'What – *still*?'

'Not a dicky-bird. I'm at my wits' end.'

'*Did* something happen to her, do you think, that night?'

'I haven't a clue.'

'Shall I come round again?'

'Yes please.'

Ruth talked through the door but Lizzie made no response. Eventually they heard her draw the bolt back; Ruth pushed the door open and she and Gavin entered together. There was a great claw-mark, like a scarification, down Lizzie's right cheek, made with a penknife.

'Lizzie, why did you *do* that?'

Lizzie could not decode it: it was an outer sign of her inner mutilation, but the inner and invisible wound was something she would not display in words. The cut, which was the nearest to communication she could get, was also a stigma and a means of sacrifice. Her insides felt a little better when the pain bit into the delicate fine skin of her cheek. But to the two pairs of horrified eyes she just shrugged, glancing from one to the other parent in some surprise at the novelty of seeing both of them together, with herself as their centre of attention.

'What is it, Lizzie? You can tell us.' After bathing the cut, which was not deep, they sat at either side of her on the bed, each taking and softly, tentatively, stroking a hand. Once, in the beginning, there had been this perfect sandwich: they the enclosing bread, she the filling.

She perceived the wear on her father's face; the grief on her mother's. But she was floating far away and looking down. They had to look after themselves, she could not do anything for them.

'It's okay,' she said listlessly. 'Don't worry.'

'Did something happen?'

'*No.*'

They got *no* for an answer until they gave up asking. Morosely, she began to go about her life again, but withholding her self from everybody, even from herself, as if she had stowed it in a box in the corner of a room. She knew where it was and roughly what was in it, but she would not visit it. She played video games for hours on end, concentrating minutely on the mindless tricks and stratagems for winning packaged battles that were guaranteed meaningless.

Then her period came. She viewed the blood on her pants breathlessly, disbelievingly. She inserted a tampon and, when she drew it out a couple of hours later, nearly fainted with the relief of seeing it covered in her warm familiar blood. Not pregnant, oh Christ, not pregnant. She wanted to dash and tell someone, 'My period's come', but then they would have demanded an explanation. That just left the worry about AIDS. She froze the worry and pressed its glacial chill right down to the depths of her mind. At times it surfaced. She lay racked with tension on her bed and thought, 'I'm going to die.' Then it became unreal, as that night (though it had changed her beyond recognition) also became unreal.

One morning Gavin saw Lizzie stuff a roll of papers into the dustbin. When she'd gone off to school, he investigated. She'd thrown out her vegetarian posters, the hanged horses and the caged pigs. 'And a good thing too,' he thought, sighing with relief. She'd started to see sense at last. On the way home from work, he bought in pork chops for all three of them. Get a bit of real protein in her. Build the girl up a bit.

'*No,*' she said, and shrank back from the bloody papers. Her stomach heaved.

'Sorry, I thought you might have changed your mind.' He thrust them out of sight. 'You're getting so thin, it bothers me.'

'It's all right,' she said tonelessly, disappearing upstairs to play with her computer game.

'Cauliflower cheese,' he offered.

'Thanks.' She picked at it with a fork. He tried not to stare.

'Eat up,' he said brightly.

'I am.'

'I wish you'd be your old Bolshy self,' he said. 'It kept me on my toes.' *Where are you, Lizzie?* he wanted to call. He longed to take her in his arms but some mental equivalent to an electric fence forbade.

Lizzie scrutinised the cauliflower with apprehension. Perhaps even plants could hurt. So some people thought. Even the stones you trod on might cry out with the crushing of unseen lives. The plants and trees and grass all wanted and deserved to live. If you thought of these things for any length of time, it affected your appetite. She was finding more and more she didn't need to eat as much. She was too fat anyway.

Gavin looked on aghast. The flesh seemed to fall off her before his eyes, from day to day. He spoke to Ruth at length on the phone.

'Do you want your mother and me to get back together again, Liz? Not as husband and wife – neither of us wants that – but as your father and mother. Mummy says she would do that if you wanted it.'

Lizzie examined her father with grave, interrogative eyes. Here was the longed-for end, the eviction of Val, the removal of Bridie McKearn, the reunion of her mother and father, all accomplished within three months. She had achieved every aim she had set out to achieve. A glint of wry amusement came into her eye. She smiled at her father for the first time in weeks.

'No thanks, Dad,' she said, and with a touch of the old aloof honesty added, 'kind of you both to offer but it would be a lie, wouldn't it?'

All that was too late. But (she saw) it was not too late for her. She took over where they left off. Having muddled and scrambled their own lives, they thought they'd settle down on hers in a lovey-dovey nest with herself crammed between them like a lonely egg oppressed by the breasts of anachronistic birds brooding out of season. No thank *you*. They weren't going to bugger up *her* life; if it were going to be buggered up, it would at least be her own mess. She saw for a dizzy moment that she was well on her way to freedom – to her self. She needed their cosseting like she needed a toothache. She picked up an apple from the basket on the dresser, tossed it up and caught it slap in one hand; then snatched a deep bite, and went off crunching.

'It's my life,' she mentioned to her father. 'Not yours.'

As soon as she was out of the door, Gavin rang Ruth.

'She's eating an apple.'

'Oh *good*.'

'She doesn't want us back together.'

'Thank God for that.' They both laughed.

Val, having given in her notice, now changed her mind. Separation from the adolescent turmoil of Gavin's household had restored to Gavin much of the old magnetic power. His sad-eyed, remote gentleness, in combination with the beauty of his hands and eyes and his willowy tallness, mingled with a thousand sensual memories to rekindle her emotion. The bust-up began to seem an avoidable farce.

She waylaid him in the corridor, placing one gently detaining hand on the rough wool of his sleeve. Looking into her melting eyes, Gavin began to fall again, without the semblance of pushing, into the mire of complexity.

After all, I deserve to have a life, he thought. *Why shouldn't I?*

He kissed Val with passionate nostalgia beside the filing cabinets in his office.

'I'll come to your place, shall I?' he enquired. 'If that suits.'

Ruth had settled herself at her writing desk most mornings at first light. The more she wrote, the more she found to say. She spun a web of Bridie from the threads and clues in her own insides; a complex labyrinth woven of herself, of Bridie, and of Bridie-in-herself. Writing for more hours of the day than she slept, sipping endless mugs of coffee and stopping at lunch-time, she would read back cursorily, to find the morning gleam gone off the activity. Words were no good. They flowed from your life but died on the page into the formal fixity of epitaphs. Her account of Bridie was nothing like Bridie; but it had the energy of quest and spoke volumes of her own love. The more she wrote, the more baffled she became. Who was Bridie anyway? How could one know? It seemed her words always missed their target, falling a little wide of their focus, yet because of this they painted themselves all round a central shape, which they defined by failing to invade. This fugitive, empty shape pervaded the manuscript like a ghost. It glistened and beckoned. It challenged Ruth morning by morning to alight on the language that would fill and flesh it out.

Writing gave purpose and interest to the vacuum of Bridieless days. When, around noon, exhausted she put down her fountain pen (itself a gift from Bridie) and looked around, rubbing her eyes, the grey daylight was flat and lustreless. Grief did not slacken but it settled in, becoming tediously familiar, like bad weather after tempests. She mooched around the house, did necessary shopping and chores, and longed to get back to the refuge and release of writing; but in the afternoon, being too drained to write, she sat and doodled, or crossed out her formulaic stammerings, while the April rain lashed down and she awaited the interminable end of the day.

Lizzie's crisis had broken into this routine and forced her to make an opening in the seamless shroud of her grief. Her own life, she realised, was of no use to her any longer: it brought neither delight to herself nor service to others. It was hanging on a peg in a deteriorating house like some old shabby coat which still, however, might be reckoned to have some mileage in it, if anyone cared to put it on. Her offer to return to Gavin had been made on this utilitarian impulse – to put to some joint use what had ceased to have any value to herself. All the same, she found she was vastly relieved when Lizzie refused the kind offer. Her own spontaneous shout of laughter broke in upon her like an echo of a past self. She felt closer to the children and friendlier to Gavin. When Sarah came and wound her gentle arms around her mother's neck with such a tender and trustful gesture, Ruth hugged her back with wonder at her daughter's resilience and understanding. The beautiful, violet eyes assured her: *Whoever else has gone, I am still here.* Lizzie slouched in and slouched out, monosyllabically. She was a changed girl, a foreigner in a strange land who neither spoke the language nor admired the indigenous customs.

Lizzie had no friends; had given up the vegetarians though she still ate no meat; indeed, ate too little of anything, to the distress of her father. Ruth made low-key overtures which were rebuffed in a matter-of-fact way. She bought delicious foods to tempt Lizzie's appetite – rich fresh salads sprinkled with nuts; honeycombs, dripping with yellow sweetness. Lizzie perfunctorily ate a bit, with an air of one who is not absolutely unwilling to oblige, then as often as not wandered out into the garden. Ruth watched from the kitchen window as the tall, spike-haired figure ambled down the long lawn, hands in pockets. For a moment a trick of the pallid sunlight brought Bridie unbearably to mind. Her heart wrung as Bridie's absence closed in stiflingly upon her.

'You ought to do something about the garden,' advised Lizzie. 'It's running wild.'

'I'll get someone in,' said Ruth vaguely. 'Probably.'

Ruth dragged out the lawn-mower from the garden shed. Tendrils of Russian vine had wound their way around its handle and the blades had rusted. Ruth knelt to oil the joints, disheartened at the area of grass to be cut and the antiquity of the instrument provided for doing so. She wasn't remotely interested in gardening; had played a purely decorative role by lounging out in a deck-chair drinking tea and giving useless advice while Bridie worked sweatily all round her. Bridie wouldn't, on Green principle, have an electric mower: she prided herself on her resourceful little machine that ran on muscle power. Ruth toiled part of the way up the lawn; returned on a parallel path; with each about-turn grew more seriously involved and absorbed as the grass-clippings flew, releasing their fragrance into the air. She gleaned the grass which had fallen loose and, as she worked on, the loneliness drew off. She forgot to be lonely.

That evening, she wandered out again just as dusk was falling, and sat amongst the moss and violets that had seeded themselves around the paving-stones under the study window. Bridie had brought the original plant in a polythene bag from a friend – an antiquarian gardener – in Norfolk, and it had colonised the reclusive places of the garden with covert success, stealing into cracks and rooting down into the tenuous marginal spaces between lawn and border. The scent of new-mown grass was heavy on the air; the green gloom was a breathing plenitude of fresh and thoughtful life. What Ruth had learnt to call the 'crocus-feeling' (though the crocuses had long passed their time) came over her again. Something of Bridie was apparent here. She glimmered in the white lamps of the rhododendron bushes and seemed to sigh in an exhalation of grass-scented air that brushed the hairs on Ruth's arm. Ruth shivered slightly and, rubbing her arms, walked slowly out into the twilight.

Emma Jenkins spotted their old history teacher, Mrs Asher, behind the till in the Trust shop.

'Look – there's old Ashy,' she informed Donna Whitbread.

'Who?'

'Mrs Asher – taught us Hitler and that last year. Hello, Mrs Asher. You working here now then?'

'Just helping out. How are you then, Emma?'

'Okay, I suppose. We're doing our GCSE's in a month. Aren't you coming back to school, Mrs Asher?'

'Yes – coming back next year. Do you want to buy that bangle, Donna? By the way, I'm not called Mrs Asher any more.'

'Oh.' Emma gaped, at a loss. Mrs Asher must have got divorced and married again. Donna reluctantly replaced the copper bangle, which she had contemplated slipping into her pocket along with the Mars bar she had nicked from Terry's and the lipstick donated to her collection by Boots the Chemist. 'What are you called then?'

'I've gone back to my . . . actually my mother's . . .maiden name, Shepard.'

'So you're Miss Shepard now?'

'Ms. New name – new start in life.'

She had for some days thought of taking Bridie's name. She tried it out: 'Ruth McKearn'. It sounded good. And it pretended that her love with Bridie had enjoyed the same legal status as that which privileged every heterosexual couple who cared to walk into a registry office and pay down £52. For several days she wore the borrowed name in her fantasy like a hat. Then she'd realised it was a fake. She assessed the reflection in the mirror and took off the name, shamefacedly. Now she had no name. Having disclaimed Gavin's and shed Bridie's, she was left with a disinherited image. She studied it. Wisps of grey had appeared among her auburn curly hair; her face, which was thin and drawn, had lost its urchin look, and shed at the same time its air of apologetic hesitation. The maturer face, for all its weariness, protested a vigour sufficient for rehabilitation: it deserved better than to sink its identity in that of another – whether Bridie's, Gavin's, or her father's. But where, in any case, did you go to find a name of your own? There was no surname that was not a 'sire's name', so that properly speaking women possessed no second name for they were appropriated by the patronymic. How odd. She would have liked to have turned to Bridie and shared this recognition: 'I say, had you ever thought, Bridie . . .?' But Bridie had been, to the core, a McKearn, a chip off the old block of her father, as she herself acknowledged with a certain rueful pride. Gavin called her 'The McKearn'. Ruth chewed the cud of all this. So strange that it had taken Bridie's death to focus her mind on questions of identity, now that she felt stripped and gutted of her very self. And yet a conviction gathered in Ruth, puzzling her more than somewhat, that this very estrangement placed her in a unique position to claim a measure of freedom. She had been all but annihilated; her emptiness was also a space to recreate a self. She changed her name by deed poll to her mother's maiden name.

'Might see you then next term, if I pass my exams. Bye then.'

'See you, Mrs Asher,' added Donna, oblivious to subtleties of appellation and shooting a final covetous look at the bangle.

Ruth retired to the back of the shop and joined Marjorie in sorting the heaps of donated clothing that piled up uncontrollably and constituted at least fifty per cent junk that had to be sent for recycling or – at its most repellent – thrown away. Some of it was unwashed and smelt offensively, so that the back room was always to a degree malodorously impregnated. A small proportion was infested by fleas.

'Crikey Moses, would you take a look at this?' Her companion waved a bundle of aged vests riddled with holes, which she bundled into a black dustbin bag. 'There are some sordid so-and-so's around. Thoroughly squalid. I don't like to say so but that's how it is. Oh, you can see them coming a mile off, those Lady Bountifuls. And often it's the richest, best-dressed ones that dump the most . . . pongy . . . refuse on us . . .'

Marjorie, as she had once confessed to Ruth, customarily permitted herself one day off every fortnight or so in which to indulge her natural feelings of antipathy to the Great British Public. Otherwise, she explained, one really might go off one's rocker, undertake some desperate suffragettish deed with a brick and have to be carted off to Cheadle Royal in an ambulance. She would pull her scarf down over her ears and launch a tirade, 'Selfish . . . complacent . . . you can smell it on their breath . . .' in a booming voice, and would have to be kept out of the way until, catharsis achieved, she would emerge refreshed and full of go. Today was evidently one of these malicious sabbaths. Ruth was unsure as to whether she felt quite up to a prolonged bout.

'Hey, but look at this, Marjorie. This is nice,' she said, to cheer her up. She held out a camel coat. 'In excellent condition, lining perfect – look – and it's got all its buttons.'

'Oh *yes* – let's have that out now. We'll hang it in the window and advertise it As New.' Marjorie grabbed it and disappeared. When she returned, her spirits had taken another turn for the worse.

'There's a couple out there complaining about prices. Say they're looking for fifty pence bargains – I ask you, fifty pence bargains. "What are you going charging £3 for?" What do they think we are – *a jumble sale?*'

'Bridie always said people were only waiting to give generously if they were given a chance,' said Ruth. 'But I suppose there are exceptions.'

'Oh yes, and many of them are not only generous but aware, I'll grant them that,' said Marjorie, beginning to sort a pile of baby clothes. 'But what with the recession . . . and all this greed that's made such a virtue of . . . and human nature. . . . And Bridie never had to cope with them at the coal-face, did she? . . . *Sorry*, pet.' She put her hand on Ruth's arm. 'Don't mind me. My great mouth.' Not for the first time, she was appalled at her aberrant tongue.

'I suppose there are coal-faces and coal-faces,' Ruth observed, without taking offence.

'Bridie dug the mine. With her bare hands,' said Marjorie. 'You can't ask much more than that.'

There was a pause, in which each tried to think of something to say to salve the other's feelings.

'So it's definite about Elaine Demetrian taking over,' said Marjorie. 'What do you think of her? Bit of a cold fish, wouldn't you say? But effective.'

'No, she's a good person,' said Ruth. 'An excellent person. And she will do the job as Bridie wanted.'

She reflected that she must be making progress if she could not only say Bridie's name aloud without nearly fainting with anguish, but also mention Elaine in the same breath.

'What were the shop's takings last year?' she asked Marjorie.

'£58,000.'

'Not bad.'

'Not at all bad. We're down a bit on that this year, Beth says – so far at least.'

Ruth took a carpet-sweeper to the second-hand section of the main shop. She felt calm in here, sheltered; came every day, and was given both a warm welcome and work to do. At quiet times she mused amongst the handicrafts, handling the woven baskets, hand-painted pots and animals, carved boxes and wooden figurines, marvelling not only over their beauty but also over the destitution and courageous enterprise that had produced them; the gulf that distanced the creators from the buyers.

She trundled the old carpet-sweeper around under a rail of blouses and sweaters. She'd given up the writing binge now. It had become like an addiction, taking up every scruple of energy and concentration. Then, all of a sudden, she'd quit, thrusting the red notebooks to the back of Bridie's desk, tied with an elastic band. Perhaps in a year or two's time she'd be quiet in her spirit enough to read them. Cool enough to take the hot shock of the raw pain and remembrance scorching between the crimson covers. She'd tried to wrestle Bridie back to life through the power of the word. You couldn't. At least, she couldn't. But the words had served their turn. Working here in the shop at mundane tasks was better; and going back to teaching, if she had the nerve – for you needed nerve, at the best of times – would be better still.

Ruth Shepard.

Bridie had not known Ruth Shepard, for she was the child of Bridie's loss. She had had to assume a new name because her face had gone. That was the most peculiar thing of all. Going out into the street, she had sustained the strangest conviction of possessing *no face*. It had been skinned off like a mask. She hadn't the face to be anyone; couldn't face up; was defaced; had lost face. But her daughter came running, in shirt-sleeves, plait bouncing, yelling, 'Mum!'; the cheeky young man from over the way winked and said, 'Hiya cockle!'; Marjorie and Beth at the Trust greeted her, 'Good morning, Ruth,' as a matter of course. Each greeting supplied confirmation enough for Ruth to begin to reinvent herself, to find a face of her own to put forward, and a self to fill it. It would take long, slow years, she saw that.

A tall young man with a ring in his ear had entered the shop, leaving the door slightly ajar so that the mobile tinkled in the draught. Ruth went to shut the door but the young man's companion came in at the same time.

'Ruth Asher,' said the tall young man. 'Isn't it?'

Ruth recognised him at once but couldn't place him. She frowned, biting her lip. It all came back in a rush.

'It's Nigel, from the hospice, isn't it? Bridie's Nigel. I didn't recognise you out of your white coat.'

Emotions surged up. She put her hands out and he wrapped his arms around her.

'Who's this?' asked the friend.

'Bridie McKearn's friend. *You* remember.' He kept one arm

around her shoulders as if he'd known her for years. 'Ruth, this is Colin, my partner.'

Hardly able to speak for tears, she warmly shook the proffered hand. They talked of other matters: how the two of them had been on holiday to the Ardennes; how they'd tried growing beards but it hadn't quite been 'them' so they'd shaved them off again; how disgraceful it was about the Gulf Victory Parade scheduled for July.

'I was so glad,' said Nigel, as they were on the point of leaving, 'that it all worked out so well for you both. What I mean is . . .'

'I know what you mean,' Ruth intercepted hurriedly. She kissed his cheek and smiled; waved through the window and smiled again, through the space between the Indian rugs and the painted wooden parrot on his perch.

She went back to the clapped-out carpet-sweeper, which growled its ineffective way to and fro under the gents suits and assorted coats. They had gone off together into the shopping crowds; if only, if only Bridie and she . . . But there was no more Bridie . . . never . . . never . . . she'd never see . . . if only just once more, just once . . . but no . . . she was gone, and *I am alone*, she thought with horror, as if in receipt of sudden piercing news, pushing the carpet-sweeper backwards and forwards over the same stretch of threadbare carpet, *I am alone forever*. She hid her face amongst the old men's cast-off jackets, with their stale, mothbally smell, and howled silently. Did it ever get better? Ever?

13

Elaine, from a seat in the front stalls, craned round to assess the size of the audience and clearly recognised Ruth Shepard sitting hand in hand with a young girl who must be her daughter. She stood up and waved but Ruth, who was positioned high up near the back of the auditorium, did not catch her eye.

'Who have you spotted?' asked her companion, Lindsay Herschel, who was settling herself down, opening her programme and exclaiming that at least the seats at the Royal Northern College of Music left you plenty of room for your legs.

'Ruth Shepard – Bridie McKearn's lover.' Elaine gave up and sat down.

'Oh yes?'

'Haven't seen her for a while. I wonder how she's getting on.' Seeing Ruth up there whisked a flurry of emotions up to the surface, which Elaine, an expert in suppression, hurriedly sent dashing for cover again. Lindsay, sensing the tremor, glanced concernedly but tactfully into her friend's face. Folding her jacket, Elaine smiled reassurance, and bundled it with her briefcase under her seat. Much of fellow-feeling and an odd, disturbing magnetism drew her to Ruth but Ruth had always fended her off. She would look out for her in the ice-cream queue or at the bar in the interval. Yes: definitely. 'So what are we hearing tonight?' she asked Lindsay.

'Well, first, the Hindemith – you won't like that, Lainey, being a philistine; then Schumann's Fourth and after the break The Rite of Spring.'

'Good . . . We're more or less *in* the orchestra, aren't we? I hadn't realised it was going to be such a noisy programme when I booked – I'm sorry about that. The Stravinsky will slaughter us in our seats.'

'Doesn't bother me. The louder the better. More life.'

Elaine stole another glance up at Ruth but the view was blocked by a line of late-comers struggling through to their seats. The concert was packed out. It just went to show what a reputation the students of the college had established for themselves. Now the view had cleared. She could see Ruth deep in conversation with her daughter. Saw her throw back her head and laugh. It must be over a year since Bridie died: yes, easily that. A year of transformation in every way, not least for the Trust, whose invitation to take over as Director she had accepted with a certain reluctance and (if she were honest) mainly because of that unfair request Bridie had made at the eleventh hour. But she did not regret her choice: not at all. There had been the triumph of navigating through the Scylla and Charybdis of the Charity Commissioners' strictures, whilst at the same time not only maintaining but stepping up the foundation's political activities – activities which Elaine had no plans to modify or reduce. As Lindsay said, you had to take calculated risks. Otherwise you were just propping up the exploitative system whereby the fat North milks its creditor the South and flings it philanthropic scraps as a sop to conscience. Last month, the Trust had shipped out eight journalists to Somalia and Sudan, in an effort to make the famine and drought real to TV-watchers at home. Now, however, the country was in the throes of an election campaign and you could not get a word in edgeways. She wondered how far Bridie, in the event, would have approved of her running of the Trust. Perhaps not entirely; even at all. The Greenpeace-style stunts she'd have *hated*. But they brought the young in, caught their imaginations, and that was where the future lay – not with us old codgers, Elaine thought wryly (though it was wonderful how her arthritic problems had been alleviated in this rejuvenating whirl of meaningful action). And the mystical Earth-mother bods they'd taken on board in the process of greening the movement – she could just see the caustic expression on Bridie's face. She occasionally spared time to feel slightly, but only slightly, guilty.

'Sorry, Bridie,' she said inwardly. 'But things have to change and develop. They have to. There's no alternative.' Bridie was in the past and belonged to the past. It was strange and disorientating when you looked back, how profound changes can occur, even within a year. It had been, for her, a time of personal emancipation. She had become high-powered to a degree extraordinary to herself. Things happened because she willed and believed that they should. The poor old compensatory cat, Leah, hardly got a look-in these days: if it wanted a lap to mew in, it had to fight for it. Odd – once the cat had been a comfort object; now it symbolised a loneliness and barrenness she hoped was over for good and all.

'Did you feed Leah?' she whispered to Lindsay. The leader of the orchestra was coming on, to applause.

'Yes.'

'Good. I keep forgetting.'

'I know. Good thing I'm there, isn't it?'

'You are not kidding.' She felt for Lindsay's hand and gave it a squeeze. A good year, from all points of view.

Learning to enjoy herself again was a problematic thing, Ruth reflected, looking down into the golden space on which the musicians had gathered. It was an act of blind faith, like trusting your weight to a previously broken leg, and at the same time it brought a shimmer of remorse, as if to be happy in the moment implied a sort of betrayal of Bridie. Leaving her behind. And yet Bridie in her protectiveness would have been the first to cheer her on toward not just survival, but recovery.

The Hindemith organ *Kammermusik* had begun. After the first few minutes, Sarah stealthily got out her book, which it appeared you had to turn upside-down and scrutinise at a variety of angles, with your nose more or less on the page, in order to follow the puzzle-trail from a dark forest to a place of safety. At some stage in these proceedings, the book slipped out of Sarah's hands and glided down under the row of seats below, resisting the attempts of Sarah's feet to fish for it. She looked up at Ruth and grinned ruefully.

The Schumann took Sarah's attention. The Japanese student-conductor conducted his soul out. On the yellow sands of the stage, the burnished violins, violas, cellos and basses glowed in the light, and eighty young hands with eighty bows rose and fell from black suits and dresses, with hypnotic precision. At the interval, Sarah rescued the puzzle-book, and ate the biscuits and apple her mother had brought along. She relished every moment, darting her eyes about to taste all the flavour of the occasion.

'That woman's waving, Mummy. Look – over there. I think she knows you.'

Ruth steered Sarah away from the figure she recognised as Elaine. She wanted no ghosts. But it was too late. The shadow of Bridie's absence crept up behind her and hovered at her back, spoiling the pleasure she was taking in the fact of being here with Sarah. She took a deep breath and shrugged her off, 'Go in ghosts, your time's up.' But Bridie's lost life did not disappear: it withdrew to the front side-stalls, where Elaine was sitting in the dim bluish light with her friend, and Ruth looked studiously away.

The orchestra could hardly be wedged in to the space available. It appeared as if every student of the Royal Northern had been accorded a part in the Stravinsky. There was much scraping of chairs and music-stands backwards and forwards to avoid collisions and jabbings in the eye. They tuned up, cacophonously. Sarah laced her fingers in her mother's with that unconscious tenderness which the rough school world and sibling rivalry seemed unable to knock out of the child. She spent a week of every month at Ruth's house, a balance which suited them both, without tearing her in two. Gavin's house remained the children's primary home. But Lizzie, being over seventeen and a student at Elizabeth Fairfax College, hardly seemed a child any longer: she went her own way, confiding herself neither to father nor mother. Her dedication to causes was more fanatical than ever. Ruth had the feeling that Lizzie would do something terrific in life, if she didn't do something catastrophic instead. Bridie had moved over and ceded place to the children. It was with a little quiver of dismay that Ruth realised that her present attachment to her daughters would not have come about if Bridie had not died. Bridie had been her life. Simply that, life itself. The enormity of that commitment, the passionate unwisdom of it. Never again would she entrust the safekeeping of her self to another person. She wouldn't dare.

' "Le sacre du printemps", ' Sarah read from her programme. ' "The Something of Spring". The What of Spring?'

' "The Rite of Spring", Sarah.'

'Not the Wrong of Spring?'

'Not "Rite" in that sense. In the sense of a religious rite.'

At the word 'religious', Sarah suppressed a yawn, and

fidgeted with her fingers. Ruth hastened to reassure her, 'No, Sarah, it's not like *church* – no, you're going to love this. It's going to be raw and wild – it'll knock us into next week. So loud we'll end up concussed and go home reeling.'

'Oh,' said Sarah, disbelievingly. She enjoyed coming out to the concerts but you had really had enough of the music by half-time.

'The rite is a sort of fertility myth: it started as a ballet. The tribe chooses a maiden as a sacrificial victim, and they kill her to make the gods give them a good spring and harvest.'

'Why did they have to kill the maiden?'

'To make the corn grow.'

Sarah nodded as if this made unexceptionable sense. She still practised her violin assiduously but, for all her musicality, it did not really touch her soul. She was happier with her oil-paints, pastels and acrylics. Through painting you could change the world into what you wanted it to be, doodling from inauspicious beginnings so that an accidental orange blodge found its way into becoming a sunset with chrysanthemums, or thin black lines brought a skeleton to life. Playing the violin was just scraping horsehair coated with resin over a wire.

Or perhaps it wasn't. The throbbing and pounding of the orchestra resonated in Sarah's ribcage, combining with the banging of her own heartbeat in a savage rhythm which made her sit up in her seat, lips parted. The excitement of the music electrified her. In her imagination the young girls danced half-naked on the stage where the musicians attacked their instruments and the melancholy flute and clarinet in the interludes of thunder played their tremulous solos. *Why* did the girl have to die for spring to irrupt? The music insisted that it did. The power of the girl bled back into the green. The green could not come if the girl did not die. The corn was sown in her blood. Sarah sat up quiveringly erect and the music seemed to penetrate not just her head but her guts. Her book of puzzles again slid to the floor.

The young woman on the kettle drums stared at her score with fierce concentration, her long black frizzy hair fanning out around her head. She began to pound, her eyes wide. The music rose as an unbearably high wave towering over their heads, and broke with the clash of the gong into a thousand echoes; and again the gong smashed into the rhythm, and the bass drummer took a colossal swipe at the drum; and then there was silence.

Silence.

A fair-haired clarinettist took up a far-away melody pianissimo out of this silence like a girl in a trance. The strings came in, gently at first, and then surging forward relentlessly toward the frenzy of another climax.

Ruth gave in to the excitement, reluctantly but with growing abandon. It was fitting that these young people should be playing their hearts out on this barbarous, beautiful theme. For herself, there was an ebb, a drag-back, which the music resisted, forcing her as if bodily into a future predicated on bloodshed. She began to slide, to give way. She left the old year behind and was beaten forward into the fresh cruelty of the new April. And it seemed to her that they all together, like orgiasts, danced on Bridie's grave, pounding with the bare soles of their blood-shod feet on the green and brown mother-planet. The tender grass-blades pierced up like knives. The firstborn tipped the rival eggs from the nest and the smashed shells spilt yolk. The frenzied rut went on over the scene of destruction.

Let it be so.

Let Bridie die.

Ruth would live.

Eighty hands under the discipline of a manic rhythm sawed their bows up and down, faster and faster; the brass blared a fanfare of discordancy and the girl on the gong held out her stick to strike.

She waited.

Yes: strike it; smash it. Now. Ruth willed her not to wait but to finish it off *now*. The girl struck the metal. Detonated sound exploded in the inner ear, and it was over. After a moment's stunned silence, the auditorium burst into a hullabaloo of applause and stamping of feet; Sarah tried out a medley of wolf-whistles and cat calls. Ruth sat spent and elated with her hands in her lap.

'It was marvellous, brilliantly played, and I *hated* it,' said an elderly man in the row behind. 'Barbarous. I kept finding myself wishing I could hear a Haydn quartet instead.'

'He's just too civilised, bless him,' said his wife to her neighbour, rather proudly. 'I sometimes wonder if there's any violence in him at all.'

'Now don't forget,' said Comrade Johnson. 'We are a professional outfit. We function as a unit, with total military discipline. No buggering about. No change of plans at the last minute.'

His beady brown eyes peered from one to another from the holes provided in the bilious camouflage-green of the balaclava helmet his gran had unsuspectingly knitted for him. Wearing the helmet and carrying the bomb in his nervous right hand, Comrade Johnson appeared a more potently sinister figure than when he was plain Roy, an unemployed labourer wearing his hand-knitted civilian jumper and a pair of pale-blue denims. 'Everyone know what they're going to do, right? Synchronise watches. 02.25 hours precisely. Comrade Asher, you're not going to chicken out again, are you? If you think there's the slightest chance, tell me now.'

Comrade Asher, still a somewhat raw recruit, smothered a nervous giggle at the idea of chickening out at a turkey farm. They had been moving in to liberate the turkeys from their mass-confinement when Lizzie had simply frozen with fear at the sound of a barking dog, nearly sabotaging the get-away. Since then she had endured several months of commando-training, and was now being entrusted with one of the grenades for tonight's raid on a meat-packaging warehouse near Sale. The Petersgate Animal Liberation Front had too few active members willing to take personal risks to keep an eager recruit like Lizzie out of the firing-line.

The bad time last year now seemed just a nasty but fading memory: something that happened to happen. Avoiding intimacy, she had hardened her outer skin. She wore tough gear and a rind of sarcasm.

'I'm well ready,' said Lizzie.

She crept out with her partner Benjy and together they made a crouching dash beind the bushes to the warehouse, avoiding the orange light from the lamp-post on the corner, and making for the unlit back of the building. Here it was pitch-black except for a thin filtering of moonlight which cast a dull gleam on the high windows of the Victorian factory building. Benjy would, at the agreed time, smash the glass (had been target practising for weeks) and Lizzie would lob in the grenade.

'*Time*,' said Benjy.

He hurled first one brick, then another. The windows smithereened, one after another, followed within seconds by the echo of smashing glass on two other sides of the building.

Now, thought Lizzie.

The blood roared in her eyes. She had drawn back her arm into the throwing position. It wouldn't move. An age seemed to pass while she held it there tense as a bent bow, with the activated grenade in her hand. She couldn't.

Come on, she told herself.

Explosions went off. The dark world seemed to rock on its foundations. The moon wildly bounced on a tree-top.

Think of the cruelty, she told herself.

With all her violent, retributive might, she hurled her bomb through the hole into the butchery.

Her heart exulted, terrified. A series of explosions within drowned out her cheers. Fire blazed up and the factory became a furnace.

Alarms went off; sirens. The night was split apart by the stridor of blaring horns and a crashing timpani somewhere between drum and gong.

'Right. Split,' urged Comrade Benjy, dry-mouthed, and plunged head-down into the undergrowth, to vault a fence and streak off in the darkness toward the Volvo waiting in a nearby lane.

Burning masonry came crashing down. More small explosions went off within, and the whole structure appeared to totter. Lizzie gave one more deafened yell, whether of joy or horror she would never know; and scarpered.